NORTHAMPTON
GLOUCESTER
oxford
BAMPTON PARISH
ABINGDON-ON-THAMES
READING
London
bristol
MARLBOROUGH
ROCHESTER
GLASTONBURY
STRAIGHT OF DOVER
wareham
BOULOGNE
KINGDOM OF ENGLAND
CHERBOURG
ROUEN
CAEN
DUCHY OF NORMANDY
PARIS
SEES
DUCHY OF BRITTANY
DUCHY OF MAINE
DUCHY OF BLOIS
DUCHY OF ANJOU
KINGDOM OF FRANCE

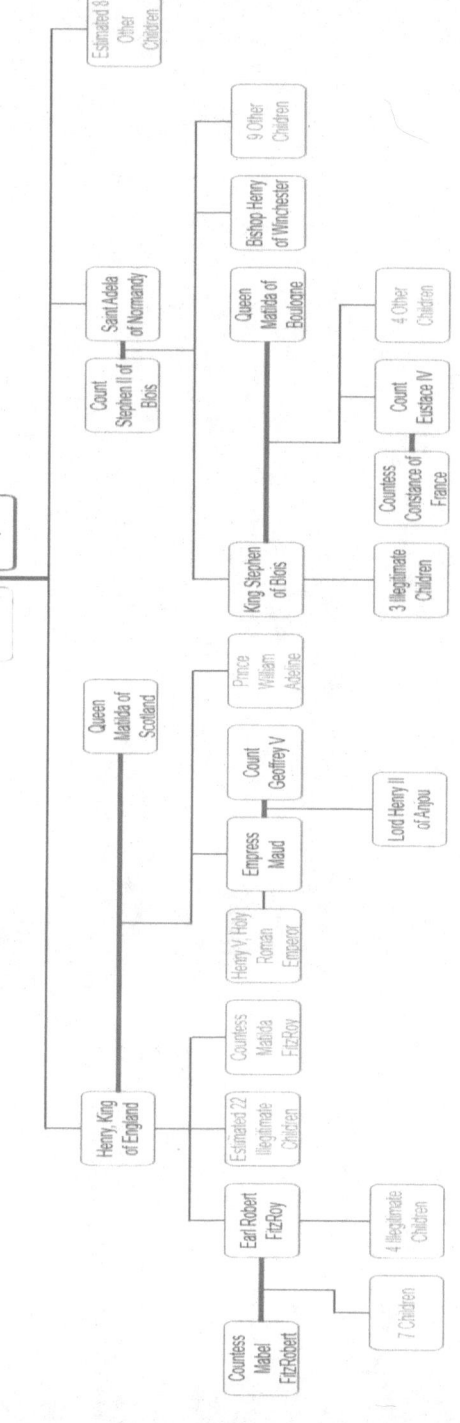

A Battlefield of Scarlet Snow
a 12th Century Revenge Odyssey

Derek Roy

Derek Roy Stories

A BATTLEFIELD OF SCARLET SNOW: A 12th CENTURY REVENGE ODYSSEY

by

Derek Roy

https://www.derekroystories.com/

A Battlefield of Scarlet Snow © Copyright 2026 by Derek Roy

All rights reserved. No part of this publication may be reproduced, distributed, or transmitted in any form or by any means, including photocopying, recording, or other electronic or mechanical methods, without the prior written permission of the publisher, except in the case of brief quotations embodied in critical reviews and certain other noncommercial uses permitted by copyright law.

This is a work of fiction. Any references to historical events, real people, or real places are used fictitiously. Other names, characters, places, and incidents are either the product of the author's imagination or are used fictitiously. Any resemblance to actual person, living or dead, businesses, companies, events, or locales is entirely coincidental.

First Derek Roy Stories trade paperback edition March 2026

ISBN: 979-8-9856219-2-1

ISBN: 979-8-9856219-3-8 (ebook)

*to all who protect those they love,
even when history forgets them*

Author's Note

Dear reader,

A Battlefield of Scarlet Snow can be enjoyed by all.

Before you ask, the answer is a resounding "no!" You *do not* need to read any other installments within The Anarchy Saga to enjoy the story told within; so, whether you're embarking on your first or second venture into the High Middle Ages, I want to sincerely thank you for embracing the lives of Lucia, Gilbert, Eadric, and Emma. *A Battlefield of Scarlet Snow* is an **entertaining**, **emotional**, and **unforgiving** story first, while it is an intriguing exploration into medieval society second. I did my best to appease history buffs and character/plot-driven readers alike. I've included an appendix at the back of this novel, where you can find information on medieval terminology and more.

Warning: this is a mature book for mature audiences. You'll find vulgar language and themes which branch into guilt, physical and sexual abuse, mental health, faith, and more; so please, take this as a trigger warning for those sensitive to such content.

—Derek Roy (February, 2026)

A BATTLEFIELD OF SCARLET SNOW

a 12th Century Revenge Odyssey

PROLOGUE
THE ROYAL MATRIMONY OF LORD MEREK AND LADY LORENA

SPRING, 1132 A.D.

CHAPTER I
LUCIA

Lady Lucia of Rockingham cared not for the queer glances she received from the pretentious Norman aristocrats, many of whom openly declared her licentious, nor for the obtuse self-righteousness those same men betrayed by leering at her salaciously, for she was far too preoccupied with enjoying life rather than dreading the repercussions of a few impotent cretins.

Oops, mocked Lucia devilishly, *that's not very lady-like of you, is it, Lucia?*

She "accidentally" rubbed her body against a count of some who-cares province as she squeezed past him. The older gentleman blushed, and she chuckled with enjoyment. The invigorating air of her cousin's wedding was not to be understated. Uncle Rowan sure knew how to throw a party. And she should know; she's been to a shit ton of them.

Lucia giggled at the crude word.

Shit, shite, shitty-shite! What would these fucking knaves think if they heard me speaking like this?

That would be something worth trying out! She grinned a rakishly mischievous grin. Another time perhaps, for she needed to meet Father inside the keep before it got too late. Eadric, baron of Rockingham and northern Northamptonshire, steward of Rockingham Castle, was many things to many people—including a personal confidant of King Henry—but all that was naught compared to his greatest accomplishment: fathering the perfect daughter.

Lucia swiped a half-full tankard of wine off a table. She downed the drink in one swift gulp, barely acknowledging its fruity flavor and grainy texture. Father didn't like it when she drank. *It's unseemly for a fair maiden to do so,* as he would say. Lucia sighed. The stigma of maidens and their inherent purity was of great detriment to her and her friends, for they all shared a penchant for alcohol and the intoxicating chaos it could imbue into the tedious routine of being a nobleman's daughter.

It was a blessed thing that her father didn't know she'd lost her maidenhead. Dear Lord Jesus, was it a good thing! That would be an awkward conversation indeed.

Lucia stretched her arms and gazed about Uncle Rowan's inner bailey, where the core of the festivities was centered. The whirling whine of a flute, mixed with the surging plucks of a lute, and hammered home by the coursing beat of tabors, sent waves of enjoyment through the courtyard. Lord Merek and Lady Lorena's wedding had drawn in thousands of people—most of whom were peasants, to Lucia's surprise—and they openly bore all the freedoms granted to them by the liberating powers of liquor.

The bailey of Uncle Rowan's castle was a sizeable expanse of flat land with a meandering pathway that led from the gatehouse to the entrance of the keep. A field of trimmed grass usually occupied most of the space; however, the vibrant grass was being molested and trampled upon by the exuberance of human merriment. The last sliver of daylight, shining over the cold stones of the castle's fortifications, shimmered off their densely garnished dresses and tunics. As Lucia stood by the gatehouse and ogled at the wonderful intermingling of peasant and noble, Saxon and Norman, she became inebriated by the gaiety of it all. The human spirit, when restored by the warmth of companionship, hospitality, and, perhaps, a *few* carnal indulgences, was a spectacle worthy of the glory of Heaven. God made humans imperfect, and those imperfections were infectious.

Lucia crossed the oval shape of the bailey. Her uncle's castle was of ringwork design, erected nearly a century ago in the early days of the Norman conquest. While the original castle was built of earthwork and timber, it had since been renovated to adopt a more modern and defensible design of stone masonry. Lucia hated—nay—*loathed* the fact that she knew all this. Her father was insistent, however, that she should learn the layouts of all the varied castles found throughout their kingdom. He forced Lucia, time and time again, to study the very secrets and hidden posterns that are shielded within these fortifications. She still didn't understand why her father wanted her to know these things so badly, for she had every intention of living out all her days at their Rockingham estate, being pampered and spoiled until her dying breath.

But the happier her father was, the more leeway Lucia got. Life's a little more fun when taking advantage of others . . . in a non-churlish way, of course. She wasn't a whoreson now.

Or, whoredaughter, I suppose.

She hummed happily to herself as she created new combinations of vulgar slang. She understood why the peasantry loved their foul language so much, as it could be quite creative and witty. The haughty discourse of the aristocracy got on her nerves more often than not. Where was the fun in four-syllable words if simpler banter had more humor and bite?

"Lucia, 'tis you?!"

She spun around to face the high-pitched voice. Lady Yvette of Bayeux laid out her arms wide, and Lucia wedged herself into the embrace.

"I didn't know you crossed the channel," said Lucia excitedly.

"We arrived only a week back. I didn't believe we'd make it in time. We thought Father was going to flog one of our deckhands, we did. But Lord Jesus blessed us with good and powerful winds."

Lucia and Yvette sized each other up; it had been many long months since they last saw one another. Yvette had splendidly long brunette hair that she coiled back to hide beneath a light-blue wimple. Lucia could tell from Yvette's curious glance that she didn't agree with her more scandalous approach. Lucia hated covering her lustrous, curly black locks. She spent her entire childhood growing it out and combing it daily, and thus she could never imagine doing anything to make her hair less prominent. People were going to gaze upon her beautiful hair with all its elaborate braiding, whether they thought it obscene or not!

Now, of course, she wore a thin veil around it tonight, as she would see her father later. She had to maintain her pure and youthful veneer for him.

Other than the hair, Yvette dressed very similarly to Lucia; she wore a form-fitted purple dress that tied snugly around her waist by a three-foot-long leather belt. The dress billowed out as it reached the stone walkway. It took up a significant amount of space, all things considered.

"I see you still like to stand out," said Yvette with her heavy French accent. Lucia used to have an accent like hers; however, her time spent living in the northern half of the kingdom had chipped it away like the wind does upon stone.

"Stop it," said Lucia. "All eyes will be upon your beauty."

"Or more likely on your bare skin!" Yvette laughed.

Lucia didn't see what was so incredulous about her outfit. Her orange dress was much like Yvette's—tied so it hugged her curves, yet remained loose enough by the girdle to not be salacious—except that the hemline ended right at the top of her feet where Yvette's covered hers entirely.

What? Am I not supposed to show off my toes or my stockings after all the effort I went through dressing myself?

"We have to catch up later," she said.

"Can't we share that drink now?"

"I have to speak with Father first. I'll meet you in the upper hall later." Lucia peeked up at the darkening sky. Indeed, all the festivities would move indoors once it got dark. They can't have a party without lights; although that *did* sound like it could be fun.

"It's a date then," said Yvette, her eyes locking onto a young count a few feet away.

"Be wary, love, that your husband doesn't catch you staring."

"Oh, everyone has their own muse nowadays. Courtly love is all the rage."

Lucia bit her lip and grinned. Courtly love was the new loophole that arranged-marriage couples used to have a love life outside holy matrimony, thus letting them maintain their social and spiritual dignity. As long as the two lovers kept everything purely romantic and didn't practice sexual deviancy outside wedlock, they would avoid any unscrupulous scandals.

"But really, *that one*?" asked Lucia.

"What's wrong with him?"

"Do you not see that nose? And then those shoes with that embroidery?"

"Says the woman who always goes for peasants."

"You're telling me you haven't noticed some of these peasant boys?"

Yvette tried to hold back a fierce blush. Lucia nudged her playfully. Yvette was only fifteen years old, while Lucia was four years her elder. The two have been close friends since Yvette's birth; they grew up together near Rouen in the Duchy of Normandy. Yvette's father had married her off a year ago, but through the word of an embarrassed courier, Lucia had discovered that Yvette and her spouse didn't find each other particularly arousing. She suspected that might be an age gap problem. *Twenty-two years apart . . . I certainly wouldn't be happy.*

"They do seem to have a certain charm to them," Yvette admitted. Lucia nodded in agreement. She looked around her at the mixture of peasants and noblemen. The distinction between those of Anglo-Saxon descent and those of Norman descent was clear. The Normans preferred to be clean shaven, their clothing emphasized style over function, while the Anglo-Saxons were scruffier and more muscular—undoubtedly thanks to their Germanic heritage. The main allure of the Anglo-Saxon men though, with their thick facial hair and simple tunics and *very* large hands . . .

Lucia pushed down a fiery urge. She could indulge herself later.

"Speaking of which," Yvette continued, "what happened to that blacksmith boy you told me about?"

"I haven't seen him since the party last year."

"Have you been inquiring about him?"

"Why would I?" Lucia scanned through the crowd again. In truth, she had been searching for that blacksmith boy who had run into her a year past. He'd been one of her more memorable lovers, and she was hoping they could rekindle some of that wonderful night. Lucia sighed. It wasn't a big deal, of course. Bachelors ran amok within their kingdom, and she had enough trouble already staving off the endless boys her father kept tossing at her.

"I think I'm going to talk to him," said Yvette, nodding at the Norman boy.

"May God grant you luck."

"See you soon."

Lucia continued to cross the bailey. Hundreds of people swarmed around her as she navigated her way toward the keep. Along the way she passed the band, who played their songs with ecstatic glee and rejuvenating alacrity. She glanced up at the sky.

I still have time.

She joined in with the mass of dancing bodies. The group comprised mostly of peasants and lower nobility, and as such, the dance felt livelier, more focused around flow and pure expressionism than the structured steps of courtly festivities. Indeed, it was easy for Lucia to get lost within the rhythm. The energy of the drums vibrated through the beat of all their hearts, and their limbs extended those vibrations to the participant next to them. Lucia came alive with the collective energy of a few dozen people, their human experience interlocked with her own; sweat became one with existence, and the radiance of the strings strung them together into a common understanding. Everyone from every class tried their best to stay separate from those above or below them; but the power of the human spirit, transcended through the rhythm of song and conjured through the carousing of love, brought the barriers of social disunion to a harmonious collapse.

Overwhelmed with the pleasure of the many, Lucia let that passion sweep her off her feet and into the center of the circular dance. All eyes turned toward her, and the band stuttered for a beat as they recognized a change in the wind.

Life was about taking control, and *that* was where Lucia shined.

She switched into a three-step. Most courtly dances revolved around a repetitive one- or two-step motion with added flourishes and an occasional bow or curtsy. Well, this night wouldn't be a simple moment with periodic treats; no, tonight they'd experience the arousal of the human form, the romping of human passion. Lucia loved being the center of attention. The only people who hated attention were those who were too afraid to embrace their inner melody. Lucia knew who she was, what she inspired, and whom she affected. There was nothing wrong with championing the might of femininity and the thirst for existence.

Lucia let every emotion, every thought, wash over her. She expressed it all in her movements, The Dance of Lucia: her keen intellect that she trained daily, the long nights she spent praying for the salvation of her mother, the constant pressure of trying to achieve her father's expectations, the lustful thrill of coveting young love, the naughty joy of perverted words caressing her lips, the amusing mischief she instigated with other girls ... every moment of her life was revealed in the motions of her dance.

And it was addictive. Potent.

The band changed tune, adapting their beat, their cadence, so it matched with her. She no longer danced to the music; the music danced to her. Men hooted and hollered from the forming crowd. A middle-aged woman sang, and her Latin lyrics harmonized with the spectacle. Men and women alike clapped their hands.

How about this for a show ...

She grabbed the hemline of her dress, gripping the fabric between her fingers, and lifted. Mouths gaped. One musician plucked a discordant string. A cool wind brushed over her exposed legs, and Lucia blushed with excitement at the chaos she caused. She spun, holding the bottom of her dress. The fabric twirled about her at mid-waist. She swung her arms up and down, causing the dress to flow into crests and troughs around her body. The crowd cheered themselves into a chorus of delirium as the band upped their tempo.

Lucia closed her eyes. She swayed her hips and bent her knees and curtsied and stepped and flung her hair and yelled with delight.

What a night. What a life. What a—

"Lucia?!"

Lucia stumbled as she tripped over her own feet. The crowd split in half behind her, and she twisted about to find none other than the devourer of joy himself, Don Álvaro de León.

Well, fuck me properly. Here we go again.

CHAPTER II
LUCIA

Álvaro stormed up to Lucia and grabbed her forcefully by the arm. The band went silent.

"What are you doing, exposing yourself to these swine?" whispered Álvaro. He glared back at the surrounding crowd.

"Don't act like you didn't enjoy the show." Lucia grinned coyly. "I understand your envy can be blinding, but now you're just causing a ruckus."

"What if the abbot saw you? The archbishop? Any of the parishes? Do you have the faintest idea what the penalty for such a sin would be?"

"They know my father. They would never touch me."

"Your father doesn't outrank the servicemen of God, Lucia. King Henry's influence must be seductive if you've already forgotten that."

"Have you anything of actual value to tell me, Don León, or are you just stalling to hold me longer?"

Álvaro glowered. Lucia grinned. She learned he hated being called by his foreign homeland. It was something of a sore spot. Most people called him León, however, since many found it hard to pronounce his first name. Álvaro tugged her away with him. A few peasants tried to block him from fleeing with her, but a sharp glance from Álvaro, with a minor threat as he moved his free hand to the sword tied about his waist, did enough to make them back off.

The don quickly towed her across the courtyard. When they were a few steps from entering the keep, Lucia yanked her arm free from his grasp.

"You can let go of me now. I know how to walk on my own, thank-you-very-much."

"With the way you whore yourself around, I'm impressed you can stand at all."

"Charming. I ever wonder why I turned you down?"

"Belt it, woman. I have no time for your insolent games."

"Mature as ever, Count Prickhead."

Álvaro huffed and thundered past the sentries that were posted outside the keep's main entrance. Lucia waved at them. They smiled back at her.

Thank God not every man is an ass.

They walked down a hallway that had a long red carpet running the entire length of it. Dozens of torches kept the hall lit. The walls were whitewashed and painted over with vibrant colors, all of which portrayed the historic conquest of England that their Norman ancestors had accomplished less than a century ago.

"Try to keep up," said Álvaro. "You're already late in meeting your father."

Lucia ignored him. Don Álvaro was the most recent swain that her father had tried to arrange a marriage with. Only a few years older than herself, the count had traveled all the way from his estate in northern Spain to her father's castle in Rockingham. A rumor was going about that he had tried to swoon over a hundred maidens throughout France and England. Lucia now understood why they all turned him down. He was the first Spanish man she'd ever met, and she wondered if all men in that distant kingdom sounded like him? His voice was overly sweet and sultry, almost queerly seductive. It made her suspicious, like a red wine that was so violet it could be poisoned. Today he wore a doublet woven with the finest green silk, trimmed with the kingly thread of purple. He embellished the outfit with a long cloak that billowed behind him as he walked. The sword he carried on his hip was a family heirloom. It had a handle made of pure Spanish silver. Her father informed her that the count's sword was more ceremonial than practical. The don had tried his best over the last few months to be a proper suitor for Lucia. Too bad he was a crazed, imbecilic churl.

"I can't believe you—"

"What?" asked Lucia innocently. "Thou can't believe that I would have my own tastes or ambitions. Oh, I know. 'Tis a pity that I should refuse to move across the world for a man I barely know."

"Sometimes you have to think beyond your own wants. I believe that's called maturity."

"No, you simply don't wish for me to have *any* wants."

Álvaro pivoted on his heel and faced her. Lucia grinned. There was the scab she was looking to pick!

"Maybe you believe yourself to be an advocate? Perhaps that's why you back the king's incompetent daughter to succeed the throne. But let me tell you this, maiden Lucia, you're holding your father back. Don't forget he is only a baron, on the losing side of what's coming. Stephen *will* be king, and only through him can we craft a better future. You believe my allegiance to Stephen and my support of traditional values makes us incompatible. You are mistaken. If you truly wanted a better world for women, you'd join the side that's going to write history." Álvaro looked Lucia up and down. "You'd be with me. Maybe we wouldn't love each other, but I'd give you the freedom to pursue your political aspirations. At least you'd have the chance to achieve them with me."

His eyes, almost black in their hazel depth, coaxed her into listening to him earnestly. The length of his jaw and chin sprouted deep, brown hairs that had grown in since he shaved this morning. She hated to admit how handsome he looked. He was a silver-tongued devil with a propensity for prideful narcissism, but he knew how to portray the guise he wanted.

Lucia raised her hands and cupped his face between her palms. He brushed his cheek against it and closed his eyes. She took a gentle breath and said, "Oh, León, my darling. That was quite possibly the daftest thing you've ever lectured me on."

The don shoved her hands off his face. Lucia grinned and hopped with a light skip in her gait as she followed the scowling man into her uncle's great hall. Immediately her senses were overloaded. It smelled of sulfur and amber; the chatter of barons, knights, dukes, and monks filled the lofted air. The ceiling rose well above them, braced up by a series of grand wooden arches. Lined against the wall were large tapestries that framed depictions of their Norman ancestors. Two tremendous tables used most of the floor space. Halfway along the southern wall of the great hall, nestled between two of the multiple archways, was a magnificent hearth that was large enough for Lucia to walk into. The elaborate overmantel had decorative carvings of swirling flowers that blossomed around ancient Latin writing; all these majestic works of artisanship allowed the eyes of the beholder to ease upward to the actual centerpiece of the hall: a short sword used by William the Conqueror, the celebrated king of kings. The sheath of his sword hung alongside it, adorned with the golden cross of William.

All things considered though, the great hall of Duke Rowan's castle was smaller than many of the exquisite keeps and palaces found within the northern duchies of France or the eastern shires of England. It even paled in comparison to some halls within the manors of the obscenely rich. Moments like these reminded Lucia that her uncle wasn't much of a duke at all.

Her eyes finally drifted to her father, Baron Eadric of Rockingham.

He was a hulking presence with broad shoulders, thick arms, and a voice so deep it could shatter the very rock of the earth. His multiplying wrinkles were making him age like the finest of wines. It was a shame he never grew out a beard like the Saxons; his striking black hair would've made him reminiscent of the Vikings of lore. Lucia followed Álvaro as he approached her father.

"Ah, Lucia, there you are," said Eadric happily, the fires of liquor blotching his face red.

Seated around her father were two viscounts about Lucia's age, two lesser-barons and their wives, a priest, a knight, and finally her aunt and uncle, Duke Rowan and Duchess Adeline. Her father must have been entertaining them; he had a habit of doing so when inebriated. Even after the death of her mother, he'd always been a beacon of light and laughter to the world. She would be forever grateful for that.

Plus, he loved to put on a show for others. Like father, like daughter.

"For those not privy to the scathingly obvious, this here is my daughter I was talking about. Look at her! As beautiful and comely as ever!"

"Thank you, Daddy."

"I apologize for taking so long to retrieve her, my lord," said Álvaro, standing up taller than usual. "She was . . . preoccupied when I found her."

"In other words, she was interested in something other than you!" Eadric slapped Álvaro across the back and guffawed. Lucia grinned as she watched the don hold back his anger. "Don't worry, lad. No man will ever get enough attention from my lovely Lucia. She used to cling to me like a babe does to their mother's swollen tit. Now look at her; she barely gives me any mind."

"That's *not* true," said Lucia.

"Have a seat, honey. Your aunt, uncle, and I have some friends we'd like you to meet."

Álvaro coughed and grunted loudly. It was such a boyishly petulant action that Lucia gaped at the unabashed shamelessness of it. Her father waved him off.

"Ah, yes. You may have your leave, Don León."

"What about our discussion?" asked Álvaro. Eadric sighed and placed his tankard down.

"I thought we settled this?"

"Actually, I find the matter particularly *un*settled."

The group sitting around her father glance at one another. Now *this* was entertainment—young arrogance against aged empowerment. Prime gossip material.

"Have I offended you, Don León?"

"Yes. You have. I find our whole arrangement offensive. You offer her to me, saying this marriage will be beneficial to both our families, yet you let her beat me around like a useless hunting dog when I arrive. How am I not to take offense?"

Eadric smiled. He turned to Lucia. "Honey?"

"Yes, Daddy?"

"What was it you told me when Don León first tried to court you?"

The don reddened. Lucia licked her lips. She was ready to enter this crusade.

"Which part?" she asked innocently. "The one where he compared my breasts to that of an overripe fruit, or when he asked what my dead mother looked like so he could picture my curves in a few decades?"

Their table guests snickered aloud. Álvaro held his jaw taunt and glared at them, noting all those who were laughing. Her father rubbed his chin.

"No, no. The other one!"

"Ah. You mean when I caught him in a brothel! He was so embarrassed and wrought with shame that he offered to buy me a man!"

Everyone nearby burst into laughter. Eadric slammed down his tankard and wiped away his laughter-imbued tears.

"Yes! That would be the one!" He turned to the priest that sat next to him. The poor man's face was aghast with shock. "My apologies, Father. You probably shouldn't have heard that."

Álvaro gripped Eadric's shoulder. Her father whipped around and grasped the don's wrist. The table went silent; Lucia gasped. No one dared touch the Baron of Rockingham and live. Álvaro tried to suppress the pain as her father's hands constricted around his arm.

"You don't want to make an enemy of me," said Don Álvaro.

"I've fought in battles you could never imagine, son," said Eadric, growling under his deep, snarled voice. The table turned tense.

"You've gotten old. You'd be disgraced."

"I think you'll be astounded by how much ruin I can still cause."

"What are you trying to accomplish with this display?"

Eadric cocked his head slightly. "I'm pointing out how pathetic your attempts at courtship were. I trust the words of my daughter. I listen to her, and I don't believe you'd do the same. You aren't worthy of my daughter, *boy*. You come to my fucking realm and dare haggle with me on the value of her dowry?! You aren't worthy of the spit I'd give you for a dowry. Hell, you and your foul Spanish blood aren't worthy of any daughter of England."

Don Álvaro had tears in his eyes. Tears! Lucia could almost laugh at how pathetic he was. Álvaro scowled at her father with his red-stained eyes and said, "I will not forget this humiliation, this shame."

"Excellent. In return, I'll make sure no father in all of England, France, or beyond takes you as a son. Don't shed tears, boy. Maybe you'll finally become a man."

They stared at one another, as silent and tense as a drawn bowstring. Lucia's breath caught in her throat as the hearth crackled in the distance. Álvaro released his grip and slinked away. He stopped next to Lucia before he left; his eyes smoldered with festering fury.

"You'll pay for this," he said.

"Oh, darling." Lucia sighed. "A beggar could pay for you. And I'm filthy rich."

Don Álvaro de León, the knave of knaves, ground his teeth and stomped away, his long cape fluttering behind him. Eadric held his tankard toward Lucia.

"How'd I do?" he asked her.

"That was absolutely stupendous!"

"I did good?"

"You did great!" She squealed as she wrapped her arms around her father. His jolly laugh made her body shake. Her father downed the rest of his ale.

"What'd I tell you all?" Eadric smiled at his table. "I'm a slave to my daughter!"

"You certainly are, Eadric," said Uncle Rowan. "You're a far cry from the stoic brother I knew growing up."

Lucia kissed her father on the cheek. He blushed at the show of affection. "Sit, Lucia. Stay awhile. We're sharing wonderful stories."

Lucia rubbed his back and shook her head. "I can't. I promised Lady Yvette I would meet with her soon."

"Can you not stay but a little while?"

Her father's sorrowful voice broke her heart. She should stay, but the prospect of drinking with her friend and potentially having fun with the other young counts and countesses was too alluring for her to miss.

"I'm sorry, Daddy. I gave my word."

"Very well. I'm sorry to say it, but my daughter will not bless us with her beauty tonight." Lucia rolled her eyes and hugged her father again. "I'm sorry I'm so bad at picking suitable men for you."

"Not that I'm much better," she said.

"I'll blame your mother for that one. After all, she chose me."

Lucia snickered. "I love you."

"You have my heart, always." Then, after a brief pause, he asked, "Are you keeping her close?"

Lucia reached into her dress and pulled out a handkerchief. It was a small white piece of linen with the name *Anabel* embroidered on it with red threads. Her mother's name. She had embroidered it herself. Lucia always kept it near her, usually under her dress and pressed up against her heart. "I always do," she said.

"Good," said her father. "Don't stay up too late tonight."

"What?! I would never."

"Humph. You certainly *are* like your mother."

"What does that mean?"

"It means I have every right to be concerned!" Eadric slammed his tankard on the table, startling the priest and sending waves of vibration down the length of the table. "Cupbearer!"

Lucia congratulated Uncle Rowan and Aunt Adeline on their son's marriage and strutted away from the table. She listened to her father's laughter behind her as he sang praises of her accomplishments and boasted about her loveliness, both to those interested and those not. Lucia smiled. Not a single person alive could escape the joy in her father's heart for having raised such a wonderful daughter.

Lucia wandered through the keep's many hallways, heading for her meeting spot with Lady Yvette. Golden firelight pranced within its caged housings along the walls, and the heat of its liveliness contrasted wondrously with the coolness of the stone.

"Leave me alone!"

Lucia rounded a corner and found a young girl, somewhere around twelve or thirteen years old, surrounded by four older men. They pinned her against the wall. A nearby chamber cast the hallway in a deep red hue, giving the illusion that they were standing before the pits of Hell, holding this poor girl hostage on the precipice of endless atrocities.

Lucia glanced around, hoping to spot a guard. She didn't see one. That was odd. She hadn't seen many guards or housecarls *at all* since she had arrived at Uncle Rowan's castle. Where were his knights, his retainers? At the very least, she expected to see Commander Rayner harassing the peasants as usual. But no. Lucia alone was the witness of this sinful act. As the men slunk around the girl and placed their filthy hands upon her, the fighting screams of her dissent rammed into Lucia like a wild boar.

She flew down the hall toward them, scrounging up her courage and bracing herself for this to turn ill. Her smaller body thundered after these towering men. She gripped her hands into hammers. A final scream from the girl solidified the resolve in Lucia's heart. Not tonight. Not to this girl.

"Hey! What do you think you're doing?"

The men and girl faced her. Her sweat-stained yellow dress, clearly an article of clothing passed down through generations, suggested she was a peasant.

"Bugger off," said the tallest man with a sword.

"This doesn't seem like comely manners for a highborn," said Lucia. "And what of you three? Why must you wait for his sloppy seconds? Are you too stupid, too ugly, or too impotent to enchant a woman yourselves?"

"I wouldn't speak to us that way, wench."

"Don't forget, you're alone here too," said one of the other men.

Lucia held her head high. She will not bow down to these smug bastards. Not her. Not the Lady of Rockingham. Nothing in this kingdom could touch her, and she knew it.

"My father is Baron Eadric, and lest you wish for the wrath of divinity to fall upon you, I would not threaten me."

The man stood back from the threat, and Lucia smiled in satisfaction. The other men shared glances with him. Now that his honor and pride were on the line, Lucia had to be careful. The social ridicule of faltering masculinity made men do stupid things, things like standing up to Lady Lucia.

"We caught this peasant snooping about the kitchen," said the man with the sword. "She was stealing food. We were giving her an alternative to being punished."

"An alternative?"

"Should we take her to the bailiff instead, where she may be hung or beheaded?"

Lucia glanced at the girl. Her eyes were closed, and tears streaked down her cheeks.

"Leave her with me," said Lucia, glaring back into the eyes of this snake.

"And if we refuse?"

"I'm going to give you one last chance not to think with your prick. For if you choose to touch any of us, I'll make certain that you lose the capability to think with it ever again."

Her voice was careful, deliberate. The fiendish red light seemed to contort around the men. Lucia's heart fluttered in her chest as the piercing anger in his eyes made her fear she'd be ignored.

"I heard peasant cunt was dry as bones anyway," he said finally. "People say you already know a thing or two about that, *Lady* Lucia." The man spat on the ground next to her before he waved for the others to follow. They did so with bowed heads and blued balls. *Serves them right.*

"Thank ye, madam," said the peasant girl after they left.

"What's your name?"

"Anna."

"How'd you sneak in here?"

"There were no guards. T'wasn't hard. Mostly peasants 'round here t'night."

"What caught your attention in the kitchen?"

"The bread."

"It's always the bread," said Lucia, nodding in agreement. "Let's go steal some."

"Why would ye need to steal? Ain't ye a noble?" she asked suspiciously.

"It sounds like a fun excursion."

"Excursion?"

"A fun distraction."

"Me wasn't tryin' to have fun.".

"I didn't mean—"

"I knew what I was gettin' into. Me knew the danger." Anna glared at Lucia with her haunting brown eyes. "Do ye think I want to steal?"

"I'm sorry—"

"Stealin' ain't fun."

"I wasn't—"

"I did it for my little brothers. Me thought maybe with everyone drinkin'..." Anna shook her head. She turned and ran down the hallway, leaving Lucia stranded in the red glow. Before the peasant girl disappeared around the corner, she looked back at her one last time.

"Thank ye for savin' me," she said, "but don't try to be like us." She hesitated, but finally added, "Me am sorry."

"For what?"

Anna vanished around the corner. The faint sound of the band drifted down the hall. Lost in her own head, musing about Anna's words, Lucia didn't notice when the music stopped; she didn't notice when footsteps retreated; she didn't notice the stirring of the still air nor the faint shattering noise of tables and chairs.

She did, however, notice the screaming of Anna, the peasant girl.

Lucia sprinted down the hallway and turned another corner. Anna stared wide-eyed at the nobleman with a sword who had just tried to rape her. He was butchered. His body slinked down the stone wall, brushing a streak of blood against it. Three peasants, dressed in simple tunics, held knives and bludgeons in their hands. Lucia's eyes flickered to the stab wounds in the nobleman's gut and the bashed brain that oozed from his fragmented skull.

The peasants turned toward Lucia.

"Run!" Anna yelled. "RUN!"

CHAPTER III
LUCIA

THE PEASANTS SHOVED ANNA aside and sprinted after Lucia, their knives and bludgeons held aloft. Lucia pivoted on her heels, but her leather shoes slipped on the stone ground. She righted herself and ducked under the swing of a knife. It missed, grazing the fabric of her veil. Lucia, spurred on by survival but clumsy with fear, tripped on a rug. She jumped in time to avoid the crack of the bludgeon.

Lucia bolted for the red-lit door and engulfed herself in the colors of Hell. The murderous peasants gave chase. Her mind raced, split halfway between embracing the thundering footsteps behind her and processing the information of the chamber before her.

A kitchen. A large hearth along the wall. Smoke plumed from its bowels. A lone door on the far side. Footsteps. Death.

"She ran in there!"

Lucia wanted to scream, but her mind focused, sharpening and powering her to move before she knew where to. She lurched behind two barrels that were pressed into the corner. Right as she did so, the three men slid into the kitchen.

Lucia covered her mouth. She accidentally kicked the barrel; its contents tumbled inside. Lucia held it steady, and fortunately the peasants' heavy breathing covered the sound of rolling carrots and potatoes.

"Try there!"

Lucia sent out a brief prayer. The peasants rushed through the opposite door, not expecting her to have hidden in the first room. She now understood what her mind had already calculated. Thanks to the countless hours spent studying castle layouts by her father's dictation, she knew that a small kitchen such as this would only have one chamber connected to it: a cellar. Her brain, in the split instant she had to decide, had told her that the cellar would be a dead end. She would've been trapped. But now...

Lucia slammed the cellar door closed behind them and rolled the barrel of vegetables in front of it. The peasants, realizing their mistake, shouted in protest and smashed into the door. It shuddered. She stumbled back as they repeatedly rammed against her blockade. She knew they'd break through soon, so Lucia snatched a candle sitting on the nearby table and hurled it at the door. It caught alight. The flames spread rapidly.

Move, Lucia, move!

Lucia pivoted and ran from the kitchen. The trapped peasants screamed from the cellar. She was lucky that Uncle Rowan had an older castle. More modern palaces and keeps didn't have an interior kitchen; they kept their kitchens separate in case...

What are you doing, Lucia?! Stop thinking and run!

Shouts and pleas echoed through the corridors. They seemed to come from every direction. Lucia finally burst back into the great hall.

It was a massacre.

Bodies lay mutilated everywhere, their forms broken over tables and their insides splayed out over the stone ground. Four, five, six dead. Tears trickled down Lucia's face. The sounds of fighting seeped in from the long hallway leading to the bailey. Lucia scrambled up to the table her father was at. Fortunately, he wasn't one of the corpses. Her relief didn't last long, though, as she recognized one of the dead to be the priest. Who would dare kill a priest?

She heard feet slapping upon stone. Lucia dived under the long table and hid in the shadows, her loose hair draping over her face and obscuring her vision as two of Uncle Rowan's soldiers sprinted across the hall.

"Where'd they come from?" asked one, his voice a slew of exhaustion and panic.

"Who fucking knows. Hurry! We must protect the duke."

They disappeared into the hallway. Lucia hesitated under the sturdy oak table. *Drip-drip*. Blood fell from the priest's body onto the stone floor. *Drip-drip.* Her fingers scratched into the floor, peeling back a thin layer of mortar, and her knees throbbed from diving to the ground. She attempted to recall every political lesson she'd been forced to learn.

Think, think! The castle is under attack. Who'd want Uncle Rowan dead? Who'd kill all these people?

Her first instinct, the intuition that she always trusted and loved, told her it had something to do with Duke Richard. Uncle Rowan and Duke Richard had been contesting the same lands for years now, and this wedding was a royal decree from King Henry—a vain hope that it would unite the rival barons before his death. Lucia scrunched her face as a swarm of lingering questions pelted her with their insoluble annoyance.

Where are Uncle Rowan's knights though? Shouldn't they be here protecting us? What of Richard's? Wouldn't he have his own knights here if this were a hasty siege?

Uncle Rowan was a faithful patron of King Henry; he even swore an oath to back the king's daughter, Empress Maud, after King Henry's death. *Why would Duke Richard then—*

Lucia's string of thoughts stopped dead when the overpowering scent of sulfur suffocated her nose. She swiveled her head and spotted black smoke filtering into the grand hall from the kitchen hallway. As if her senses suddenly adjusted to this new reality, her ears tuned in to the constant, buzzing drone of a well-fed fire.

She dared to crawl forward, and when she reached the benches beside the table, she dared to look up, high, high up at the lofted ceiling with its ancient wooden support beams, and the sight made her heart jump twice, and it made her perspiring hands stick to the stone floor. Her intuition betrayed her, vanishing behind the thick bulwarks of fear, as Lucia cried out in a forgotten wail. Flames engulfed the entire ceiling.

Uncle Rowan's castle would burn.

Lucia used all her strength to push the wooden bench away. She spun out from under the table. At that instant, one of the support beams snapped in half. It collapsed down from the inferno, cleaving the wooden table she was just hiding under in two.

Lucia ran. Her feet were swift, but her mind was swifter. Even above the rushing cacophony of fire, her keen ears could still distinguish it from the clanking of steel on steel, the crushing of bone against iron. She slammed into the hallway. Her face lit up as she spotted the gentle glow of moonlight from the keep's main entrance. A new vigor flooded through her, and she pushed through the rising pain in her legs. Her feet flew out from beneath her dress and carried her across the red rug. Lucia smirked as she realized her shorter-hemmed dress might actually save her life today. If she wore a longer one like Yvette had, she'd never be able to run with the haste she did now.

I'm never wearing a long dress again!

Lucia exploded out of the keep and had to stomp her heels into the earth. She covered her gaping mouth as she watched carnage engulf the inner bailey. Men and women fought for their lives. Scattered noblemen fended off the swarming peasants. They swung their swords in wide arching movements, but the peasants, using farming instruments like pitchforks, scythes, and the like, had a lethal reach advantage. Noblewomen held chairs or solid sticks, wrangling back their children, as the lowest of society, the ones they've kept beneath them all their lives, stalked around them like a pack of ferocious predators.

Lucia finally grasped the situation.

The peasantry started this bloodbath. She watched as a strong, muscular tradesman hurled his hammer into a small batch of nobles. The weapon split a man's skull; the handle broke off, spinning into one woman's eye and bursting it into mush. Another peasant, one of the musicians from earlier, had somehow retrieved a spear and gored it into another count's stomach.

Lucia set her eyes on the far end of the inner bailey, where the fighting was at its fiercest. Knights, barons, and bishops fought for their lives against a host of furious lowborn at the gatehouse. Her mind raced to piece together an escape plan. The castle didn't have a secret back exit or postern; thus, her only path to freedom was through the courtyard and, maddeningly, through that skirmish at the gate. It seemed the peasants had taken full control of the bailey, and the noblemen who'd originally escaped its confines were trying to break back into the castle.

Lucia ducked behind a barrel of horse tacks as two elderly peasant women holding butcher knives scurried past her. An idea fluttered into Lucia's mind. She remembered the map she'd studied during one of her father's teachings and how it explained the design of ringwork castles. She glanced a few meters to her side and spotted the exterior staircase. The wooden stairs switchbacked up the keep's walls, allowing quick entrance to the upper floors of the keep.

They also led to the battlements surrounding the bailey, the same ramparts that led to the gatehouse.

Lucia waited for the opportune moment when no one would spot her. Without chancing a look back, Lucia ran and reached for the stairwell. Her fingers gripped the wooden railing.

In a split instant, Lucia was up the stairs and entering the walkway above the walls. She gingerly stepped around a dead guard who was pierced in the neck by an arrow. She ducked down, now trying to keep an eye out for any dangerous archers on the prowl. Dukes and barons always fancied themselves good shots when they hunted in their pristinely kept forests and abundant woodlands, but they'd never reach the potential of those who hunted to keep their families alive and fed, those who did it because they must.

Lucia navigated from parapet to parapet, zipping across the brief gaps of the crenels as quickly as she could. The stone walkway rounded before her as the castle's walls bent toward the gatehouse. She heard the last breaths of the living moan into the moonlit night, and Lucia shivered as those tormented souls evaporate around her.

The first and only tower along the castle's eastern walls approached her. Her only way to reach the gatehouse was to go through it. The square tower obliterated the pale moonlight as she entered its shadow. Her bones chilled to ice, and her heart failed to add warmth as she reached for the iron-reinforced oak door. She pushed it open.

A rank smell slapped her. She ripped her veil off her head and used it to cover her nose. *What is that stench?!*

The tower's interior was dark, with only a faint sconce emitting any relief from the inky abyss. Dust danced around the cold interior. Her feet hit something. She scrunched her brow and tested the object with her toes. It was soft, almost elastic, and radiated a slight warmth. Lucia stooped. Her eyes adjusted.

No words could adequately describe what she saw; no tears could fully portray the extent of her pain. Of all human capabilities, nothing could be used to relate this moment.

Her friend was dead. Yvette was *dead*. And so was the crooked-nosed count. And Aunt Adeline. And her cousin, Merek. And half a dozen others. All their bodies lay mangled and destroyed under the soft, flickering glow of the torch, abandoned in the eternal darkness of Uncle Rowan's tower.

Lucia couldn't find the energy to cry. Her feelings choked within her throat, and she swallowed them down with bitter emptiness.

Rage. Fury. And then, finally, nothingness.

It swelled into the hollowness of her being. She didn't take notice of what killed them. They were dead. That was all she needed to know. The only thing Lucia's sanity could grasp onto was that her father wasn't one of them.

He was still alive, and she needed to find him. To save him.

Lucia barreled across the tower and pushed out the opposite side, exiting into moonlight and the last stretch of battlements. As she crossed the crenellations, she peeked down upon the wreckage of her uncle's castle. Blood soaked into the trampled grass as the outer bailey turned into a storm of bickering. Confusion and chaos reigned supreme. Innocent peasants mixed with frightened nobles, and thus the outer bailey became filled with accusations and assaults. Highborn beat and whipped every lowborn they saw, while the actual usurpers at the front lines were holding against the armed counter-ambush the aristocrats were putting up. Even from fifteen feet up, Lucia could tell that this was about to get much worse.

The bedlam transformed the tide of anarchy into brutal class warfare. Guiltless peasants defended themselves from persecuting knights and guards, while noble families caught in the crossfire, marred from a nebulous state of shock, lashed out at anyone who seemed to be lesser than them.

Why has God abandoned us?

Smoke rose from the outskirts of Rowan's castle, and Lucia could smell from the ever-rising wind that the surrounding village was burning. Her uncle's entire domain was collapsing into a pile of smoldering ruin, destroyed and butchered by the hands of its inhabitants. Lucia would never look at peasants the same way again.

"Hurray! Hurray!"

The traitorous vassals cheered and hollered down in the inner bailey. Lucia couldn't help but look over at their commotion. A crowd had formed in the courtyard, and a figure was being harassed in its center. Lucia hid behind the inner parapet. Staring through the arrow slit, she watched as the crowd broke its bubble around the poor, beaten soul.

Uncle Rowan.

Her uncle fell to his knees amongst a swarm of knives, whips, hammers, and cudgels. His long black hair was drenched to his scalp. Blood wound its way from a gash in the back of his skull and soiled his purple cape. Lucia pressed her hands against the parapet.

For a brief moment, no one moved. The fighting crawled to a halt at the gatehouse. The armed peasants, men and women alike, stood quietly around the kneeling lord.

"Look up, uncle, look up," said Lucia to herself. "Beg. Do something."

But Duke Rowan didn't grovel beneath the weight of his death; rather, he lifted his head up high enough that he stared past the circle of villains, past the boundaries of his castle and his home, and up to the fathomless sky with its innumerable stars. He was a single man, small and isolated in his courtyard of bloodied stones, but in that moment of defiance, he appeared content in his insignificance; and thus, he looked regal. For the first time in Lucia's life, her uncle looked to be a real duke.

Then, the first peasant stabbed him. Then the second. The third. The fourth. Lucia stumbled back from the crenellations as the twentieth knife punctured his mangled corpse.

"What the fuck!"

Her chest barely contained the erratic beating of her heart. Her legs no longer working, she crawled desperately to escape. She entered the armory above the gatehouse and found that most of the weapons were missing. Lucia was such a sniveling, distraught mess that she never noticed the muscular peasant at the edge of the raised portcullis.

The man gripped Lucia by her shoulders. She screamed in surprise. She tried to fight back against his muscular arms and powerful grip, but there was little she could do. He was too strong, and her tired muscles too weak. She bit the man's hand. He yelled and tumbled her into the staircase. The man hauled her backward. Lucia's feet thudded against each step until they descended to the ground floor. They passed two men who grasped at the wheel that worked the portcullis, waiting for their chance to lower the gate.

The sounds of fighting grew to their extreme; the clanking of spears against shields and swords against armor filled the night sky. The man dragged her by the hair, and she strained as he ripped out full strands. He threw her onto the ground.

Lucia crumbled. New scratches formed on her legs and arms. They burned intensely. Tears fell down her trembling face.

"Lucia!"

The voice rang around her. She lay on the courtyard just outside the gatehouse, listening as footsteps approached.

"Lucia!"

She finally looked up. At the gatehouse, noblemen and peasants fought for every square inch. The peasants used shields and pikes to force the highborn to the other side of the portcullis, while the noblemen attempted to tear their way back inside. Lucia's eyes drifted over the menagerie of pained and exhausted faces. She spotted her father.

He stared at her in pure horror. He screamed. His face was bloodied and his clothes tattered. The veins in his neck bulged as he yelled for her.

"Lucia! I'm coming! Get to her! That's my daughter!"

The men around her father surged forward, but they could do little as the death of one of their men thwarted their leverage.

"No! Not my daughter! Not her! Please! I beg of you!"

"Daddy . . ." Lucia wept at seeing her father in such a state. She had never seen him cry before. She'd never seen him distraught and pale with fear. "Daddy!"

"Lucia! NO!"

A stern hand yanked Lucia upright. Something cool press against her back. For the first time, she noticed Don Álvaro standing next to her father, trying to help him get to her. They chopped at the prodding spears and redirected the blades with their shields.

"Watch out!"

The portcullis plunged to the earth from its hanging position. Highborn and lowborn alike leaped out of the way, lest they be impaled by the gate's spikes. Eadric pushed himself up from the ground first. He wrapped his large hands around the thick timber of the portcullis. Like a trapped bear, he shook the latticed grille, making it strain and groan. His eyes were stained red; his mouth snarled with foam.

"Let my daughter go! Please take me! Take me!"

"Daddy, don't cry," said Lucia.

"LET HER GO! GOD, PLEASE LET HER GO!"

Serrated teeth pressed against her throat, and her windpipe strained with anguish. Her father looked her in the eyes, and what Lucia saw was the most frightful sight she'd ever seen.

"Lucia!"

The knife pressed firmer against her neck. Blood trickled out. The peasants who had been fighting at the gatehouse backed up from the portcullis as her father attempted to tear down the stone battlements with his might. Those who stood near her father's rage knew pure terror.

A hot, odorous breath blew against her ear. Her hair stuck up on end, and her focus shifted onto the man holding her.

"I am sorry," said the voice. It sent a shiver down Lucia's spine as she realized the person holding her, the one who pressed the knife to her throat, was not the muscular man who dragged her down from the gatehouse.

It wasn't a man at all.

"Your lot did this to us," said Anna, the girl she saved from being raped. "And it is ye who must pay."

Her father screamed again, but Lucia no longer heard his voice. She heard nothing, not a sound in the entire world, except for Anna's last whisper to her...

Lucia always believed she knew life. She thought she understood what it meant to be alive. But now she was uncertain. Her world had gone mad.

The bridge to the bailey raised up. Her father screeched and thrashed and bellowed as the edge of the blade sliced across her throat.

Lucia's last image before her existence faded into darkness, before the raised bridge blocked Eadric's sight of her, was the image of a father who'll bring Hell unto earth.

It was of a father who'll make the rain of brimstone and fire upon the wickedness of Sodom and ancient Gomorrah appear like the work of an amateur.

It was the image of a father who had lost his only daughter, and with her, his entire world.

PART ONE
BRIMSTONE AND FIRE

SPRING, 1142 A.D.

CHAPTER IV
GILBERT

A LONG THE SERPENTINE SHORE of the Côte d'Opale, the sunburnt brambles vibrated from the passing wind. Under the energy of the turbulent, wind-trembled surface, the Strait of Dover settled into its deep indigo color, and the dawning light glistened the sky into a lapis hue. That cool breeze trekked inland, stirring the ocean into a frenzy that showered a trio of cloaked figures. Those figures leaned back into the dirt embankment and warmed their hands over a smoldering flame.

Comforted by the kindling fire, they could almost ignore the sounds of battle coming from the nearby town.

Gilbert pressed the soles of his aching feet closer to the heat. His brother William sat across from him and twitched. His brother had a strange tic, which caused the right side of his body to tense up. It happened more frequently when William was anxious or contemplative.

"Don't ye worry, Will," said Gilbert. "They only want the strong ones, and you're far too weak to be a proper slave."

"Ha ha," William mocked back. "Your jests will mean not when they put an axe through our skulls." His voice had dropped to a much deeper tone over the last few months, and Gilbert still squirmed at hearing his kid brother speak with such . . . oomph?

"Belt it, the pair of ye," said Jacques as he appraised the battle next to them.

The morning sun, veiled behind the smoke of burning homes, turned blackish-red. The sweltering inferno acted as a persistent backdrop to the agonies of war: clashing steel and iron, shouting soldiers and generals.

William stood suddenly. He took up his spear and kite shield, pointed toward the battle, and said, "Maybe we should go. They'll know we hid. They'll know we deserted."

Gilbert grabbed his brother by the armor and yanked him so hard that William's butt bounced off the sand embankment.

"You sure as Hell are stupider than a slave," said Gilbert. "You'll get yourself killed if ye go out there. And worse yet, they'll see ye enter halfway through the battle. Then if we do live, we'll surely get tried as traitors."

"We can't just stay 'ere."

"Sure we can. We'll win; you'll see. And when that happens, we swoop back in, dirty ourselves with soot, and they'll be none the wiser."

William's right side twitched again. Gilbert knew his half-brother well enough to understand that meant he'd conceded, albeit not confidently. Gilbert couldn't blame him. To know such carnage at fifteen was cruel. Death wasn't uncommon, and everyone saw their fair allotment of it: mothers died during childbirth, newborn babes starved during the harsh winters, peasants caught illnesses and plagues, farmers collapsed in the fields.

But to be killed at the hands of a terrorizing, foreign army—now that was a way to die that few have seen. When he was his brother's age, Gilbert was busy causing mischief with Hawk or Bartholomew, sneaking peeks at women bathing in the river or pranking the local clergy. He certainly wasn't going to war against William of Ypres and the Hellhound of Rutland.

It had been the wee hours of the morn, long before the sun shed any light onto the duchy of Flanders, when Gilbert, William, and Jacques snuck out of their war camp. Jacques ran guard duty during the night and knew the spots where the guards usually fell asleep. It had been easy, easier than Gilbert expected, to sneak between the tents of their fellow countrymen and vanish into the night. By the time their commanders had gathered the troops for the invasion, the three of them were safely a kilometer away and enjoying breakfast.

"I think they're gettin' closer," said William.

"They're not," said Jacques. He leaned back against the bank, using his cloak as a pillow.

"Your eyes aren't even open."

"They don't need to be. I've got ears."

Gilbert followed William's line of sight. The battle had moved away from the streets and toward the docks, which, admittedly, *was* closer to their hiding spot. Gilbert ruffled William's hair. His brother's gray eyes stared back at him.

"Just try to relax. We'll be all right," Gilbert said with a hesitant smile.

The three of them, and the army they stationed with, were part of an outer squadron meant to monitor any naval movement along the coast of Boulogne. The leader of their army, Geoffrey V, Count of Anjou and Maine—plus any other lengthy title the lords in power gave each other—was on a quest to capture all of Normandy. They positioned their squadron on the northernmost edge of Geoffrey's domain, technically within the duchy of Flanders. Outwardly, the purpose of their loyal watch was to rebut Stephen of Blois, King of England, if his army attempted to make landfall anywhere near their realm, especially since Count Geoffrey's wife, Empress Maud, was causing endless chaos in the kingdom of England.

Their real purpose, however, was twofold. For one, Geoffrey was at war with many barons throughout Normandy, Maine, and Blois. He wanted their squadron to repel any reinforcements coming from Flanders or Brabant. But more importantly to Geoffrey, their secondary purpose was to watch for King Louis VII; the king of France seemed content with staying hands off of the civil skirmishes happening between the barons of his province, but eventually he'd feel threatened by the power Count Geoffrey was gaining in his conquest. They all knew it could mean war eventually, and thus they were to betray any movements they spotted from King Louis's army.

Politics was a tricky thing, Gilbert decided. In times like these, when anarchy ran rampant and leadership keeled over in battle after battle, it seemed impossible to ignore. Politics were a philosophical self-indulgence during times of peace, but a horrifying usurpation during times of war, especially to the paupers like Gilbert and William . . . like the family they left behind.

Their family was dying. Gilbert and William's little sister passed away three winters ago; she was only three. Their mother went stupid afterwards. She never ate and rarely worked. Their father had to take up the breadwinning, quite literally, wherever he could. They were lucky he had a skillful trade as a freemason. They traveled throughout Normandy, Gilbert and his brother taking refuge with their mother while their father found work building up whichever castle or cathedral was needing repair. In times of war like these, with sieges and battles happening regularly, he was quite busy. And it had been enough for the four of them.

But then four became five. Their mother came of child yet again, and as this babe grew inside her, she found new vigor for life yet again. William, Gilbert, and their father were ecstatic to see her moving, to see her interacting with other villagers. Her skin's sickly color became a healthier red, and her gray hair grew back blonde. The only issue was they weren't earning enough to feed five people. Their mother was due a few months before winter, and they knew losing another child might be all she could bear.

And thus, Gilbert and William did the only thing they could think of—well, that Gilbert could think of, as William was hoping he could continue to learn the craft of reading and writing from his real father. They joined Geoffrey's army and left the life they knew behind. It gave their parents the means to raise their sibling as a healthy newborn. Plus, they could have parental comfort in knowing Gilbert and William would be well fed in the military, if they lived.

"RETREAT! RETREAT!" bellowed one of King Stephen's commanders at his troops. They formed ranks down by the water, creating a formidable line against Geoffrey's oppressing Norman army.

"See, William? We're winning," said Gilbert.

The clashing became more brutal. They watched their brethren slaughter and be slaughtered. Each side fought for every inch. Their army pushed back the invaders to the waterline, trapping them against the forces of nature. The town burned to cinders next to them. Gilbert was quite pleased that he wasn't in the fight, getting broken and bashed with all the rest. It would be terrible if he or his brother died, and Mon Maman would blame him, as always.

"Something doesn't seem right," said William.

Jacques peeked an eye open at him. "Oh yeah? And why's that?"

"They're giving up really easily. Why would they retreat toward their own ships? Wouldn't that corner them?"

"They're overwhelmed," said Gilbert. "Men do foolish things when they panic."

"I don't like this." William's breath trembled out of his mouth. His shaking hand pointed to the ship that Stephen's army crossed the strait with. "See that? There are men moving aboard."

"The sailors are prepping the ladders so Stephen's army can try to escape. They'll prance away like the cowardly dogs they are," said Jacques.

"But why are we surging them head on? Shouldn't we flank them from both sides? Cut them off from all directions? Hark! Archers! I see archers on the boat!"

"Son, ye ain't a damn commander. Those in charge know what they're doin'."

Gilbert sighed. It was time to be an older brother. Gilbert stood and pulled William with him. They walked down the beach, keeping behind the fluttering brambles to remain hidden from the battlefield.

"Look out there," Gilbert said, motioning across the Strait of Dover. "What do you see?"

The retreating high tide left sticks, algae, and other plants that once hid in the ocean's depths scattered across the beach. He waited for his little brother to answer.

"I see nothing."

"Look harder."

"'Tis just the ocean."

"Exactly." Gilbert stood triumphantly. William glanced at him sideways. He waited for Gilbert to elaborate, and it took several confounding moments to pass before William realized he wasn't going to. Another one of his brother's annoying tricks? William groaned.

"What is that supposed to mean?" he asked.

"It means—"

Gilbert shoved William into the sea. William yelped as the freezing water washed over him and seaweed wrapped around his legs. He coughed up water. "What the Hell, Gil?!"

"Feelin' refreshed?"

"No!"

"Oh, well, let's try again."

Gilbert reached down and pulled William up. His brother fought back, slapping Gilbert's hands. But Gilbert had two years on him, and two years meant quite a bit at their age. He tossed William back into the sea. The wave collided around him with a giant splash.

"Stop it!" yelled William.

"What?!"

"STOP IT!"

William covered his mouth, suddenly realizing he was yelling when they were supposed to be hiding. The incoming waves continued to slam into his back. Gilbert leaned down closer to his brother. William might be the smart one, the one who can read and write and is the chosen scribe for his wealthy father, but his older brother still had more wisdom. Survival skills, as his friend Hawk would call it; so here comes the brotherly lesson, Gilbert's gift to his superior younger brother.

"Do you get it now?" asked Gilbert, this time layering love into his tone.

". . . I'm wet."

"Yes, yes you are. We're also screaming at each other on the edge of a battle, at the corners of our kingdom which neighbor enemy territory."

"I don't understand you, Gilbert," said William, standing up before another wave drenched him. His teeth chattered from the cold. He kicked off the seaweed.

"Hark. I may not be a bastard in the traditional sense like ye, but I've been called one plenty of times. And as a bastard of the world, I've learned one or two things. Now this? This is something I learned from Hawk and Beatriz well before we took ye with us. We call it *relativus*. You see: we can yell because the battle is too loud for them to hear us. We can hide because the world is too big for them to find us. I can shove you because you're too small to fight back. Do ye understand now? We can't control the world around us, but we *can* control what we stand next to. We decide whether we want our strengths to be stronger, or our weaknesses to be weaker."

William stared at Gilbert in disbelief. "Have ye been drinkin' again?"

"What? No."

"Gilbert! Will! Get back here!"

William and Gilbert spun around. Down at the shoreline, it was impossible for either of them to see Jacques or the firepit clearly; however, reaching up into the blue sky was a cloud of pitch black. It hung in the clouds for a fleeting moment, before it arced its way downwards behind the embankment. The screams of a few hundred men followed it.

"Gilbert . . . ?"

"Arrows," he said. "Those were lots and lots of arrows."

Gilbert raced up the beach, not waiting for his kid brother. He crested the hill and appraised the battlefield. Jacques stood next to the fire; he pressed his hands against his head. He fell to his knees.

They'd lost.

Geoffrey's army, *their* army, had pressed the enemy all the way to their docked ship. They had King Stephen's invaders trapped between landfall and the expansive ocean. It should've been over. It *was* over . . . until a hundred archers appeared aboard the docked ship from their hidden spot below deck. With their army pressing their attack, the hidden archers had sprung up and let loose a barrage of arrows so terrible it darkened the sky. Those arrows fell down onto the squadron that Gilbert, William, and Jacques had abandoned, and those who had the rotten luck to recognize their danger too late became pierced with fathomless arrows.

The archers released another volley. Geoffrey's men screamed. The arrows found their mark. Normans died by the dozens. The front line of Stephen's army advanced under the leadership of their commanders, who had, only minutes prior, given the signal to retreat. They slew the front row of Normans who had avoided the aerial onslaught.

The battle ended as quickly as it had begun.

"Oh fuck," said Gilbert.

The remaining Normans, those not pierced by arrow or butchered by spear, fled the battle toward Gilbert, his brother, and Jacques. The invading army turned all their attention to those trying to escape. And they gave chase.

Gilbert threw William onto their gear. Jacques kicked sand over the fire. The flames smothered as the trio hefted their weapons and shields.

They spent all morning staying clear of the bloodshed, and it was only now that the battle had climaxed that they found themselves in grave danger. Gilbert couldn't help but laugh at the irony.

Gilbert, William, and Jacques turned and ran as the first men from their squadron caught up to them. Behind them all, they heard the battle cry of King Stephen's army, and they heard the *twang* of a volley of arrows.

CHAPTER V
EADRIC

Eadric impaled a peasant on his pike. He flung the corpse off the blade, leaving the hemorrhaging husk for the dogs. He spat on the corpse. *That was for my daughter.*

The filthy peasants and the abominable Duke Richard betrayed her. It'd been ten long years since she had died, since the night he had failed her. How dare he ever believe himself to be a father? A father wouldn't stand and watch as their child died. A father wouldn't fail.

Ten long years.

But today was the day that Baron Eadric of Rockingham, at the smoldering age of fifty-two, became vengeance. Today was the day that he finally let loose. The day of rampage.

And it started with a simple command.

"RETREAT! RETREAT!"

Eadric's men fell back toward the sea. Their inferno had already enraptured much of the small coastal town. The thatch roofing made them particularly prone to fire. It pleased Eadric greatly to hear the screams of peasants and livestock commingle in their rapturous blaze.

"They've routed us along the waterfront," said Sir Álvaro upon his steed. "The ship is almost in position behind our back flank."

Sir Álvaro de León, the former suitor of Eadric's daughter, had earned much esteem in his military service since the outbreak of war. Back when he was an egotistical bachelor, Eadric detested him. Outside his prestigious estate and wealth in Spain, he was never good enough for *his* daughter. But the man he was now, a masterful battle tactician with a spotless pedigree, had granted him respect and reconsideration from Eadric and the other noblemen. War has always held the power to irrevocably change the fortune of a man . . . while he kept winning.

"Give the orders," said Eadric, his voice booming with pleasure.

"Yes, my lord."

"Remember to keep the commanders alive."

"Are you sure he's here?"

"This was the only regiment we've seen along the coast."

"If you're mistaken, and he's not, they'll give us Hell when we return."

"I'm never wrong."

"Yes, my lord. I'll remind the men to spare the commanders." Sir Álvaro snapped the reins on his horse and pranced off. Eadric took a deep breath. Only an idiot like Sir León would doubt him. He had to be here. That disgusting peasant woman had sworn up and down that her son would be in Geoffrey's army. She wasn't lying either. Eadric had a knack for seeing through lies. No, her son would be here.

I'm getting close, Richard. Can you feel me? You were foolish to have forgotten him.

Eadric stepped over the corpses he'd made and proceeded to the most elevated position in the village. From this vantage point, he could appraise the full battlefield below him. It appeared, as was the intended effect, that they were on the precipice of defeat.

The Norman army had them "trapped" between their force and the sea. Escape seemed inconceivable. That was the key to Eadric's plan. It gave the Norman army the courage to advance heedlessly. Men always become blindly confident when they spot victory.

"Help . . ." a voice croaked, hoarse and destitute.

Eadric glanced over. The feeble voice came from a young enemy soldier. The unranked teenage militiaman bled from a wound in his lower stomach. Eadric had been in enough battles to know a fatal wound from a salvageable one; this one was survivable. He wondered if he was the one who had gored this boy. Throughout his long and violent life, he'd killed so many people that most of their faces were forgotten to him. The kid lay on his back, his eyes searching for some salvation in the sky above him.

"Help . . ."

"Come here," said Eadric, yanking the boy up by his shoulders. The boy squealed. His hands pressed down on the wound to keep the blood from pouring out. Eadric sat the boy on his lap as if he were a toddler. He reeked of adrenaline, a stench not dissimilar to that of a dog after it takes an anxiety-induced shit. Eadric twisted the boy's head to stare at the clashing armies.

"Watch this," said Eadric plainly.

Sir Álvaro blew a horn, and the sound sundered the crisp morning air. From the massive boat that Eadric and his war party traversed from England on, a squadron of archers popped up from below deck. They released their arrows. The morning sun, which just rose above the horizon, disappeared behind the volley.

"Helpless," said the boy.

"Yes, as are all who cross me." Eadric brushed the boy's hair out of his eyes. "I'm sorry. I can't let you go, lest you chase me down in vengeance."

"I wouldn't—"

"And I have something too important to do first," said Eadric, ignoring the boy. "One of your commanders is the son of a very bad man. I mean to kill him. It was unlucky that you and this village should've been harboring him. Can you do me a favor, boy? When you're up in Heaven and seeing Him in all His glory, remind Him. Remind God to damn me well."

Eadric slit the boy's throat. His blood gushed warmly over Eadric's fingers. The soldier spasmed, but Eadric timed his demise perfectly. The boy's body fought for life just long enough to watch as the arrows fell on his comrades in a deadly wave. All his friends and commanders were obliterated in a flail of desperate cries.

"Helpless are the righteous," said Eadric to the lifeless boy. The survivors of Geoffrey's army retreated down the coastline. The commanders, who stayed back from the assault, were among them. Eadric smiled. It was time for him to join the fray.

Good, thought Eadric, *I was getting bored*.

Eadric charged down the village as his army pounced from their once trapped position. Blood pumped through his veins like racehorses down a track. Eadric may not be as young or nimble as he was in his prime, but ever since Lucia's death, he had done little else than dedicate his life to King Stephen and the physical toil of war, forging him into the best condition he'd ever been in. He grinned as he bore down on his enemy.

Indiscriminate revenge was his only salvation. Eadric began the slaughter.

King Stephen of Blois, Count of Boulogne and Duke of Normandy, led the hunt ahead of Eadric. Duke Richard and Don Álvaro trailed with him. King Stephen loved to hunt in the forested countryside of northern England. The hunting party comprised of them four plus another fifteen housecarls, nobility, and even a few clergymen. The four dogs they brought with them sniffed and scoured the surrounding underbrush.

It took little for King Stephen to find a reason to hunt, but the excuse today was that tomorrow would be the royal knighting of Don Álvaro. In the brief skirmishes since Stephen took control of the crown, Don Álvaro had squandered Geoffrey's every attempt to enter the kingdom. As long as they kept Geoffrey, or more specifically his wife, Empress Maud, contained off the island, then Stephen could continue to garner favor among the clergy and aristocrats unabated. And that was how the crown would be won.

All of that was to say, Eadric had to go through another dreadfully boring hunt.

"I think we should turn in, Your Majesty," said Eadric. "Night falls upon us."

"I won't return empty-handed, my friend," said the king.

"Perhaps Lord Eadric is right, my liege," said Duke Richard. "None will dare think less of you if you venture back without game."

"Silence, Richard. War is here. Every move, every action I make will be scrutinized and maligned until the filth that flows through London has trampled my exploits." King Stephen shook his head. "Even returning from a hunt empty will be heralded as a symbol of my weakness. Our country is too brittle for that to happen."

"But who would smear you in such a manner?"

Don Álvaro and Eadric shared a look. Duke Richard was already on thin ice with the king. The only reason he was here was that Stephen wished to maintain a powerful alliance with the southern nobility. Southern England was, after all, where Geoffrey and Empress Maud would attempt to establish a foothold first.

"The bitch's spies will," said Stephen, alluding to Empress Maud. Even though the king wouldn't admit it, it was clearly not the Count of Anjou and his foreign army that Stephen feared, but Empress Maud. It didn't help Stephen any that Maud was his cousin, *and* the only legitimate child of the late King Henry, may God rest his soul.

"In the war ahead," began the king, "we'll have to be crafty. Resourceful. Like this hunt, we must make sacrifices to save face. We must care what others think of us. We cannot, and shall not, leave any bush unturned, nor any wood unscoured. My cousin, she will be like the boar we seek, loud and inelegant, like any woman with the heart of a man. *But* she'll be ferocious and deadly when cornered."

Eadric rolled his eyes. King Stephen's routine dismissal of the empress by taking constant jabs at her womanhood made him appear intimidated, like a young boy trying to overcompensate for his lack of puberty. It was unbecoming. Empress Maud being a woman was already a tired joke amongst the citizens of England. Everyone knew she didn't have a cock between her legs. So? What of it? She even shared the same name as King Stephen's wife; Empress Maud, wife of Geoffrey of Anjou, and Queen Maud, wife of King Stephen. The jokes practically wrote themselves. Stephen's wife went by the name Queen Matilda now to avoid confusion. Some aristocrats considered the name change a defeat on King Stephen's part.

God, I fucking hate politics, thought Eadric.

King Stephen *was* right about one thing, though. This war *would* be like a hunt.

The dogs stopped in their tracks, sniffing the spoor. The hair on their backs stood upright. King Stephen stooped next to them as they snarled. The king looked funny when bent over. His tall, skinny frame made his spine protrude beneath his overcoat, and his curly light-brown hair hung loosely over his eyes. Stephen followed the hounds' gaze. He snarled with them.

"Our enemies are everywhere," said King Stephen. "When I took the throne, I took on all the paranoia of the world. I see my cousin's face in every alley. Every wood. Every reflection. I glimpse the betrayal in her eyes, fresh as if I had gutted her father myself. I realized, despite her manliness, that the empress does cry."

Stephen of Blois, king of England, usurper of thrones and devourer of successions, unleashed the dogs from their ropes.

"I kept my hounds near at hand, chained up for far too long," he said quietly. "Bribery and promises can only get a man so far."

One dog barked. They sprinted off. The forest came alive with noise. A flurry of ruffled feathers and a shrill, throaty jumble of panic-induced yells leaped from a nearby bush. The hounds descend on the area. Four wild turkeys—one gobbler and three hens—ran for their lives.

"I shall be indolent no longer," declared King Stephen.

The turkeys screeched as the hounds bit into them. Their brittle legs snapped in half under the force of the dogs' weight. Blood squirted onto the underbrush. In the violent tussle of life and death, feathers and blood and saliva slobbered together into a muddy texture.

"It's time I released my dogs."

The king looked back at Don Álvaro, at Duke Richard, at Eadric, at all of them. Eadric smiled with glee; he was tired of this bullshit. After so many years of waiting, the time had come for him to get revenge against the peasants that killed his daughter, and eventually, one day, when Duke Richard inevitably abandons the king like the coward he is, against Duke Richard too. For now, though, they were allies. But Eadric would never forget that Duke Richard had pulled his housecarls and knights from the wedding. The slimy bastard had let his own wife and daughter get murdered on her wedding day, all so he could take over that fiefdom for himself. Richard was equally responsible for Lucia's death, and Eadric would *never* forgive him.

He was ready to be unleashed.

The gobbler cried as it watched the hens get torn limb from limb. It didn't know whether to flee or fight. Neither choice would matter in the end; it would be ravaged all the same.

The troops fled from Eadric and his army. He lifted his arm into the air and commanded the release of another volley. The sky turned dark, and dozens more fell to their demise on this accursed beach. Eadric ran as fast as he could, his blood pumping through his body, each maddening step emboldening the next. He reached a Norman soldier, no older than Eadric's daughter was when she died, and he pierced his sword through the back of their throat.

By the end, bodies littered the coast of Boulogne, and the town that once stood along its shoreline was now an endless column of black smoke rising into the sky. The sun appeared like a singular hot coal behind the dark fumes. Eadric kicked up sand behind him as he oversaw his army claiming their spoils. They stripped the dead bodies naked, stealing armor, jewelry, and anything else of worth. Another group was rounding up the commanders.

Eadric prepared himself to interrogate them. He had followed the rumors of Richard's infidelity to every corner of his kingdom. Little did he expect that Richard, after being thoroughly soused with southern wine during one of his trips to Normandy, had lost control of his prick and slept with a peasant woman. Now that his son was grown, he'd make a spectacular hostage. Perhaps Eadric could ransom him to find where Richard hid.

A scream diverted his attention. Clanging steel told him that someone was still alive. Eadric sprinted to where a circle of his men had formed around a single soldier, a boy who must be in his mid-teens. His soldiers prodded at him with their spears—a bunch of wolves playing with their food. The boy had a leg wound and a gash that clipped off a portion of his right ear.

Eadric let the soldiers have their fun for a bit. The boy eventually collapsed onto the sand, his chest heaving from such heavy exertion. He dropped the mace he was holding. The crowd booed.

"That's enough. Step aside," said Eadric. The circle parted for him. He approached the kneeling boy. The soldier laboriously glanced up at him. The right side of his body twitched. Eadric knew he must look intimidating to the lad. Even compared to a lifelong soldier, Eadric was *huge*. Large-shouldered, vascular, and with eyes hardened from a painful life.

"What's your name, son?" asked Eadric.

The boy hesitated. When he opened his mouth, a small rivulet of blood seeped out from the corner of his lips. The boy winced in pain, his own words painfully contorting his lungs.

"William," said the boy. He had a harsh accent.

"You're the last of your army. Did you know this?"

William's lips quivered. His eyes sparkled with something resembling fury. His body twitched again, as if a shock went through his entire system. "Where are you from?"

"Does it matter?"

"It may."

"I'm from Rouen."

Whenever Eadric became shocked, he reached for his sword. It was trained into him since his early days of service under the late King Henry. He gripped his sword now.

William from Rouen? No, no. This cannot be. It's a large city. There must be many Williams from there. Richard's bastard would have to be a general. He would never let his honor be tarnished further by letting his lowborn son be infantry.

Eadric gave the boy another glance over. He seemed the right age too.

"I've been there," said Eadric, calming his emotions. "Rested for a day on my way to Paris. It sits beautifully on the River Reine, doesn't it? I was there recently, actually."

William ticked. Eadric grinned down at him. The crowd of soldiers waited expectantly. "Do you know who I am?" he asked the boy.

William nodded his head.

"Do you know what they call me?" Eadric unsheathed his blade and placed it under William's chin, lifting his head up to look him in the eyes.

"The Hellhound of Rutland."

"That's right," said Eadric.

"I tried to warn 'em about the trap. Pike infantry can hold their ground when trapped. Allows time for others to come to aid."

"We would've beaten you all the same. Whether you flee or fight, I always win."

"That's why we hid. Tried to, anyways. Commanders weren't smart. I told them we should give up ground inland. Allow the fight to become a siege. Could 'ave sent a messenger to bring ships and defend us from the sea."

Eadric started to sweat. He felt the crowd's agitation from behind them. This wasn't how they thought this conversation would go. But this boy, could he be . . . ?

"*You* told your commanders this?" Eadric asked.

"No one listens to a boy," he said.

"And where did you learn military tactics? A common foot soldier wouldn't know fundamental battle strategy, and they certainly wouldn't have the nerve to give commands to a ranked officer."

William hesitated. "Back in Rouen I studied with my father, and for a brief time, Earl Robert was there."

The crowd went silent around them. Eadric gripped the boy by the shoulders. Urgency overpowered him. "You know Robert?"

"The Earl? Briefly, yes."

"You worked with Robert of Gloucester? The empress's half-brother?" Eadric stared into the boy's eyes, searching for the truth.

"My father had me aiding the earl when he stayed in Rouen. He sometimes discussed battle plans."

Eadric swallowed his salivating mouth. The woman Richard slept with was a peasant. Eadric had met her, talked to her in her house at the edge of the forest. The villagers called her family cursed. And they were right. Eadric would kill Richard's entire family.

The question remained. Was this the boy he had sailed from England for? A boy they almost killed because he wasn't a commander?

"When was the last time you saw Robert?" asked Eadric.

"Two years past now, after he was freed in exchange for Stephen."

"And who is this father of yours? What connection does he have to grant a peasant like you such high honors?"

"I'm a bastard, my lord. My father isn't a peasant. He goes by Duke Richard of Wilton."

Eadric tensed up. Excitement and anxiousness climbed into his voice. "You're Richard's bastard? Your cousin was Lorena?"

William nodded his head. Some kind of pus trickled out of his cleaved right ear. Eadric stood up and turned to the crowd. Duke Richard abandoned King Stephen three years ago now. Their intel said he was now one of Empress Maud's top advisors, which meant he was a traitor to the throne. It gave Eadric the right to slay him at long last; he'd been searching for him ever since. And now, finally, he may have a way to find him.

Through his son. The Lord had finally blessed his vengeance.

"Bound and gag him!" shouted Eadric. "Ready the boat. Send word to the king: we're returning to Kent!"

CHAPTER VI
EMMA

Emma stood back and admired her work. The thatched roof wasn't easy to repair. Many men had stopped along the street, gazing up at this girl balancing precariously atop a steep roof, and taken it as their moment of destiny, where they could show off their manhood and help this damsel in distress. Although it *was* annoyingly distracting, Emma was grateful that so many men would help her should she need it. It wasn't necessarily their fault. They probably grew up hearing stories about knights from far-off lands who helped fight heretics and save defenseless women.

The issue, of course, was that she wasn't defenseless at all in this current moment. She was sure of her footing and confident in her ability to lay and bind thatching over a small hole in a simple roof. She enjoyed being self-reliant, and she adored being able to affect the world around her. Even if the impact was only a few sheets of straw atop a humble house, Emma could look up at that small patch when a storm passed through and know in her heart of hearts that she existed, that she had sway over the appearance of the world, and that she could fix her own problems thank-you-very-much.

Godrick was the next man to stop under the bright glare of the sun and stare up at her sweating body. He was one of the hired masons rebuilding the parish church on the east side of town. Like most of the men who've stopped, he was well over twenty years her senior; he had a wife and two kids, who she sometimes played with after she finished her odd jobs. Emma smiled and waved at him kindly as he offered his services. She turned him down, explaining that the job was already finished, and any effort imparted by him at this point would be a waste of his good energy. He thus continued on his way, and Emma enjoyed her solitude again.

"Showing off now, ain't ye?"

Emma spun on the roof and smiled down at Alice, her best friend of five-going-on-six summers. Ever since she and her mother first moved to Marlborough, Emma had been fond of Alice. She became engaged to a slow-witted but gentle boy named Roger recently, saddening Emma because she now saw her much less than she'd like. Emma, at the exciting and prosperous age of fourteen, realized that most of her girlfriends—like Alice, who was only two years her elder—were already off getting married. In tough times like these, any extra family member meant a better chance of surviving these dismal winters.

"Only for ye, my love," said Emma. She bear-crawled her way to the ladder and scurried down to Alice. They shared a warm embrace before heading to the market.

The pair chatted along the way, catching up about each other's families and the few exotic experiences they'd had with the odd foreigner that passed through their city. On top of that, other than discussions about church, the juicy rumors swirling about folk their age always became the prime subject of their talks.

When they reached the market, Alice and Emma bought bread, spices, and game meat. The air was full of the textured aroma of sweets and delicacies.

"When'd ye get so much money?" asked Alice.

"Been doin' plenty of odd jobs," said Emma. "Fixing roofs. Delivering letters."

"And do they know you can read?"

"They wouldn't hand me important letters if they did."

"You're going to get yourself into trouble." Alice and Emma smiled conspiratorially.

"Ye want to know the best one I've read yet?"

"Yes! Must you even ask?"

They pulled each other into an isolated corner away from any prying ears. They giggled to each other. "Lord Hunnington has professed a new love life," whispered Emma.

"Ooooh. To whom? Prithee tell. Come, come."

"Peace, Alice!" They smiled and pushed into each other. Nobles were weird. They rarely married for romance, and it made Emma *very* confused. Why were they so content with being unhappy? Like, they're rich . . . just be rich and marry someone dashing. But alas, the eccentric highborn found a way to neglect their marriage that confused her even more. Each noble had the person they were married to, the man or woman they had their personal and . . . *sexual* duties with—the word sex still made Emma feel naughty—but then, the nobles had their actual admirers, the person they really loved but couldn't be with for whatever stupid reasons. They called it a "love life." The life of amour they could experience away from their wife or husband.

And the part that scrambled Emma's brain the most? The wife or husband usually allowed it.

WHAT?!

It made no sense to her. She would be furious! Why can't they just be with the person they love? The one who makes them feel warm and cozy, like the sun exploded inside their chest. If Emma found out Tom would even consider a love life—

"Emma," Alice moaned. "Tell me who!"

"He has a love life with Isabeau of Wareham."

Alice gasped. "He chose someone from the empress's land? Why would he do that? He'll never get to see her."

"He said, 'love is love,' or some silliness like that. Ye want to hear the best part?"

"Yes, spit it out."

"Guess how old she is?"

"Emma, how'm I supposed to guess that?"

"Just do it."

"Seventeen?"

"Forty-five."

"HOLY SHIT!"

Emma spat out a laugh. Alice ducked down, embarrassed by her own outburst. Some older women walking by gave them dirty looks. Emma and Alice grabbed each other for support.

"My God, Lord Hunnington must be stupid or insane or both," said Alice.

"She's older than his wife."

"Jesus Christ, that's older than me mum. He could have had any young girl he pleased, yet he chose an old hag on the other side of the war?"

"'Tis his love life. Besides, forty-five isn't that old."

Alice raised her eyebrow. "I know *four* women who died last winter who were over that age. If being that age makes me die easier, then I'd call that old."

A sudden commotion on the next street aroused their attention. They swarmed to the excitement, for they were addicted to intrigue and novel experiences like most young people confined to a single town; any scandal worth gossiping about was met with the utmost pleasure. Emma couldn't wait to tell all her other friends about her good fortune of being able to see whatever was happening. They pushed through a small crowd and spotted Lady Colette.

Emma gasped. Lady Colette, the daughter of Lord Deorwine, was like the princess of their knightly tales brought to life, unfathomably beautiful and perfect in all ways. Today, the fair lady wore a brilliant, burned-orange dress with a lovely floral design decorated up the skirt. She didn't need to wear a belt, as her bodice was perfectly tailored to fit around her waist. It was striking. Daring. It gave a hint of her figure, while still allowing her the grace that would be expected of a lord's daughter. Emma imagined what the dress would feel like on her—the fabric brushing against her legs and the power she'd command from feeling so elegant.

"She's so pretty," said Emma.

"Me knows," said Alice. "And I hate it."

Emma knew what she meant. Anytime Lady Colette granted the citizens of Marlborough a chance to gaze upon her, she made certain she was adequately graceful and handsome. Just like Emma, she had raven-black hair that hid behind a thick wimple and veil. The only thing she didn't have was Emma's eyes. *Green as springtime grass*, as her mother would say. Lady Colette had dark auburn ones. So, Emma might not have wealth, or a well-fed body, or ornate clothes, or hundreds of admirers, or the ability to travel, or a warm bedchamber at night, *but* Emma had some beautiful green eyes that her mother complimented all the time.

At least she had that?

"Actually, I hate her too," said Emma. She sighed. "Why is it that God makes some of us look like angels while He makes the rest of us look like the rear end of an ass?"

"Because we're peasants. If we ate as much as they do, we'd look lovely too."

The crowd around the illustrious Lady Colette dissipated as she moved down the street. And with it, Emma saw an opportunity. She glanced over at Alice, and her friend caught the look in her eye.

"Oh no," said Alice.

"Let's do it!"

"It will never work."

"We don't know that."

"It didn't work when Lady Sabina came to town."

"That's because I fell right on top of her. As long as I fall *next to* her, it'll be fine."

Alice sighed and gave in. Emma did a little jump, needing to get the bottled-up energy out of her system somehow. They moved, both knowing the plan. It was bound to work one of these days. Emma just needed to make sure she didn't almost cripple the royal maiden; she still had sores from Lady Sabina.

Emma climbed up a ladder leaning against the apothecary's shack. She slipped off her shoes. The straw roof felt spongy underneath her. She ducked as a city guardsman with an intimidating halberd walked by. She waited for him to pass, and then she jumped.

She leaped across the narrow gap between the apothecary's shop and the adjacent building, owned by a tailor named Oswald. She landed cleanly and smiled. From above the muck and stench of Marlborough, the fresh spring breeze could hit her unimpeded, giving her lungs a refreshing surge of clean air.

Emma smiled. This must be what it feels like to be a princess. She could have clean air every day if she were noble. Now, all she needed to do was to be accepted by one. Lady Colette certainly wasn't her top choice, but, hey! A noblewoman was a noblewoman.

Emma chased after the moving entourage. She spotted Alice. She was keeping close at hand while watching out for guards. Lady Colette's group took a left turn down a dusty old street before pausing to allow a pony-drawn cart to go by. It gave Emma the opportunity to get directly above them.

A few nearby townsfolk noticed her up on the roofs and grimaced. Emma imagined what they must be saying: *Not the cripple's girl again. Whose roofing is she going to ruin and have to fix this time? She* is *mighty sure-footed up there, though. Great balance! Oh, she can certainly hop farther than any boy her age. Maybe she* is *as skilled as a noble woman. She should be a princess with how daring and confident and pretty and—*

Alice hissed at her, desperately waving her arms. Emma glanced down and noticed with horror that Lady Colette was halfway down the road. She cursed. Her mother routinely berated her for getting lost in her daydreams. Thoughts, like imagining what her life would be like after she fell next to Lady Colette; she would take Emma under her care, and bring her back to her estate where there would be endless food and constant pampering, and Colette would decide to make Emma her little sister, and—

"Emma!" Alice shouted.

Right! Stop thinking, Emma! She shook her head and sprinted across the rooftops. Lady Colette headed for the townhouses at the outskirts of town, whose roofs were much too high for Emma to jump up on. She needed to act fast. This was her dream, and dreams don't magically come true like in children's tales.

Her foot slipped. *Oh no, not again!*

A bundle of thatch flew up and caught in the breeze above her. Her stomach lifted into her throat. Her scream thundered out to the wide blue sky. The next thing she knew, she slammed onto the dirt road; the air blasted out of her chest. She sucked in pure dust, and it burned her lungs. A crowd flocked around her as she focused her eyes on some pigeons flying way above her. She moaned.

The sun blinded her until a dark shadow blocked it out. She gazed up at this phantom and recognized it to be the beautiful noblewoman. For a split second, Emma saw her own reflection looking down at her. Yes, she would make a proper aristocrat one day.

"What's wrong with you?" asked Lady Colette.

Right, time to put on a show.

"Oi! Oh! It hurts so much." Emma winced, not having to act much on account of how badly it *did* hurt. The men in the crowd attempted to help her up, but Emma pushed them away. "Nay! Don't touch me. You there."

"Me?" Lady Colette looked down at her confused.

"Yes, ye fair maiden. Please help—no, no, not ye men. You. Pretty madam. Perhaps ye have a nice infirmary bed inside your estate where I can rest me woes?"

"Uh, no. We don't have any extra beds."

"Oh, well, ye wouldn't need a little sister, would ya?"

"Huh?"

A loud shout came from behind the crowd. Alice pushed her way up to the front and was pulling Emma off the ground before she could object. "Emma, we got to go."

"Move aside!" yelled a commanding voice.

"The guards are after ye!"

Emma tried to wave goodbye to Lady Colette. She really was gorgeous up close. Behind the crowd, she spotted a halberd thrusting up and down in the air.

"Move!" shouted the guardsman. "Let me get to her!"

"Bye, Lady Colette!" Emma screamed. "Let me know if ye change your mind about having a sister!"

Before the bewildered noblewoman could respond, Alice had towed Emma through the crowd and out a back alleyway. They ran and ran until the crowd and guard and all the hubbub around the main street of Marlborough were far behind them. Eventually Emma caught her breath, and she could enjoy Alice's company once more.

"Can ye do me a favor?"

Alice sighed. She knew what was coming next. "Don't make me lie to your mum."

"It'll be just once."

"'Tis never just once. You know she doesn't like him."

"Please, Alice. I want to see him so badly."

"Where is he now?"

"In Reading. 'Tis not very far."

"How far isn't the point. It's dangerous for us. Girls can't be out on the road alone."

"I won't be alone," she said timidly. She raised an eyebrow in an inviting gesture.

"You want me to travel all the way to Reading so ye can see Tom?"

"Please? I'll love ye forever! Please, please, please?"

Alice moaned. "Only if Roger comes with us. But I'm *not* lying to your mum."

"You're the best! Thank ye." She paused. "At least I didn't land on her this time."

"I think it's time for you to admit that peasants and nobles don't get along."

"I'll be a princess one day. You'll see."

"If ye do, you better take me with you."

Emma and Alice smiled, interlocked their arms, and headed for the edge of town. Underneath the crystal-clear sky, the spring weather bloomed the natural wonders of Marlborough into a visual treat. Fresh streams snaked along the stone paths, and the constant trickle provided a soothing backdrop to the eager gossip of the townsfolk.

Soldiers of King Stephen's army patrolled the town. They made hungry, wanting eyes at Emma and Alice. The recent influx of military activity had been an active concern for the locals. Robert FitzRoy, the Earl of Gloucester, had been building his forces in the southwestern regions of the kingdom. Under his immaculate military leadership, he and Empress Maud were expected to make a heavy push inland, hoping to capture London at the heart of England. King Stephen retaliated against this threat by stationing more soldiers in the minor towns throughout Emma's region, which bordered the territory held by Earl Robert.

They reached Emma's home as the sun set far in the west. Her simple abode rested underneath a large oak tree, whose leaves had reached that magical time of year where they shimmered in a vibrant-green wave. Emma pushed open the front door.

"Mama, I'm home. Look who I have with me."

Emma and Alice navigated a tight entryway until they reached the main chamber, where a small, central fire pit in the dirt floor gave off a comforting heat. Edith, Emma's mom, kneeled next to the fire and stoked it with a large poker. She glanced back at the girls.

"Alice! How joyous it is to see ye again," said Edith. "Here, give me a hug." Edith tried to push herself onto her feet, but she stumbled down as her lame left leg gave out. It erupted a series of deep coughs from within her lungs. Emma and Alice rushed over.

"We'll help ye, Mama."

"No. No. 'Tis fine. Me gots it."

"Don't be silly," said Alice. "Let us help."

With a bit of grunting effort, Alice and Emma lifted Edith to a chair next to the fire. Her mother had injured her leg in a freak accident when Emma was very young, and since then, she hadn't been able to find any long-standing work. At first this wasn't much of a problem, as Emma's godparents, Verona and Paris, helped provide for them. For a time, they even had Emma's childhood friend, Lief—whose own parents had died long ago—living with them. He started working after he came of age for an apprenticeship with a scribe, and together all three, including Emma performing the odd job here and there, made enough money to survive despite Edith's injury.

But now, because of some troubling events that Emma would rather not think about, it was just her and her mother. And last winter had her awfully worried.

Emma had been the sole provider all year, and she'd been unable to save up enough provisions to last the full winter. In a desperate attempt to feed herself and her poor mother, she succumbed to thievery, which was how she met Alice. They both teamed up to steal a loaf of bread here, or snatch a coin purse off a drunk traveler there. One of the few benefits of being a woman was that they could get away with a lot by behaving innocently.

"Did you get everything you needed?" asked Edith.

"Yes, Mama." She placed the goods they bought on a rickety trestle table. Her house had only two chambers: the main area for cooking and staying warm, and a side bedchamber to sleep in. It was a far cry from how she imagined the luxurious abodes of the fair maidens and princesses.

"Did you have any trouble?"

"No. No trouble at all, right, Alice?"

"Nothing that got us killed," said Alice. She glanced at Emma, waiting for her to tell her mother about her planned venture to Reading.

Emma took a deep breath. She blew air into her closed mouth and puffed out her cheeks. Her mom gave her a discouraging look. Edith could always read whatever Emma was thinking. She wondered how her mom did that.

"What do ye want?" asked Edith.

"Mama, don't be mad . . ."

"You're not going, and that's the end of it!"

Alice scratched the back of her head awkwardly. Emma and Edith had been arguing for the last quarter of an hour. There were many times when Emma had asked Alice for aid, but Edith had been way too kind to her over the last few months to risk interjecting. Eventually, the argument moved to the bedroom, and Alice was left waiting next to the fire.

Emma slunk out of the bedroom looking defeated, annoyed, and utterly devastated. She sat down on the ground next to Alice and poked at the fire. She glanced over at her best friend, and the flames radiating in Emma's eyes reflected the passion flaring in her chest.

"I don't like that look," Alice remarked.

"She said I couldn't go."

"I got that impression."

"So, I think I'll leave tomorrow." Emma gave Alice a devilish smirk.

"She's goin' to kill ye, you know that? And then she'll murder me for helpin' you."

"We'll run then. What she goin' to do? She can't keep up with us."

"I hope this boy is worth it."

"He's a *man*, not a boy. And he's a squire. Means he'll be a knight soon. And when he's a knight, that'll make *me* his princess."

"You're obsessed with this princess idea."

Edith stumbled back into the room. It struck Emma how alike she and her mother looked. Her hair was jet black, just like Emma's, and they had the same tanned skin color. The only obvious difference was in their eyes. Her mom told Emma she had her father's eyes.

"It's not about the princess thing," whispered Emma to Alice as her mom prepared dinner. "Ye know what happened last year. I want to make sure we don't starve again, and he might be our best chance."

"Ye can tell yourself that, but I know the real reason is that you think he's ravishing."

"Yes, that too." Emma smiled. "Why can't a girl have both?"

CHAPTER VII
GILBERT

GILBERT REGAINED CONSCIOUSNESS.

Mist from the sea showered over him, leaving Gilbert cold and stiff. The wet sand clumped on his clothes and hair, and it stuck to his skin irritatingly. His head throbbed. All around him lay the bodies of those he'd deserted.

"William?" croaked Gilbert, struggling to lift his upper body off the ground. He was famished. His stomach growled something fierce, but his soul was now filled with dread. A thick fog rolled over him, strangling him with its heaviness. Faint patches in the fog glowed an eerie orange, places where the fires of war still lingered.

Gilbert mustered himself to say his brother's name louder. "William?" His bones creaked and popped as he forced himself to stand. The corpses that littered the beach all donned the crest of the Angevins—three golden lions upon an azure sky. He stumbled toward the nearest body. As the wisps of fog dispersed around the cadaver, Gilbert saw that it lay face down with three fletched arrows piercing its back. The congealed blood below it had turned the sand to mud. The corpse was roughly the same height and had the same brown hair as his baby brother.

"Will?" Gilbert asked, hoping some act of God would move the body with renewed vigor, and begging beyond hope it would be his brother, alive and well, so he wouldn't have to discover that William was dead. But the body did not move.

Gilbert gathered courage, at least as much as a deserting coward like him could, and he flipped over the body. The arrows snapped in half as the corpse's weight fell on top of them. Gilbert nearly toppled backwards. It was a young boy, his eyes opened and frightened. A swollen tongue, oozing with some black substance, protruded from his mouth like a violet slug. Gilbert pushed the fallen soldier away. His heart thundered in his chest; his body shivered relentlessly from the dank air. "William!" he yelled. "Will!"

Gilbert strained to recall what had happened. But the events that transpired following the surprise attack by Stephen's archers were as clouded in his mind as the dense mist around him.

"What 'ave ye got there?" whispered the fog.

Gilbert jumped. He reached for the knife that he always kept on his belt, but the tiny scabbard lay empty. Someone had stolen it.

"Oh my. Is this for me?"

It was too dark, and the fog too thick, to see the source of the coarse voice. A part of Gilbert leaped at the possibility that it could be his baby brother. "Will?"

He heard a shush. A muted muffling noise. And then nothing else.

"William?! Is that you?" asked Gilbert. The rational part of his brain, the part that begged him to remain quiet, warning him it could be the enemy, was defeated by the insatiable desire to no longer be alone. Gilbert moved toward the sound.

A sharp wind fluttered over the beach and blasted into him. He wrapped his arms around his body, and he discovered he was bleeding. A superficial cut ran up the length of his arm. *How did I get that?* The thought didn't linger very long as another strong gust pierced him. Gilbert imagined himself back home in central Normandy, away from these damn border disputes and the horrid English weather. He forced himself to remember the warm French summers, when Hawk, Bartholomew, Beatriz, Will and he would stay up until dawn drinking, smoking, and celebrating life. So alluring and so comforting were the images that Gilbert could taste the warm mead cascading down his parched throat; it loosened his stiff joints and softened his provoking headache. He even smiled.

Then he tripped over another corpse. Gilbert lifted his hands up to stop his fall, but he was much weaker than he expected. He crashed into the beach, breathing in coarse sand. He pushed it out of his eyes and coughed it out in an excruciating spasm. His lungs were still burning when a shadow loomed over him.

"What's this? One still alive, and handsome too?"

Gilbert faced the shadow. It was a woman, and an ugly one at that. She smiled leeringly at him. Half her teeth were missing, and the ones that remained were rotten and brown. Her tangled hair was gray, fraying at the ends, and her skin was covered in filth or shit or both. Her torn simple tunic revealed protruding ribs and bright red rashes. "Why do ye appear startled so? Dist find anythin' on him?"

The woman bent down to the corpse and started stripping his armor. Gilbert was in shock. "What are you doing?" he demanded.

"Seein' what he gots." She patted him down, letting her fingers glide over the dead man's body. "Nothin' up here."

"You're robbing him?"

"Can't rob what's dead. Nothin' in here either." She pulled the man's trousers below his waist and stuck her hand inside. "Pity, pity. He had a big cock. Ha!"

Her hand gripped it under his pants and stroked it. Gilbert nearly threw up. He shoved the woman away. She rolled onto her back and hissed at him. He saw a flash as she swung a knife. Gilbert stepped back. "Pretty boy scared?" she asked.

"Stop that," Gilbert said. His voice failed him; it trembled with fright.

"Ah, a coward then! 'Tis always the brave who die." She smiled. Her tongue moistened her lips. "But they isn't usually so handsome. Mmm. Why don't ye come with me? Warm shelter, just for us. Cozy beds, yes. With hordes of treasure from the dead."

"Shut up."

"T'ain't hard. Oft have I taken two at once."

"Belt it!" Gilbert yelled. The woman lunged forward. The knife flashed. It missed him by inches. The woman cackled. Her spit hit him square in the mouth. He wiped it away and heaved. If he had any fluids left inside of him, it would have covered the beach by now.

"*You* belt it, foolish boy. I 'ave a man t'would like to meet ye. Ha! It be warm, safe. Oh-so safe, for us three." She waved for him to follow. Gilbert considered running; he could try hiding in the fog. But if this crazed woman was a local, she'd know these lands which were a mystery to him. That was, of course, assuming he could even escape. "We 'ave food too. He can feed you. And then, we can 'ave fun. So much fun." She bit her lip.

His stomach trembled. There were many winters when Gilbert, William, and their family could only eat a slice of bread a day to survive. But this hunger was different; it was ravenous and frenzied. Once she mentioned food, and the potential of getting away from the frigid wetness, he decided he would chance it.

"Follow!" she said. "Follow."

She led him to an isolated shack outside the nearby village. Its open door shone out one of those ghostly orange lights that he'd seen earlier; it made him desperate to enter. Once he was warmed and fed, he could redouble his efforts to find Will. Gilbert barely took three steps into the warm shack when he felt a sharp poke in his abdomen. The woman laughed and pinched her knife into him. Gilbert cursed himself for being such a fool.

"Lookst at who me found," said the woman, shoving him toward the below-ground firepit within the empty chamber.

"I'll be damned," said another familiar voice. Gilbert slowly turned, letting the blade slip around his torso, and found Jacques holding a short sword. "My, my, Perrete. You did *real* good."

"Don't me always?" Perrete laughed. She pushed Gilbert away, opening her cloak and upturning the bag she hid beneath it. The stolen goods of their fallen comrades clanged against the other spoils that she and Jacques had stolen, which lay in an ever-increasing pile. Jacques lowered the sword.

"Welcome back from the dead."

Many thoughts swarmed through Gilbert's mind. *Do you know what happened to William? How did you escape? What happened to me?* But as he shivered in the damp air, his body could only focus on the overpowering urge to get close to the fire. Jacques sensed this too, for he upturned his hand and motioned to the flames. Gilbert nodded his thanks and collapsed next to the firepit. He stripped off his freezing *maille* and soaked gambeson, followed by his boots and mittens. It was like he peeled off his incessant agonies one by one, grating off his animalistic desires until he was finally closer to his right, God-given mind again.

"He's hungry," said Perrete. "Ha! Look how he starves."

"Then shut your bitching mouth and feed him," said Jacques. "Get."

Perrete lowered her head and scurried to a door on the far side of the room. She gave a sly glance back at Gilbert before she cautiously opened the door and entered the dark chamber beyond. Jacques sat down next to Gilbert. A biting wind blasted against the shack, rattling the shingles and penetrating the wooden walls.

"How'd ye get out?" asked Gilbert.

"I hid better than you. You're a worse coward than you are a soldier. Don't play the rat if you can't escape the cat."

"What happened? I remember them routing our army and fleeing toward us. I got separated from you and Will, but after that . . ."

"'Tis no wonder with a gash like that." Jacques pointed to his head. Gilbert gingerly touched the wound there, an incision an inch across that he wasn't aware he had. His fingers came away red. "You ran, but not far. I think you maybe got twenty feet before–*bam!* Enemy's shield bashed you real hard. You fell."

"How am I not dead?"

"T'would be your brother's doing, that. Good lad . . . stupid lad."

Perrete slithered back into the room—being mindful to close the door behind her—before Gilbert could ask where his brother was. She ruffled Jacques's hair and tossed a sausage to Gilbert. "Is he warm yet?" she asked.

Jacques wrapped his arm around her legs. "Getting there, ain't ye, Gilbert? Go on, eat. A battle is always tiring, especially one you ran from."

An intense desire to defend himself overcame Gilbert. How could, of all people, a graverobber belittle him? He was trying to save himself. No, to save his brother! This was about protecting those he loved.

It was . . . it was . . .

Gilbert shoved the sausage into his mouth. God, he was hungry.

"Look at 'im gobble that up. HA!"

"I bet you're wondering where I met this *feisty* woman," said Jacques. "T'was love at first sight."

"Shut up. I was speaking." He waited for her to go quiet, then went on. "As I was saying, I found her walkin' along the sea, waving at those

Saxon bastards as they fled. There were so many bodies all around, I asked her if she could help me lighten 'em."

"T'was your idea then?" asked Gilbert. "To rob our brethren?"

"Don't be angry because I'm a better weasel than you. You can be shite at being a shit human, but I aim for greatness." Jacques squeezed Perrete's ass. She hollered in surprise. "You can join me. Plenty of loot for the two of us."

"Three of us," Perrete corrected.

"Quiet! What'd I say?"

Having been thoroughly warmed, fed, and dried, Gilbert decided he was disgusted enough to end this conversation. He glared at Jacques and braced to finally learn the truth. "What happened to Will?"

"He saw you get your head smashed by that shield. Will wanted to save you. I tried to pull him away, but the fucker was determined to die with you. So, I let him. Better him than me."

"And I was here," Perrete interjected. "Quieting their screams."

Gilbert frowned. Whose screams was she quieting?

"And you know what that crazy brother of yours did?" asked Jacques. "He picked up a spear and yelled. And I mean loud. So loudly that the cunt who did that to your head turned after him for making him deaf. He wailed and swung that spear and led half the fuckin' army down the beach. Hell, I guess I have to thank him. Damn good distraction, all things told."

"*Relativus*," whispered Gilbert shakily. He was a man who rarely cried, even after losing his siblings, even after hearing his mother say horrible things about herself, about him, and about God. Without shedding a tear, he bore it all. Maybe it was because he wanted to be strong for Will, or for his mother. But now that William sacrificed himself to save a deserter like Gilbert . . .

"Tell him," said Perrete. "Tell him who ye saw."

"I thought your brother was as good as dead," Jacques began.

"He's alive?!" Hope exploded in Gilbert's chest.

"I don't know if he still is, but he was."

"Tell 'im, my love! Tell 'im who came!"

"The Hellhound of Rutland. And my, was he a mighty big prick. Strong. Demanding. He and Robert had to be of the same cloth. I couldn't take my eyes off him, and so I hid behind the brambles, careful to keep myself concealed. He came up to William and put a stop to his harassment. I don't know what he and your brother said, but Will convinced the large bastard to spare him."

"He is alive!"

"I told you; he *was*. They took him hostage. Bound, gagged him, oared him to their boat. If he's still alive, he's halfway to that accursed island kingdom by now."

Gilbert's world stopped. He saw William before him as clearly as the flickering flames, befouled and emaciated, chained by the neck in a dank crypt below an indomitable castle, with the notorious Hellhound of Rutland watching over him like a sentinel of Satan. The flames reflected in his brother's eyes, betraying all his fear and abandonment.

Gilbert grimaced. A long-submerged memory struck him, like an axe had fractured the headache deep in his skull and shattered his psyche with tempestuous guilt. He saw *her*. Dying. Wailing. Her small body, and his unthinkable mistake—*no, it wasn't a mistake. It was more than that. It was everything.*

Gilbert clung desperately to his broken mind, trying to mend it with forgetfulness. He pushed the memory away, burying his emotions with it.

Again, I'm a coward.

Gilbert imagined William with another captive in that cellar, equally befouled and emaciated because of his curse, her skeleton chained to the wall . . .

No. Not again. I need to be strong for them.

"I have to save him." The words flew out of his mouth as soon as his mind thought them. "I need to."

"He's beyond saving," said Jacques. "He's the Hellhound's property now and well past your reach."

"All my life, I've hurt the people I've loved with my feebleness. But not again." Gilbert nodded to himself, layering any courage he had one by one, like the foundations of stone beneath a grand cathedral, until he could finally rouse himself to bravery. "I must be off to Rouen. There's some people there who'll help me. We can save him. I *must* save him."

Gilbert, not wanting to waste a moment, turned to run out the door. Jacques was faster. He raised the sword and crossed in front of the doorway, leveling the blade at Gilbert's sternum. "Where do you think you're going, friend?"

"What's this?"

"Ha!" Perrete yipped excitedly. "Look at 'im squirm!"

"Jacques, please. Let me leave."

"I'm sorry," said Jacques. "But I can't let you return home. Lest ye forget, we're deserters. If anyone finds out, we'll be hunted and beheaded for such a crime, and I like my body whole."

"Then flee."

"Ah, but I can't if you get caught. I know your type. The moment they have you, you'll betray me and your brother and every other sin you've committed. I like my chances a lot more if you're with me."

"Jacques—"

"Or the alternative." Jacques smiled. His grip tightened around the hilt of the sword. "No one dares listen to the dead."

Gilbert's throat went dry. His ears rang with the pounding of his blood. He raised his hands. "I promise I won't tell a soul. I just want to save William."

"Perrete, why don't you show him where we keep the food?"

"Oh, ho. Anything," she said. She tugged him toward the back chamber, using her free hand to threaten him with her knife. She threw open the door. Gilbert's knees wobbled. The sight was grisly; three young children lay dead. They sat in the corner, cowering, their faces still frozen with fear.

"They were hidin' in the pantry," she said. "But they aren't as good at hiding as me. Too much cryin', so I silenced them. HA! Now I'll have enough food for winter. No more starvin' for me. No more eating bugs and gross plants. No more."

"You passed the parents outside," Jacques explained. "They must have been in town when Stephen attacked. Perrete was showin' me her wonderful work with the kids when they returned. Really, I did an honorable thing in killing them. No parent should see their babies in such a state. They should make me a knight for such nobility!"

"Yes, and make me a princess!"

Gilbert pushed down his nausea. This was too much for one person in one day. Perrete pressed her knife into his side. It gave him an idea. He lowered his voice so that only Perrete could hear him. "Come with me," he said.

"What?"

"He doesn't care about you, Perrete. Look at all this . . . this . . ." He struggled to find the right words. "This good work you've done. He'll ruin it—take it all for himself."

"You don't know us."

"No, but you can know me." Gilbert caressed her body with his hand. He shuddered at the thought of lying with her. She gave a devilish grin and reached down between his legs. Right as she touched him, Gilbert snatched the knife from her hand. She tried to turn and run, but Gilbert flung his arm around her neck and pulled her against him. "Hark. Listen to him betray you."

Gilbert spun her so she faced Jacques. He pinned the knife against her throat. The smell coming from her made him gag.

"What is this nonsense, Gilbert?" asked Jacques.

"Let me go, or I'll kill her."

Jacques shrugged. "You think I'll throw my life away for this infested whore? You must be stupider than your brother as well."

"I ain't a whore," said Perrete.

"Silence. He won't kill you anyway. He's a coward through-and-through. As if he'd ever sail across the sea and save his brother. The man fears his own shadow. Go on, cut her throat."

"Jacques . . ." moaned Perrete.

"Do it. I'd actually like to see it."

Gilbert smiled. He handed the knife back to Perrete and threw her away from him. She rubbed her throat. Jacques laughed and took a step closer. The firelight glistened off the short sword he held.

"Now you'll stay put," he ordered Gilbert. "We'll be off soon. I'm thinking we should head for Spain. What say you, Perrete?"

She didn't answer him. Jacques was careful not to take his eyes off Gilbert. He waved her off. "Women don't know what they want. Start packing, love. I'll make sure he doesn't move an inch—AGH!"

Jacques swatted back, but his body already betrayed him. Perrete shredded her knife out from between his spine. She plunged the dagger into his throat, slicing and tearing and shredding it to bits. She became covered in his blood. "I'm not a whore!"

Gilbert didn't wait to see how far this would go. He sprinted out of that God-forsaken shack at the edge of Geoffrey's empire. He ran deep into the fog-enshrouded night until all he heard behind him was the distant shouts of Perrete.

"Gilbert! Gilbert! Come back! Come back!"

But the memory of Perrete's face was already forgotten in his mind, just as he'd done with his sister on that terrible night so long ago. He had a skill for forgetting, and abandoning, and running. Eventually, he fled so far that his legs gave out, and he collapsed into the dense foliage of the nearest wood. Somewhere on the beach far behind, the ghosts of the Côte d'Opale moaned in misery while listening to the endless cries of the accursed Perrete.

CHAPTER VIII
EADRIC

S TANDING AT THE BOW of his ship, Eadric endured the night air while it pierced his gambeson. He embraced it—this final frigid breath from the brutal winter. Spring germinated more and more each day, yet his soul never left the desolation of the English tundra. The horrid cold of winter more acutely accentuated the hollowness inside him. The shell of a parent after losing a child.

I hate crossing the Channel.

This was his fourth time sailing across the Strait of Dover. After King Henry's death in 1135, it became immediately clear that the war for England's succession wouldn't be fought solely on domestic shores. The duchies of Flanders, Brabant, and Normandy would all be under contention. Stephen and his wife, Matilda, already had a strong foothold in southeast England, and thus it became paramount to their early campaign to control Flanders and Brabant, the two duchies closest to them opposite the strait.

Stephen was careful with Eadric, much to his dismay. The king sent him to fight only when a victory was completely necessary. The first time Eadric crossed was to fight a brief battle against some dukes in Normandy. Eadric dismantled their armies and even captured a castle on the border of Flanders. Matilda, who seemed the cunning half of the royal matrimony, convinced Stephen to grant the castle to a Flemish commander. In one swoop, it increased the landmass of the duchy *and* secured the admiration of multiple Flemish mercenary armies. King Stephen would be dead by now if not for them.

This second time, however, was under very different pretenses. It wasn't exactly at the behest of the king or his generals. In fact, Eadric expected them to be quite furious when he returned.

"How you holding up?" asked Sir Álvaro.

Eadric turned to face the knight. Sir Álvaro's tan face appeared pale in the brisk wind. Since the days of him courting his daughter, the knight had grown a large bushy mustache and thick eyebrows that sat snuggly over his upper eyelids. He placed a hand on Eadric's shoulder, apparently trying to be friendly.

"The mission was a success," said Eadric simply.

"Yes, miraculously. But I was referencing your stoic solitude. Usually when someone stands on the edge of a boat or battlements, I get the feeling they're going to jump."

"I'm not suicidal."

"Not in the standard sense, at least."

"What do you want?" Eadric never truly lost his suspicion of Sir Álvaro. His daughter was a better judge of character than Eadric ever was, and *she* disliked him. That was enough foundation for him to remain apprehensive.

"No need to get upset. I just care about you."

"I'm ruminating on the war."

"Ruminating outside on a nippy night?"

"The Hell do you want?! I told you how I feel, and that's the fucking end of it."

"I apologize for asking. Maybe it's my own demons coming forth. On a night like this, I find myself thinking of your daughter—"

Eadric swung up his gauntleted hand, as if to strike the knight across the cheek. He pulled back at the last second. Sir Álvaro didn't flinch; instead, his mouth twitched somewhere between a smile and a grimace.

"Hold your tongue," said Eadric. "Now piss off before I drown you like the late king's son."

"Forgive my presumptuous spirit. Knighthood has destined me to be so," said Sir Álvaro. Before he walked away, he added, "Oh, and check up on that hostage of yours. They're crying up a storm down below. It's infuriating some of the crew. You wouldn't want him murdered before we reached Kent. He is the reason we came all this way, after all."

Eadric glowered at the knight as he walked off. *That fucking bastard thinks he can bring up Lucia to me? And so abruptly? So . . . rationally?!*

Eadric clenched and unclenched his fists. His legs held firm on the tilting deck. The wind blew around him like a stream around a boulder. That reassurance—the fortitude that he was strong and stern and mighty against the elements of God—calmed him down.

Lucia: my darling angel with the slit throat.

This was why he hated crossing the channel between England and the mainland. It's where the war started. In these very waters, the son of King Henry, William Adeline, and his other illegitimate children drowned. Their ship rammed into a rock off the coast of Normandy, capsizing with the royal passengers into the bleak depths. It was said William would've survived had he not heard the cries of his half-sister, who was still trapped in the sinking ship. William swam back to save her, but he found only an eternal tomb at the bottom of the sea.

Helpless are the righteous.

An act of bravery begot the tumultuous succession crisis, which led to war, to banditry, to civil unrest, to peasant revolts—

"What did You want?! Why did You take her?!"

Eadric's screams echoed into the black sky. God didn't answer. The nearby crew scuttled away from him. Eadric straightened his armor, suddenly embarrassed by his outburst. Why'd that damnable Sir Álvaro make him think of her?

Eadric sighed. He felt drained. His sagging skin and armor hung heavy on him. His stomach growled, and an ache grew in his head. That was the one thing that amazed him after Lucia's death. No matter how much the wretchedness of despair wracked his soul, his body continued to function normally. He expected himself to lose all appetite, for his muscles to stop growing and his hair to shrivel up and his prick to stop hardening . . . but his body went through its normal routine as it had every day of his life.

Well, except for the prick part, he supposed.

Eadric determined long ago that because his body hadn't quit on him, that meant God hadn't either. He'd continue to fight until someone blessed enough struck him down. But until that day came, and he was finally reunited with Lucia, he would continue to combine the forces of Heaven and Hell to destroy all those who wronged him.

The city of Lincoln burned. Eadric backed up against King Stephen as they butchered the advancing Angevin infantry, listening gleefully while men screamed and cried. Eadric had never been in a lost contest before, but this had all the hallmarks of certain death. The battle seemed clear at first. Stephen and his chosen knights were at the center of their formation with two thousand troops, while two other companies of five hundred men each, one led by William of Ypres and the other by a band of earls from various provinces, protected them at their wings. And then on the opposite side of the battlefield was Empress Maud's army, led by her cunning half-brother Robert of Gloucester. They had a similar arrangement, only with a few thousand more troops and a Welsh free company led by Ranulf de Gernon.

Those cowardly fucking Welsh, thought Eadric. How Stephen's flanks had yielded to Welshmen of all people—horrid fighters with barely any training—was beyond him.

"Fight for your country!" shouted King Stephen. "Fight the invaders! Channel your blood; the blood of conquerors!"

With their wings disbanded, the empress's army surrounded them on all sides. Eadric heard his fellow countrymen die by the dozens. Pikes, swords, and spears punctured them. Arrows darkened the sky and sprayed the battlefield with deadly randomness. An honorable knight by the name of Sir Frederick stumbled over a corpse. Before he had time to react, one of Robert's soldiers impaled their spear through the knight's throat, ejecting his spine out the back.

Eadric roared. He jumped in close to the soldier, grappling their spear so they couldn't use it. He stabbed his dagger into the soldier's ear, right beneath his helm. The man's eyes exploded like popped grapes as the blade ruptured them.

"Eadric, fall to me!" Stephen ordered him to protect his flank. The king, for all his grandiose dramatics, was truly a determined and passionate fighter. He battled like Eadric, like a bull trapped by wolves. Stephen and he took out dozens of Robert's men before their weapons shattered in half from overuse.

"We're being routed!"

"William has abandoned us!"

"They're breaking through the east guard!"

In the distance, Eadric spotted Robert of Gloucester commanding his troops. He had a special aura around him, one that the poets of old wrote about. His men rallied about him, no matter the odds. If he were in battle against anyone else in the world, Eadric knew he could fight his way out. But not against the empress's brother; Robert of Gloucester didn't lose. Deep down in Eadric's soul, he knew Robert was the only man who could best him.

"My king, we need to get you out of here," said Eadric.

"No. I will not surrender. I will not bow to my cousin."

"We cannot win."

"I will *not* abandon them," said the king. He reached out and held Eadric's arm. "But you must."

"What is your command?"

"Flee. Find the queen and tell her what happened."

"And what of you, my lord?"

"Maud won't kill me. My cousin's pride is too great. She'd hold me hostage."

"What should I tell the queen?"

"The truth. I've been captured, and it's time for her to prove her love."

"I will, my lord. Stay strong."

"Fight for my wife, Eadric. Fight for the queen, and I shall reward you handsomely. I will find who's responsible for your daughter's death. I swear it."

"My king!" Tears swelled in Eadric's eyes. He wouldn't let King Stephen down. They clanked their helms against each other in parting.

Eadric turned and fought his way to the southern edge of the battlefield, where a long dike circled the city. Once there, he frantically ripped off his armor, stripped down to his undergarments, and swam across the river. Other men fleeing the battle tried the same, but in their fear-stricken minds, most of the deserters forgot to strip their armor before crossing. They cried for help as the river dragged them beneath the surface like anchors.

Eadric ended up being one of only a dozen who made it across the River Witham. The other five hundred who tried all drowned. Archers took aim and fired at him when he reached the opposite shoreline. Eadric raced off. Far back on the battlefield behind him, the rest of King Stephen's army was slaughtered, and the indomitable Robert of Gloucester took the king as his prisoner, only two short years after the war had begun.

The below decks were much rowdier than the main deck. Eadric pushed his way past dozens of troops, a mix of both Queen Matilda's Flemish mercenaries and King Stephen's English loyalists. The mass of bodies swayed in perfect synchrony with the vessel, the hull groaning and rumbling like the men as they clanked their tankards of ale and laughed over games of dice. There was a time when Eadric would engage in such debauchery, when alcohol wasn't a crutch to overcome his crippling insomnia and guilt.

But that wasn't his life now, so why dwell on it?

Eadric reached the stern of the lowest deck, where cages held hostages and prisoners. The keeping of hostages was a common wartime practice; it allowed both sides to have leverage in trade negotiations, while also keeping opposing armies from heedlessly invading the other.

Eadric heard the boy weeping before he even shoved through the final bit of crowd. William, their captive, the bastard son of Duke Richard and previous aide to Earl Robert of Gloucester, laid on his side in the dog-sized cage they kept him in. The conjoined body heat of the lower decks sweltered back here; the smell—an odorous mixture of fish, sweat, vomit, piss, and fecal matter—made it near unbearable. A soldier kicked the cage, making Will roll over.

"Shut ye'r whinnin', ye fuckin' ass," the soldier ordered.

"Yeah! Can't ye see we're tryin' to party?" said another drunkard.

"Wait, wait, wait. He's had a tough day," said a third. "Methinks he needs a drink."

The third soldier flung his ale onto the hostage. William recoiled and whimpered. The sticky ale clumped into globs on him. The group of soldiers laughed.

"Leave the hostage alone," said Eadric. The group turned to argue, but as soon as they saw it was the Hellhound, they quickly shut up and squeezed past him. Eadric turned to a fourth soldier who was half drunk and standing idly by. He seemed strong and foreboding enough.

"What's your name?" Eadric asked him.

"Alfwin."

"You've been promoted. You're now a gaoler. Watch over this prisoner with your life, lest you wish to forfeit your own. Understood?"

"Yes, milord," said Alfwin, stumbling for his weapon.

Eadric stooped to William's level. The boy twitched. "You best learn to stifle those cries," he said to the sniveling husk. "You aren't getting out anytime soon."

"Why do ye care?" asked the boy.

"Because I need you to live and not get throttled by your guards. Something tells me I'm going to need you." Eadric hit the cage as William sobbed again. "Stop that blubbering. What happened to the soldier who stood up to all my men?"

"I was being brave then. For me brother."

"Find something else that'll make you brave, then. Even if its vengeance."

William glared up through the confines of his dog cage and said, "*Relativus.*"

Eadric furrowed his brow and frowned. *The Hell does* relativus *mean?*

An audible uproar came from behind them. Sir Álvaro pushed through the crowd to reach him. "We have a problem," said the knight.

Eadric and Sir Álvaro stormed onto the top deck. A ring of soldiers formed around the central mast. They forced their way to the front. In the center of the riot were two men. Eadric knew one of them—Duke Pascal de Aalst, a conniving, shrewd, lesser nobleman with some estate in eastern Flanders. He was the worst type of duke; the kind always searching for the next way he could rise on the social ladder. He reminded him of Richard.

"What's the meaning of this?" asked Eadric, thundering his voice over the crowd.

"This man has stolen from His Majesty," said Duke Pascal in his rough accent.

"I have not," said the soldier. "He fibs on account of losing a game of chance."

"You devilish fiend. You dare insult a liege lord?!"

The crowd rumbled into an uproar again. Eadric glanced around. This fight filtered through to the infantry. A tale as old as time: the wealthy versus the poor, the nobility pitted against the peasantry. Eadric knew if he didn't act decisively, then the crew could turn against one another. Trapped on a boat, it would be a bloodbath.

"How has he stolen from the king?" asked Eadric.

"By stealing from my purse, he has stolen from the king's treasury," said Duke Pascal. "How can I pay my due taxes when they are stolen from me? Taxes that *they* are unwilling to pay, on all accounts." Half of the crowd thundered against the disgust in the duke's voice. "How can I fund the king's campaign and aid his conquest while worrying about theft?!"

"I'm not a thief! I won the purse. Won it fairly. He lost the game, and rightly thus, I claimed my award."

"Did anyone see this game they played?" Eadric asked the crowd. They went silent. "Did no one witness the exchange of niceties and agreement of winnings?"

Again, the crowd was silent.

"We played it in our own corner," said the soldier. "T'was a spat between the two of us alone."

"Horseshit!" said the duke. "He stole my coin from right under my nose."

The crowd shouted again. Duke Pascal and the soldier reached for their weapons. Eadric crossed to them. The thumping of his boots on the wooden deck echoed into the blistering wind, quieting the crowd.

"My lord, I would never lie to you," said Duke Pascal, bowing before him. Eadric glanced at the soldier expectantly.

"This is a farce," he said instead. "I am in the right. T'was a game, and now his hurt pride from losin' to a peasant has caused him to form this lie about me. I'll not have it." The soldier stuck out his chin, high and proud against the tyranny of the highborn.

Eadric punched him in the throat.

His leather mitten cracked the soldier's brittle windpipe. The crowd gasped. Eadric gripped the soldier by the tunic and dragged him across the deck. The peasant's breath escaped in compressed wheezes. Eadric slammed him against the gunwale.

"Me didn't—"

Before he could finish his sentence, the Hellhound kneed the peasant in the sternum. Sir Álvaro and the other high-ranking officers held back the crowd. Eadric raised the peasant to his feet.

"I will not tolerate theft," said Eadric.

Duke Pascal grinned triumphantly at the corner of Eadric's vision. Eadric rifled through the peasant's pockets until he found the coin purse. He threw it across the deck at the duke.

"Why?" coughed out the peasant. His name suddenly came to Eadric. *Clementus*. Clementus drooled blood. "Why do ye not believe me?"

Eadric leaned in so only Clementus could hear him. "I *do* believe you."

He elbowed the soldier in the face. The peasant's nose split in half. In an act of strength astounding even to the strongest aboard, the Hellhound of Rutland flipped Clementus over the gunwale. The soldier splashed into the accursed depths, not even releasing a scream before the waves swallowed him. Just as the five hundred souls had perished in the River Witham, his armor plunged him into the infinite darkness to join Prince William in his eternal slumber.

Ahead of them, becoming discernible under a dawning sky, the marbled cliffs of Dover came into glorious view. They were almost home. Eadric turned back to the crowd behind him. Many were stunned into silence.

Eadric smiled. He spread his arms wide. "Who's ready to celebrate?"

CHAPTER IX
EMMA

EMMA SNUCK AWAY IN the wee hours of the morning, while her mother was tossing and turning in bed. There've been many nights when Emma was kept awake by the fitful nightmares that harassed her mother. They often woke in the morning with the sheepskin blankets soaked through with sweat. Emma never dared ask what she dreamed about, as there were some sins that a child should never know about their parents; for when they learn about them, they might become a different person entirely . . .

. . . but sometimes Edith would mumble in her sleep, and Emma would listen. Faint words stirred and blended together like a drunkard. Names occasionally. Emma knew some of them, like *Lief*—her childhood friend and kind-of brother. But most of them she didn't know. *Rayner. Algor. Warin. Kendrick.* Other times, Edith would cry in her sleep, and those nights were particularly hard on Emma.

There were few things in life more traumatizing than a child seeing their parent weep.

This was one of those nights. Before she left, Emma leaned over to her twisting-and-turning mother and wiped away her tears. She wrapped her arms around Edith's body. Her mother looked tired and old in the darkness of night. She coughed her deep, ugly cough—the kind where Emma expected smoke to leave her mother's lungs. Edith placed her wrinkled hand on Emma's arm and rubbed it.

"Was I doing it again?"

"'Tis okay, mama."

"I'm sorry."

"Don't be. Get some rest."

Emma kissed her mother on the cheek and lay with her until she fell back asleep. Then she snuck out of the bed and through the front door. She met Alice and her husband, Roger, at the edge of town as the first light of dawn spread over the countryside. The air was crisp and chill, but without the foreboding sense of never-ending cold that winter gave. This was spring, and the world would get warmer. It made the frigid weather feel better.

"Did your mother see you?" asked Alice as they started their journey.

"No," said Emma. "Methinks she's seeing ghosts again."

It took a little over a day's travel to reach Reading. Emma had anticipated it to be more tiring, but the journey was mostly downhill and without complications. They stopped overnight at a small village called Newbury and continued on the next morning. The sun had not passed midday when they all saw the town from a distance. Roger was quite a bit taller than both Emma and Alice, and he seemed to feel the length of their trek a lot less than they did. He had a mop of brown hair that lay unsullied atop his round head; how he managed that was beyond Emma's comprehension. She was an absolute mess. Sweating. Stinking. Sore. She needed to freshen up before she visited Tom. He couldn't see her like this.

"Alice?" asked Roger with his reedy voice.

"Yes, Roger?"

"Methinks I sees Reading. Look over there. That be it, no?"

"Yes, love. We told you we were close." Alice sighed and lifted her eyebrows at Emma. They brought Roger along because it was undeniably safer to travel across the realm with a man than without; however, if they let Roger lead the way (to put it as politely and with as little disrespect as possible), he would've managed to lead them into Welsh country but think he'd actually discovered Spain.

"Me don't think t'would be a fanciful idea to stay and leave on the same day, girls. Me could protect you well enough under the light of day, but the nighttime woods would be darker. My navigation expertise can only save us so much." Roger plucked at his fingernails anxiously.

"Don't worry, love. We know bandits can be scary—"

"Me ain't scared of no bandits. Really." Roger licked his lips. His eyes darted at the scattered trees. "Really, me can fight any man. I would for you. But it be the beasts of the night that frighten . . . frighten ye girls, me means. Not I. But boars. Snakes. Owls."

"Owls wouldn't hurt us," said Emma.

"Seen their devil heads? They spin all around and gaze evil-like."

"Roger, calm down before ye hurt yourself," said Alice. "Here, have another drink."

Alice handed Roger the wineskin again. When they left this morning, it had been filled with some alcoholic concoction, but now it was nearly empty from the many times Alice forced it on her husband so he'd shut his mouth for a few blissful minutes. He was a lovable man, but he had a dangerous desire for booze. Plus, he was a simpleton . . . respectfully.

Reading was a busy trading center in the center of southern England. Two rivers, the River Thames and River Kennet, met at a T-intersection, splitting the city into three even sections. As the three of them entered the outskirts, Alice and Emma formed a plan: Emma would meet Tom at a bathhouse in the southwestern section of the city, while Alice would wait with Roger in a nearby tavern in case things got carried away.

They reached the palisade right before the sun kissed the western horizon. City watchmen were preparing to close the gates when they arrived, and the guards hastily waved them through so they could lock up the city for the night. Emma stared wide-eyed at all these new experiences. Different faces. Different bodies. Different buildings. A wholly novel existence. Kids kicked mud at each other in the street, playing and laughing. It wasn't too long ago that Emma would've joined in with them. She loved getting dirty and wrestling the other children.

But now that she was older, she had many more things on her mind than simply playing in filth. Things like dreaming about courting cute squires. She swooned not-so-subtly as she imagined Tom waiting for her at the bathhouse. How could her mother say no to this? Why wouldn't she want her daughter to know love and joy and the thrills of visiting unknown places?

"I'm nervous," admitted Emma as they approached the bathhouse.

"Shush," said Alice. "You're young, beautiful, smart. Just be careful. Soldiers like him have lots to lose and much to gain. Here, let's clean you. Don't want ye scarin' him off!"

"I hate ye."

"Love you too." Alice helped Emma wash off the gunk of their journey at a nearby trough. Once she felt clean enough to feign confidence, they went to the large tents that made up the bathhouse, all while Alice pressured Roger into complimenting Emma's appearance so she'd feel better about herself. Emma didn't feel very pretty wearing her travel garbs and sweat-soaked wimple, but she appreciated both of them for trying their best to make her feel so. She knew, however, that there was only one person who could make her feel like a princess, and that man was inside one of those erected tents.

"All the baths are full up," said the maiden who worked the entrance. She had dark hazel eyes and soft, clean skin. She looked lovely, and it made Emma even more self-conscious. If these were the types of women who attended and bathed the men here, she wouldn't stand a chance at all.

"I'm visitin' someone," she said shyly. The bath maid glared at her skeptically.

"*You* are? And who might that be?"

"A . . ." Emma struggled to admit it. Her cheeks blushed, her skin sizzling like a fire simmered underneath. She glanced back at Alice and Roger, who waved her on encouragingly from the opposite side of the road. "I'm meeting . . . you know."

"No, I don't know."

"A man," she said hastily.

"We don't allow sexual games here."

AHHH! Emma almost lost control of her legs. "No, no, no! Nothin' like that. He's a friend. Well, we're courtin', but he's a soldier. I mean, a squire now. We weren't gonna . . ." Emma felt gassed. Bloated.

I should leave. This is a disaster. Mama was right.

"Emma!"

AHHHHHHH!

And just like that, her knight in shining armor was running to her rescue. Tom was twenty-three years old and much more mature than any boy her age. For one, he was tall. *Very tall!* Emma was still taller than most of the boys her age. Tom had a deep voice, like it was steeped in heavy soup and glazed over with warm honey. The boys her age sounded like whiny toddlers. He had a beard, one that was dark and stiff and perfectly accented his green eyes, and his close-shaven head made him look manlier and more brutish than any boy she knew.

And he's a soldier, Emma swooned. *No, a squire. Don't get that wrong, or he'll get mad like last time. He'll be a knight soon. And then I'll have my knight and an estate and be just like those rich, beautiful noblewomen.*

"This girl with ye?" the bath maid asked Tom.

"This *lady* is, yes," said Tom with a biting undertone. He grabbed Emma's hand and held it tightly. "Come on. Our bath is this way, my lady."

"No fooling around in the baths!"

"Take it up with the king's army." Tom pushed Emma ahead of him and rubbed her back. "Ye look dashing. Utterly beautiful. Most divine."

"Oh," said Emma stupidly, trying not to giggle. "In these old clothes?"

"You'd look great in anything . . . or nothing."

Oh, dear Lord Jesus, help me.

Numerous tents within a fenced-off plot of land made up the Reading bathhouse. There were fifteen private bathing tents, and one giant pavilion that held a multitude of baths inside it. The bath maids went between them all, making sure the coals and embers were kept stoked and the water warmed. For a few shillings extra, men could pay for the maids to help them bathe. Emma imagined that seedier bathhouses also allowed for some extra . . . services.

"How was the trip?" asked Tom. "I'm sorry I couldn't visit you closer. William won't let us stray too far from Kent. And I've told you the way my knight—"

"Don't worry. I don't mind," said Emma. Her mind raced faster than she could think. She blushed just looking at the man. "T'was a simple trip, really."

"Good. I'd hate for something to happen to you because of me."

They entered one of the private tents. It took less than five minutes for her to change behind the courtesy screen into a modesty dress—a thick piece of sheep's wool, stiff as a plank of wood, that allowed her to cover most of her body while bathing. Tom waited for her next to the tub. He had changed out of his uniform into some tan breeches and a loose blouse that exposed his upper chest.

Were those chest hairs? AHHHH—

"I've warmed it for you."

"You're too sweet."

She stepped onto a stool and tested the water with her big toe. It was perfect. Warm, but not burning; steaming, but not boiling. She felt the same way inside. Tom smiled as she submerged herself. She immediately felt better, as if the water's surface was a net that caught all the tedious toil of the day and left her engulfed in pure bliss. Emma burst out of the water, her cheeks swelling from the clean water she held in her mouth.

"Is all well?" he asked.

Emma spat her mouthful of water at him in an impulsive spur of childlike mischief. It hit him square in the face. Tom flinched. "What the fuck?!"

Emma cackled to herself. "I'm sorry, but look at your face!"

"Do I look funny?"

"Aye, like a tomato!"

Tom wiped away the water dripping off her face. She saw him rein in his embarrassment or anger or whatever he was feeling and come back to his alluring self. "There, you've had your fun. Now turn yourself around and let me wash ye."

Emma leaned against the back of the tub, the hairs on her arm and leg prickling up in the warm water. She grinned and held back a moan as Tom lifted her long hair out of the bath. She always forgot how heavy her hair was, and the unburdened weight, literally lifted off her shoulders, made her dizzy.

"God, Thou art a wondrous creator," said Tom.

Emma laughed. "That supposed to be a compliment?"

"My, did He ever bless you with such beauty. Close your eyes."

Emma closed them. Tom pressed his fingers against her temples and massaged them in a circular motion. She melted under his firm touch. He picked up a pitcher from a nearby table and dipped it into the bathwater. He pulled back her head, gently stretching the skin of her scalp, and poured the warmth through her hair. Emma opened her eyes. She saw the veins in his arm jutting out beneath his skin. His deep green eyes followed his precise and delicate work. He caught her staring. She quickly shut her eyes again.

Emma smiled, feeling giddy and free. They'd only known each other for a few months, but she'd never known anyone who could make her feel like this before. Enjoying the tranquility of each other's presence, she listened noiselessly as he gently soaped her hair, washed it out, and massaged her head. So thoroughly did she lose herself in the sweet smell of his fragrance, and in the softness of her hair on her nape, that she eventually thought herself to be dreaming; she believed she had fallen asleep in Tom's vascular, nurturing arms, until the sound of his voice stirred her from near-unconsciousness.

"Have ye considered my offer?" he asked.

Emma winced. She had hoped to avoid this conversation. She kept her voice calm, undramatic. *Don't be a crybaby, Emma. Don't turn this into a fight.* "I can't leave my mum."

"I told you I'd watch over her. If anything, she'll be safer than now. I can't protect you both when you're halfway across the kingdom."

"You know she can't travel all the way to Kent. Her leg won't let her."

"Emma, we can't be together while the kingdom remains in tatters. As long as this war is ongoing, I'll always be needed elsewhere. I can't keep leaving camp and traveling to small towns, especially in the whore's territory."

"Empress Maud."

"What?"

"Her name is Empress Maud, Queen consort of the Romans. She isn't some random woman calling herself an empress. And she's not a whore."

Tom laughed. He leaned his head against hers. "See? This is why you're perfect for this. Ye know all about them, their lineages and titles."

"I'm not a spy . . . I can't do what ye ask of me."

"Do you want us to be together?"

The water sloshed, grimy and dirt-filled, against her skin. Her mind was a torrent of complicated thoughts. She twisted around so she could look him in the face. "Of course I want to be with you."

"Then this may be the only way," he said somberly. "A union can't be formed under present conditions. I can't court that which is distant, and poor. The countryside is unsafe. Peasants will continue to die in droves. What I'm offering is a solution that can solve both. Work for the king's army. Don't you understand? The king needs someone who can get inside the empress's circle. He needs a woman who nobody knows. Someone smart, preceptive, trustworthy."

"I'm scared."

"I know. I don't want you to get hurt, either, but I must become a knight if I'm ever to save us from poverty. You and your mom will be killed if that doesn't happen soon. The fastest way for me to become knighted is if I help capture the empress herself. Emma, love, all I've ever wanted was to become a knight. To become *your* knight." He stroked her cheek and continued, "This new kingdom wasn't built for the poor. We need to become better, or it'll kill us. Luckily, there *is* a war; war can make a hero of a coward and a lord of a serf."

"Only for men."

"And what am I? Are these not the lips of a man?" She almost gasped as his lips parted hers. They've only kissed a few times in the past, but each time felt as exciting as the first. "Are these not the hands of a man? The desires of a man?"

Emma would usually tease him for making such an eye-roll inducing comment, but she discovered that the more physical he got, the more quickly she abandoned rational thoughts for animalistic urges. She leaned forward for another kiss, but Tom pulled away and left her puckering air. Emma grinned in pleasurable exasperation. An overwhelming urge came over her, something primal but new, to kiss him again and again and again and again—

"I wouldn't want to make a sinner of ye," said Tom coyly. "If we're to be together, I need to know. I need to know you are on King Stephen's side."

"Me am," said Emma.

"He is the true king. Your womanly ways can contort your mind and make you believe a woman like Maud can rule. But she's evil. Vindictive. Manipulative in all the ways a woman can be. Do you understand?"

Emma was annoyed. This conversation had her emotions whiplashing one way and another. *I don't give a damn who rules. I just want to kiss you again, ye stupid dolt.*

"Yes," she said instead.

"Then convince your mum to come to Kent. Become a spy for the king, and together we'll rise so high that any castle in England can be yours."

Emma's eyes lit up. She could see her future now. Large, belly-aching banquets. Scores of laughter and music and wonder. Beautiful, ornate dresses. Servants and parties and a warm bed for her mother to rest her lame leg. It would all be perfect if it weren't so impossible.

"I'll think about it," said Emma, "but only if you kiss me like that again."

Tom smirked and gave her a long kiss, his breath hot and inviting.

"Good," he said. "Now let's get dressed before that bath wench believes we're doing something ungodly."

CHAPTER X
EADRIC

"Will ye do nothing about it?" cried Viviane, an older peasant woman with graying brunette hair that slipped out from beneath her veil. It made Eadric uncomfortable. Only a peasant woman would be so nonchalant about revealing so much skin and hair. Fucking barbarians.

Except your daughter did that often.

"King Stephen says he is a ruler of our people," said James, the peasant man with her. The intensity of his anger slurred his speech. "He claims to be the protector of the men, women, and children of England. Yet he lets Maud an' her band run free all along our southern shires!"

"Watch your tongue," said William of Ypres. "You speak of your king, who is currently protecting your realm from Scottish invaders in the north."

"Then why don't ye do something?!" asked Viviane. She flung tears off her face. "We saw our town butchered by the knights of the empress."

Eadric watched the commotion from the side. The man and woman—made refugees by a raiding party sent by Empress Maud—had arrived earlier this morning. Their town was safely within Maud's territory in Hampshire, yet she had pillaged and torched their village nonetheless. Their skin was still black from soot, and they wore their scorched and tattered clothing. Eadric tensed his fingers. His breath became shallow. The news had been getting worse since they had arrived in Kent a few weeks back.

"Why would the empress destroy her own holdings?" asked William.

"What?!" Viviane looked around incredulously. Higher officers, nobility, and influential clergymen filled the temporary council tent. "How are we supposed to know?!"

"Hunny, 'tis all right," said James. He reached out his hand to calm her—

"'Tis not," she said, pushing back his hand. "Is it not *your* responsibility to protect us? Isn't it your job to know why? Ye extend this war year after year, while ye watch us die by the thousands. Each winter we starve more-n-more because our food is being taken for the army. And then each summer we die from these endless battles that are fought in our yards."

"We understand your frustration," said William.

"I'm *beyond* frustration; I am without hope." Her husband rubbed his hands on her arms and kissed her head from behind. It was a simple, encouraging gesture, and it almost stirred something in Eadric. It was an intimate gesture that he rarely saw among the highborn.

"I see no path to a future," said Viviane. "We saw our town burnt by a ruler who claimed she'd protect us. Her men slaughtered our cattle, raped our women, murdered our children. Then ye ask us, 'Why would she do this?' I ask you: why would Satan stir evil? I know not why she would command this. She didn't steal our food, our coin. She wanted not our fealty nor our labor. All she wanted was to burn us to the ground for daring to exist."

Viviane, her eyes bereft of tears, searched for the meaning in the violence. Eadric glanced around the room. The officers and clergy became silent. William of Ypres hesitated, as if full of shame. Only this peasant woman's voice echoed in the hollow tent.

"I'm very sorry for your loss, madam," said William. He motioned for the guards to lead them out. "I can assure you that we are investigating these skirmishes and plan on putting a full stop to them. King Stephen *will* take back your land, and he *will* protect it."

"I don't see how it'll be any different then," she said. James hushed her quickly. Once they were taken from the tent, Eadric and the other chief officials surrounded William.

As third in command behind only King Stephen and Bishop Henry of Winchester, William of Ypres was the focal leader of their military expeditions. Eadric believed he wasn't capable of the task. He was there when William failed King Stephen at the Battle of Lincoln, and now William was failing to even stave off Empress Maud's skirmishers on the borders of their land. What the king saw in him was beyond Eadric. The man had even failed to become a noble in his home duchy of Flanders.

The officers assaulted William with questions. They asked about the skirmishes, what their next moves should be, and what they should tell their troops. The commander thought for a long moment. He rubbed his light-blonde beard that stretched down to his chest. He was a heavyset man, tall and intimidating, with the shrewdness to find an excuse for every failure.

"I believe this is precisely what the empress wants," said William stupidly.

Obviously that's what she wants, thought Eadric. *That was why she fucking did it.*

"But she's devaluing her own land," said Sir Haworth of Norwich, an older knight and close confidant of William. "Why take over England if there's no one left to bow?"

"These skirmishes are for the sole purpose of creating unrest. You heard the peasant woman as she left. Empress Maud's goal is to turn the peasantry against the noble class. Her assaults on them creates animosity toward *all* authority. The peasants will see us no differently than they see her." William sighed and rubbed his temples. "I believe she wants a quick end to the war. It's been raging for almost five years now, and more than that if you include Normandy. She hopes that if she turns them against us, win or lose, she'll still spurn Stephen's legacy."

"Fuckin' peasants," said Eadric, way louder than he intended. His cheeks flared up as everyone faced him. William gave him a stern look.

"That, Eadric, is exactly what we don't need."

Eadric spat on the ground just to distract himself with something. Discontent had been growing in their army as well; the infantry, which mostly comprised of peasants, and the officers, who came from powerful families, often fought in drunken brawls. William berated Eadric mightily when his division returned from Flanders. And his stunt on the boat, allegedly, didn't help the lowborn-highborn hostility.

The remainder of the counsel was uneventful and boring by Eadric's standards. They scoured maps and heard spy intel on Empress Maud and Earl Robert's troop placements, even though they had no idea where the empress even was. Their best guess was she was hiding somewhere in Berks or Oxford, perhaps at Oxford Castle itself. Word traveled slowly, especially through enemy territory. It wasn't easy for couriers and spies to cross battle-scarred lands. After the meeting concluded, William doled out duties to each officer and sent them on their way. Eadric was among the last to leave. And right before he stepped out of the flaps of the tent, he heard William call out to him from behind.

"And please, Eadric, antagonize no more of our peasant troops. I'm tired of hearing their complaints of you."

"She's done this before. Were you aware?" asked Eadric.

"Who?"

"Empress Maud. She's used the peasants against us before. It's how the uprising that sacked Rowan's castle started. How my daughter—"

"Yes, yes," said William of Ypres, sighing with annoyance. "We're all aware of what happened to your daughter. Just please, for my sake, for your king's sake, use that frustration for our benefit rather than our detriment."

Eadric bowed to William. "Of course, my lord. I would never think of doing otherwise."

Eadric slammed the peasant soldier to the ground. What was his name?

Jonathan? Sure, why not? Jonathan was a large man, like Eadric. Most of the scrawnier, younger troops wouldn't come near the Hellhound during a sparring session. A burly type with giant hands and protruding muscles, Jonathan seemed to be a hunter before the war.

He was the perfect type for Eadric to get his frustrations out on.

Eadric kicked him in the side. Jonathan grimaced. He sprung forward, trying to wrap his arms around Eadric's legs. He went with Jonathan's momentum and allowed himself to scramble down to his knees. Eadric pressed both his elbows into the big peasant's back and shoved downward. He heard Jonathan's spine crack. Eadric smiled. He may be in his fifties, but he was as light and quick as ever. Eadric kicked—

"I yield! I yield!"

He pulled back at the last second. Jonathan coughed up blood over his waving hands. "I yield. Ye bested me," he said.

Eadric sighed in disappointment. Those troops who dared to watch looked away, hoping not to catch his eye and be forced to spar. Eadric wiped his hands on his training tunic and walked away, while Jonathan writhed on the ground moaning.

The midday sun glistened off Eadric's sweat-glazed skin. He stretched his muscles. It felt good to spar. For the brief moments during glorious combat, he could forget about his history. The past and future matter not amid battle. To feel his blood coursing through his veins, and to experience the joy of domination, gave Eadric the illusion of having control. Stability.

On the untrampled grassland surrounding the camp, wildflowers sprouted in a menagerie of colors, hosting a frenzy of bees, butterflies, and dragonflies, which danced around their fragrant aromas. Women and children, carrying baskets full of clothes, passed by as they headed for the River Medway to do laundry.

War camps function similarly to a small town; not a village, but a town. Inside the war camp, when no immediate battle loomed, the troops who possessed a special trade outside their recruitment performed those jobs: butchers, bakers, tanners, stonemasons, cobblers, carpenters, blacksmith, and the like; meanwhile, the laymen troops took on the typical wartime duties that were expected of a soldier, such as mending armor, sharpening weapons, cleaning trash, and other similar activities. Since their war camp was in the shire of Kent, just outside the city of Rochester, and securely within allied territory, William of Ypres allowed the families of officers and troops to join them in camp. Those women and children did their part to upkeep the camp, often aiding as cooks, basket weavers, gardeners, or water fetchers.

Eadric's duties were odd in comparison. His position was a unique one, granted to him by King Stephen, that placed him in equal power to that of an earl. As a war constable, not too dissimilar to a quartermaster,

Eadric interacted with most of the trades found within their temporary settlement. He settled labor disputes, endured intelligence meetings, trained with troops, and evaluated letters they received from throughout the land. For the first few days after they returned from Flanders, that was what took up most of his time.

As the weeks passed on, one boring, uneventful day after the next, Eadric often wandered to the outskirts, like many soldiers, to block out the foulness of sweat and oil that commingled inside the encampment. Sometimes, on the best of days, he lost himself in thought while he took these walks under the warm springtime sun. He caught younger soldiers who were only in their early-to-mid teenage years flirting with young maidens from the nearby city. The other superior officers and he knew that many of these young men sneaked into Rochester during the night to enjoy the revelry of city life. They allowed it, as it raised morale.

Their youthful exuberance, like many other things, reminded him of Lucia. How she was, what she did. He often turned away from the sight of these young men and women before the anger boiled out of him, and he did something he would regret. So many joyful moments had been stolen from him, experiences he should have shared with his daughter. To make matters worse, the brutality of her death forever tarnished the few memories he had of her.

Day by day, Eadric went through this routine as they awaited word from the king in York. They had sent a messenger weeks before they sailed to France, but they expected it to still take another week to hear back. He hated times like this. Information traveled slowly, and it was a burden to those prone to unrest. Each day he waited was another day he was kept from avenging his daughter; another day he had to wait to meet her in Paradise.

The walls of London stood elegantly before Queen Matilda and her host. The queen glanced back at Eadric. In the deep blue of her eyes, Eadric gleamed the hope and despair that so often obliterated himself.

He understood the emotions that streamed through her, yet the magnitude of repercussions that she must navigate exceeded his mightily.

Here, in the hands of this woman, laid half the fate of England. And there, within the walls of London, laid the fate of the other half, also in the hands of a woman.

"What do you believe I should do?" asked Queen Matilda. She had the regal elegance and beauty that should be expected from a queen. Like her husband, she wore the color of kings; her lilac-hued dress, tied snugly around the waist, gave off a sense of predestined greatness. Her posture demanded respect.

"I believe this to be the best way to save your husband," said Eadric.

Empress Maud had been scheming inside London for months now. She was trying to convince the population to coronate her as queen regent until her young son in Anjou came of age. The city had seemingly refused, or at the very least, argued itself into gridlock. Dozens of wealthy and influential citizens had sneaked out of the city and pledged their fealty to Queen Matilda, and by extension King Stephen, if she invaded the city and liberated them of the empress's tyranny.

If all went right in the ensuing siege, they could capture the shrewd empress and bargain with her half-brother to get Stephen back from imprisonment. Eadric grimaced as he thought of the day Stephen got captured at Lincoln. His wife had been leading his army and the realm all by herself since. It was truly impressive how Matilda held everything together.

"If we fail, and Maud escapes again, then it may convince her to execute my husband and end this madness," said the queen.

"Or it may force her to see that she is in more danger than she thought. Perhaps it will show her that you, my lady, are not powerless without your husband."

"Is that so?" Queen Matilda smiled warmly at him. "I don't believe she, of all the maidens in the world, needs to be convinced of the power a woman can yield."

"Then we teach her a different lesson, my queen. We show her that the God-fearing people of England won't bow to hubris and vanity."

"You believe her to be prideful?"

"I do."

"Then what do you believe I to be?" she asked. Eadric watched her scan the army behind them. Queen Matilda stood, resilient and husbandless, leading the charge of destiny.

"I believe you to be charming," said Eadric.

Matilda blushed. She brushed him off with a wave of her hand. "I've made up my mind. We will attack. Bring Empress Maud to me."

Eadric gave the order. The troops advanced.

"Baron Eadric, do you know what I have that the empress doesn't? The one thing the citizens of London can't accept about her, that they can about me?"

"Your sincerity?" He thought a little more. "And your lenient tax provisions."

Queen Matilda laughed at his joke. Although when she responded, there wasn't a single ounce of levity in it. "No, my dear. It's that I have a man to hide behind. And she doesn't."

Beyond the chimneyed houses and spired churches of Rochester, a flock of doves fluttered before the setting sun. Long wispy clouds dissolved from white to tangerine to magenta. Stars began to shine out crystal clear, piercing the invading darkness. The last of the city folk meandered their way back behind the safety of the walls, for outside such battlements, in the bleakness of night, banditry and brutality ran amok.

Sir Álvaro rode up to Eadric upon a fine steed with long white hair and a bushy tail. The knight dismounted carefully, balancing two pewter dishes with cutlery. He handed one to Eadric.

"I don't remember requesting food," said Eadric.

"Before she left with His and Her Majesty and traveled to York, your wife entrusted me with your care," said Sir Álvaro. "That involves making sure you eat."

"Does it include climaxing me too?"

"Tsk, tsk. Vulgar tongue for a vulgar man. I hope you've been pleading for salvation at church."

"God will do with me what He must."

They sat silently as they ate their grub. It was a standard military dish, stew with loads of cabbage and carrots but minimal meat.

"The king has fallen ill," said Sir Álvaro after some time. All at once, the weight of the world fell on Eadric. If King Stephen were to die, the war would be over in an instant.

"Has word arrived?"

"Stephen and Matilda are stationed in Northampton. The herald tells us he got sick in York, and it got worse as they traveled south."

"Will he die?"

"It sounds like he'll need Christ to perform another miracle."

Sir Álvaro waited for him to respond, but Eadric sat in silence, letting the quietness of dusk wash over him. Would his quest for revenge end before it even started? He didn't know where Duke Richard was, only that he was now a loyalist to Empress Maud. If Stephen were to die and Maud won the war, she'd persecute and execute Eadric long before he ever laid eyes on the duke and his worthless knights.

"The soldiers are growing discontent."

"Fuck the soldiers," Eadric snapped. He glared as two peasant archers walked by.

"We need to retaliate against these skirmishes the empress is organizing. William doesn't want to send a party and risk losing lives. He wants us to be full strength if the queen comes back widowed, but I believe we need to strike back. Eadric, we'll lose the army if we don't act fast. Think about it from their perspective. Their homes and families are being sacked and disgraced while they wait idly for a king who might never return."

Eadric's mind drifted to Queen Matilda. She held them together for years while the king remained imprisoned by Earl Robert and Empress Maud. She was strong when they were hesitant. She *grew* their army by winning the hearts of London and by making pacts with Flanders and Brabant. Eadric also thought of their eldest son, Prince Eustace, and how he and Matilda must be praying over Stephen's decaying body.

"If we go against William again," said Eadric carefully, "he can try us for treason."

"Only if we fail. We saw that with our expedition south. He would've tried you, had you not actually found Richard's bastard. We need to quell the discontent among our troops. And we can only do that by winning battles, by gaining back every town and village she razed to ashes."

"Do we know where she'll attack next?"

"Our scouts report they are heading north, closer to Oxford. My guess would be Marlborough, or the lands thereabouts. Maybe Reading or Wallingford."

"Why do you care so much about these peasants?"

Sir Álvaro shrugged his shoulders. "I'm a knight. It's what I was christened to do."

Eadric looked him in the eye. Could it be that his daughter was mistaken about this man? Could he be honorable after all?

Sir Álvaro reached out his hand for Eadric to shake. Eadric smiled devilishly.

I was getting bored around here anyway.

CHAPTER XI
GILBERT

It took less than a week for Gilbert to trek from the sandy embankments of Boulogne to the vibrant farmlands that surround Rouen, and when he finally passed through those bountiful lots that gave food to the thirty-thousand residents of his home city, he couldn't have been more grateful. With the events following William's capture being almost fully forgotten—

Although that's not true, was it? I still see them when I sleep. Her face . . . what was her name?

Gilbert shook his head. If God wanted him to remember such things, they wouldn't be banished from his mind so quickly. Just like *her*. Just like—

Where am I?

He stepped off the dirt road, making room for some peasants and their cow to amble past him. He reached out and touched the weeds growing off the side of the road. It grounded his anxious mind by connecting him to the earth and the Almighty. Thinking about that night on the Côte d'Opale, or about that frozen night in the woods long ago, gave him a throbbing headache. Better if he not consider it at all.

After another half hour, Gilbert saw the city walls. Rouen stretched along the northeastern side of the River Seine, safe-guarded by strong stone ramparts. It made him deeply homesick. He and William had only been in the army for a little over a year, yet he would fully admit he missed the skyline of Rouen. The villages and hamlets he ventured through to get here had their charm, but the bustle of city life was where he felt most comforted—a place where he could get lost in the crowd.

As he overlooked the city, watching the smoke billow out from the single-story homes and the sun glint off the towering steepled cathedrals, the memories flooded back to him. Happy moments; never the rotten ones.

Gilbert took a deep breath. Somewhere past those granite walls were his parents, his infant sibling, and a whole life he and his brother abandoned to give them a chance to live. He was going to have to tell them what had happened to his brother.

The throbbing returned to his head.

First things first: find Hawk, Bartholomew, and Beatriz. They'll help me. Maybe it'll make it easier on Ma Maman and Mon Papa if I come to them with a plan and some support.

The clouds parted, and the sun blazed down onto him as if God gave approval to his decision. From beyond the walls, he could hear and smell the excitement of a thriving city. Rouen waited eagerly just for him. What a beautiful day to return home.

"Your queen is a fucking whore!"

"And what has Stephen done for our country? All he cares for is his little island to the north. A true Norman would never abandon his homeland to Angevin swine!"

The crowd cheered. Gilbert stood back and watched the chaos unfold. Throughout the streets of Rouen, heated arguments arose and trickled out of every home, storefront, and alleyway; he'd never seen such turmoil in his city before. The two squabbling nobles had stirred up quite the crowd, maybe a little over four dozen total, and they wore the insignias of the notorious House of Bellême and the powerful House of Angoulême.

"You prove my point, sir!" said the Angoulême nobleman. "Your lady empress enlists the aid of Welshmen and Scottish mercenaries. She abandoned her husband here to raise foreign armies!"

"Oh, shut your beleaguered mouth, swine," said the Bellême. "When have our people ever not torn at each other's throats? Geoffrey's attempt to unite the royal houses is commendable. Lest anyone forgets, he was *chosen* by the late English king, God rest his soul, to bewed his daughter. That makes Geoffrey a chosen descendant of William the Conqueror. Makes him our brethren. My father's father fought alongside William as he reclaimed England from those Saxon bastards, and I'll be damned if I let a sniveling boy become king of it."

The Angoulême nobleman took out his sword, and all Hell broke loose. He lunged through the crowd and after the Bellême, who looked equally enthused to start a fight. The guards from both houses joined in. Gilbert and the multitude of peasants knew this was their time to get lost. He ducked away and avoided the clashing of blades and the Rouen city watchmen who ran past to break it up. He made a mental note not to mention the ongoing war to anyone with a sizable iron blade.

Bulging out from the Rue des Minimes was one of the most historic buildings in all of Rouen. Most commonly referred to as Denier's Treatise, the alehouse became the favorite destination for weary sailors and merchants along the River Seine. It overlooked the majestic river and swelled close to bursting with lively companionship and rowdy debauchery. From dusk-till-dawn-till-dusk again, the shutters of Denier's Treatise would remain open, letting out the pungent odors and warm lights from within. Citizens from all around the kingdom of France and beyond would find their way here, united by the human desire for warmth, comfort, and hospitality. Gilbert, Hawk, Bartholomew, Beatriz, and William would routinely spend their evenings soaking in the varied visitors and getting into all kinds of trouble.

Gilbert only expected to find Hawk here though, for last he heard, Bart and Beatriz had eloped to Caen. Gilbert shuddered. It still made him uncomfortable to think of Bartholomew and Beatriz as husband and wife. They'd all been friends since childhood, and that the two of them had been nurturing a secret romance had become quite the surprise for Gilbert, Hawk, and William.

The interior of Denier's Treatise was just as exciting as Gilbert had left it a year ago, when he, William, and Hawk had shared their last drink together before they joined Geoffrey's army. Gilbert swam through a sea of men; the debarked sailors, either unsteady from standing upon unwavering land, or unmoored because of the intoxications of liquor, stumbled into one another, sloshing their drinks over the cusp of their tankards and soaking the straw-covered ground in a sticky residue. The smell was rank and putrid and, to Gilbert, reminiscent of better times.

As he'd hoped in coming to the largest alehouse in the harbor, his best friend was as easy to spot as a cock in a nunnery. Hawk sat perched in his favorite spot, crowing his strange, shrill laughter that brightened the dour expressions of all those around him. Gilbert could recognize it from a mile away, like the ringing church bells of the Rouen Cathedral. The bartender motioned for Hawk, and he strutted up to the counter. His bright-red Phrygian hat—which he rarely left the house without—bobbed atop his head, displayed proudly for all the world to admire. He loved his outfits, and today he wore a bright-purple tunic, closely fitted to his arms, which flared around the wrists. A dark-green supertunic hung over everything else and drooped to his ankles. If it weren't for Gilbert's friendship with Hawk, he'd not even know what a supertunic was. Only recently had it gained some popularity with the younger aristocrats; it was a loose, sleeveless wool coat that could be belted around the hips to give some figure to the wearer. Knowing Hawk, he'd probably stolen it from some wayfarer's wagon as he was preparing to sell the garment for an exorbitant price.

Gilbert smiled; it was damn good seeing his friend again.

Hawk retrieved six tankards and plopped them onto a nearby table occupied by five fiery-tempered sailors. Gilbert wandered closer, eager to see what his friend wanted to do with such unsavory company. Something mischievous, no doubt. Hawk handed out the drinks and began in his bassy, boisterous voice, "Aight lads, you can keep going now!"

"I have nothin' to say to these lots that ain't already been said," huffed a middle-aged man to Hawk's right.

"What?" asked Hawk incredulously. "What is this? Nothing to say? When I left, you claimed that these pleasant folk over here were tarnished moneylenders with not a semblance of Christendom in their meager hearts."

The two younger men to Hawk's left gave Middle-aged Man and his two older companions a low growl.

"No, no, no," said Middle-aged Man defensively. "I called 'em warmongers for encouraging Geoffrey's butchering of the houses that opposed him."

"Ah, did you hear that?!" Hawk said to the younger men to his left. "He just said you were a bunch of dirty, murderous Vikings!"

"I did not!"

"Aye, you did. You just called him a pagan rapist."

"Hark," said one of the younger men. "I think you're misrepresenting him, friend. What's your name, good sir?"

"Friends call me Hawk."

"Hawk, if I may call ye so on friendly terms?"

"You may."

"Me and my friend here were havin' a . . . uh . . . what is it called, Grisham?"

"An intellectual joust," said his other young companion, Grisham.

"Aye. An intellectual jousting with these . . . old-fashioned minds." The younger man put up his hands defensively when that brought out meaner rumbles from the older men. "I mean no offense. Simply that ye grew up in a time when Henry was still very much alive, and when he arranged the marriage of Geoffrey and Empress Maud in this very city. We were younglings then, and all we've known is the strife between the Angevins and the other royal houses."

"Perhaps we started off on the wrong foot," said Middle-aged Man. "There is no need for us to be barbarians because we feel differently about the war. We are good sons of Christ, after all. To let civil strife enrapture us in more sin would make us no different from those fiendish Muslims that are invading the far south. Now them, there's no reasoning with."

"I think we can all agree with that," said the younger man.

Hawk picked up his drink and sighed. He gulped down his tankard in one long swig. Gilbert smirked. Even without being able to see Hawk's face, he could sense his friend's immense displeasure at the amicable turn of events. Gilbert tapped Hawk on his back shoulder. His friend turned, and his eyes went wide.

"Well, I'll be! If it ain't the red devil himself," said Hawk. Gilbert grimaced. It was a lighthearted jab, but Gilbert knew Hawk had meant it to have a scolding bite. "Aren't you still fighting Geoffrey's war?"

"Me was," Gilbert admitted.

"Don't want to talk about it?"

"Not here."

"Very well." Hawk read his expression and frowned in response. He punched Gilbert in the arm and turned back to the table. "New friends! Since we are good and tolerant folk suddenly, let me introduce you all to my old friend Gilbert. Now. Before we all go our separate ways and continue to joust intellectually and whatnot, let us have a toast to friendship and the joyous demise of those terrible Muslims from the far south that cause *so much* bloodshed."

"Here, here!" they shouted.

As they all sipped from their tankards, Hawk turned to Gilbert and spoke in a low voice, "Can you do me a favor?"

There was no hesitation in Gilbert's heart. "Sure."

"Punch that one over there." Hawk motioned to the younger peasant. "I'll take the older three."

"Ye want to start a fight?"

"Aye, fuck this boring shite. I wanted a good tussle before Lent starts, and it seems to me you need to let out some frustration."

"How can you tell?"

"It's all over your face, brother. You can't hide that from me." And then, after a brief pause, "I missed you."

"Missed you, too," said Gilbert.

He punched the younger man. The tankard he drank from flew across the tavern, spilling onto some nearby guests. In that same instant, Hawk upper cut Middle-aged Man, knocking him into his two companions. It took all of thirty seconds for the truce between the two sides to revert to animosity. They fought back against Gilbert and Hawk, but also against one another. By the time the city watchmen arrived with their spears and bludgeons, half of the occupants within Denier's Treatise were involved in the tussle. Gilbert was bruised and battered and bleeding from a cut on his lower lip, but he didn't care. He needed to get his mind off Will and his parents, and the dreaded memories he had long ago submerged.

And he wasn't alone. He felt it in the room as the watchmen subdued the violence. He couldn't put his finger on it until it was extinguished, but there was a heaviness that lay over everyone and everything since he arrived in Rouen—a deep, unfathomable apprehension that was crushing everyone. The fight was like the opening of a sluice gate; their fears and anxieties poured out in a wash of physical barbarity. When it was over, and the only sound remaining was Hawk's uniquely crazed laughter, the air felt inexplicably lighter. They'd hurt each other, but they had released their animosity at the same instant.

Was that why Hawk was laughing? Not because he enjoyed the savagery, but because he had rid them all of that infectious disquietude?

The city guards locked Gilbert and Hawk into the pillory. His body ached from the brawl, and having his head and arms stuck in such an awkward position was not doing him any favors. But on the bright side, he would at least be publicly humiliated alongside his best friend. The Rouen bailiff, a stern-looking man carrying a heavy cudgel, walked in front of them and gave Hawk a stern look.

"How many times this month are we goin' to have to go through this?" he asked him.

His friend flicked his fingers up in an attempt at shrugging. "Maybe that'll be the last time," said Hawk.

The bailiff huffed and walked off, leaving the two friends alone to the whims of passing citizens and whatever elements nature tossed at them. Hawk strained to peek over at Gilbert. He smiled; his teeth were bloodied.

"Didn't that feel great?!" asked Hawk unsarcastically.

"It did," said Gilbert. "Although my back is goin' to hurt something fierce when we're freed from here."

"Aye, but this is the best time of year to be in the pillory."

"And why's that?"

"Because everyone is too hungry to throw vegetables at us. They won't be wasting food when their stomachs are still growling from the winter. That's why I only get in trouble during the spring."

"But what if they start throwin' rocks?"

"Yes, well, let us hope no children come by with such thoughts." Hawk flicked his brown hair aside and gazed at Gilbert with his keen, dark eyes. "Now that we have some alone time, why are you here? Shouldn't you be fighting some battle? And where's Will?"

Gilbert took a deep breath before he explained what had happened in Boulogne. It was easier than he expected, and much of the late afternoon passed them by before he finished. Hawk stood quietly, only moving occasionally to stretch out his bent-over spine. They were lucky. None of the Rouen citizens seemed bothered enough to shame them, and there were no children bored enough to pelt them with dirt or rocks. When Gilbert finished, his mouth parched from talking so much, Hawk nodded his head—well, as much as a pilloried man *could* nod his head—and whistled.

"Captured by the Hellhound, you say?" asked Hawk.

"Yes. I understand what I'm askin' you to go against. I've been a coward twice over, and it may have cost me my brother. But I can't leave him to rot in a dungeon. I don't even know how we'll get to England, or how we'll find him once we're there. If ye don't want—"

"Oh, belt your blabbering. I'm tired of hearing you speak. Of course I'll help, you dolt."

"Oh . . . ye do realize—"

"I realize. I've always wondered what it'd be like to fight a Saxon lord. Suppose it'd be a great deal of fun."

"Fun isn't the word I had in mind."

"And that's why you're a fucking coward. Lucky for you, I make you not so." Hawk swung his hips and bumped into Gilbert playfully. "Does that mean we're goin' to the coast?"

"I need to find my parents first and tell them about William."

"Oh. They ain't here anymore."

"What? But where could they've gone?"

"Caen, from what your neighbor told me. Your folks wouldn't tell me, of course, after they described me as a demonic bugger and whatnot. I don't understand what they could mean by that. I'm perfectly lovable."

A few teenage peasants walked by and yelled some obscenities at them. Hawk stuck his tongue out at them until they walked off. "Good kids, those," he said. "Wondered how long it'd take for us to be properly told off. So, off to Caen then, yeah?"

"Off to Caen then."

Hawk nodded contentedly as if he'd woken up that morning expecting to be found by his best friend, and thereafter told he was to go venturing off on a journey beyond the sea to rescue his friend's half-brother from a vicious warlord. An overpowering warmth of appreciation for Hawk and the brotherhood they'd developed washed through Gilbert. He was fortunate to have a friend like him in such disagreeable times.

"Beautiful day, isn't it?" asked Hawk.

A single-masted cog sailed by on the River Seine, its sailors lighting lanterns aboard as they furled the sails and organized their wares. High above the boat flew a wedge of swans, their formation piercing the stars like an arrow. They honked pleasantly as they passed overhead. Gilbert smelled the fresh air that blew in with the breeze they glided on.

"Yes," said Gilbert. "'Tis a beautiful day indeed."

CHAPTER XII
EMMA

Emma, Alice, and Roger reached Marlborough a little before noon. Emma kept herself entertained during the trip by remembering the conversations with Tom. After they had washed in the bathhouse, they had visited Alice and her husband at a tavern. They shared a few drinks, devoured some salty stew, and separated for the night. The last thing Tom said to her was a question: *Would you stay with me in Reading for a few more weeks?*

She wanted to, of course, but she had to reluctantly decline. From then on, she prepared herself for the scolding she would receive from her mother. She still wasn't ready for it. It had been four days since she had left home, and it was the longest she'd ever gone without being with her mother.

Emma said goodbye to Alice and Roger and entered her house. Her mother was working on her vertical loom, weaving together a tapestry for some paying customer. Edith didn't look up from her work; instead, she strung one string tighter and simply said, "Welcome back."

Oh boy.

"I'm sorry," said Emma rapidly.

"Sure."

Oh shite.

Emma paced to the bedchamber, stopped, and paced back. She repeated this a few times as she gathered the courage to address her. Her mother looked exhausted, as if she'd been up for days, and her fingers struggled to work the loom. She was shaking. Emma took a deep breath, waited for her mother to finish a series of coughs, and asked, "Are ye mad?"

Emma winced. She spent all that time thinking, and she came up with something *that* stupid?

"I'm irritated," said Edith. Her hazel eyes glistened with tears. "And I don't want to talk about it."

"Are ye certain?"

"Quite certain."

"Oh . . ." Emma turned to leave, but her legs had turned to putty. "I am really sorry."

"I heard ye."

"Me knows. I just . . . I'm just goin' to sit here." Emma shed her mantle, placed it on the bare floor, and sat on it. She picked at the loose chunks of dirt, glanced up at her mother, flicked the dirt, looked down, and then glanced back up at her. "Do ye want to talk about it now?"

"You're making me angrier."

"I'll be silent then."

Emma waited.

And waited.

And won.

"What the Hell were ye thinkin'?!" asked Edith.

"I—"

"No! I know what ye were thinkin'. Immature, selfish, doltish thoughts! You're lucky you weren't murdered, or raped, or worse. This world isn't kind to us."

"Me knows—"

"I'm not done! This boy—"

"His name's Tom."

"This boy that you're infatuated with is a knight—"

"He's a squire."

"A knight, a squire—they're all whoresons, the lot! I forbid this thing between the two of you. Ye clearly don't know how dangerous they can be."

"I'm safe. Look at me. I'm here."

"Because for some reason unbeknownst to myself, God seems to have endless grace. The Lord knows I deserve it not, yet luckily for us both, His benevolence expands to you."

"That's good, right?"

"People who rely on God's better judgment ignore the lesser notions of men," said Edith sternly. She pushed the loom to the side so she could stare daggers at her daughter.

Emma was more confused now than ever. "Is this still about Tom?"

"Emma. I told you not to go."

"I went with Alice and Roger."

"This isn't about them."

"Mama, I can take care of my own!" Emma knew the exact moment she lost control, when a wildfire incinerated through her body. It was as if she could reach out and touch those furious flames. "If it weren't for me, we would 'ave starved last winter! I labored all year—"

"That's beside the point—"

"'Tis the full point. You're a cripple! Ye can't help at all. What good is a mum who can't feed her child?!"

"Emma," her mother's voice cracked. "You don't know what I've gone through, what I've *done* for ye."

"I do all this work now. So, who cares if I found someone?"

"He's a knight."

"What do you have against knights?"

"Your father was a knight. And he was the most putrid, evil man I've ever met. Vile. Barbaric. Ruthless. As were all the knights under his tutelage."

"Tom is different."

"Emma, you're fourteen. You have no one to compare him with. I've only ever met one—"

"He's not even a knight," said Emma defensively. "He's a squire."

"I've only met one *squire* that was ever decent, and he died long before he could ever make a change. Believe me, they're all evil."

"I said I'm sorry." Tears streaked down Emma's face.

"I don't care about your apology. Tell me you'll never see him again."

Emma stood up, her hands gripped into fists, her teeth gnashing against each other. Somewhere outside, they heard someone yell. Something like thunder sounded around them.

"Why are ye doing this?" asked Emma.

"Because I love you," said Edith, "and I love your beautiful eyes that remind me of your wicked father. I love your stupid habits, and the way your body is growing into mine. I love you, and I'd do anythin' to see you live a full life."

"Ye aren't helping me live a full life! You're taking mine away from me!"

That shut her mother up. Emma nearly collapsed. She lost control of her breath; she panted, expelling the last of her fumes.

"I want what's best for us," said Emma. "And Tom does too."

"Emma..."

"He does, Mama. He wants us to move to Kent, and for me to join the king's army as a spy. And I'll do it. We'll keep you safe. I'm goin' to help him become a knight."

"Stop."

"And I'll become one of those princesses who always come through town."

"Stop lyin' to yourself."

"We'll own a castle and always have food, and it'll be wonderful."

"You're a peasant, Emma! A fucking peasant! As am I. As is Tom. Nothing will change that for *them*. They'll never let you be one of them. It doesn't matter if it's Stephen or Maud or the ghost of Prince Willliam. You need to accept the truth: they would rather let the world burn to the ground than let someone like us rise to them."

The front door flew open. They jumped. Alice and Roger sprinted in. Roger winced in pain. He had an ugly gash on his left arm that he was cupping. Both of them were covered in soot. Emma had never seen Alice like this before; she was petrified.

"What's wrong?" asked Edith.

"We're under attack!"

The next few minutes were a blur. Emma had never seen her mother move as quickly as she did then. They threw their clothes into a sack and left all other valuables behind in that small, two-chamber hovel on the outer edge of Marlborough. Emma never expected an assault to happen in broad daylight. Childhood fables told tales of ghouls and witches that lurked deep within the woods under a full moon, and those same stories warned that terrible things only happened to bad people who were awake at night rather than asleep. Perhaps that was why she expected something like this to only happen at night?

But it was a perfect day; it was violent and bloody and terrible. Emma couldn't unsee the things she saw, for the sun shone too brilliantly to hide the bodies, the gore, the death.

Emma, Edith, Alice, and Roger sprinted out the front of the house. Townsfolk that Emma had known for most of her young life ran for their lives. A horseman clad in a surcoat embroidered with three lions stampeded down the street. He swung down his pike at Lionel, the tanner's son, and slit halfway through his ribs, severing his torso to the navel. This was the first time she had ever seen someone murdered; she would see over twenty more by the end.

"This way!" screamed Roger, trying his hardest to seem confident and brave. They ran through a narrow alleyway between Emma's home and the next. When they came out the backside, an older woman by the name of Susanna wandered out ahead of them. Her skirt was soaked red, and her skin was a pale-blue color. Foot soldiers of Maud's army approached behind her. One of them pushed her over, and Susanna fell face-first onto the earth.

A crowd of townsfolk swarmed away from the violence, right into the four of them. Edith twirled Emma around, blocking her daughter from taking the brunt force of the crowd. They slammed into them. All at once, they got caught in it. They stumbled onward with the panicked villagers. Emma couldn't see over the press of bodies. She'd never forget the smell; the stench of fear was repulsive and contagious. Like a plague that jumped between hosts, the smell swelled around Emma and galvanized her into a frenzy. Edith pushed her forward, trying to keep her from tripping and becoming trampled under the swarm. It reminded

Emma of a school of fish in a river, zigzagging away from the unknown predator together. If one moved, they all moved.

Suddenly the crowd stopped; the villagers screamed. The man in front of Emma collapsed, his neck snapping in half as he hit the ground. An arrow stuck out between his eyes. She gazed into his lifeless eyes, and the world went still. More arrows stuck into the surrounding ground.

"Emma! This way!" Her mother took her by the hand and yanked her off the street. Roger, Alice, Edith, and Emma squeezed themselves through the crowd and pushed out the other side. They saw the village gardens, which hadn't yet bloomed, burning to ashes. A dog lay butchered on the ground, its intestines spilled out and squished flat by someone's feet.

"Watch out!"

A raider slammed their shield into Alice and Roger. Alice fell to the ground, her head bleeding from the wound. Emma tried to grab her friend to pull her off the ground, but her mother seized her first and kept her back. Edith pulled her into a small shed that was out of view of the street.

"Alice!" yelled Emma. "Alice!"

Edith covered her mouth, suppressing her cries. "Be silent."

"*Let me go!*" Emma whined under her mother's suppressing arm. She dug her elbows into Edith's side, but she refused to let go.

Three other soldiers carried Alice off the ground. Roger gave chase, but an armored knight blindsided him with a punch. The knight stood over Roger. He grasped a two-handed longsword that glistened crimson under the afternoon sun. "By the decree of Empress Maud, you shall lead us to your food stockpile. She has ordered its occupation for the war effort."

"Alice!" Roger reached for his wife. The knight kicked him in the ribs. Roger doubled over.

"Belt it!" commanded the knight, "Lest you wish to be keeled over and sodomized?"

"Fuck you!"

The knight pressed his sword against Roger's throat. "I am Sir Commander Hurst, knighted by my liege lord, Duke Richard the Just. Following his guidance and the wishes of the Holy Empress, I will raid and pillage, as is my right. Now, for the last time, lead me to your food stockpile."

The knight kicked him in the side again. Roger groaned and scrambled up, crawling back toward their house as the knight followed. Once they were clear of danger, her mother finally let go of her.

Emma spun around and slapped her mother across the face. Edith flinched. Her cheek glowed red from the hit.

"I must save Alice," said Emma. Her eyes burned with her forming tears.

"I'm sorry, Emma," said Edith gently. "'Tis too late for her. We need to go."

"No! I won't leave her."

"We 'ave to. We can leave on the south road."

"You go if ye must!" Emma had never known hatred like this before, especially not toward her mother. Her willingness to abandon Alice disgusted Emma. Tom would never do such a thing. No one should do such a thing!

"Emma, be smart. Please," Edith begged.

Her mother, like always, seemed to have read her mind. It annoyed her to no end. Emma even suspected that her mother had known she was going to visit Tom, but she'd allowed it to happen anyway. Thus, it was no surprise to Emma that her mother jumped forward to catch her as she spun away. Emma dodged to the left, narrowly avoiding Edith's grasping arms, and hurled herself out onto the street.

She ignored her mother's fleeting cries. Emma flung away her tears and tossed off her wimple, allowing her hair to dance behind her. Her feet almost slid out from under her as she rounded the corner. This secondary street was littered with people. Some of them were soldiers, some villagers; some of them were dead, but most were injured. The empress's soldiers were sacking the homes here, tossing out bundles of food and provisions. They stacked everything onto a large wagon at the far end of the road. Children stood in the middle of the street, crying out for parents who were nowhere to be found.

It horrified Emma to find that two different women—Margaret, the butcher's wife, and Agnes, the tailor's daughter—were being dragged by soldiers into vacated houses. She could pick out their specific screams from all the other cries for mercy. Finally, she spotted Alice. The three soldiers hoisted her onto the large wagon, where a fourth pinned her down.

Emma thought fast. She would never get down the street in time. And even if she did, they'd doubtlessly catch her. There were too many soldiers, too many fleeing villagers. Alice reached up for someone to save her, but there was no knight in shining armor to rescue her.

There was only Emma.

T'would have to be enough, she thought, rousing herself to action.

Maud's soldiers snapped the reins. The two yoked horses pulled. Emma moved, giving little thought to caution and self-preservation. Before she knew it, she was scrambling up the side of blacksmith Orvyn's home. Emma had helped repair his roof last fall, and she knew the handholds to grab to climb it fast. She was already atop Orvyn's home when the wagon carrying Alice turned down a side street. Emma leaped from one house to another, avoiding the chaos of the streets below. She would have to trust her footing not to betray her again. This wouldn't be like chasing princesses, hoping that she could fall into a life of luxury; failing this time would mean losing her best friend forever.

Emma kept the wagon in her sight. She was sore from exertion and had difficulty breathing. All around her, she heard screams and shouts and perverted moans. Dozens of knights and soldiers raided every home, store, and barn in town. She saw more dead bodies than she ever hoped to see, all left discarded for the dogs and crows, rotting in the gutters between homes. She ignored them and kept her eyes on Alice.

Don't miss a step, Emma. Don't miss.

Maud's soldiers struggled to maneuver the horses and wagon through the pillaging. Other foot soldiers and townsfolk kept getting in the way, slowing them down and causing delays. But on the rooftops, the way was cleared. Her only enemy was stumbling upon a gap too big to hurdle.

THUNK!

An arrow pierced the roof next to her foot. Emma almost fell. She leaped to the side, narrowly avoiding a second. She hurriedly searched for the archer, but the arrows seemed to have appeared from midair.

THUNK! THUNK! Two more arrows stuck into the surrounding roof.

Emma dashed forward. She caught up to the wagon, just clearing her final leap between a home and the low roof of a shed. She calculated the distance between herself and the wagon. Emma jumped—

THUNK!

An arrow sliced the side of Emma's arm. She cried out and plummeted into the wagon. Her body slammed into the soldier who held Alice, his arm snapping backward as he tried to brace himself.

Alice pushed herself up and saw with amazement that it was Emma. Jubilee ran rampant across her face. She reached down and pulled her friend up. Emma groaned; her arm and body shook from the pain. The soldier with the broken arm stirred behind them. They jumped off and hit the dirt street with a hard *thud*.

"I got ye," said Alice. She braced Emma using her shoulder, and they limped down the nearest alleyway. The soldiers in the wagon didn't give chase.

Ten minutes later, Alice and Emma hid themselves in the nearby forest with a group of other women from the village. They watched their home get ripped apart by the savage army of Empress Maud. Someone touched Emma's shoulder.

She jumped, spun around, and found herself in the arms of her mother. Edith held her daughter tight, letting her tears of relief fall down her cheek freely.

"Don't ye ever do that to me again," said Edith. "Ye hark, Emma? Never be that foolish again!"

"Yes, Mama."

Emma hugged her mother back. The hidden women of the forest all held each other and prayed that they could forget the horrors of Maud's army.

CHAPTER XIII
EADRIC

The southern shires were a vast realm of long, rolling hills that appeared flat when standing upon them. Patches of dense foliage broke up expansive green meadows, and those small forests housed hundreds of trees, plants, and animals. During the height of summer, the lovely songs of birds and insects could lull even the hungriest of babes to sleep; but right now, the sweet smell of honey carried by the warm breeze made Eadric content with the joy of springtime. He was alarmed at how quickly summer approached. Easter was to arrive in a few days, yet they were still waiting to hear news from Northampton about King Stephen, if he had weathered the illness or had been allured by the gentle beckoning of death. Eadric wasn't in any hurry, though. His second wife was stationed with the king, and she would be with them when they finally traveled south to Kent. In the meantime, he, Sir Álvaro, and their party of thirty men were trying their best to enjoy the summer weather, although the monsoon rain, sprinkling down on them from low, gray clouds, made that tougher.

As did the fact that they marched to war.

Their scouts had returned the previous night with word that the empress had sacked the town of Marlborough and savaged its inhabitants only two days past. They had woken their men early. If they were lucky, her troops might try invading one of the nearby towns.

"My lords, I see smoke!" yelled Sir Francis, one of the few knights they brought with them. He pointed over the summit of trees, where a cloud of black smoke billowed.

"That's Reading, is it not?" asked Sir Álvaro.

Eadric grimaced. They'd wanted to reach the city by midday, but the soggy weather had slowed their horses quite a bit.

"Quickly! Ride with me!" yelled Sir Álvaro. He whipped the reins, and his steed jumped to a gallop. Eadric kicked his horse until it obediently followed. Soon the entire batch of them rounded the bend of the road and stampeded through one of the many copses that blotched the land. The vacuous sounds they'd been enjoying all day—that of water dripping off high boughs and splashing into thorny thickets—vanished beneath the thundering of hooves. They fled the grove and entered the town of Reading.

It was being assailed.

The screams of the townsfolk carried to the high ground their unit stood upon. Down in the pandemonium, horsemen bearing torches lit up the thatch-roofed buildings. Even in the suppressing rainfall, the homes caught fire immediately. Dozens of bodies lay bleeding on the outskirts of town. The River Thames and River Kennet, which divided the town into three subsections, carried debris downstream in massive congealed chunks; its waters ran black with ash and blood. The stench was unbearable to anyone but the most perverted of souls—people immune to the scent of burning flesh, those like Eadric.

"Jesus Christ, have mercy," said Sir Francis.

Sir Álvaro hoisted his sword from its scabbard and pointed its steel tip before him so the spreading flames of the town gleamed off its razor edge. Eadric adjusted the leather straps of his plated armor. He was the only one in their company who wore additional plate armor on his chest and back above his hauberk. Some knights in the realm were even testing the use of a full suit of plated armor, although Eadric had heard that blacksmiths still needed to improve those, as they too often came loose and left openings for the enemy. The rest of their loyal company wore *maille* above padded gambesons with surcoats of various colors to designate their liege lords. Sir Álvaro, unbeholden to any lord, had dyed his harness and surcoat as black as the tarred pits of perdition. It truly seemed he had left his Spanish roots well behind him.

Eadric flared his nostrils as he watched his enemies, both Empress Maud's army *and* the fleeing peasants, fight desperately on the roads and alleyways within the town.

"Sir Francis, take a company of fifteen and flank from the north," commanded Eadric. "Sir León, lead a small band of five from the south. The rest with me. We'll pierce the heart of the city from the east. Fight your way across the rivers! We'll meet in the center of town!"

"Let God shine upon us," said Sir Álvaro. "May He light the path of justice and devour the evil of Satan! May Christ allow our swords to run red!"

As Eadric roared a mighty war cry, and the stampede of their unit announced their arrival to battle, a single crow glided down beside his horse from the heavens above. It glanced at him with its beady eye, glossy and black and pure in the chaos of battle, and it cawed. Its shrill voice pierced even the densest of coifs. It flapped its wings and withdrew into the gray clouds.

Fiery Hell. What's taking so long?

Eadric awaited his greatest battle yet.

He sat in the wooden tub and splashed the water impatiently. It was lukewarm and getting colder. A servant woman poured a pitcher of soapy water onto his nude back, while Eadric glanced over at the empty tub next to his. A member of the surrounding crowd coughed. Then someone else did. Then another.

King Stephen and Queen Matilda watched patiently atop their royal thrones, which were brought into the antechamber of Eadric's estate. After forcing Empress Maud out of London, the queen had expertly commanded her troops and captured Maud's half-brother, Earl Robert of Gloucester, after defeating his army in Winchester. They recently exchanged the empress's captured half-brother for Matilda's imprisoned husband.

Eadric sighed. The bathing of newlyweds was a big event in highborn weddings; it symbolized the cleansing of past sins to make room for new love.

Well, if this could even be called love. Hardly anyone married who they actually adored, and that was no exception for Eadric. This would be both Eadric and Eleanor's second spouse.

"Have you fetched a cold yet, Eadric?" the king jested. The crowd politely laughed.

"I fear I will soon if she doesn't arrive," said Eadric to a roar of more polite laughter. The grand double doors of his Rockingham estate pushed open. A breeze passed through the crowd, making him shiver in the tub.

The crowd parted, and Viscountess Eleanor of the Holy Roman Empire strutted into the antechamber. She had changed out of her gown from earlier and now wore a blue dress that hung loosely to the top of her feet. Her hair, like all women of this day and age, was covered with a long veil that disguised her thinning brunette locks. This matrimonial event was usually embarrassing for young maidens, but Eleanor had been through this before. And while her foreign body and sheer dress may prove exotic for some of the lonelier men in attendance, most of them saw this as an insipid ritual.

Besides, both she and Eadric held the same feelings about this *lovely* marriage.

"Ready to get this shit over with?" Eleanor asked with her deep, rough voice.

"I was cleaned before you even undressed yourself," said Eadric.

"Hah. I doubt that. I could smell you from outside, you shit-stained bastard." Eleanor smiled smugly at him. Eadric groaned. He tried to keep on a cheerful face for the crowd. His wife stepped into her tub, leaving her dress on for modesty's sake. She made a small yelp and glared at the servant. "Virgin Mary's divine blessing! This water's frigid. My nipples are going to poke through my damn dress."

"Giving the watchers what they want?"

"Belt it. They could've kept it warm at least." She lowered herself into the tub. The water sloshed over the side and wet the ground. "They didn't need to fill it up so high either. Making me feel like a pig."

"You could pretend to enjoy this. If the king didn't want our houses joined, I wouldn't marry you either. So don't be offended."

"Oh, I'm not offended, darling. In fact, I'm quite allured by the prospect of lavishing myself inside your lovely home here."

"My estate goes to the king after I die. Don't think you can marry into it."

"Yes, yes. I've heard all about your tragic story. I lost my husband and son too. This war takes from us all, indiscriminately."

The servants dumped soapy water over their heads, dousing their heated words. The crowd cheered. King Stephen and Queen Matilda smiled at one another. Eadric amused himself by glancing from their royal love over to the unabashed disgust on Eleanor's face. She looked over at him, and Eadric knew she read that same disgust on him.

It made them smile; they had something in common after all.

Her sheer dress stuck closely to her body. Eadric gazed over it. He noticed Eleanor doing the same to him. She was beautiful. And he was . . . fit.

"Ready to consummate?" she asked in a blasé tone.

"I see a great number of men who are going to be eager to watch," said Eadric. Much to his dismay, Eleanor didn't blush at all.

"Let them come and watch," she said. "I'm just here for your estate."

Eadric crossed the bridge into Hell.

Flames leaped from one home to the next, leaving behind a trail of cinders; the ashes flailed to the ground in a gray sludge after being battered by the mist. Townsfolk wailed on the street next to the bodies of their fallen parents, children, and spouses. Others sprinted from one alleyway to the next, desperate to evade the roaming horsemen and knights. Eadric's steed spooked as an elderly peasant sprung out from behind a cart. He tried to calm the beast, but she reared up and almost toppled him onto the ground. Annoyed and flustered, Eadric dismounted and slapped the horse's rear end, causing it to gallop away.

Eadric spotted his first enemy. Based on the embroidery of their surcoat, he must be a knight. Only someone with significant wealth could afford a seamster of such skill. The knight, unlike Eadric, didn't have any plate armor atop his padded gambeson and hauberk. Eadric was at an advantage.

"In the name of King Stephen of Blois, I command you kneel! Swear fealty to his holy name!" shouted Eadric across the thoroughfare that separated them. The knight gripped his mace nervously. It was easy for them to remain calm when they were slaughtering peasants; at the most, they would only have axes, hammers, or pitchforks to fight back with. But the lowborn weren't versed in warfare. They didn't have the ferocity that Eadric trained into every muscle.

The fight lasted only a few seconds. Eadric cut him down with ease, using his sword to knock the mace from the knight's hand. He then took up the knight's mace, splintered his beater shield, and exploded his head like a melon. He then sheathed his sword and took the mace with him. He needed more practice with bludgeoning weapons. Eadric slew two, three, four of Maud's soldiers in quick succession as he plowed his way forward.

The center of Reading had three major streets that branched off into each subsection of the city. Eadric smiled at himself, satisfied with his work. His once reflective and polished armor was stained red with the lifeblood of his enemies. All around him, endlessly high pillars of black smoke rose into the air. He glanced around for the company he was leading, but it appeared he'd lost them in the thrill of battle.

A woman screamed inside a nearby tailor's shop. Eadric shrugged. He had time until the others caught up with him. The scream came again, and he kicked open the door. The inside of the shop was trashed with fabric; it lay everywhere in tangled clumps of brazen colors. Eadric had to step over a dead shop guard on the ground, his throat slit from ear to ear.

"Please stop!" A female voice again, but different from the one screaming earlier.

Eadric crossed into the storage room in the back. Three women cowered in the corner. And standing in front of them, holding a longsword that dripped with fresh blood, was a knight in black-plated armor.

"Álvaro?"

The black knight glanced back at him. This wasn't the man Eadric had seen a mere half hour ago. No, standing here before him was a demon in a man's body. Glaring from the depths of his dark pupils, the knight placed one hand on the nearest woman's breast.

"Help us, please!" she begged. Eadric glanced at her.

He wished he didn't.

She looked like Lucia; she had fair skin with freckles that were haphazardly splattered across the bridge of her nose. Her veil had fallen off her head, revealing long, black locks that rested upon her shoulder. The most frightening similarity of all, however, was that she had the same elegant brown eyes.

Eadric couldn't stop the tears from boiling down his cheeks. He saw in front of him not Sir Álvaro nor the three peasant women, but his daughter. Lucia smiled at him and held out her arms for a hug. Eadric stepped forward, hoping beyond hope to feel his daughter one last time. But just as he took that step, his daughter fell to her knees. Eadric trembled. He reached for her.

Lucia whipped her head up to stare up at him. What were once beautiful brown eyes were now glazed red; she wept blood. Her throat, like that of the shop guard, was sliced from one side to the other. She opened her mouth as if to speak, but no words came out.

"NO!" yelled Eadric. He leaped forward. Lucia disappeared, and he crashed into Sir Álvaro. He pinned the black knight against the wall. "Leave them alone!"

"Don't—" Sir Álvaro began.

Eadric slammed him against the wall again. "Leave them."

Sir Álvaro hesitated. He had a dangerous look in his eyes, and Eadric spied a hint of hatred in them. But eventually, the knight nodded. The women sprinted out of the room, stumbling over their long dresses. He watched Sir Álvaro for a long moment while the darkness receded from his eyes.

Eadric knew that look. He'd seen it countless times. To survive during war, to best an enemy in combat, a soldier had to lose all sense of self. A soldier must become something inhuman, one of God's angels put on earth only to extinguish the flames of life. There must be no empathy, no reluctance, no morality. In this state, a person became nothing more than a vessel for wrath. Eadric had lost himself in it before.

"Come back to me, León," Eadric said to him, bracing the knight upright. Sir Álvaro grimaced. His bushy mustache raised to reveal blood-stained teeth. Finally, at long last, after holding the knight for what seemed like minutes, the demon dropped out of him. "There you are."

"I'm . . . I'm sorry, Eadric. I don't know what overcame me."

"Don't let it happen again. Now begone." Eadric shoved Sir Álvaro out of the backroom.

"I'm sorry," Sir Álvaro said. He turned to exit but halted in his tracks. "Fuck."

Four large knights blocked the front door. Two of them carried longswords, while the other two held war hammers. The one who stood in front wore a harness. Its craftsmanship almost appeared as good as Eadric's. The Hellhound took a step closer to get a better look at the man. Then it hit him . . .

Commander Hurst.

He lost thought of all else; his one goal in life was to annihilate the man standing before him. Commander Hurst's dark eyes and chiseled jawline jutted out around the thin steel helm that protected his head and nose.

"I recognize you," said Commander Hurst. "You're Stephen's Hellhound. The one who's been causing us all our problems."

"Aye. And you're the one who abandoned us at Rowan's castle."

Duke Richard's knights, led by Commander Hurst and another man by the name of Commander Braxton, were supposed to be keeping the peace that night. They were the ones who should've been protecting them all from the peasant uprising. But rather than doing their duty, they abandoned them all, leaving Duke Rowan and all his relatives, including Lucia, to die.

"You had a daughter there, did you not?" Commander Hurst smiled at him.

"Leave me," Eadric said to Sir Álvaro. "This is my fight."

"I won't," said Sir Álvaro. "We'll avenge Lucia together."

Eadric huffed. He pointed his mace toward the commander. "Tell me where to find Richard, and I'll grant you a quick death."

Commander Hurst laughed. The three knights around him readied themselves.

"I'll enjoy this," jeered the commander.

He lunged. Eadric and Sir Álvaro pounced. The three knights charged.

Eadric swung his mace twice, and two dead bodies collapsed onto the floor. He bounced off two other fighters as they all threw themselves against each other. The shop was in turmoil. Iron, fabric, and arms flung everywhere. He guarded instinctively and blocked a flurry of blows from Commander Hurst. Eadric kept himself centered, focusing on his breath work. Something stabbed him from behind, but he remained alive. Good! His armor was doing its job.

Eadric pivoted, using his momentum to slam his mace in a downward bash at whoever tried piercing him. Commander Hurst parried the blow, aiming to nick Eadric below his armpit where his armor tied together. Realizing this, Eadric spun, twisting his armor enough to deflect the sword off his breastplate. He threw his knee upward into Commander Hurst's stomach.

Sir Álvaro came up behind the commander and swept his legs out from under him. Hurst stumbled prone. Eadric kicked him in the head. Hurst spat blood as Eadric booted the commander's helm across the store.

The room went silent. The three other knights lay dead on the ground, some of them missing limbs. Sir Álvaro had continued his streak of never losing a battle.

Commander Hurst tried to stand, but the black knight pinned him to the ground with a strong stomp. Commander Hurst yelped. Eadric kneeled next to him and brought out a long hunting knife from his belt. The weakest part of a knight's armor was in the groin, under the hauberk and between the chausses. Luckily for Eadric, and unluckily for the commander, a major artery also ran through there. Eadric stuck the dagger between the commander's legs.

"Wait! Wait! WAIT!"

"Where can I find Duke Richard?" asked Eadric.

"I don't know! I don't know where he is."

"You lie." Eadric sawed the knife into Commander Hurst's groin. It tore through the skin. The commander's body spasmed. Sir Álvaro kept the crying man still as Eadric twisted the knife inside him. The serrated edge of the blade did even more damage, ripping and shredding muscle from tendon. Blood pooled below them.

"P-p-please! I don't!"

"Tell me."

"I left! Please, God. I left. I left his service." Commander Hurst whined. Eadric tried to read his blanching face. Blood squirted from the commander's mouth. Seems he bit off his own tongue. Neat.

"I'm waiting!" Eadric pushed the knife farther in. Commander Hurst could barely muster a moan. His eyes grew wide.

"C-commander Braxton . . . He'll know. He still h-holds fealty to . . . to the duke."

"You know where Commander Braxton is?"

Commander Hurst nodded. Eadric pulled the knife out, slashing through the artery. Blood spewed, gushing in a concentrated arc. Commander Hurst spasmed below him.

"Tell me where," said Eadric, "and I promise I'll give him a worse death than you."

Eadric and Sir Álvaro listened as he gave them the whereabouts of the Hellhound's next victim.

CHAPTER XIV
EMMA

EMMA REMEMBERED THEIR ESCAPE in scattered pieces; jagged and raw, they'd tear into her at random times of the day, both solicited and not so—a dark, endless nightmare pestering her until it became impossible to know peace, for she always feared when the next grim reminder would overtake her. It left the order of events forever ingrained yet eternally missing from her memory. It molded the flight from her home into a spiraling, internal maze.

"I need a break," said Edith. Emma's mother sat on a boulder that jutted out from a creek bank. Emma groaned and tapped Alice to hold up. They were on the third day of their trek to Reading, a trip that had only taken Emma, Alice, and Roger two days to cover previously. But barely able to shuffle her left leg, Edith had to take multiple long rests along the way. The small group of a dozen refugees they'd fled with had either diverted off or left them far behind.

"How long do ye need *this* time?" Emma asked with a huff.

"Not long. Just need to stretch."

Edith lengthened her leg. A brief ray of sunshine glimpsed through the foliage above and shone upon her protruding scar. It was ugly and scabbed over and zigzagged across her thigh like a branching lightning strike. Emma shook her head; she still couldn't believe her mom tried to stop her from saving Alice. Surely, her mom saw all their unlucky, dead neighbors? Surely, she knew what evil, despicable, disgusting things soldiers did to women during raids?

Alice and Emma sat on the massive root of a willow tree that snaked out of the ground. In truth, they were all feeling the emotional and physical exertion of the last few days. Alice rubbed her tummy. "I'm hungry."

"Me too," said Emma. "We should be in Reading by now, with Tom. He'd 'ave given us a big meat pie and rented us a warm room. Should've been there yester morn."

"'Tis not her fault."

Emma glanced over at her mom and lowered her voice. "She'd be quicker with that leg chopped clean off."

"At least ye have your mum." Alice gave her a stern look, and Emma had to look away. This attack had been especially hard on Alice. She still didn't know whether her parents or sisters were alive. The former residents of Marlborough had fled in all directions. Every family was likely separated, and it was near impossible to find a lost child, sibling, or parent in the aftermath of such extreme chaos.

Emma sighed. Her friend was right, of course. At least she had her family, even if it was only a single person.

"I'm gonna see if I can find any fruits or nuts for us to eat," said Emma as she stood. It was a damp, overcast day, and she wanted to move to stay warm.

"Where ye goin'?" asked Edith.

"Finding us food."

"Please don't leave our sight, ye hark? 'Tis too dangerous."

"We need food."

"Emma, we're almost to Reading—"

"And we'd be there already if it weren't for you!" Emma grimaced. She hadn't meant to yell, but all the suppressed turmoil that bubbled within her gut had been waiting for a violent release. "We haven't ate in over a day. I'll be fine."

"Then I'll help ye."

"Why? So ye can hide again when we're attacked? Would ye let me get taken away too?"

"Watch your tone."

"Would ye not help me if I were being butchered?"

"'Course I would! How could ye say that?"

"But not Alice? Not others?!" The faces of dead villagers flashed through Emma's mind. Squished skulls. Lifeless eyes. "You criticize

Tom, but he's willing to save us from what happened! I would too. So'd Alice. And Roger. And anyone with a proper heart. Yet ye—"

"Confine your words within your chest, Emma! Ye speaketh with a tongue that has yet to taste the breadth of futility. You know not what I've been through. Helpfulness did *this* to me." Edith showed Emma her scar. "Tryin' to aid others almost killed me and almost made you an orphan! No knight will come and save ye, Emma, so don't call me malicious for doing the only thing I could to save you."

"I'll be fine." Emma took off into the forest without listening to another word.

She followed the creek downstream, kicking rocks and twigs into the swift current. Staring at the water as it danced and bounced over the pebbles, Emma ignored the torrent of thoughts threatening her sanity. She meandered along the creek bed until she eventually heard a soft squeak, followed by the frantic rustling of some leaves. She focused on the source: a bunny caught in a trap.

The small creature lay on its side, a snare wrapped around its left rear-leg. Emma could tell it was broken. The bunny glanced up at her and twitched its tiny brown nose; its belly heaved rapidly from exertion, its breath scattering the fallen leaves around it. Emma's stomach growled.

Who laid the snare trap here? Would they notice if she took the creature for herself?

She reached down and removed the snare from around the forest critter. It tried to kick away, but all it did was further dislocate its back leg. It was too exhausted; the bunny gave up and didn't move. Emma grasped its neck.

Back in Cudworth, the village they lived in prior to Marlborough, a boy by the name of Rodrick had shown her how to do it. Rodrick's father was a trapper and forester, and thus he'd instructed his son where to hunt. They'd found one in its trap. Rodrick told her that his father had taught him the secret to killing it instantly. Emma was curious; she'd never seen someone kill an animal before. Rodrick, after taking care to have her undivided attention, seized the rabbit by its head and body. But his father must have taught him wrong. He pulled and twisted in one startling motion. The rabbit shrieked and spasmed in his arms as its spine ripped; yet it remained conscious, feeling every terrifying inch of it get yanked apart.

Emma could still hear the rabbit's death throes to this day.

The brown-nosed bunny rested helplessly in her hands. Her mouth was salivating. Her mind buzzed with the excitement of rabbit stew filling her rumbling tummy. She wrapped her hand around the bunny's head. Its breath felt cold and forceful against her middle fingers; its fur was rough and prickly.

A quick tug and twist, just like Rodrick said. No pain.

The critter made a soft whimper in her hand. Emma steeled herself, ready to pull. She saw, suddenly and violently, the deceased form of an elderly woman, her neck broken. She remembered seeing this unfortunate woman as they fled Marlborough. Her body was so badly trampled that Emma couldn't recognize who it was.

Emma collapsed to the ground and released the bunny. It limped off into the underbrush.

She cried. Loud and hard. A light sprinkle of rain fell between the canvas of the trees, and her heart lightened, for in that moment it seemed as if God was mourning with her. She sat on the soft embankment next to the creek for a while... until laughter broke the calmness of nature.

Men.

Her blood froze in her veins. Her heart hammered in her ears. Still confident in her ability to be silent and stealthy, Emma crept toward the noise. After blowing up at her mother, she felt committed to finding food. And where there were people, there were provisions. She rounded a tree trunk and found herself on the upper side of a hill that overlooked Reading.

It was on fire.

Smoke billowed up from its wooden homes and houses until the collective ashes of the town were indistinguishable from the gray clouds above. A battle coursed through the streets far below, but Emma couldn't tell who was fighting whom.

Was it the town guards? Bandits? King Stephen's army? Was Tom down there?

More laughter drew her attention toward a small encampment of two soldiers, their surcoats bearing the three golden lions of the Angevins. Empress Maud's army, then. Their *maille*, battleaxes, and shields glistened wet as beads of water stuck to them in the drizzle. A burlap sack full of plundered loot lay next to them. Visible within the bag, much to Emma's satisfaction, was a pile of food provisions.

I can do this. Stay silent. Be patient.

She crept closer until she could hear them speaking. The two soldiers were dividing their stolen jewelry and cutlery and bickered about who got what. They called one another Bernard and Joshua, and she guessed they were in their late thirties. Though dried blood soiled their surcoats, there wasn't a single scratch visible on them.

"Stupid fathers always get their families killed," said Bernard, the taller of the two.

"Shame too," bemoaned Joshua. "Wouldn't have 'ad to touch his ugly wife if he didn't attack. Show me them rings."

Emma dropped onto her belly, trying to keep cover behind the shrubbery. She painstakingly crawled across the cold mud. The spring rain made her shiver.

"What's that?" Bernard asked.

Emma froze. Was it the noise of her dress snagging on weeds? She lay still, keeping her breath as muted and controlled as possible. Fear and anxiety mixed within her. Everyone went silent. She gazed at the burlap sack only a few feet in front of her. The rain bounced off it.

Tap, tap, tap, tap, tap.

The soldiers rushed to their weapons. "Shite! Move! Quick-like!"

Joshua and Bernard turned to grab their loot, but Emma leaped up and stole the sack. The soldiers shouted. She threw the sack over her shoulder and sprinted into the forest. Gambling a look back, she saw they were giving chase. She also saw something else; multiple horsemen thundered behind them. One galloped up to Joshua. He drove his pike down through the soldier's back.

Not on their side then, thought Emma frantically. She pranced between trees and over thickets like a scared doe, somehow being both graceful and quick.

"Get back 'ere!"

Emma wasn't sure if the command was directed at her, Bernard, or both of them. She ran and ran with the sack bouncing against her back until the sounds of hooves had faded into the constant rumbling of the creek. She made her way upstream.

THUNK! THUNK!

Two arrows struck the tree next to her, chipping bark off in all directions. Emma screamed. She jumped prone onto the ground. The next thing she knew, she had lost all control of her breath. Her insides contorted. Bernard lifted her off the ground as she wheezed.

"I'll take that," he said, hoisting the bag over his shoulder. Emma tried to speak back, but her throat closed up.

Bernard gave her one last curious look before he turned and—

Tom smashed a mace into his face.

Bernard's head caved inward. He fell face-first into the creek, where his bright-red blood was carried away from him in string-like cords. Emma pushed herself up and ran into Tom's arms. She hugged him tightly, uncaring of how disgusting she must look and smell.

"I told ye I'd save you," he said.

"I knew ye would." Emma smiled. She didn't know exactly where the decision came from, but the answer explode out of her all at once.

"I want to," she said.

"What?"

"She killed my home. Murdered my friends."

"I know." Tom stroked her back. It felt good to be comforted.

"I want to help," said Emma again. "*Fuck* the empress. Fuck her and those vile men who serve her. I'll do what ye want, Tom. Whatever can make us live a normal life again."

"You'll be a spy then?"

"Emma?!"

Edith and Alice rushed through the forest. Her mother ripped her from Tom's arms and into a hug of her own. Edith's fingers desperately grasped at her, as if she would disappear if she stopped pulling at her.

"What happened?" asked Alice.

"I got us food," said Emma, "like I said I would."

"Thank God you're all right," her mother said.

"T'was Tom who saved me."

Edith glanced over at the young squire. "Thank you for saving me daughter."

Emma grinned. That was one of the few nice things her mother had ever said about him. She glanced back at Tom and saw that he was looking at her expectantly. There was no ideal time to let her mother know, so she might as well do it now while he could help.

"I'm leavin' with Tom," Emma said, speaking fast. "I'm goin' to help him and the king and everyone, so they don't lose their homes and friends and family like us."

"Emma, don't be stupid."

"I'm not. 'Tis my choice, my life. Tom will protect me."

"I pledge my honor to her, madam," said Tom, bowing to Edith.

"I don't give a rat's ass who ye pledge your honor to," said Edith. "I've told ye once, and I'll say it now before the Lord again, stay away from me daughter."

"That's not what she wants."

"It's not her choice, ye prick! She's *my* daughter."

"Mama," Emma yelped. Her heart was heavy. She struggled to hold back her tears. "It *is* my choice. Why don't ye understand? I want to help people."

"Alice, take Emma back. I'll deal with Tom."

"I'm sorry," Alice whispered as she grabbed Emma's arms. Emma ripped herself away from her friend's grasp.

"No! I want to go with Tom. He'll protect me."

"Emma." It was Tom's voice. She was mortified when she glanced over at him; he looked like a whipped puppy. "Do as your mother commands."

Alice rubbed Emma's back and pulled her away. The last thing she saw as her friend directed her around the bend was Tom handing over the sack of food while her mother berated him.

Emma was roused awake in the middle of the night, the warm weather hanging around them like a heavy quilt. Tom stood over her. Emma couldn't contain her smile.

"What are ye—?"

Tom shushed her. He glanced over his shoulder at Edith. Emma's mother moaned in her sleep like she usually did. "Come with me," he whispered. "Alice is waiting."

Emma packed the few things she had with her from Marlborough. She leaned over her mother's sleeping body, just as she did when she left for Reading, and said goodbye yet again. It felt different this time, though. She knew there was no going back, not from this. This wasn't simply goodbye; this was something more. She kissed her mother on the forehead.

"I'm sorry, Mama." She tried to think of something more to say, but when nothing else came to her, she turned around and walked away with Tom. She regretted not having further contemplated those last words.

Tom and Emma met Alice along the main road. Alice gave her friend a sad smile, hugged her tightly, and said, "I'm going to miss ye."

"You're not comin'?" Emma asked. She didn't know it was possible for her heart to sting so much. The last few weeks were a whirlwind of unfathomable loss.

"I need to stay. Roger might still be alive. He's a dolt, but he's my husband. And someone must calm your mother down before she does something crazy. I'll make sure she's well while you're gone."

No words could express Emma's gratitude for her friend, so she hugged her again, tighter than before, and said, "I hope ye find Roger."

"Me too."

"After I take you to Oxford," Tom began, "I'll come back and watch over Alice and your mother. My knight will want me back in camp soon. There'll be fallout for us counter-raiding the empress in Reading, but he'll be grateful we got a spy in such an important castle."

"Just promise me you'll take care of her," Alice said to Tom.

"I promise."

Alice and Emma hugged a third time. Her friend felt warm and comforting and lovely in her arms. In that moment, Emma made a vow that she would see Alice and her mother again one day, when the world became a better place because of her actions; one day, when she had her own home, and she could invite her mother to live with her; one day, when the world made sense once more.

A haunting howl erupted from down the main road. The three of them jumped. Emma gasped.

A wild dog, appearing silver under the waning moonlight, crossed the wide dirt path. In its mouth hung the limp form of a bunny. It twitched between the dog's sharp canines, blood pooling from its broken leg.

CHAPTER XV
GILBERT

G ILBERT AND HAWK WERE starving for some meat. Delicious, salted meat. Crispy skin and tender center. God, wouldn't it be glorious? But God wouldn't be happy with that, for the Church reminded them that Lent was still ongoing even on Holy Thursday, which celebrated the start of the Holy Triduum, which celebrated the final days of Jesus's life, or, more importantly, the final three days before they could start eating meat again.

Gilbert and Hawk had arrived at Caen early the day before, and although they had asked around for their wedded friends, Bartholomew and Beatriz, they had found no one who knew them. Well, at least they knew where they'd be today.

Easter was, inarguably, the largest and most important holiday of the year, with not a single soul in all the duchies of France and beyond ordered to work. The Easter festivities began on Holy Thursday, and all eyes and ears turned toward the Church. And Caen, being perhaps the biggest hub of commerce and trade in all of Normandy, would be swarmed with peasants, nobles, clergy, vagabonds, merchants, charlatans, minstrels and more from every corner of the realm. If there was ever a single day that gave every peasant hope during the coldest, dreariest nights of winter, it would be Easter Sunday. The streets of Caen were jammed packed, and the mass of bodies flowed toward the towering cathedrals. The bells tolled throughout the city, tolling for life, for salvation, and for all of Christendom. Gilbert still didn't know if Pope Innocent II down in Paris, or if Pope Anacletus in distant Rome was the *true* pope, but the church bells tolled regardless; thus, it made little difference to the poorly lived common folk, who festered hungrily for eternal salvation, which side of the papal schism prevailed.

It was a race to the western edge of the Caen, where the Abbey of Saint-Étienne stood erected as the sacred heart of the city. The towering structure was as magnificent as it was ostentatious, equal parts mesmerizing and horrifying. If one were to stand in the lowliest parts of the city to the south, they could look north and see the true power of the glorious sister cathedrals of Caen: Saint-Étienne to the west and the Abbey of Saint-Trinité to the east. Both cathedrals framed Caen Castle perfectly between them, as if the historic keep of William the Conqueror and the city below were divinely planned by God Himself. Over the last few decades, Archbishop Hugh IV had been updating the ancient cathedrals about Rouen and Caen, paying countless coin for stonemasons to chip away at the facades like angels eroding the face of mountains. The cathedral at the heart of Saint-Étienne had multiple half-cylinder towers with tall spires that speared the heavens above, giving shape around the central nave. Scaffolding scarred the sides of the cathedral, where additional chapels or wings were being added. The disarray of the construction site gave Gilbert the impression that an Easter deadline was planned and not met.

All along the Rue de St. Pierre leading up to the abbey, traders arranged stalls and organized events for the citizens of Normandy to enjoy. But first, before the revelry could truly begin, a mighty procession lined up outside the cathedral. Gilbert and Hawk guessed that the best place to find their old friends would be here, as no good Christian would dare enjoy the Easter festivities without first doing their mandatory spiritual cleansing: giving alms to the Church.

"Please stand orderly," shouted a nearby priest, his face shrouded by the cassock that drooped around him. "Everyone shall have time to gaze upon the wonders of Christ and the blessed Holy Mother. Please do not touch the Relics!"

"Is there a new tithe to be revealed?" Hawk asked him.

The priest gazed at Hawk and took in his outfit. Hawk wore, like always, his bright-red hat, along with a finely woven tunic and a dark-green cloak. It was his chosen outfit for the task assigned to him by Gilbert.

"Today we've been honored to showcase the very shroud that covered Christ when he was entombed," said the priest after assessing incorrectly that Hawk was of high birth. "We also have a tankard that was touched by the very lips of the Virgin Mother."

"Oh, shit."

"My lord! Have some decency."

"My apologies," Hawk said quickly, remembering he was supposed to be a nobleman and *not* someone who cursed openly. "Father, if I may ask you something further, might I request that the Church, the glorious earthly government of His empire, reconsider the ban of meat consumption during Lent?"

"What?"

"On account of the starvation and thievery and taxation and alm-giving and general suffering, it seems rather cruel to not finally feast when winter abates. Do you not agree?"

"I could have you thrown into the pillory for such heresy," said the priest. His face turned red from the blasphemy.

"Wouldn't be the first time. You think they'd feed me the spare meat before it spoils while I'm entrapped?"

Gilbert smiled and turned away. He scanned the massive crowd and finally found one of his friends; Beatriz appeared from the dense line of the congregation, shuffling her way with everyone else as they crammed through the archway leading into Saint-Étienne. Gilbert tapped on Hawk's shoulders. "Beatriz is here. C'mon, Hawk."

"Anyway," said Hawk to the priest, "think on it, yeah? I'll give extra alms in the hopes God lets you know He agrees."

"Excuse us! Excuse us! Royal blood comin' through," shouted Gilbert.

"That's right!" said Hawk proudly. "Give way, ye lesser men. Christ loves us equally, but the Church adores the rich most. Give way!"

"Oi! Me don't recognize ye from any prominent house," said a peasant in line.

"Aye," said Hawk, "nor does God. Henceforth, I must make myself known to Him promptly and orderly. Now, if you'd please."

They crammed themselves into line only a few people behind Beatriz. They ignored most of the crude gestures and vibrant cursing they received as they pushed forward.

The cathedral was vast and tall; massive stone archways lined the nave, and windows cut into the walls let glorious sunlight fill the heavenly air. The congregation moved even more slowly inside, shuffling down the main walkway between the many wooden seats bracketing the path. It was loud with the voices of thousands. Peasants and nobles spoke to each other excitedly, trying to glance ahead at the holy Relics on display at the end of the nave. Those who already looked upon the tithing were spreading around against the far stone walls and exiting out doors on either side.

It made Gilbert sick. The crowd reminded him of things he wished to forget. Darker times, deep in a frozen forest—of pitchforks and torches and angry, blank faces. He tried to keep his composure, but his stomach tied into knots within his bowels.

How many times had he asked for forgiveness for his crime? How often had he begged God to kill him instead of . . . no, he couldn't think of that. He had to save his brother now. Forget everything else. He may go to Hell one day, but as long as he lived, Gilbert would not let the Devil tempt him further.

"Are you okay?" asked Hawk, a knowing look in his eyes.

"Yes. Let's just get some help. Beatriz!"

It had been well over a year since they'd last seen their friends. Gilbert had expected some changes, sure, especially on account of his two friends getting married. But he absolutely, positively, never would've suspected that the bald man who turned around next to Beatriz was his childhood best friend.

"Bartholomew?!" Hawk hissed with disgust. "What the *fuck* happened to you?"

"Hawk?! Gilbert?! What are ye doing in Caen?" asked Bartholomew with a bewildered but overjoyed grin spreading across his face. The smile and crooked front teeth were immediately recognizable, as was the warmth radiating off him, but Gilbert could not get over—

"Your hair . . . Bart, what happened?" asked Gilbert aghast.

Beatriz, who looked much the same as she always had since entering womanhood, elbowed Bartholomew before he hugged them. "Why don't you greet them properly, dear."

Their friend bowed, dropping his exuberance, and said, "May God be with you, friends."

"Very good," said Beatriz in her quick cutting voice. It was as if each word must start before the last one finished. "May God be with you, Hawk." She smiled. "And Gilbert." She smiled slightly less.

Gilbert and Hawk glanced at each other. *What's happening here?*

"So . . . the hair?" asked Hawk.

"Bartholomew has let go of his sinful past," Beatriz answered for him. "Like a monk, he shaved his hair to clear any barrier between him and Christ." She rubbed his arm and added, "And it looks good on him."

"Um, well, congratulations," said Gilbert, stumbling over his own tongue. "On the marriage, that is. We didn't—or at least, I didn't realize—"

"Beatriz, my love and stars," Bartholomew began, "had helped me gain a . . ." He peeked at her, searching for the right word, until she finally nodded when she spied it on the precipice of his lips. ". . . deeper understanding of the sacrifice our Lord and Savior made. She has proposed, even, that she should become a nun, detesting of all worldly pleasure, a fact she *decidedly* didn't tell me until *after* we married."

"Bart!" Beatriz punched him in the arm.

"What?" he asked, rubbing where she had hit. "Was that not what you said?"

"Lord God, give me strength. Do *not* bring up bedroom affairs in public."

"I wasn't . . . sorry. What brings ye both here? Aren't you supposed to be in the king's army, Gilbert?"

"I hope God gave you strength," Beatriz whispered.

"I hope God gave you strength," Bartholomew repeated.

"And guidance."

"And guidance."

"And grace."

Bartholomew turned to her. "Okay, I'm not sayin' all of that every time."

"You need to be serious about this!"

"I AM BEING—"

"*Shush.*" The nearby clergymen glared at them. One of them spoke up, "Keep your voices down. This is a place of worship."

"Sorry, Fathers," said Beatriz.

Gilbert and Hawk shared a glance. These weren't the two friends they'd known their whole lives; these were almost new people entirely. Beatriz turned and pointed at them, making the pair shrink beneath her long finger.

Christ, when did she become so scary?

"Now listen here," she said, "the both of ye. Bart and me have turned a new leaf. We're followers of Christ now, and we'll have none of your rabble-rousing. We've come a long way from the stunts you had us pulling."

"We're not here to pull a prank," said Gilbert. Hawk nodded encouragingly, but Beatriz raised an eyebrow in suspicion. "Or a con." The eyebrow stayed raised. "Or to steal." *Damn, the eyebrow is still up?* "Or to otherwise sin in any fashion that may be unbecoming to your new turned leaf."

"Is that true?"

". . . Mostly?"

The line slowed as they reached the far end of the nave. The congregation rounded an altar, which had a strange contraption on it. Monks stood around the choir chanting a long Latin prayer, and a few bishops were carefully monitoring the peasants whom approached the holy artifacts.

"So," Bartholomew began, "if not a prank or a con or a sin, why're ye here?"

"Can't friends just come to say hello?" asked Gilbert. Beatriz was about to open her mouth again, so Gilbert quickly added, "And to congratulate the lovely newlyweds?"

"We married eight months ago," said Beatriz.

"I was at war."

"And I was busy," said Hawk.

"Busy doin' what?"

"Conning and thieving."

Beatriz sighed mightily. Gilbert lifted his hands up in defense. "Hark, Beatriz, we came because we need you. Both of you. *Not* that I'm not happy to see you both, hair or no hair, married or not, but we need your help."

"Let me guess. You tricked some general in the king's army to let ye leave, and now you have to fake your death so they don't behead you?"

"What is with ye and people fakin' death?" Bartholomew asked his wife. "This is the fourth time this week you've brought this up."

"I think I could do it rather convincingly."

"Nay," said Hawk, cutting them off. "'Tis about William."

That changed their mood at once; they became sober and serious, concern prodding at them. Beatriz had every reason to be antagonistic, or downright hostile, with Gilbert and Hawk. They were often the ones who begot trouble or came up with the "genius" idea to earn some coin, gathering them and William to go fulfill said plan. But William was always the emotional center of the group. He was who everyone could turn to if a plan turned sour and went awry.

He was the best of us, thought Gilbert. The hole in his heart continued to eat away at him.

"What happened to Will?" asked Beatriz.

"He was taken as a war spoil," said Gilbert. "Shipped to England."

"Poor lad," said Bartholomew.

"We're sorry, Gilbert." Beatriz rubbed his shoulder. She could be as tender as she was fiery—a woman whose emotions were as clear as day. That was one of the things Gilbert loved about her.

"We mean to get him back," said Gilbert, his voice hardening.

"From England?" Bartholomew gasped.

"And how do ye plan on doin' that?" asked Beatriz. "I'm sorry, but don't be a dolt. That island is terrorized by war. I love Will, me does. But he's gone now."

"No," said Gilbert. "We can find passage and sail to Wareham. From what I overheard in Flanders, the southwest of England is still largely untouched by war. If we hurry, we can get ashore and trek inland before they fortify the ports."

"Let's say you even get there. What next? Do ye have the means to pay his ransom? Do you mean to siege whatever city he's imprisoned within? Or will you simply sneak inside and fuck the prison guard in the arse so he'll let you—*Oh!*" Beatriz huffed. "God blessed! Look at what ye made me do. Dear Lord Christ, forgive my serpent tongue."

"I don't know yet. We can figure it out when we get there. And I do mean *when*. He needs all of us, Beatriz."

"This is insane. And you said yes to this?"

Hawk nodded. "Ye know me."

"You're an idiot."

"Yeah. Me knows."

"Fuck it," Bartholomew said. "I'm in."

Beatriz slapped him. "You most certainly are not."

"It's Will."

"It's *me*, your wife! What are we talking about? Going to England? Freeing a captive hostage?"

"He's not just some hostage," said Gilbert. "He's my brother, *our* friend."

Beatriz sighed. She raised her hands in prayer. "God, Christ, and all the rest, please give me strength before I strike these fools. My husband: the biggest of them all."

"Quit acting so high and mighty, love," said Bartholomew. "You were the one who came up with half our plans."

"Shush."

"Don't ye remember the night before Lammas? Or . . ."

"I said, *shush*! Lest God hears you all and banishes me to Hell."

"I thought ye said God remembers everything."

"Don't be stupid. There be far too much goin' on for Him to remember everything I've done."

"That sounds a lot like blasphemy," said Bartholomew, smiling.

"Damn you! And you! And *you*," she said finally to Gilbert, "most of all! You can all go to Hell, while I'm pampered and fed like a right, fat lord in Heaven. Humph." She flicked her hair and spun away.

They finally approached the altar with the holy relics, and Gilbert could see what the otherworldly contraption was. A box? No, not quite, because he could see his own reflection; only . . . he could also see through it like a window. Gilbert let out an audible gasp, as did many other peasants around him. He and his friends glared at this see-through, not-see-through box with equal parts awe and horror.

"What is this witchcraft?" asked Bartholomew.

"It's called *glass*," said the nearest bishop, who was tasked with watching over the relics. He looked unamused, perhaps at telling the thousands who flocked through Saint-Étienne about this wonderment rather than the holy artifacts.

"Glass?"

"It allows one to see things with a barrier in between."

"It's like frozen water," said Gilbert.

"Is it made that way?" asked Beatriz.

The bishop shrugged. "I am unsure of its construction. It comes from the east. But I can assure you, it is *not* devilry."

"Whoa," said every peasant who could hear him. Inside the glass box were the two tithes that were announced, a long dirty cloth that must be the shroud of Christ, and a goblet adorned with jewels that must've been touched by the Mother's lips.

"I feel holier already," said Beatriz lovingly.

Bartholomew, Gilbert, and Hawk all chuckled at her comment. She gave them a harsh glance. She didn't find what she said to be as amusingly dirty as they did.

"So, what say you, Beatriz?" asked Gilbert again.

His childhood friend, a woman he'd known and grown with since the dark ages of his youth, turned to face her husband. He held out his hand, and she took it in hers. Bartholomew still appeared absurd to Gilbert, but he was getting used to the lack of hair now. He could finally see how the couple suited each other. There was a tenderness there, an earnestness in the way they clasped hands, both supportive and gentle.

"No," she told him. "I'm sorry, Gilbert. I'm not the woman I was. We have a chance to start anew with God, and, if blessed, with child one day. I cannot throw that life away for an impossible task in a country that would have me dead. I'm sorry."

"Is that what ye want, Bart?" asked Hawk from behind Gilbert.

Bartholomew nodded and said, "I want to be with Beatriz. Forever. But I don't want to lose you either. Is there any way we can convince ye to stay?"

Gilbert thought of it, as he had many times since he escaped that God-forsaken beach. It would be so easy to be a coward once more. He could wave his hand, banish his brother from his mind like he did his . . . like he'd done . . .

Not again. I will be brave.

"It's somethin' I must do," said Gilbert. Hawk patted his back as if praising him. Beatriz and Bartholomew smiled, and it made the day seem slightly brighter than before.

"You're a good man," said Beatriz. "Even if you annoy me to no end, I would hate for this to be goodbye."

They hugged, and Gilbert remembered he had one last thing to ask them. "Do ye know where my parents are? I've been told they live here now."

Beatriz and Bartholomew glanced at each other. "Are ye sure you want to do that?" asked Bartholomew.

"No," said Gilbert honestly. "But I need to do it anyway."

CHAPTER XVI
EADRIC

"**I** won't tolerate insubordination!" said William of Ypres.

Eadric held strong. "I wasn't asking for permission," he said.

"Lest you desire death by the executioner's axe, I'd suggest you control yourself. *Now!*"

Eadric's blood burned through his skin. He ground his teeth. Before he said something he would regret, Sir Álvaro pulled him aside and stepped in front of William. Bowing, the knight said, "My lordship, please excuse the actions of Baron Eadric. His mind is like that of an animal. Can you blame him for being so hostile after he finally found a clue for the man responsible for his daughter's butchering?"

"That's no excuse to disparage your superior and abandon your post. *Twice*, might I add, after your equally errant actions in Flanders."

"I'm not fleeing his lordship," said Eadric sternly.

"Explain. How does losing my top officer help us purge the foreigners from this land?" William of Ypres raised his eyebrows.

"Given that Duke Richard is a high-ranking noble in Empress Maud's favor, *and* that he betrayed King Stephen by swapping allegiance after Lincoln, I would consider his assassination a *very* rewarding success to His Majesty. And as for Flanders, I captured the bastard son of that very same lord who betrayed our king."

"And what will you do after he's dead? What would you have done with Richard's estate? With the peasants of his province? With his bastard?"

"King Stephen can do with them as he pleases. He can give the estate to some baron or clergyman. I don't rightly care."

"Eadric, I don't believe you're seeing my perspective." William sighed, brushing back his thinning white hair. His leathery skin shimmered in the harsh sunlight that streamed through the tent's flaps. "I can't have my officers divided between personal matters and affairs of state. And I certainly can't have them taking entire squadrons and heading off into enemy lands for their own quests of vengeance."

"I—"

"Let me finish, damnit! For all I know, King Stephen—and may God fucking protect him—he may be dead from that accursed plague. Rochester wants us gone. We've used up their entire stockpile of food, and the citizens are ready to torch our tents. The soldiers are restless after our extended bout of inactivity. I fear these rumors of desertion are true."

Eadric nodded despite himself. Even he had caught himself falling victim to this horrendous hesitation. Over a month had passed since they saved Reading from Maud's skirmishers, and they still haven't heard word from the king or queen. Summer was peeking around the edge of the earth, ready to scorch the final dreadful memories of winter from everyone's mind; but truthfully, dread often made the best motivator for war, and summer made one yearn for the company of friends and family, to drink ale and laugh cheerfully at the close of each long day rather than consume stale porridge and take watch duty. Eadric liked to imagine that he could partake in those wonderful summer activities. It helped him keep his mind off the demons that provoked him from within, the uncontainable fury that stirred in the bowels of his soul, craving for escape.

Eadric struggled to contain the madness too, as it sometimes felt like anger was the only emotion he had left. *God, what has happened to my life?*

"I'm sorry, Eadric," said William of Ypres at long last, "but you're too important for King Stephen to lose. I cannot allow you to go."

Eadric and Sir Álvaro crossed two large drawbridges that spanned the length of the River Medway. They passed through the gatehouse and entered Rochester. Townsfolk swarmed between the buildings like ants. Eadric stayed along the outer walls.

"Eadric, please." Sir Álvaro grabbed him by the shoulder.

"Don't put your hands on me!"

"Prithee, peace. I won't. Just hark my words, please, as a friend. I don't wish to see you beheaded for desertion, certainly not before you get your vengeance."

"I'd like to see that churl stop me."

"All I'm asking is for you to give me some time. We know Commander Braxton is in Bristol. He isn't going anywhere. Do you know the wonderful thing about a stalemate? 'Tis that Robert and the empress won't advance their troops either. He isn't leaving his post."

"I can't take that chance."

"I know. I know. Please. Give me some time, and I'll figure something out. I'll find a way for us to campaign west. I just need you not to do anything rash in the meanwhile."

"When have I ever been rash?"

Rochester housed the war prisoners and hostages, for a guarded location behind stone walls and a moat offered better security than the openness of a war camp. The dungeon was beneath the bailiff's chambers, and the gaoler Alfwin—who Eadric had apparently promoted, although he didn't remember doing that—led him through its dark passageways under the twitching light of a torch. Deep, red shadows danced under its bright light. They eventually reached the cells, which were full of pickpockets, drunkards, and other disturbers of the peace; those who committed worse crimes were often killed on the spot.

At the very back of the dungeon were the war prisoners, and in the farthest cell in the darkest corner, sat a scrawny lad who was barely recognizable as the feisty soldier Eadric encountered on the beach in Flanders.

"Will? That's your name, is it not?" Eadric asked the pile of bones.

"Yes, my lord," replied the bones.

"I'll be honest, Will, I'd nearly forgotten you entirely."

"It seems everyone has."

"I have a proposition for you, boy."

The pile of bones stood and approached the cell door. Eadric appraised the boy hostage. His ribs protruded from his thin tunic, and his hair draped to his shoulders in a knotted, waxy mess. The trembling torchlight made his eyes jump to life within the hollowness of their sockets. Eadric had purposefully waited a few months to confront his hostage. He didn't want to use energy to break someone outside of a battlefield, and he discovered the most effective method for getting what he wanted from a prisoner was to allow them to dwell on their thoughts long enough that they believed themselves to be deserted.

Will leaned forward. His fingers gripped the bars, his knuckles bare white. He twitched. Eadric smiled to himself. This was exactly what he needed him to be. Broken. A whipped and neutered shell of his former self.

"You can earn your freedom if you work with me to capture your father."

"I don't know where he is." Will licked his parched lips. His eyes were eager.

"But you claimed to have aided him and Earl Robert in Normandy. Or was that a lie?"

"No. T'wasn't a lie, my lord. I promise."

"Let me be very clear. I intend to slaughter your father. I've tried sending word to him that I've captured you. But he either doesn't care enough to respond, or he has redoubled his efforts to hide from me. Either way, you are becoming less and less valuable by the day. But if you can help me navigate through his defenses, and through Earl Robert's protection, I will grant you your freedom."

There wasn't any hesitation. "Yes, my lord. I'll do it."

"Swear to me," said Eadric, holding out his hand to the cowering hostage bathed in red torchlight. "Swear to me you'll betray your kin."

Will kissed Eadric's hand. "You have my fealty."

Lucia waved her hand through the stream. She shrieked as the cold water rushed between her fingers. Eadric chuckled. He could watch her play all day. His daughter was nearing the tender age of six, and he could see her actively forming her personality, her spirit. She loved nothing more than interacting with everything around her. She seemed to adore the fact that she could, even in such a minor way, affect the world surrounding her. Whether it was throwing pebbles down a hill and causing a rockslide, or tearing up her dresses to create senseless objects from her imagination—much to the dismay of her governess and tailor—she always found joy in testing the limits of herself and their beautiful world.

"Daddy, look! What's that?" She pointed to something in the stream. Eadric kneeled next to her. He placed his hand on her back and grinned pleasantly to himself. His hand took up the entire length of her back, and he could feel her lean against him for support.

"Those are tadpoles," he said.

"Tadpoles?" His daughter cocked her head at him like he was lying. It *was* a funny word when he thought about it.

"Can you guess what they grow up to become?"

"Fishies?"

"Frogs."

"WHAT?" Lucia recoiled from the swarming tadpoles. She groaned and snuggled up against his shoulder for protection. "Yuck, yuck, yuck!"

I guess she hates frogs now. What she loved and hated daily was often a roll of the dice. Eadric was pretty sure their cook was fed up with how often Lucia preferred one meal over another, only to swap her opinion before they even finished prepping.

"Don't be afraid, honey," he said, nuzzling her hair behind her ears. "You're safe with me. You're always safe with Daddy."

"They don't look like frogs," said Lucia. From within her fortified position in the nook of his shoulder, she peeked her little face and large eyes upward at him. Eadric kissed her forehead.

"Many things in the world can be surprising," he said. "It's not our place to question why the Lord made things the way He did."

"But what if God makes me look different when I'm older?"

"Are you a toad?"

"No," she said confidently.

"Well, that's a relief." Eadric shook her until Lucia gave in to an infectious bout of giggles. "But even if you turned into an old, wrinkled, slimy-skinned toad, I would love every bit of you."

"No, you wouldn't!"

"Yes, I would. Because that's the way God created you. And he promised me he would make me the perfect daughter."

Lucia hugged his side. Eadric wrapped his arms around her, pressing her fragile body close to his heart. She looked so much like her mother that it made his heart ache, but Lucia filled every crack of his fractured soul and then some.

Along the bank of the stream, listening to the gentle noise of the water and the melodic songs of the birds, the pair of them savored this moment forever.

"I love you, honey."

"I love you, Daddy."

"You're the last woman I'll ever love," he said truthfully. "And don't you forget it."

Chaos erupted in camp. Soldiers swarmed around their isolated pockets like hornets about their hives, yelling and screaming, getting into fistfights and throwing insults. The peasant-soldiers were packing their belongings in a mass exodus, while officers tried desperately to staunch the festering rumors. One group caught Eadric's attention. Seven soldiers, all much younger than he, were galvanizing themselves into a frenzy. A peasant-soldier by the name of Hugo was leading them in this uproar.

"We must stand tall, brothers! The end is nigh, and all who stand alone will be slain. We've seen what they think of us! Oft they show how they feel in their hearts." The crowd cheered him on, banging their chests and strutting out their chins like they were the lone cock on a hen farm.

"What're you blabbering about?" questioned Eadric. They froze up and lost their cockiness as they saw him. Hugo, who had a patchy beard that reminded Eadric of pubic hair, attempted to stand tall—a rooster against a wolf.

"We knows ye," he said. "Ye noble types can turn sides, switch allegiances at a snap. But we peasants can't. Whereas your lot can surrender and become pawns, we get butchered by the 'undreds all in the name of lordly comeuppance."

"What's the meaning of all this chaos? Speak quick, for I tire of your insouciance."

"The queen has returned without 'er husband. Hark! O, she's returned alone! What do you glean from that?"

"I glean nothing. Only that our illustrious queen has returned."

"Aye, like a lord to see the leaves on the ground but not dread the doom of winter. We see it as it is. The king is dead! And for us, t'would mean we're doomed. Of what good is a woman without her husband?"

He punched the young soldier in the face. The others reached for their weapons, but not before Eadric unsheathed his sword and held it to the peasant's throat.

"You dare besmirch the grace of our queen? You'd belittle the woman who alone, while her husband remained captive for years, grew an army and marched on London?! A woman who did the Lord's work to free her husband against all odds?! Who captured Earl Robert?!"

Eadric pressed the blade against the soldier's windpipe. He expected him to beg for mercy, but instead, the madman laughed a throaty cackle that reverberated through his whole body.

"We all knows what ye are," said Hugo. "A peasant killer. The only respect ye've earned is by the viciousness of ye're blade! Ye're not a man, but a perverse angel of Satan!"

Eadric grimaced, ready to pierce the sword right through—

"I see you're still trying to murder everyone on Earth, darling," said a deep, feminine voice from behind him. Eadric reluctantly pulled the blade away from Hugo's neck. The others dragged him away from the Hellhound.

"Believe it or not, I did not start this one," said Eadric, turning to face his wife.

Eleanor looked at him crossly. She'd aged quite a bit since he last saw her. Her face seemed squarer than it once was, and new wrinkles had formed crevasses on once-smooth skin. She had her hair tucked behind a silk scarf, and a long orange dress stiffly hid her figure. "What are you doing here?" he asked.

"I return with the queen. And I must admit, I had high hopes of finding you deceased."

"It's my honor to disappoint you. Is it true? Does Stephen lie dead?"

"Which answer would dissatisfy you most?"

"Just tell me, woman."

"He's alive and has made a full recovery. I'm sure Matilda will give you more commands, but she's currently resting from our extended travel, as I plan soon to be." Eleanor scanned him up and down. "You seem clean enough. Come on."

"What?"

"I want to have sex." She looked Eadric dead in the eyes. "It's been eight months. Are you telling me you don't want to?"

He hesitated and clumsily sheathed his sword. "Very well. I'll join you if we must."

"I mean truly, what good is our marriage if not to have God-sanctioned copulation?"

Their lovemaking went as it did most of the time: violently and short-lived. Eadric mused that it was almost like wrestling, with one opponent trying to grapple atop another. This was a power match between them, a physical manifestation of their mutual anguish for one another. Sloppy and animalistic, but undeniably passionate.

This bout ended as a tie in all regards, with neither side fully satisfied but everyone glad it was finally over. This wasn't an unusual experience for most married couples, as both of them were from aristocratic origins and had grown up surrounded by reluctantly arranged nuptials. Especially as a woman, Eleanor knew it was typically their lot to go through unloving matrimonies. The only occasional bright spot—if both sides were, at minimum, physically attracted to one another—was that they could release their lust without sin.

"It's quite remarkable how you've been fighting in a war for years and still managed to gain weight," Eleanor said while poking his stomach.

"After all this time, that was the best insult you could think of?"

"I'll be honest, I did little thinking about you at all."

"Makes two of us then."

Eleanor raised an eyebrow. She studied him. "You lie. You're a terrible liar, you know? You're far too emotional."

Eadric huffed. He threw the covers off him and breathed in the warm air. He hated when she was right, and she was almost always right. Damn woman! There were multiple times when the thought of Eleanor jumped unsolicited into his mind. Sometimes it could be explained away as prurience, or the laziness to cook and clean, but other times it was impossible to excuse, especially on nights when he was alone and forgot the memory of Lucia—nights when his thoughts wandered to the present world. In those times, Eleanor could slip into the deep recesses of his mind, and he wondered how she was doing or if she was thinking about him too, which she apparently wasn't...

"Eadric, are you decent?" asked a voice from outside their private tent.

"Yes, come in," said Eadric before his wife could cover herself. She scrambled for the animal-skin blankets as William of Ypres pushed himself through the tent flaps. Seeing Eleanor's partially nude body, and Eadric's *entirely* nude one, he immediately blushed.

"What the Hell, Eadric!" William covered his eyes.

"What do you need, William?" Eadric asked, stretching his legs so two particular body parts dangled more than usual. "Something bothering you?"

"Are you planning on covering yourself first?"

"Nay. You're in my tent after all."

"What's taking so long?" asked Sir Álvaro from outside. He peeked into the tent. "Eadric we're—oh, what the fuck."

Eleanor sighed and pulled the blankets up to her chin. Eadric waved Sir Álvaro in. "Come on, Sir León. The more the merrier."

"Eadric, stop this nonsense and get dressed," said William, his cheeks still blushing.

"What's happening?"

"We're marching to Wareham," said Sir Álvaro excitedly. "King Stephen is ready to strike!"

Eadric frowned. This all sounded unbelievable to him. They've spent countless months, and honestly the better part of two years, doing nothing. The king had been reluctant to aggravate Empress Maud and Earl Robert in the slightest. "Do you know something I don't?" asked Eadric. "This doesn't sound like something Stephen would order."

"Thanks to a spy in close confidence to Maud, we've learned that Earl Robert has left England for Normandy," said William. "Apparently Count Geoffrey is reluctant to aid his wife, and she has sent forth her half-brother to parley between the two."

"Look at that, darling." Eadric nudged Eleanor in the ribs. "We aren't the only ones with a shite marriage."

"Piss off," she responded hoarsely.

"Eadric, this is it," said Sir Álvaro. "With Robert out of the kingdom, King Stephen finally has the courage to attack the empress."

"His Royal Majesty wants us to take Wareham," William continued. "That's the only major southern port not under our control. If we burn it to the ground, Robert can't easily dock back in England. He'd have to skirt all the way around to Bristol. We'd have Empress Maud surrounded. Marooned in the middle of the country, bereft of her best commander, she won't stand a chance."

Yes, thinks Eadric, *this'll work nicely*.

He smiled at Sir Álvaro, who nodded back. He was thinking the same thing. By marching west and besieging all of Empress Maud's castles, they would eventually reach Commander Braxton, or even better, Duke Richard, the only man alive who was fully culpable for Lucia's murder. This meant Eadric didn't have to desert the army to get vengeance; he could do so with the blessing of a king. God had truly worked His magic.

"Eadric, I need you with me as we do this," said William of Ypres. "Queen Matilda wants you by her side. We'll march from the east, and King Stephen from the north. Together we can capture Empress Maud and end this festering civil war."

"Don't worry, William," Eadric said in a relaxed tone. "God has shown me the light."

CHAPTER XVII
EMMA

On the fringe of Oxford, hidden behind densely packed trees and shrubs, was a poorly constructed and thoroughly dilapidated shack that had two missing walls and a roof peppered with holes. It amazed Emma that it still stood at all. Spiderwebs clung to the ceiling, and thin animal bones were scattered in the corner.

Emma and Tom sat up. Footsteps approached. A woman and young boy walked through one of the missing walls. The woman looked a little older than Emma's mother. Moles and sunspots molested her wrinkled skin. Her hands in particular seemed unique; they were almost black, like they'd been smudged with charcoal. She wore a thick beige blouse and a skirt that draped to the ground. Patchworked together with a dozen other fabrics of varying patterns and colors, her skirt appeared every bit as old as the woman herself.

Tom cleared his throat and greeted her. "Mildritha."

"Belt your filthy mouth from uttering my name, Thomas, for I wish not to be bewitched by thee." Mildritha sucked in snot from her nose and spat it out. "Is this the girl?"

Emma mustered as much cheer as she could. "Hello. I'm Emma."

"She's pretty," the boy behind Mildritha said shyly.

"Shush!" scolded Mildritha. She swatted back at the boy. "Hold your tongue."

"Sorry, Mama."

"Me said, *shush*. Now Thomas, the message I received from your lord said ye were bringing a young woman."

"I did," he said.

"This here is a *girl*, ye dumb knave, not a woman. Do ye expect me to put our lives on the line for her?"

"How dare ye call a knight a knave, you vile—"

"Oh, sit your ass down. You're not a knight any more than I'm a bare-tit wet nurse. Now, I'll ask again since you're too daft to hear. Do you expect me to put our lives on the line for this *girl* to spy on the Holy Roman Empress?"

"I'm fourteen," said Emma defiantly. She reached out and held Tom's arm. She could feel his intensity. He took his pride very seriously.

"Oh, wonderful!" Mildritha smiled at her. "Thank you, O, glorious Virgin Mary and your holy cunt, for blessing me with the presence of a fourteen-year-old babe. I am overwhelmed with reverence for Your mysterious ways, O, Lord. Say, 'O, Lord,' Crispin."

The boy, Crispin, said, "O, Lord."

"O, Lord, is right! O, Lord, why do ye challenge me so?"

"Are ye done?" Tom asked with a huff.

"Tell me, Thomas. Did you at least wait for this one to bleed before ye courted her?"

"Damnit!" Tom stomped forward. "Enough of this! Her name is Emma, and you'll find her to be adept in all the ways needed for this job. She's capable, agile, stealthy. She'll help you and me and the king capture this bitch trespassing on our land."

Mildritha took a long sigh. The boy tugged on his mother's blouse. "She seems safe, Mama. We'll be okay."

Emma glanced the boy over. He was a little shorter than she was, but much rounder in frame. He reminded her of a pig; not that he was particularly filthy or anything, but rather that he was ruddy in the cheeks and had a content, full belly he seemed proud of. It didn't help that his hair was cut short, and he had dark eyes like those of swine.

"I won't protect her if she gets caught," said Mildritha.

"Me won't get caught," said Emma. She locked eyes with Mildritha for the first time. "She killed my friends, my village. Raided it. And did . . . other things too." Emma had to stop before the nightmares came again.

"*Humph*. Very well. But if she tries backstabbing us, I'll slit her throat meself."

"I'll be back every month," Tom said to Emma. "We'll meet here, where it's safe, and ye can tell me any news you hear at the castle. Anything about Count Geoffrey, Earl Robert, or her other lords. Anything that will help the king."

"I will."

"I know ye will. We'll pull this off and become Stephen's favorites. Then nothing can stop us."

Emma nodded. They embraced and kissed one another. A thought, or more so a feeling, fluttered across her mind. It was so immediate and intense that the words drenched her tongue and dripped out before she could think of what she was saying.

"I love you," she said.

"O, Jesus Christ, help me." Mildritha groaned from the corner, rolling her eyes.

Tom placed his hand on Emma's cheek. She smiled up at him. She could see the world sparkling in his eyes. "Succeed for our love," he said.

Oxford was unlike anything she'd ever seen before. There seemed to her to be two cities, one inside the stone walls and one outside. The outer city was larger than all the villages she'd lived in combined, overrun with goats, chickens, cats, dogs, cows, donkeys, and even loose sheep; hundreds of peasant-farmers sweltered under the hot late-spring sun as they harvested crops from the vast arable land surrounding the city proper, loading them up onto carts pulled by yoked oxen which were filled with other goods and riches; all these sundries were flaunted through the busy streets by their owners to be bartered and traded with locals and visitors alike. At the edge nearest them in this outer city, a large group of war refugees had camped together and created an intimate commune of their own.

Emma couldn't believe it. Her senses were assaulted from all directions. Awe and wonder overtook her, for towering above it all, even over the height of the city's ramparts, was Oxford Castle. It boasted impressive square towers, which reminded her of the romantic tales she'd heard as a little girl. This was her first time seeing a grand keep in all its proud, stoic beauty. She imagined herself up in its highest window, gazing out and admiring how all this land was hers. She'd be pampered and dressed in the softest silk dresses while servants attended her, and she'd be invited to lunch dates with other royal women like Constance FitzGilbert, the great arts patron, or maybe Adeliza, the dowager queen of the late King Henry, or perhaps even Adela de Warenne, Countess of Surrey; and afterwards, she'd stay up late with Tom and relay to him all the juicy gossip that the noblewomen—

"Has your hair always been like that?" asked Crispin.

"What?" Emma shook herself from her daydream. The boy wobbled next to her, trying his best to keep pace, while they followed his mother toward the castle. "No. Obviously not. I was a baby once. Didn't 'ave long hair then."

"I like dark hair."

"... And?"

"Your eyes are very green."

"I know."

"Ye see that house?" Crispin pointed to a massive home near the forest north of Oxford. Gardeners were pruning the plants and shrubbery around it.

"What about it?"

"That was built by King Henry," he said, sounding proud of himself. "T'was his own hunting lodge here. We call it Beaumont Palace. Was supposed to be given to his son, but, y'know." Crispin slid his finger across his throat. It grossed her out. She didn't want to think of what happened on the white ship. "I'm fourteen too, y'know."

"No lying, Crispin," said his mother. "'Tis a sin, son."

"I'm *almost* fourteen," he added reluctantly. Emma raised her eyebrows suspiciously. She couldn't believe that he was the same age as she was. Like all other boys her age, he was shorter and frailer and had a higher-pitched voice than her. It amazed her that these boys would turn into men like Tom eventually, especially a pudgy, round-featured one like this.

"I am though," he began stubbornly, "almost fourteen. Your eyes are really, really green."

"You've already said that," she replied.

"Stop hassling the poor girl," Mildritha ordered. "What 'ave I told you about hassling?"

"Leave the hassling to men with small pricks but big sticks," Crispin said.

"That's right. Women get violated enough as it is. They don't need extra harassment from lowly men who believe it'll make them royalty to be a knave like the rich folk."

"Doesn't God get angry with such foul talk?" asked Emma.

"Hark my words, girl. I learned long ago that there is no word that can't be forgiven at penitence. Ye think Jesus didn't mutter the occasional 'Goddamn', 'holy shit', or 'Jesus Christ'?"

"Why would he say Jesus Christ? Isn't that him?"

"Of course it's Him. Don't ye know your history? Where does the term come from if not from Him? And even if He didn't curse, 'tis only because He was a man. There hasn't ever been a woman who didn't have reason to curse, let me tell ye. I know damn well the Virgin—may God bless her—shouted some Lord-abashing comments. Whether at her son, her husband, or someone else, I know not; but, it was certainly at a man. And if the good Lord does indeed have a problem with all the cussing I do, then He best believe I have a list of sacramental violations that many-a-men have trumpeted around me. If I'm goin' to Hell, then I'm dragging every man who's wronged me down there as well."

"Mama says even I'm on that list!" said Crispin.

"That's right. Almost killed me coming out the womb, he did. Made me lose half my blood and curse the Lord in all the ways He hates. My body was never the same. Fat baby!"

They came upon the city's southern gate. Five guards, all wearing the red and gold colors of the Angevins, assessed visitors under the raised portcullis. One of them tried to stop Mildritha, but she hastily raised her finger at them and said, "Move! Castle cook comin' through. I have a loaf in the oven, and ye won't be the reason it fuckin' burns!"

The guard backed off after that. Once they passed through the gatehouse, Emma let out a breath she hadn't known she'd been suppressing. Maud's militiamen surrounded her, but she survived the first step. Mildritha quickly ushered them to the castle before Emma could give the city a proper evaluation, but what she did briefly notice were stacked townhomes, dark alleyways, and dense swathes of people, rich and poor, with the odd drunkard, charlatan, and troubadour thrown between them.

Oxford Castle stood atop a grassy mound in the western part of town. A moat, which connected to the nearby Castle Mill Stream, separated the hill from the rest of town. Castle Mill Stream was the lifeblood of Oxford; a wide white-capped river around forty-feet across at its widest point, it branched off from the larger River Thames and flowed exuberantly around Oxford city and the castle's western walls. Fish jumped out of the river as they approached a drawbridge that spanned the moat. They crossed the drawbridge, passing through stone ramparts which protected and marked the outer boundary of the castle, and arrived at a second gatehouse. The guards here seemed to have long ago learned their lesson; they gave Mildritha a wide berth as they passed through.

"Heed my counsel, Emma," said Mildritha. "You are to become a handmaiden, ye understand? That means you are to be respectable, courteous, and well-mannered. A castle is no place for a lowborn girl. A few ground rules..."

Emma tried her best to pay attention. She really did. But once they made it past the gates and entered the bailey, she was officially royalty—or, at least, that was what she imagined it would be like.

"Ew. What's that stench?" Emma asked, covering her nose from a putrid smell.

"Horse shite, mostly," said Mildritha. "Best hold your skirt up."

"If ye stay on the path, you won't step on any," Crispin added with a friendly smile.

The inside of the castle couldn't be any different from Emma's imagination. She had expected vibrant buildings, sparkling towers, and majestic pathways, with a flurry of servants, merchants, and scholars doing business in between; instead, the inner bailey was almost completely barren, like a large farm plot that had been trampled too thoroughly to grow anything other than weeds and thorns. The three of them followed a narrow path of upturned dirt that led up the motte to the keep. What really surprised her most was the lack of people. The bailey was desolate. Temporary stables were erected along the southern wall, which was surrounded by piles of manure, and there was a small collection of crammed shacks that must have been where the servants slept. But the only proper building on the hill, outside the towering keep, was a medium-sized chapel off the dirt path that Mildritha called the Church of St. George. On the way up to the keep, they only passed a half-dozen soldiers and two artisans who were bickering to themselves in a language Emma couldn't understand. Unlike the battlements, the keep was still made of wood, which also surprised her. Why would the empress choose a fortification that could be burned so easily as one of her epicenters for strategizing the war?

Why would any empress want to live in a stinky place like this at all, thought Emma repulsively. She certainly wouldn't. A pile of granite blocks from some nearby quarry suggested that a renovation might be possible soon, but she was still disgusted with the reality that she'd have to live here for the next few months.

Mildritha led her and Crispin through a side door on the bottom corner of the keep. The passageway inside was, admittedly, nicely furnished with warm candlelight and vibrant tapestries along the mahogany-stained walls. It made her feel a little more like a princess. They walked a little way before the sound of music stopped her in her tracks. It made Emma's heart sing, for she'd only heard the lovely strings of an instrument once before. She ran ahead, overcome with the anxiety to experience the music in her soul before it concluded.

"Emma, wait!" yelled Mildritha after her.

Emma sprinted into the kitchen. She stumbled upon two men who reclined against wooden chairs around a table full of bread, cheese, and vegetables. They were laughing, their mouths full of the edible delights laid out before them. One of them, a lanky fellow with light-blonde curly hair, strummed an instrument. The sound was bright and playful, and it swept through her like a raging, jovial tempest.

"What's that?" Emma asked excitedly.

"'Tis called a mandolin," said the musician with a broad smile.

"It's beautiful. Well, go on! Keep playin'."

"Prithee, peace," said the other man, an older fellow with barely any hair left atop his head. "Where'd ye come from, young maiden? Lookin' for someone?"

"Nay. I heard the music and ran for it. T'was the most lovely sound."

"God bless ye. I thank you kindly," said the musician.

"Would ye mind playin' some more?"

"Not at all." The bard plucked at the mandolin and carried on with the tune like a random girl hadn't just careened into their chamber. Emma let the music swell over her; however, she felt overly tense, like a bow pulled taut, ready to fire.

"I think the girl likes it, Jory," said the old man. "But why on God's gracious earth is she standin' stiff as a board? What are ye doin', young maiden?"

"What do ye mean?"

"It looks like ye desperately want to dance."

"I don't know what that is."

"Dancing? You've never danced before?"

The bard, Jory, turned to his companion with the veiny skin and balding hair and said, "Reginald, why don't ye teach the poor girl? The world is too cruel without dance."

"As ye wish," said Reginald. He stood up and groaned in pain. He wrung his hands together and shook them off. His bones creaked as he crossed to her. "Very well, young maiden, can you move your body better than mine?"

"Yes?"

"Then that's all ye need. Follow me." The old man crossed his feet oddly. His arms moved back and forth in rhythm with his steps. Emma tried to follow along.

"Yeah!" Jory yelled heartily. "Now you're gettin' it. Old-Codger, let her spin!"

Reginald spun her around. The bard hooted and hollered. Emma let out a big laugh. If this were dancing, she wanted to do it every day for the rest of her life. It felt *right*. "Like this?" she asked.

"'Tis impossible to dance wrong," said Old-Codger Reginald, smiling at her.

So lost had she become in the thrill of her newfound skill that she didn't realize the music stopped. Jory cursed under his breath, and Old-Codger Reginald almost knocked the cheese right off the table as he fell back suddenly.

"What is this?!"

The shrill voice made Emma jump. She followed the horrified gaze of the two workers to the entrance of the kitchen. Mildritha and Crispin, their heads hung like whipped dogs, stood behind a stern-looking woman of indistinguishable age. She had short black hair that was tucked perfectly behind an age-worn coif. Her body drowned in fabric, with not a single inch of skin showing other than that present on her sour face. She had a few wrinkles on her forehead, but something about the keenness of her eyes made Emma think she was still fairly young. Whatever the case, she clearly had power, for the entire room became insignificant when she entered.

The woman stomped over to Jory and ripped the mandolin from his grasp. Even though he was a solid foot taller than her, the bard seemed to shrink below her penetrating gaze. "What did I say about fiddlin' with your toys during working hours?" asked the woman.

"I'm sorry, madam."

"No, you're not. Five times I've caught ye now. Five!" She threw the mandolin across the room, where it slammed into the wall. The instrument made a hollow sound as it cracked around the strings. A flash of anger passed through Jory's eyes before tears covered them. Emma glanced over at Old-Codger Reginald. He looked away guiltily. Emma blew out hot air.

"Ye can't do that!" she roared.

The woman glared over at her. She took Emma in for a split second and made an aggravating smirk. "And who in God's name are you?"

Mildritha stepped in front of Emma before she could respond. "This is the new handmaiden, m'lady," she said. "I apologize for her petulance. She comes from a lowly lineage and a father who aspired to be rid of her. She knows not how things are run."

The woman appraised Emma with a newfound interest, her investigative eyes peering over every pore of her skin, each fold of her dress, and Emma's insecurities gave way like the release of a sluice. When she approached her, Emma realized how tall the head handmaiden was. There was something regal in the way she carried herself—an air about her that entranced and commandeered the very space around her.

"What's your name?" she asked.

"Emma."

"You will not speak to me that way again, Emma. Do you hark?"

Emma nodded.

"I am Madame Beatrice. You may refer to me as Madame B, if you wish. Go with Mildritha. She'll show you to our bedchamber. Go there at once and change."

"Change into what?"

"Out of those horrendous clothes. You will not greet our lords in such unsavory clothing. You'll then meet me in our lady's chambers. I'll be expecting you in a half-hour's time. Do not be late."

"Of course."

"Of course, *madame*."

Emma straightened her back. She tried to shake her head of the fog that Madame Beatrice had blown into her mind. She was so beautiful and so ugly all at once. How could a woman be both things?

"Well?" Madame B waited expectantly.

"Of course, *madame*," said Emma. She bowed for greater effect.

"Then off with you."

Right as Mildritha placed her hand on Emma to lead her out of the kitchen, Madame B added, "Oh, and one last thing. If I see you dancing again, Emma, I'll have your legs cut off and fed to the pigs. There is no fun here. Our duties are to be proper ladies and to serve the Holy Roman Empress. Never forget that."

Emma nodded. The madame dismissed her, and she left with Mildritha and Crispin. All she could think about over and over in her head was, *what was her problem?*

And then Emma thought rather mischievously, *I wonder if I can steal those fancy clothes from her? I would surely be a princess then.*

CHAPTER XVIII
GILBERT

Beatriz and Bartholomew led Gilbert and Hawk to a dirty slum outside the city walls of Caen, a place where the piss and shit of the city drained and settled between the moldy walls of the inhabitants. A few stray goats ate the growing weeds nearby, while chickens in a nearby pen bawked at their egg laying. A drunkard stumbled by, spilling his ale and adding to the filth.

"This is where they ended up?" asked Gilbert. "Will and me went to war for this?"

"Want us to come with you?" asked Hawk.

Gilbert shook his head. "No." He took a deep breath. "This I must do on my own."

His parents' house—a narrow place crammed between all the other narrow homes—had walls of a putrid, rotten color and a roof made of warped shingles. Gilbert pushed open the front door, the hinges whining, and was confronted with a gust of fiendishly cold air, as if frozen death had claimed hold of the interior.

He saw his mother. Agnes. She looked so much like *her*. She had blonde hair, only a little longer than her shoulders, that was a frizzled mess, poking out in all directions as if a bird's nest was buried deep within her strands. Her wrinkled and leathery skin, further blemished with dark brown spots, betrayed her years spent farming in open fields. She had brownish-yellow teeth, and her eyes . . . her deep blue eyes repelled his gaze like blinding sunlight.

"Ma Maman," Gilbert called out hesitantly.

Her neck twisted, spinning her head like an owl so her blue eyes could pierce through him. Her hand rested on the cradle. Inside the crib, Gilbert could see the slight movement of his baby brother—fast asleep and unaware of this upturning in his life.

"What are *ye* doin' here?" his mother said. Her eyes went wide and ferocious. "Ye pissant, shouldn't thou be at war?"

"I've come home, Ma Maman."

"O, a spectre ye ain't then?"

"No, 'tis me. And only me."

She shushed him and tenderly stroked the baby in the cradle. "Not too loud; you'll wake him. I asked, what are ye doin' here?"

"I've come to see you and Mon Papa. To see my baby brother."

"Thou hath seen. Now begone."

His mother turned her eyes down to the baby, releasing Gilbert from her spell and allowing him to glance back up. He stood awkwardly in the doorframe, waiting for his mother to say anything more. When she did not, he stepped closer.

"What did I say?" asked his mother hastily.

"I have more to tell ye."

"Hear it, I will not. I hearken not to a son who defiles all he touches. Shan't ye be in the army of our new lord? Shan't ye be with the other sibling you stole? The blight of the moon darkens all our blood, doesn't it, me baby boy?"

Gilbert froze. "I did not steal my sibling."

"*Siblings*," Agnes corrected him. "Do not play games with me like I'm some whore ye bought off the streets. I am your mother. I *birthed* you."

"Ma Maman—"

"Ye split me from navel to ass, bleeding me like a stuck boar. Only through the mighty grace of God did I survive. And only by witchcraft did you." His mother turned her sharp blue eyes to him again. This time, he did not look away. The air went still; the house dust froze in place. His baby brother rolled in the crib, moaning faintly. Gilbert didn't even know his name. This entire home was bewitched. All because of him.

"William is gone," said Gilbert.

"Ha. Is he now?" Agnes hummed, almost joyfully. "And what did ye do with this one?"

"He was taken as a hostage during battle, by a Saxon lord they herald as the Hellhound of Rutland. He's still alive, I believe. I intend to go there and free him, Ma Maman."

"You shall do no such thing."

"What? Why ever not?"

"Would ye have him butchered, Gilbert? Would ye make certain your curse damns him as it did her? As it did the twins? No, you will not go to that Godless kingdom."

"I will," said Gilbert defiantly. "You will not stop me."

"Do not kill my son!"

That stirred the baby. He cried, his wails coming out in sudden bursts, almost like he was hiccupping tears. Agnes lifted him up and cradled him to her breast. "Shush now, me baby. Ma Maman is sorry for yelling."

"How is he?"

"He survived the winter. That's more than most can say of their newborns. More than we could say of angelic Olive—God watch over her little soul."

"Can I see him?" Gilbert walked up to her, but his mother threw herself back against the crib. She *snarled* at him, her teeth appearing menacing and wicked.

"Ye will *not* touch him, devil! I'd devour ye myself before I let you place your hex upon him!"

Gilbert stepped back. His head throbbed with memories he had long since abandoned. The chill of winter came back to him, along with the darkness of the woods and the crying of children and the faceless torchbearers with their weapons held aloft.

Gilbert grimaced. He broke into a sweat as he tried and failed to remember...

"Don't ye see?" asked Agnes. "All the woes we've carried all these years come from ye."

He felt the truth of it in his bones. The *wrongness* of him. The endless despair and suffering, all because of what he was born to be: a child of the red moon, the spawn of deviltry. He stepped away while his baby brother, still nameless to him, cried harder.

"I'm sorry, Ma Maman. This was a mistake."

"I've prayed for your return," said Agnes. Gilbert's heart fluttered. Even after all the abuse, all the uproar and pain she'd ordained as his sins, *his* mistakes, he hoped that there was still a mother's love willing to embrace him. "I begged and begged His Majesty: 'O, Lord Jesus Christ, little and unbecoming as I am, may Ye grace me once more with the presence of my firstborn. Bless me, so I may gaze upon his villainous form and harken unto him one last time: seek forgiveness for your transgressions, son, seek absolution in the Lord. Take your soul and purify it. Purify it in the pits of Hell.' And I prayed. O! I prayed, son. Prayed that I would have this moment with ye . . . and He delivered! My wondrous, beautiful, handsome God delivers."

The foundations of Gilbert's soul shook. He felt small and feeble, like the little boy he was on that cold, forsaken night so many years before. His mother's eyes were crystals of ice, frigid and deadly. "I'll bring him back," Gilbert whispered. "I'll bring Will back. I swear it."

Agnes was half distracted trying to calm the baby. She lowered her tunic, exposing one malnourished breast, and pressed the baby's mouth to her nipple. She glared at him over the baby's suckling head. "Why did you have to take him?"

"We did it for you." Gilbert pointed at his baby brother. "For him. For Mon Papa. We were goin' to starve. Will and me—"

"No, just *ye*. Will could 'ave saved us. He had training from his father, a real lord. He could read, write, do so much more than your worthless actions. William wasn't a thief, a whore, a leech. He alone could 'ave dragged us from this hell. You spent your life corrupting my son."

"*I'm* your son."

"Nay!" Agnes bellowed. "Nay. Will could 'ave been a lord, and our family raised from the torment of poverty. But *ye* . . . oh, ye couldn't let him be better than thou. No, instead you told desperate tales of our starvation. Ye snake! You convinced him that only war could free us of death. Ye took two babes from me in life, devil! And two more yet in the womb! Nay, you are not my son. I gave birth to the offspring of Satan."

Gilbert's tears built up. He heard crying, so much crying from the dark, snow-covered woods . . .

"It wasn't my fault."

"T'was." His mother's face twitched with disgust. "Born under a crimson night, I knew you would be ruinous to this family. A full blood moon! The devil's own calamity upon our celestial heaven, and *you* were born from it. They told me you would be evil—a plague, an omen of most baleful repugnance. I should 'ave slit your throat with the knife that cut the umbilical cord. I had it in my hand, the moon shining red off it. I saw ye. Ugly. Putrid.

"Yet I couldn't do it. My cowardice overwhelmed me. The Adversary, he sowed love in my heart for ye. O, damn him, Lord Jesus! But he did. And now . . . now my greatest sin has been ingested by thee. My cowardice on that night has been given to you, and it has killed this family. First, the twins. Then, your sister. And now . . . now ye've come for your brother."

"No."

"All of them, because they're royalty!"

The words of his mother slammed into him and nearly made him topple. The implications were vast and horrifying. *Royalty*, she'd said. Did that mean—?

"Yes," said his mother, as if gazing into his thoughts like a witch. She rubbed the head of his baby brother as his parched mouth strained for any milk from her teat. "He is the son of a lord too. As was your sister. And the twins."

"They're all bastards like Will?" asked Gilbert, aghast.

"Each was *my* way out of this torment. They were supposed to get me away from ye. I knew your father was no good when he seeded you inside me—a demon. I knew I could never let a feeble man like that place in my womb another son of omens and grief. So, I slept with lords and dukes and anyone with a gilded prick, anyone who could sire a bastard of nobility. I let them overwhelm me with their warmth. Once I was of child, I hunted down these stained highborn and threatened them with the child they begot. I threatened to expose their dishonor, their sins, and send their legacy into ruin. But I would not, if they helped raise the sired child as a ward. If they gave us wealth and means. William, Olive, the twins, my baby boy . . . they were all cleansed from the defilement of your father's cock, that which planted you."

Tears boiled out of his mother's eyes. Gilbert's face was red with a hundred pains and a thousand thoughts. Unable to suckle nourishment from his mother's breast, the baby grew louder and louder, its wails resounding deep within Gilbert's soul.

"But you've ruined it," said his mother. "You took away all those nobly sired."

The hinges of the front door squeaked open, and Gilbert's father entered. Albert was tall and willowy; dirt and grime covered his body. He'd been working during Easter celebrations then? That was a terrible crime. They were still desperate for food? It pained Gilbert to see the life his baby brother had been born into. Their sacrifice to join the army was for naught.

"Gilbert?" Albert rubbed his eyes. His brows were sweating, and the way he wrung his hands let Gilbert know his nerves were continuing to get the best of him. "What are ye—?"

"He abandoned the war," said Agnes.

"But that would mean—"

"Aye, he's a deserter. Just like you, he continues to bring great shame to our family."

"Will was taken hostage in battle," Gilbert said to his father. "He was brought to England, and I'm going to free him."

"Did anyone follow you here?" asked Albert. "Do they know ye deserted?"

"They're all dead. By sheer luck, me and Will were the only survivors."

Agnes scoffed. "*Luck*," she said faintly. "I'm sure it was."

"Why is Robin crying?" asked his father.

So, his name is Robin, thought Gilbert. *My brother's name is Robin.*

"Gilbert disturbed him," she said. "He was about to leave."

Albert looked back at his son. He nodded and said, "T'would be for the best."

"Is there anything I can help with—?"

"No," said Agnes. "Get out."

Gilbert looked at his father. "Is there anything—"

"Get. Out." Agnes's blue eyes held onto him.

"I know ye don't love me, Ma Maman, but I *will* bring Will back. I swear it. Then he can become a lord like the man you slept with. All the turmoil that you created to push us away, to make our family fall apart, will all be redeemed through him. Is that what ye believe?"

"Yes, that's why I sent him after ye."

That stopped him. Gilbert looked at her crossly. "Sent who?"

"The large man. Big as an oak tree. As frightening as the perverted angels of Satan. He came here looking for the son of Duke Richard. Looking for Will."

"And ye told him where to find him?" The anger inside Gilbert vibrated through his body. His fingers buzzed with rage.

"He threatened to kill baby Robin! He threatened to kill *me*! But I saw the truth in what he asked for. He wanted only William."

"So ye knew? You knew the Hellhound was coming for William, but ye sent him anyways."

"Yes."

"Because you wanted to get Will away from me?"

"Yes."

"And you'd hoped he would kill me?"

Agnes smiled. "My soul is satiated, devil. Is yours?"

A child crying in the woods . . . the villagers screaming his name . . .

"Come on, Gilbert," said a voice from behind him. Gilbert spun around and found, much to his surprise, that his friends had entered the home. "There's nothin' left for ye here."

"Go back to your tainted friendships," said Agnes. "You think they'll help ye save him? Will was doomed the moment you loved him." She turned to his friends. "Do you intend to go with him on this fool's errand? His love is a poison that'll bury ye into the deepest pits of oblivion."

"Aye," said Hawk, standing taller. "I will venture with him into the abyss, for that is what family does."

Then, even more so to Gilbert's surprise, his other two friends nodded.

"Aye," said Beatriz. "As will I."

"And I," said Bartholomew.

Gilbert felt a thread of joy. Like the first glimmers of sunlight, they banished the darkness that his parent's hospitality had encumbered him with. *This* was the family he had chosen, and even if he was cursed, even if he had the mark of the red moon from the first moment he drew breath, he had *not* damned his friends.

At least . . . he hadn't yet.

"Beware ye," Agnes warned them, "for if he drags you to that war-torn kingdom, he will corrupt ye and beget your deaths, as he has to all his family. To hellfire he will bring ye."

"Then to Hell we'll go," said Hawk. "I've grown quite tired of the cold."

Gilbert smiled. Beatriz looked moderately concerned about going to Hell, but she didn't voice any opposition.

"Bye, Ma Maman," said Gilbert. "Bye, Mon Papa." He looked at his baby brother. "Bye, Robin."

"Don't speak his name." His mother hissed.

"Bye, Robin," Gilbert said again. "When I return with Will, I'll save ye too."

"Get out!" screamed Agnes. "I command thee, begone!"

Gilbert bowed and left the home of his parents. He, Hawk, Bartholomew, and Beatriz walked toward the docks. They had a ship to catch, and a new realm to sail for. And to Gilbert, he had a new family to embrace.

He would not let his curse, nor his innate cowardice, doom this one.

William, your family is on the way.

PART TWO
GOD FORSWORN & CHRIST FORSAKEN

SUMMER, 1142 A.D.

CHAPTER XIX
EADRIC

Formless shapes awoke in the dark chamber. He touched the bed beneath him. Not a military cot, but an actual bed stuffed with soft feathers and bundles of hay. His fingers grazed warmth; Eleanor slept next to him, naked, her back turned to him so he could see the protrusion of her spine beneath her skin, stretching the freckles that ran down her back.

Eadric realized, suddenly and completely, that they were at his Rockingham estate. *Yes*, he nodded, *this is my home.*

Long, lavender-colored drapes sagged in elegant swathes from the towering timbered bedframe. A beeswax candle hummed sweetly on the bedstand, its wick burned to the base. Through a narrow window on the opposite wall, far across the large and opulent bedchamber, Eadric gleamed absolute darkness, suggesting it must be the middle of the night. A beautiful gown rested on a wooden bench below it. Eleanor's wedding dress.

It's my wedding night, then.

The bedroom door creaked open.

"Who's there?" Eadric asked.

No one answered.

Eleanor stirred next to him. He monitored the shadowed hallway beyond the door. He *felt* something on the other side. After a moment's hesitation, he decided to investigate. He dressed himself in a simple robe, moved to the door, and pushed it open. The hall outside the bedchamber was vacant. Only a single candle atop a stand shed any light.

"Daddy."

Eadric jumped. The voice came from the far end of the hall. His heart hammered in his chest. His breathing quickened; he knew that voice. "Lucia?"

He sped down the corridor and turned a corner. A slim figure quickly dipped down another hall. Eadric followed. The figure always seemed one step farther away, leading him down one corridor to the next. He ascended a flight of stairs and exited outside.

Lucia stood on the edge of the first-floor balcony, facing away from him. Her body appeared ghostly white against the black, moonless night. A sharp wind made him shiver. She turned. Eadric gasped. His knees buckled. She had no color to her skin, and her slit throat was scabbed over, leaving behind a jagged maze of protrusions from one ear to the other. Her body seemed to glow, like a hallowed painting of Saint Mary.

"You said I'd be the last woman you'd ever love," she said.

"You are, honey." Eadric barely managed a whisper. "I don't love *her*. I was ordered to marry her."

"I see how you stare at me. You think me a monster."

"No, honey. I don't."

"You promised you'd love me no matter how I looked. Even if I were a toad."

"I do, Lucia."

"Then why do you keep glancing away?"

Eadric forced himself to stare at his daughter. She was horrifying. Her voice carried the same biting frost as a mid-winter breeze. Tears clouded his vision. "You're beautiful," he lied.

"I'm not. But I would've been." She tilted her head as if searching for the right words to say. "'Tis okay, you know. To forget me."

"No, honey. I'll never forget you."

"You can love that woman more than me."

"I won't!"

"You can abandon me again. Leave me to rot away with time. My body is already defiled. You can't hurt me anymore."

"I never meant to hurt you."

"You can't disappoint me anymore, Daddy."

Eadric cried out, falling to his knees, but his voice vanished into the abyss. Naught could hear him; even God wouldn't lend His ear. Lucia watched her father weep.

Eadric startled himself awake. He sweated right through his clothing. He gripped the animal furs around him, tightening his grip on them until he convinced himself that they were real, that he was actually awake.

"Your nightmares are getting worse," said Eleanor. He looked over at the cot on the far side of the room where his wife sat. She wore a nightgown and was sewing up his tattered surcoat. Eleanor and he had slept in different beds since she'd arrived. A gust of warm wind rustled their tent. The air inside, however, seemed stagnant. Eadric rubbed the bridge of his nose, disgusted by the smell of his own sweat. "What did you dream about this time?" she asked.

"What else?" he answered.

She set down her needle and looked at him with an expression somewhere between dejection and pity. Somehow, both were worse than her simply being vexed. "I'm sorry," she said softly.

"You need not to pretend to care."

"Well, I do. Firstly, because it keeps me awake all night. It's hard to sleep when you're crying out during all hours. But mostly, I can see how much it hurts you."

"I wouldn't fret. All it's doing is killing me faster. Then you can finally have my estate all to yourself."

"I pray to God that you stop having them. Honestly, I do. I don't know why He besieges you with such dreams."

"What hour is it?" He sat up and rubbed his eyes, for he was no longer in the mood for sleeping.

"A few hours 'til dawn yet. You wish to talk about it?"

"No."

"Know what I think, Eadric? We should move back to Rockingham. This war isn't good for you. There you could start a business, command a fief with some arable land. I can finally tend to the duties of our estate and grow that dream garden like I've always wanted. I can help you track our expenses. We wouldn't have a marriage, but we'd at least have a partnership then. Seems like the best we could ask for."

"I can't. I know this isn't what you thought you were getting into."

"I'm not a fool, love. I knew you could never love me. But I *did* believe I could distract myself by attending your estate. That can never happen, though. Not when you're across the kingdom, always fighting other people's battles, keeping me from the home we share. It's unfair to us both."

"I'm sorry, Eleanor. But I can't move back. Ever."

"Why not?" She gave him a pleading look. She'd been trying for years to get them situated back at Rockingham. Eadric sighed. He needed to give her a real answer.

"It's not a home to me any longer," he said. "Those halls are forever haunted."

Eleanor lowered her head in defeat. After a long silence, she finally glanced up at him with a smile that appeared genuine. "And I'm afraid, with your persistence, darling, those halls will be haunted long after you pass too."

Eadric smirked. It wasn't often that they actually smiled at each other. "I'm sorry for keeping you awake. I'll leave so you can get some sleep."

"Praise the Lord. Maybe you *do* love me."

Eadric dressed himself and exited the tent. Unlike that dreadful night in his dream, the moon was bright and gleaming today. The bivouac, even in the middle of the night, bustled with soldiers and officers, some of them wobbling after an extended bout of drinking, others wandering aimlessly, cursed with nightmares like Eadric.

They were seventy kilometers away from Wareham, and it should only take four more days until they reach the port city, where they'll make their first proper battle against Empress Maud in years. Their army had settled for the night in a low valley between two large forests. The trees stood like ghastly sentinels, tall and dark, hiding unknown terrors behind them. Somewhere in the forest, an owl hooted multiple times. The noise gave the night a sense of grandeur, like the earth was underneath a splendid cathedral that stretched out into the heavens far above; the hooting echoed between the invisible, lofted ceiling and reverberated back to Eadric, making him feel insignificantly small within God's massive sanctuary.

He walked around the fringes of the camp, careful to think about nothing in particular. Unlike their semi-permanent settlement outside of Rochester, there were only six tents pitched in the entirety of their current encampment. The vast majority of soldiers slept outside under the stars, as it took too much time each day to set up and strike thousands of tents. Only the highest-ranking captains, usually earls or commanders, could sleep in tents; even knights didn't have that prestigious luxury.

Eventually Eadric discovered he had wandered into the camp prison. Here, they only had three wagons, each with a cage built on them, which could hold prisoners and hostages. The horses that pulled the wagons were nearby on a picket line. He walked to one cage.

"Are you awake?"

Will rolled over in his cage. He glanced up groggily at Eadric. "Yes, my lord."

"I couldn't sleep either."

Will pushed himself up into a seated position, leaned back against the bars, and waited for the Hellhound to say something.

"What keeps you up at night?" Eadric asked eventually.

"My lord?"

"What's your affliction? What demon curses you?"

"Other than being held hostage?"

Eadric almost laughed. Yes, obviously that would do it. He shook his head. What was he doing here? "You mentioned a brother in Boulogne. What men were you?"

"I don't rightly know. That's something for God to decide."

"Were you troublemakers? Good Christians? Or did you chase women? What was life like as a bastard of a foreign lord in Normandy?"

"We were just . . . boys. Average. Our parents were poor."

"I should have guessed, of course a fiend like Richard wouldn't support his bastard."

"He does," said Will hastily. "But not enough to feed a family through the winters we've had recently."

"Is that why you're reluctant to turn on Richard? You fear that if you do, your father will stop supporting your mother?"

Will nodded. Another silence passed between them, and Eadric wondered why his feet had carried him here. He hadn't left the tent intending to talk to the hostage; yet he had to admit, it felt good to talk. Maybe he needed something more than a void to release his thoughts into.

"What do you like to eat?" asked Eadric. The boy froze, as if he were afraid of being caught in a trap. "Come on, lad. Spit it out. Hare? Chicken? Fowl?"

"Chicken," Will said, daring to test the waters.

"Very well. I'll get us chicken."

"And bread," Will added feverishly. "Butter too, if ye 'ave that. And cabbage. And carrots. Or fowl too. Whatever you have."

"A feast it is then."

Ten minutes later, a hefty meal was brought to them. Will devoured it. His teeth gnawed and tore the chicken, launching bits of juice and rogue meat through the cell. Eadric filled a wooden mug with ale and slid it through the bars, where Will nodded his thanks and downed it greedily. The pair sat like this for a while, not speaking a word, for neither side felt concerned with ruining a peaceful night with more unimportant talk. Alfwin the gaoler watched begrudgingly from his stool about twenty feet away; the poor man looked torn between exhaustion from serving night duty and starvation from hearing them have such a feast.

They finished their meals and reclined back, while their digestive systems did the rest of the work. The hostage stared at him. Perhaps he expected Eadric to drop the sledgehammer, that all this feeding and pampering after months of inhospitable bondage was, in a sense, like the fattening of a pig before a holiday banquet. That wouldn't be entirely inaccurate, as he did indeed have plans for Will; for here, in this unlikeliest of individuals, a filthy, rotten peasant like the ones who murdered his daughter, was a young man who could be the key to finding Duke Richard.

The only issue? There were too many doors this key could unlock, and Eadric still needed to decide if that key would truthfully tell him which door to enter when the time came.

If he were to get the hostage to that state, first he'd need to break his soul. The process of breaking a man was both incredibly easy and arduously tedious. The easiest thing to break was the body, and they've already accomplished that. Next was to break the mind, which could range in time based on the individual; some torturers attempted to accomplish that by tormenting the body further, pushing the limits of what the mind could comprehend as pain.

Eadric wasn't of that mindset; jam a key too hard into a lock and it would break. He held a different belief. The paramount goal should be to combine the process of bending the mind with that of shattering the soul. These two methods were intermingled, and succeeding with one without the other was nigh on impossible. *If* Eadric could get Will to see things from his perspective, and *if* he could get him to see the horrors that his father allowed to be committed, then perhaps Will might believe in his vengeance. Then, and only then, would the key willingly unlock the right door.

"Have you heard," Eadric began hesitantly, breaking the lengthy silence, "of what your father did to my daughter?"

"Yes."

"Oh . . . you have?"

"Yes, my lord. Everyone talks about it. The guard over there said ye would probably bring it up to me too. Like ye do to everyone else."

Eadric glowered at Alfwin, who stiffened and faced the other way, humming a hasty tune to distract himself. "I see," said Eadric, feeling stupid. "Then I suppose you know why I'm doing what I am. Make no mistake, I will kill your father. Whether it happens now with your aid, or decades in the future long after you've rotted to dust in a dungeon, I will have my vengeance. I'd rather it were the former than the latter, wouldn't you? You've seen me fight, heard my exploits. You know I can't be stopped."

Will nodded. Eadric reached into the bag that he had brought with the food earlier. He took out a map detailing the layout of Wareham and a candlestick to light the surrounding space.

"What do you know about Wareham?" he asked.

"Only that it's a port city," said Will.

"Not precisely. It *is* the only port of entry from the English Channel, but what makes Wareham unique is this." He pointed to a river that serpented from the coast in the northeast to the city. "The only way a ship can get to the port from the sea is by traveling a distance down the River Frome."

"'Tis a wedge point."

"Yes. The waters on the coast are too hectic to dock, but a port inland, on a river, has a much calmer surface."

"But that's not it, is it?" Will studied the map further, his eyes scanning the brown leaves. He pointed at a building a few kilometers away from Wareham. "It's not a true port city because they need it close by that castle."

"Castle Corfe." Eadric smiled approvingly. This lad caught on quickly. "One of the most magnificent, impregnable castles in all of England."

"Built by William the Conqueror," said Will. He got eager, and his body involuntarily twitched again. "I heard Earl Robert call it a pillar of might, a symbol of resolve from your Saxon ancestors. It towers on a large hill, and you can see the entire southern peninsula from it, right? It's unique. Built mostly of stone."

"And it's surrounded by a strong palisade, yes," Eadric said, slightly taken aback by Will's knowledge; even firstborns of prestigious houses didn't have such vast educations on steadfast fortifications. "You know quite a bit about castles."

"Me does. I think how they're built and defended is interesting. They're goin' to be important to the future of the world."

"I agree. I taught my daughter that it was paramount to understand castles and their layouts. She hated me for it, but I thought it could help her one day." Eadric lost himself in that sentence, as his mind drifted off to a simpler time. Will jolted him back to the present.

"But attacking Castle Corfe isn't the goal, is it? Ye want to sack Wareham only."

"Do you know why?"

"Because ye don't think the empress is in the castle. And if she isn't there, then there's no point in wasting effort on a siege."

"Our goal is to cut the umbilical cord between Earl Robert and Empress Maud. He's in your home realm currently, but eventually he'll hear of our gamble. He'll know we're cornering his half-sister, and that the king is pushing to end the war. But by then, if Wareham is in ashes, and all the ports in southern England are under our command, Robert will have no choice but to circumnavigate us completely and dock ashore somewhere in Bristol or Scotland."

"So ye don't want to destroy all of England, but only the least amount needed to secure victory? Like how ye only want to find my father, and not kill everyone to get to him?"

Eadric paused. The flame danced on the wick. He lied.

"Yes, that's what I want. But I need your help. You know more about him than you let on. If you help me with this, I won't need to keep doing terrible things. You can save me, lad. And with each step we take, you'll be one step closer to freedom."

"Yes, my lord," said Will more firmly than last time. "And I think I know where my father's knight may be located inside the city . . ."

Eadric leaned closer to the cell, while Will told him of the potential whereabouts of Commander Braxton, the two of them bouncing battle tactics off one another until the sun rose and the bright moon was dim in the early blue of dawn. Eadric rubbed his eyes, exhausted from staring at the map under minimal light. He was also a little sore from the march they had taken from York to Dorset. He wasn't the young man he used to be; his muscles grew weary.

He folded up the map once they were content that they had thought out each action he'd take once they invaded the city. Will looked equally tired, but more satisfied than he'd been in months. In fact, he looked proud of himself. Sometimes joy came from the simple pleasure of thinking productively.

"What was your daughter like?" Will asked as Eadric turned to leave. He glanced back at the hostage, and he saw the boy's eyes glimmer under the orange canopy of God's cathedral.

"She was like the rising sun, full of promise and beauty and forgiveness. She'd shed her light on everyone, noble and peasant alike. She was everything I am not."

CHAPTER XX
EMMA

All of Oxford gathered for the Holy Roman Empress. She entered the city on horseback; a vibrant gown of unequal beauty was draped around her rigid posture. Her posse, made up of numerous knights, lords, and barons, waved the heraldic flags of the Duchy of Anjou—three golden lily flowers (that the Normans called *fleur-de-lis*) floating on an azure lake, surrounded by a blood-red border. A trumpeter in the retinue quieted the murmurs of the crowd.

Whether the citizens of Oxford believed in their hearts that the empress was the proper Queen of England like her father had declared before his death, or if they believed, rather, that she was a foreign invader sent by her Angevin husband like King Stephen continuously claimed, it mattered little to them in this moment. That Empress Maud was here meant they were denizens of her rule; any thoughts to the contrary were punishable by death.

Their destinies, whether wanted or not, were tied to the empress. *That* was the truth of the peasantry. Only those lucky enough to be born into riches have the luxury of choosing the life they want; everyone else was only lucky if they survived it.

"Quit gossiping and remove that linen like I said," Madame Beatrice ordered. The two other handmaidens, Theresa and Isabella, rolled their eyes and got to work. Emma and the three of them were hastily readying the empress's ornate bedchamber before she returned from her private council. Theresa and Isabella stripped the bed and replaced it with fresh sheets while Emma stoked the flames in the hearth and checked the kettle of herbal water. Madame B hovered over them all like a watch commander who was ready to bludgeon them at the first sign of insubordination.

"Emma, why isn't that drink finished?" asked Madame B.

Because I can't make water boil faster, thought Emma irritably. She regained control of herself and said, "My apologies. Should be ready shortly."

"Organize her trunks once you finish. She'll want to be freshly clothed. Isabella! How many times have I told you? She wants her linen spread like *this*. She's not some street whore."

"S-sorry, Madame," Isabella said with her soft voice. She had a slight stutter which made her hard to understand. She spoke rarely—perhaps for that reason—and at one point, Emma had believed her to be a mute.

Ever since Empress Maud returned, the tension in the castle had increased. The hallways buzzed with the frenzied work of bishops, constables, scribes and more. Emma, for her part, had been put to work immediately on menial tasks: scrubbing floors, carrying dirty laundry to the washing well, emptying Her Highness's royal chamber pot . . . and, much to Emma's innocent dismay, being a princess *didn't* decrease how stinky their poops were. She'd only been in Oxford a fortnight now, and she clearly understood she was on the bottom rung of the handmaidens, which made her more worthless than the cow fertilizer layered on the farmland outside the city. Today was the first time she'd been allowed inside Empress Maud's bedchamber; she had yet to interact directly with the Roman queen at all. Madame Beatrice kept a tight leash on her, and it appeared she was going to have to surpass one of the other handmaidens if she were ever going to be near the empress. It was tough to be a spy when she couldn't be trusted near anything spy-worthy.

And to make matters worse, she was in a temperamental mood. Earlier she had made the unfortunate mistake of snapping at Crispin. He'd been hounding her with questions on a day in which Emma was particularly at odds with his usual, chipper countenance. Crispin eventually teased her when he caught her carrying around the foul, odor-laden chamber pot, and that finally broke something inside her; she turned to him and claimed proudly that it'd be *he* who'd one day be cleaning *Emma's* personal chamber pot once she and Tom became a count and countess, but Crispin laughed and promptly reminded her he was actually of a higher status than herself. Even hours later, Emma was irritated she couldn't come up with a witty response to his maddening cheerfulness.

"Isabella! Jesus Christ. Neat corners. Straight angles. Must I teach you how to do this once more?" Madame B shoved her aside and flattened the bedding herself.

"Madame, excuse my sayin' so, but must ye be so hard on her?" Theresa asked as she consoled Isabella. "Never has Her Highness been anal about the angle of her sheets."

"Silence. You clearly know not what you speak of. The point isn't whether the empress cares, but rather the insistence of our own rigor. We must do things exactly, perfectly, every time."

"But why should the linen matter? 'Tis only bedding."

"It isn't about the linen!" Madame B's tone halted suddenly, like her breath caught in her own throat. She scratched at the scarf wrapped around her neck. Eventually, the head handmaiden managed to loosen the scarf, and she took a few moments to regain her breath. Once calmed, she continued, "We do the little things perfectly so nothing slips through. Do you understand? Complacency kills. Tomfoolery kills." Madame Beatrice glanced at Emma with an enigmatic expression. "Dancing, and music, and all joyous distractions kill."

"Ye still don't need to be so rough," Theresa muttered. Madame B somehow frowned deeper. She shredded the newly made linen off the bed and scattered the pillows and sheets across the floor.

"Then prove to me you know how to be competent! Isabella, be useful and take those filthy rags down below. Emma, I want them washed by tonight. Now begone."

The dejected handmaidens got to work; Theresa fixed the bedding, Isabella carried off the dirty laundry in a basket, and Emma attended to the herbal water. Once the water was boiling, she opened up the first of the empress's many traveling chests. Aubrey de Vere knocked on the open door. He was a tall, stout fellow with an uneven jawline and a beak-like nose. De Vere always wore an unassuming outfit—today he wore green hose and a loose tunic of simple design—and thus it surprised her greatly when she discovered Empress Maud recently granted him the earldom of Oxfordshire.

"Madame Beatrice." De Vere bowed. "Fair ladies." He bowed even deeper to them.

"What is it you want?" Madame B snapped impatiently. "I've no time for pleasantries."

"Her Royal Majesty has summoned you. I am to escort you."

"Very well. You two continue. I want everything perfect when I return." Madame B readjusted her dress, keeping true to her desire not to reveal a centimeter of skin that wasn't her face.

Emma turned back to the trunks after they left, grateful that overbearing woman was no longer hovering around her. The craftsmanship of the multiple trunks was astonishingly beautiful; etched into the dark wood were swirling flowers and sharp vines, and the lid was reinforced with shiny rivets and metal clasps. Inside the first two were a menagerie of vibrantly dyed dresses and hair coverings, the fabric of which was thick and sinfully soft. Tiny individual strands of wool stuck to her hand. She clumped these fallen threads of supreme nobility and rolled them between her fingers, wondering if this was what her life could be like. What if those were her clothes, or these her chests, or this her room? Emma smiled at these fanciful dreams. It strengthened her resolve. She *would* do all that was necessary to achieve those dreams. *'Why can't my life be more than this?'* had become a motto she repeated to herself every night when she lay on her hard bed in the stuffy servant room while Madame Beatrice's guttural snoring kept her awake. *Why can't I be a princess?*

Every locked item that the Roman queen brought was always sturdily clamped shut, and that was why it startled Emma when the clamped lid of the third trunk opened as she gingerly tested it. At the slightest touch, the lock fell off and rattled on the floor. Emma, her breath caught in her throat, glanced behind her to see if Theresa noticed, but the handmaiden was murmuring curse words to herself while she hastily remade the bed. Emma examined the lock. Its metal surface was scratched up, as if scuffed with an ice pick.

Did someone else break into the empress's personal luggage? She glanced around her conspiratorially. She and Mildritha were supposed to be the only spies here. *Well*, thought Emma nervously, *now's my chance.*

She opened the chest. A plethora of bound tomes and sealed parchments were stacked inside, everything neatly in place, except for a single scroll that lay askew, puffed out, and partially unwound because of its broken seal. She opened it. Her mother, who had learned the skill herself from being a barmaid for many summers, had taught Emma how to do some basic reading. But this letter was far beyond her capabilities; the only words she recognized were *Normandy*, *kingdom*, *England*, and some words she understood to be names. Emma grimaced; she did not know if this was useful at all.

A stampede of noise erupted from the hallway. In that split second, it reminded Emma of Marlborough. She saw the dead lining the streets, turning the earth red with blood, and she heard the screams of women and children as Maud's soldiers torched their homes and stole their winter stockpiles. It brought tears to her eyes.

Anything is better than nothing, decided Emma. She stuffed the opened scroll down the top of her dress. She closed the trunk, placed the broken lock back on, and spun around right before the gaggle of aristocrats flocked in.

Emma gasped. Empress Maud, Queen of the Romans and rejected heiress to King Henry—may God rest his soul—stood at the forefront of the party. Beautiful without fault, she seemed to Emma an angel of divine womanhood, commanding all the attention one would expect from a harbinger of God. Atop her head and beige veil, she wore a crown of gold and silver with dazzling jewels inlaid. Her skin was unblemished; her eyebrows were lush and darkly contrasted with her pale complexion. Draping pleasantly around her slender arms in bold and exotic colors was her dress, and interwoven into the fabric were so many fine details that Emma's hands ached at imagining the work the seamstresses put into sewing such fine embroidery.

Madame Beatrice stood next to the empress. There was a vague resemblance between the two. Emma wondered if they were distant cousins, and if that was how the madame was given her trusted position. Empress Maud was only in her mid-forties, so she could imagine the empress looking even more like Madame B when she aged another five-to-ten summers.

"I fear they're moving to blockade us from the south, whether my brother's plea to my husband proves fruitful or not," said the empress. Her voice was deep and sultry, reminiscent of her youth spent in the distant kingdoms of Rome and France. "We must maintain an open route to Normandy at all costs, lest we give Geoffrey another excuse to stay in his realm."

"Surely he'll listen to Sir Robert," said someone in the entourage behind her.

"Nothing is sure to an idiot but their commitment to idiocy," countered Madame B.

Empress Maud gave her handmaiden a sly smile. She squeezed Madame Beatrice's arm before turning to the crowd and stating, "The point stands. We must secure passage south. If we lose access to the strait, we lose quick reinforcements from France. And even more importantly, it would be near impossible for my brother to return home."

Isabella snuck back into the bedchamber behind the queen's entourage, apologizing profusely for doing so. She glanced around for where to set her empty laundry basket before eventually deciding to hold it awkwardly while she stood next to Emma.

"That's fine and well, empress, but what of Reading?" asked Baron Baldwin de Redvers, one of the few attendants Emma recognized. "Our loss there has proven to be detrimental to our favor among the clergy. We've received word that the abbot of Reading survived the assault and has held council with Henry."

Empress Maud sighed. Emma, on the other hand, got excited. Gossip! Wonderful, juicy gossip. She always had a fascination with courtly intrigue, although she preferred topics involving princesses, queens, and similarly privileged womenfolk—usually regarding their recent amorous adventures. But this would do for now. She could at least follow along with this discussion. Henry of Blois was King Stephen's brother and, debatably, the most powerful man in England. He was the abbot of Glastonbury Abbey *and* the papal legate of Pope Innocent II, effectively making Henry the religious leader of the realm; a powerful ally for Stephen indeed.

"Hugh de Boves has always been a lapdog to Stephen," said the empress. "Our attempt to reclaim Reading simply gave him the justification needed to be open about it. If he expects an apology, he won't get one. Reading Abbey is the death palace of *my* father, not Stephen's. His occupation of the city should be seen as unholy to the Church, and anything otherwise is obviously dubious."

"Forget the damn clergy," said another well-dressed man, Earl Miles FitzWalter. "My lady, if you wish to reconcile the fears of the feudal lords, then I beg of you to reconsider the finality of this land tax you're placing on them!"

"Prithee, peace. That is enough for today. I desire to convalesce, pray, and mull over the complexities of your demands. With God's divine blessing, we may all be alive and well enough tomorrow to continue discussions. But for now, I must rest."

A slight clamor of disappointment slipped out from a few richly-adorned men. Empress Maud gave them stern looks of condemnation, and that shut most of them up for good. "Sheriff d'Oilli, would you stay but a moment? Duke Richard, Lord de Vere, you two as well."

"Of course, my empress," said Robert d'Oilli, sheriff and royal constable of Oxford Castle.

"Do you wish for me and the others to stay, my lady?" Madame Beatrice asked.

"Yes. This won't take long." Empress Maud placed her crown on the bedside table and removed her hair covering. The Roman queen had long, beautiful black hair that bounced off her shoulders as she moved; she appeared even more similar to Madame B with her wimple removed. When Empress Maud spoke next, her voice had a clinical sharpness to it that made Emma's skin crawl. The niceties that she displayed while taking counsel with those she needed to please were long gone, and she now spoke with candor; or at least, that was what Emma presumed since the empress now began to speak in her French tongue.

Emma didn't know a single word of it, but she thought the language sounded rather crass. The words seemed to jump out of the empress's mouth. She exchanged a few words back and forth between herself and the three men before she turned and crossed to the trunk with the broken lock. Emma's gut dropped into her bowels. Sweat beaded on her temples.

Empress Maud took out a key and grabbed hold of the lock. It slid open at her touch.

If the empress was surprised to find that it was already unlocked, it only showed in the slight cocking of her head. She put the lock to the side and threw open the trunk. Emma could hear her own pulse droning incessantly in her ears. Her knees ached. She felt like collapsing. Empress Maud pushed aside the contents of the chest, spitting out some sharp words that Emma could only guess were profane. Aubrey de Vere helped her look through the chest.

The bedchamber closed in on her. This couldn't be happening, not already...

Emma reached into her dress and grabbed the rolled-up scroll. She knew they were looking for it. How could she be so unlucky? How could she be so careless? Her mind scanned through a million options. Should she place the scroll on the ground somewhere and pretend she'd found it? Should she hide it? Try to eat it?

Emma, taking too long to decide any one thing, hid the scroll in the only place near her: a laundry basket with more discarded bedding. Suddenly, Empress Maud screamed in frustration. The other handmaidens jumped. Isabella pressed herself against Emma.

The empress slammed the trunk shut and turned toward Sheriff d'Oilli. "I've been robbed," she said.

"That's impossible, my empress," the sheriff said. "There are very few people who—"

"Silence! I want the room searched. Now! All of you." She pointed to the handmaidens. "Stand against the wall. Duke Richard, have them undressed. I want them patted down. This castle is to remain locked until the thief is caught."

"Yes, my empress," said Sheriff d'Oilli. He sprinted out of the bedchamber. His orders echoed down the hall.

This is it, thought Emma.

All her dreams were dashed. Even now, she could see Tom's disappointment. She'd failed him. And herself. And her mother, who would forever wait for her daughter to return to her. Emma had thrown her life away. She peeked beside her at poor, anxious Isabella, who clutched the laundry basket that Emma had just slipped the note into.

Wait! NO!

Emma tried to reach out and push the laundry basket out of her hand, but Duke Richard was already shoving them against the wall, separating them from each other. The duke was a large man with hairy arms and thick hands. He always had an unpleasant odor about him, like many of the lesser nobility.

"Give me that." He took the basket from Isabella. "Do as your lady commands. Remove your clothes."

They slowly disrobed. Duke Richard had placed the basket on the ground when the scroll rolled into his view. He picked it up and showed it to the empress. Isabella gasped.

"Is this it, my lady?"

Empress Maud yanked it from his hands and opened it up. Her eyes glazed over the leaf. She lowered it and glared at her handmaidens. "Which one?" she demanded.

"Her." Duke Richard pointed at Isabella.

"N-n-no. P-p-ple-plea—" Isabella stammered.

Duke Richard was too fast. He pinned the girl to the wall, making Emma and Theresa jump back. "Belt it, daft wench!" said the duke.

Tears streamed down Isabella's face. "It-it-it . . ."

"Silence!" commanded the empress. Her hard, fury-driven eyes turned at Madame Beatrice. "I trusted your ability to choose loyal handmaidens. Clearly, I was mistaken." Madame Beatrice lowered her head under her lady's chiding.

"What do you want done with her?" Duke Richard asked.

Empress Maud glowered at Isabella. The betrayal and embarrassment were clear on the empress's face. "Have her taken to Sheriff d'Oilli. Hang her from the drawbridge."

Emma gasped. She had thought about admitting the truth. But for some stupid, naïve reason, she'd believed that the worst thing that could happen to them was that they'd be thrown into a dungeon. The magnitude of her ineptitude and foolishness hit her all at once. She wasn't playing a game; she wasn't a little girl sneaking around a duke's manor.

"Em-Em-Empress," cried Isabella. "P-please."

"You've betrayed me, Isabella," said Empress Maud. "I took you in, and you were a thief for my enemy this whole time."

"No!"

"My lady," said Madame B frantically, "it was my fault we took her in. Please, don't punish her—"

"I may be a woman, but I am not weak. I will not tolerate such despicable actions. If I let you live, they will claim it as proof of my womanly fallacies. I will not give them the privilege. Take her away."

Duke Richard dragged Isabella as she kicked and screamed and pleaded to Maud and Madame B and the high Lord above to save her from certain damnation. Her screams echoed hollowly inside the bedchamber. Emma, wracked with guilt, stood frozen, her feet nailed to the floor. Isabella's shrieks tainted every corner of the castle, and Emma's warm tears trickled down her cheek.

Madame Beatrice stared at her for a long second. Emma noticed and wiped the tears away. If Madame B was suspicious, she said nothing of it. She simply tugged at the scarf around her neck and went back to work.

CHAPTER XXI
EADRIC

"Fear God; for through His might, He will humble you. Despise Satan; for through his cunning, he will misguide you. Be deceived not, for amongst thee on *middanearde* is the Great Serpent. Be disheartened not, for amongst thee on *middanearde* is Christ. Thus, 'tis your responsibility to behead the first trickster; thus, 'tis your responsibility to decipher when God is humbling, and when Lucifer is misguiding."

This was how Theobald of Bec, archbishop of Canterbury, finished his sermon to Eadric, William of Ypres, Sir Álvaro, and the entire congregation of soldiers on the morning of their assault on Wareham, the day the Hellhound of Rutland was betrayed twice.

"The gates are down! Run! Cover the arrow slits!"

Eadric's squadron swarmed over the toppled palisade and toward Wareham's eastern gatehouse. City guardsmen shot arrows from atop the city walls. Eadric covered his face with his splinted armbraces, feeling an arrow bounce off his chest plate and knocking him back a step. *That'll leave an ugly bruise.* More arrows flew out of arrow loops built into the gatehouse walls. This was always the most dangerous part of an invasion. Gatehouses were designed to be funnel points, where the defenders could take out multitudes of their enemy as they attempted to push into the city or castle proper.

"Cover the arrow slits!" He ordered again. Man after man fell, slain in the onslaught of arrows. The soldiers yelled and leaped over the stacked bodies, some of them slipping on the oozing blood of their brethren only to find themselves impaled with an arrow at that same instant. They used shields, armor pieces, bits of the broken portcullis, and even corpses to cover the holes—whatever they could use to stop the barrage of arrows piercing them from all sides.

A trapdoor on the gatehouse ceiling dropped a mighty stack of rubble, and it crushed the heads of many soldiers below it. Eadric cursed. It was an unexpected and clever move, which killed a dozen of them in total. Bloodlust coursed through Eadric's veins. His eyes only saw red as he and his men fought with brutish recklessness and made a final push through the death zone, muscling their way into Wareham.

However, city walls served two purposes; one, to shoot invaders outside the walls from a high vantage point; two, to shoot invaders *inside* the walls, also from a high vantage point.

Eadric took cover behind a signpost. "You eight," he told a group of his soldiers hunkering nearby. "Ascend those stairs and take these whoresons out! I'll keep you covered."

They gathered their strength and cried out as they ran for the battlement stairs. Eadric directed a few other groups to do the same. There was strength in numbers, a courageousness which couldn't be replicated when one sees they are not alone in Hell, and within a few minutes, he had his army efficiently eliminate the archers atop the walls.

All-in-all, their losses were minimal; the losses for the city garrison were not.

This didn't surprise Eadric, for the king's army finally had something worth fighting for. King Stephen, with the overdramatic zeal he liked to portray, wearing his obnoxiously bright-violet armor that drew one's eyes like a child to sweet fruits, had finally rendezvoused with their war party late last night, raising much fanfare and jubilee from those same peasant-soldiers who'd nearly deserted only a few weeks back. The king seemed eager to be on the front lines of their first major battle on this new offensive, and thus the invasion very much reminded Eadric of their horrid failure during the Battle of Lincoln. Just as they were on that battlefield, they had split into three flanks; Eadric attacked Wareham from the east, William of Ypres from the west, and King Stephen from the north.

A brave courier—who couldn't be older than ten—ran up and updated him on the other squadrons. King Stephen and William of Ypres had broken through the northern and western gatehouses using battering rams to knock down the portcullises, and they were already piercing toward the center of the city. Eadric thanked the boy, even though he learned little new information from him. As much as he detested William of Ypres and thought him a tactical fool, even he should be successful today. The Wareham garrison was mostly local citizens who were forced to defend their city, and they were sorely undertrained for such a concentrated strike. Even their commanders were only a few low-ranking knights, barons, and priests.

They were slain easily—well, not the priests. No one dared touch them. The haunting sermon given by the archbishop made certain the fear of God was in everyone's soul.

They fought inwards. Eadric stuck his blade through the ribs of a civilian who ran at him with a pitchfork. The man slumped to the ground, slapping at his wound. A woman screamed from a nearby shed. She threw herself onto the man and sobbed deeply. *Must be his wife*, thought Eadric. More stifled cries came from the shed, where four children watched from the shadows. The eldest child in this mourning family, a young boy around the age of twelve it looked like, stared at the Hellhound with a red glaze over his eyes.

He'd be yet another person in a long string of inflamed grievers that would place Eadric on the pedestal of revenge. The Hellhound of Rutland would become more than a man to this young boy; he'd become the nightmare that haunted him every night, gifting him the curse of insomnia, until the boy, fed up with the sleepless agonies of grief, trained to become a warrior so he could one day slay the bastard who took his father's life. And on that vengeful day when the boy-turned-man found the Hellhound of Rutland, he'd discover that he'd dedicated his life to destroying a man who'd kill him within two moves.

Hopefully his mother would remind him of that, and he'd realize that the most honorable thing a man could do was sacrifice his vanity to put the pieces of his family back together.

Revenge was a luxury for those left with nothing.

By the time he reached Sir Álvaro and his small band at the center of Wareham, much of Eadric's squadron had dispersed into isolated control groups. He'd directed most of them to suppress each major quadrant of the city and maintain control, so that by the end, only a small group of about twenty soldiers remained with him.

"Took you a while," Sir Álvaro teased with a smile. "What kept you?"

"We had trouble at the gatehouse," said Eadric.

"I bring orders from William. We're to clear a path to the docks. King Stephen has apparently found opposition at the central shops. William's bringing troops there for backup and will meet us at the dock houses."

"I have something I must look into first. I'll send my troops afterwards."

"What are you going on about?"

"I believe Commander Braxton is here."

"You have orders," Sir Álvaro said with a touch of disapproval. "We've gotten away with disobedience twice. I fear we may not get levity again. Where does your intel come from?"

"Do not doubt me."

"This is treachery you speak of, Eadric. You'll be tried as a traitor."

"Then let them try me."

Sir Álvaro sighed. He glanced back at his squadron awaiting orders. "Very well. I'll trust you're right; you were in Flanders. I'll buy you as much time as I can."

"Thank you, León."

Eadric gathered his measly twenty troops and navigated to a large crossroads. South of them sat the docks along the River Frome, where even now Eadric saw boats being assaulted with arrows; to their west was the central square, where their king fought against the last remnants of Wareham's city-watch; then to the north, atop a grassy knoll where their current street climbed to its ultimate destination, reigned St. Martin's Church.

A small church built during the Roman occupation two centuries past, St. Martin's was simply constructed with a narrow nave, a small chancel, and a short bell tower. As far as houses of God were concerned, this one was pretty humble and inconspicuous—aside from how it towered like a bastion on its round hill. Gleaming upon this idyllic place of worship, Eadric set his eyes on his new prize. If Commander Braxton was actually in Wareham, William the hostage was adamant he'd be commanding his troops right there inside God's holy place.

"Hark! Hearken all who are bound by oath to our king!" Eadric waved his sword in front of his troops, pointing toward the church. "Follow me, and we shall bring great glory to His Majesty. We head for the church of Saint Martin, where, God-giving, we'll slay a notorious commander of the empress's vile army!"

That didn't get the reaction he expected. His soldiers hesitated, giving each other odd looks. One soldier up front took a step forward. His surcoat was dirty and scarred from the battle thus far, and the shadow of his helm covered all facial features.

"M'lord, shan't we be fightin' to our king?" Shadowed Soldier asked. The others nodded in agreement. Something in this soldier's voice was vaguely recognizable to Eadric.

"*This* is our mission," Eadric lied. "To capture the church and expunge it of the enemy."

"But, m'lord—"

"Silence! You're under my command and will do as I dictate. Do I make myself clear?" Time slipped away from him. Commander Braxton could escape with every moment of his delay.

"Yes, m'lord," said Shadowed Soldier. Eadric grunted in assent and waved for them to follow. They charged up the northern street.

All along their path, storefronts, houses, stables, and everything with thatch and timber and furs caught fire. The Hellhound and his men advanced toward the church, trailing behind them a halo of wicked fumes. Flurries of fire fanned around them in the rising wind, and Eadric, for the briefest of fleeting moments, while watching these incandescent specks burn alive and shrivel up in the air, felt in his heart the devastation of their exploits here. All these thousands of tiny, fiery dots that littered the bright sky were homes once. They were dreams. They were hopes. They were livelihoods.

If he were a better man, one filled with morality and decency and honor, then perhaps he'd have felt something more humane in this moment. But watching the scorching death of the once pleasant city of Wareham, it wasn't pity or self-judgment that overcame him. Only waste, as if the world was depleted of all meaning. There was a time very recently when Eadric truly felt vehemence at everyone, especially at the peasants. And to a degree, he still did. But all that anger, all that suffering, had formed into a stone-like lump in his gut.

This is an extra weight I don't need to carry . . . damn woman. Eleanor had been trying to get him to see the errors of his cruelty, and it seemed she had a larger effect on him than he'd like to admit.

They reached the base of the knoll. Eadric's eyes grew wide. His grip tightened around the hilt of his sword. His throat was dry with adrenaline.

"M'lord!"

His squadron fell behind. Eadric, so caught up in his own thoughts, hadn't realized he'd raced ahead of them. And they were ambushed.

Remnants of the city garrison sprung out of the surrounding buildings and alleyways as his squadron funneled down the northern thoroughfare. The street constantly climbed uphill, and his men were further disadvantaged because of this. And even worse, they were outnumbered. Dearly outnumbered.

One of his men died beneath the hammer of their enemy, his head caved inward as the enemy slammed through the helm, skin, and bone. They screamed and swung and tried to overcome the sudden attack, but they needed their fearless leader to turn the tides of battle.

Eadric glanced back up at the church. He froze.

Upon the grassy knoll, which stood along the northern walls of Wareham, the bells of St. Martin's Church tolled like a petrifying warning from God. Four soldiers, wearing an emblem of red splotches on a bright azure sky, huddled beneath the ringing bell tower.

Eadric knew that insignia well.

Will was right. Those are Duke Richard's men. Commander Braxton is here.

Eadric couldn't believe his luck. Of all the cities and castles in all of southern England, the one person he was looking for was here. His decision was immediate and definitive. Eadric abandoned his squadron and sprinted up the hill. The four soldiers of Duke Richard retreated inside St. Martin's Church. Eadric grinned ecstatically.

God has finally blessed me. I won't let this divine favor slip away. Lucia, this is for you.

Eadric kicked open the wooden door of the church. The door rattled against the stone walls with a heavy thud. Dust scattered around him, and he yelled, "Braxton!"

Three soldiers flanked a man with a blonde scruffy beard who kneeled before a large crucifix. Commander Braxton stood and faced his death.

He and Eadric, both in plated harnesses, stared each other down across the stunted nave. The hollow air of the church felt cold. Pale sunlight filtered through narrow windows, coruscating off the dense dust that swirled between the sworn enemies. The flames of the burning city, which suddenly came back to Eadric's attention, blocked out the sunlight occasionally. And in those moments, the interior of the church tinged black-orange, making the hostile warriors appear to be inside an infernal oven.

Commander Braxton clearly recognized him. Eadric glowered at him. This man, under the dictation of Duke Richard, had ordered his men to abandon the wedding. He should've been helping Eadric, Sir Álvaro, and the other abandoned highborn fight back against the peasant revolt that had wiped out his brother's bloodline and slit Lucia's throat.

"My lord tires of hiding from you," said Commander Braxton. His voice echoed high into the sacred ceiling. Eadric stepped further into the nave.

"Then tell him to reveal himself," retorted Eadric. "I have his bastard son held hostage. There is no ransom needed but for him to give himself to me."

"He's sorry about your daughter. It was unlucky she had to be there."

"His pity means naught to me."

"I know. It was the reason I was sent here, to deal with you now." Commander Braxton picked up his helm off the altar, his *maille* ringing like the mighty bell in the tower, and placed it onto his blonde head. The soldier next to him handed him a kite shield and a mace.

So, a contest of strength, thought Eadric with glee.

Eadric roared, using the power of his voice to conjure vengeful ecstasy. He unsheathed his longsword and sprinted down the nave, passing row after row of wooden seats. He scanned between Commander Braxton and the three harnessed soldiers with him. They each carried spears. That put Eadric at an advantage as long as he could get in close. He raced through the dark, fiery glow of the church. He heard the flames outside. Popping. Roaring. God had truly abandoned this holy place.

Clunk!

A fourth soldier leaped out from one of the pews and swung his wicked cudgel at Eadric's legs. The sturdy wood slammed into his chausses. A bone cracked, reverberating like the sound of a twig snapping underfoot. The Hellhound tripped. His body toppled over itself, end over end. His *maille* scraped against the stone floor, screeching and rattling. The pain hit Eadric all at once, a fiery sensation that traveled up his body until it had to be released in one loud, monstrous yell. Eadric could barely comprehend all of this before he got jumped.

But not by one soldier, or two, or three, or even all four.

No, Eadric realized with horror, *the boy hostage lied to me. I've been ambushed.*

Half a dozen soldiers surrounded his crumpled body. They swung down on him with maces and hammers and other blunt weapons. Eadric covered his head and face with his splinted armbraces. His plated metal concaved under the force of their blows.

Eadric gasped. Ribs cracked. Bones snapped. He tried to force himself up, but his own armor weighed him down. He wasn't the strong young man he once was. One soldier hammered down at his head. Eadric redirected the blow, but his armguard broke in half.

Somewhere above the groans of the assaulting soldiers, Commander Braxton cackled heartily to himself. His laugh stoked a smoldering flame within Eadric. He gazed up into the vaulted ceiling of the church, and he fancied he saw that black-feathered crow that had appeared to him as they charged Reading. The Hellhound of Rutland wouldn't go down so easily.

In one quick motion, before any of the soldiers had time to take advantage of the opening and squash his head like a melon, Eadric swung his sword in a wide arc. The blade sliced through three legs before the men realized and jumped back.

Get up. Don't stop. The most dangerous place to be is on the ground.

Eadric rolled onto one knee. He tried to stand, but his left leg was broken beneath the kneecap. He lifted his right arm, but that was fractured at an unnatural angle. Eadric quickly appraised the fight. His arching blow took down two of Braxton's men. They hemorrhaged on the ground with their stubby legs severed. The other four, however, regained their balance and readied to rush him.

The front door of the church kicked open. Everyone turned.

Eadric's squadron of soldiers flooded into the church. Eadric laughed aloud. His squad was decimated, only eleven remained of the twenty he left Sir Álvaro with, but they had survived the ambush outside and made their way up to him. Eadric spat blood.

"M'lord, are you injured?" asked Shadowed Soldier, the one with the familiar voice.

"Sir Knights," said Eadric to Commander Braxton and his soldiers, "how about a fair fight?"

The two sides stared each other down. Eadric braced himself to have this fight on his one good knee. *This'll get very bloody*.

Shadowed Soldier stepped ahead of the others, glanced at his commander, and sheathed his weapon. Eadric's face twitched. *What the fuck is he doing?*

The soldier took off his helm, and despair dropped into Eadric's gut. It was Hugo, the man with pubic hair for a beard who Eadric humiliated the night Queen Matilda returned—the peasant-soldier he was going to kill if not for Eleanor stopping him right before.

"Sorry, *my lord*," said Hugo with pure vitriol in his voice. "All God's children get what they deserve." He spat in Eadric's direction. The rest of his squadron did the same.

This time it was Commander Braxton who laughed.

Eadric didn't know how to react to such treachery. He first felt anger, then sorrow, and then a kind-of ironic respect. He finally settled on fury. "You traitors! Every one of you! I'll behead all you myself!" Eadric screamed as they left, one by one, out the front door and vanished into the city of flames.

The church went silent.

"Your men desert you," said Commander Braxton. "Your vengeance has outstripped your dwindling respect. It seems the Hellhound of Rutland is without friends."

"Fight me, you coward," was all Eadric could weakly mutter. His body was abandoning him. His left arm twitched from the weight of his mighty longsword. It was practically impossible to wield with just one hand.

"As you wish." Commander Braxton sprang forward. Eadric sliced.

The commander deftly deflected the blow with his shield and knocked the sword from Eadric's grasp. He swung down. Eadric rolled away, but the mace clipped his right shoulder. He felt an audible *pop*.

Eadric crumbled. Everything hurt. His broken ribs made it difficult to breathe. He wheezed his final few breaths. Commander Braxton stood over him. He raised his mace—

"STOP THIS MADNESS!"

Commander Braxton, Eadric, and Duke Richard's soldiers looked toward the gigantic voice.

A priest with blood-stained robes and a bald head blackened with soot stood with his hands held high in the air; and behind him, surrounding the altar of Christ and filling out the chancel, was a militia of citizens armed with fishing instruments.

CHAPTER XXII
GILBERT & WILLIAM

A PHANTOM DRESSED IN black, wearing a wicked mask that obscured his face, visited him in the heathen hours of the night. It frightened the boy dreadfully. He ticked. William had been twitching less of late, and he supposed it was because of the lack of food and vigor. He had never been so weak in his life. He craved companionship. It was a treat any time anyone visited and distracted him from the countless hours that whittled away at his mind.

But this spirit dressed in black before him sent a shiver down his spine.

"William of Rouen," said the phantom, its voice thick and foreign, "bastard of Duke Richard of Wilton."

"What do ye want?" asked William.

"I offer thee freedom. Dost thou trust the Hellhound?"

He peeked around the phantom, looking for his gaoler. He was nowhere to be seen. How did this spirit sneak past him in the middle of camp? Most people were asleep as they were only days away from sacking Wareham, but someone should've seen this spirit enter.

"Dost thou trust the Hellhound?"

"... No."

"Good. Use thy intellect keenly. Hark my words, and thou may yet live."

"What is it ye want from me?" The world turned cold around William. His eyes were frozen on the mask hidden under the black hood. It was lifeless, hollow, and terrifying.

"The Hellhound must pay for the lives he's taken. He must pay for his sins. Guide him. Lead him toward the Church of St. Martin. It is there he'll be ambushed. And it is there that his sins shalt be atoned."

"Why would he believe me?"

"He is desperate. Tell him the church shall be where the commander will be found. Tell him your father is fearful and would rather send his best knight to fight the Hellhound than wait any longer. Thy capturer will follow any lead. Guide him to damnation, and thou shalt be freed."

"How do I know I can trust ye?"

"Thy can't. But wouldst thou rather place thy trust in a butcher than a spectre?"

The spirit fled that very moment, disappearing into the shadows of the war camp. William glared after it with a dreadful pit in his stomach. He felt another tic coming.

England differed from how Gilbert imagined it to be. The countryside expanded outward in all directions around the river, the land flat and green and full of life. It was a vast wetland, with pools of water seeping up through the abundant grass. He saw all kinds of wonderful birds, their bodies reflecting off the many pools, as they flew in tremendous numbers beneath the daytime moon, which appeared hazy and lethargic when veiled behind the thin summer clouds.

Bartholomew puked over the gunwale.

Beatriz put her hand on her husband's back, rubbing him, trying to help him feel better without actually looking at his retched insides. Bartholomew's face turned green. Hawk laughed at him from below the foremast.

"You survived all the treachery of the fathomless sea with your food securely in your belly, yet it's the calmness of the bay that introduces us to your inner acids?"

"I'm done in!" Bartholomew heaved. "Kill me now. Throw me overboard."

Beatriz slapped his bald head, and said, "Don't tempt the Lord. I didn't travel all this way for ye to die immediately."

"You can spread the Faith without me, love."

"Don't be so glum, Bart," said Gilbert. "We've been on the River Frome a while yet. I imagine we should reach Wareham shortly."

They approached a bend in the river. Within a few minutes, the flat wetlands around them disappeared, and they were shrouded between trees as the River Frome slinked through the middle of a dense forest. Hawk placed his hand on Gilbert's shoulder.

"We'll find William," he said. "He's out there somewhere."

Bartholomew turned away from the gunwale and sat down, sweat breaking out on his face. Beatriz smiled and scratched her husband's head.

"Prepare to dock!" shouted one of the many deckhands who worked the trading vessel. "Prepare to dock!"

"See," said Gilbert. "Told you we'd soon approach port."

The ship rounded the bend, exiting the forest into a clearing on the far side, which indicated they were very close to a city. The deckhand approached them.

"Please wayward step from the bow," he said. "We need must clear the way so the helmsman can spot the dock."

"Apologies," said Bartholomew. Beatriz hit him. "And God be with ye," he added.

"Aye!" the deckhand laughed. "And as yet, God hasn't failed me." He turned awa—

THUNK!

An arrow went through the deckhand's neck. Beatriz screamed.

THUNK! THUNK! THUNK!

Arrows rained down on the ship. They ducked prone, using the gunwale as protection. The sailors ran for safety, hiding behind the mast and other objects aboard. Gilbert glanced to the side and saw the deckhand gurgle his last breath. His blood pooled around him, swaying toward Gilbert and then away as the ship rocked.

"THE CITY IS UNDER ATTACK!" yelled the captain. "DON'T DOCK! KEEP GOIN'! WAREHAM IS UNDER ATTACK!"

The friends crawled to one another, arrows whizzing by their heads, while the crew desperately unfurled the mast to keep sailing. Gilbert glanced at his friends, their wide-eyed faces waiting for him to decide their next move.

"We need to jump ship," said Gilbert.

"Are ye crazy?" asked Beatriz.

"Perhaps. But we must, lest we sail back to Normandy."

"The city is under siege," Bartholomew retorted.

"I can't waste more time," said Gilbert, looking them each in the face. "William is held victim on this land. I won't turn back without him. Not this time."

"Well," Hawk grumbled, "'tis a fortunate thing we know how to swim."

"What if the archers aim at us while we swim ashore?" asked Beatriz.

"Seeing how you have the best relationship with Him, I suggest you pray for us."

Beatriz whined. She reached into her tunic, retrieved her rosary and a small wooden cross that she'd etched herself, and brought it to her lips, muttering a quick prayer. Gilbert and his friends glanced at each other. They were lucky in the sense that they hadn't brought many items with them. Gilbert had a small satchel that carried all the money they could muster up from selling some of Hawk's clothes—the first and perhaps toughest sacrifice he'd have to make on their journey—while Bartholomew owned a sack that carried the minimal spare food they brought with them. Their original plan was to use the money they had to buy provisions once they reached the city of Wareham.

It looked like they'd be keeping their money a little while longer.

Another three arrows stuck into the surrounding deck.

Hawk rubbed Gilbert and Bartholomew's shoulders playfully. "Just like old times," he jested. His high-pitched laughter almost covered the screams of the sailors.

"How is this like old times?" Bartholomew asked. Beatriz cried out. The rosary *clacked* against itself as she shook. Bartholomew hugged his wife close to him. Instinctively, Gilbert reached out and grabbed Beatriz's arm. Hawk did the same. Together, all three of them held her against the wave of fear, and she took strength from that bond.

After taking a few long breaths, she asked, "Jump on three?"

Four more arrows struck the gunwale.

"Fuck that," said Hawk. "Jump now!"

"WHA—"

All four of them leaped off the side of the cog, plummeting fifteen feet until they splashed into the river; coldness rushed over them; bubbles exploded out. Gilbert kicked. His eyes burned; the refracted light blurred the world into shimmering greens and blues. He erupted to the surface, gasping for air and spinning, hoping to spot his companions.

Bartholomew and Beatriz already swam for shore. But Hawk was screaming. Gilbert twisted around, eyes glancing over the gigantic waves coming from the ship. He found his friend swimming toward the boat.

What was he doing?!

"Aha!" Hawk screamed triumphantly, holding up his bright-red Phrygian hat. "Got you!"

Gilbert groaned. His friend pivoted and swam for shore. Gilbert followed, sending up a prayer of his own that no arrows should fall upon him. The hidden archers continued to let loose on the boat, not wanting any ships to port while they were sacking the city. Bartholomew and Beatriz helped pull them onto dry land, and they entered what looked to be the dock district. Screams echoed around them. The air smelled acidic and strangely pungent, like burned pork, and black ashes tumbled to the earth around them like perverted snowflakes. His companions glanced at him; it was the tiniest of peeks, but Gilbert knew what they must be thinking:

Is the curse of the blood moon real? Maybe their friend was *doomed for endless sorrow; perhaps his mother was right . . . he will kill them all.*

The proof was becoming undeniable; since his birth, Gilbert's life had been nothing but a series of unending catastrophes. He was about to apologize when they heard, "Psst. PSSSST."

The group turned and saw an older peasant with a receding hairline and ripped clothes waving at them from across the alleyway. Two other peasants hid behind him. "PSSST," he hissed again. "Come hither."

Gilbert looked at Hawk, who shrugged and nodded. Gilbert agreed; there was strength in numbers. They sprinted across the opening between their two buildings.

"Thank you, Jesus," said the older man when they reached him. "Was hoping to run into some strong young men. We need aid."

"What's goin' on?" asked Bartholomew. "Who's attacking?"

"The king's army. Can't ye tell from all the fires bein' started? That mad bastard loves to burn everythin' to ash. And . . . why ye soakin' wet?"

"We just swam from that ship," said Hawk.

"Oh, fancy that. Where ye coming from?"

"Normandy."

"Ah, very good. Well, welcome to England," said the peasant man as a woman screamed somewhere distantly in the city. "The name is Hann. Behind me here are my kids, Edwin and Cedric."

"I'm Gilbert. This here are Hawk, Bartholomew, and Beatriz."

"Well met! Now, if ye won't mind, one of our local priests, Father Tobias, is currently in danger of burnin' alive. He's trapped in that building over yonder with many other good folk. Me and my sons can't move the debris ourselves."

"That building looks on the verge of collapse," said Bartholomew hesitantly.

"That's why your help is needed. Please. Father Tobias is a true son of Christ."

Gilbert's instinct was to flee. The warehouse Hann pointed to was being devoured by flames. It would be more than dangerous; it could be deadly.

"I'll help," said Beatriz, shocking the rest of the group. She looked determined and solidified in her choice, like the prospect of saving a priest had somehow encouraged her. "It's our Christian duty," she said.

"The building may well kill us," her husband argued.

"Then we see God and go to glorious Paradise for sacrificing ourselves like Christ."

"Plus," added Hann, "if ye need further motivation, we are trapped at the lowest part of the city. There be no escape but to travel to one of the gates. Father Tobias can help us. None would dare attack a priest, lest they wish to be banished to Hell for all eternity, and so on. There's no one safer to flee with."

That logic did indeed galvanize them. He was correct; to kill a servant of Christ would be a sin most unholy. The clergy were practically untouchable by both sides of the war.

"Very well," said Gilbert. "Lead us."

Hann and his sons guided them across the street, ducking behind an abandoned cart as four archers navigated toward the center of town. Once the archers passed, they sprinted to the burning warehouse. Inside, they could hear the screams of children. They got to work. Wrapping their wet tunics around their hands, they pushed away the smoldering debris. Hawk and Gilbert leaned their shoulders into a long support beam that lay askew across the doorway and pushed it just enough that it collapsed into the ash pile below them, puffing up a minor explosion of fiery embers.

Hann waited for the smoke to ventilate from the opening they'd just created before he peered inside and called out, "Father Tobias? Father Tobias?!"

"Shush now, everyone," said a tender voice from somewhere beyond the smoke, followed by a series of abrupt coughs. "By God's good grace, yes! We're trapped in here."

"Make everyone stand back," said Hann. "We're going to push our way inside!"

Father Tobias relayed the message. Hann motioned for everyone to help. There were multiple fallen beams just within the entrance. All they needed to do was push past them.

They all crammed together within the doorway. Flames lurched at them from across the alley.

"Please hurry!" yelled another voice from inside. Gilbert could hear the children screaming, the adults coughing.

"One, two, three, push!"

They shoved. The beams moved a few inches. A part of the roof collapsed.

More screams. More coughs. More death.

"One, two, three, push! One, two, three, push! One, two, three, push!"

Finally, Gilbert and his friends, with Hann and his sons, shoved aside the wreckage. They coughed as black fumes blasted into their faces. "'Tis open, Father! Come to the door!"

"Go, my children," said Father Tobias from beyond the smoke. "Flee!"

There were more than Gilbert had expected; around twenty people flooded through the opening they created. Father Tobias was the last to exit. He coughed mightily as he breathed in fresh air. The priest was a tall man, about the same height as Hawk, with shredded black robes and a scratched face that seeped with blood. He was bald, like most clergy, and his eyebrows were such a light-brown color he appeared almost entirely hairless. He glanced at Gilbert and his friends with a warm stare. "God bless you all," he said. "Thank you."

"Father, is there anyone else—"

"No." Father Tobias cut off Hann. The priest had a troubled look on his face. He lifted his hands, revealing that they were stained with red. Gilbert gasped. It was scandalous for a priest to touch blood. Father Tobias, blinking away tears and looking back at the burning warehouse, wiped his soiled hands on his robes. "The rest are with God now. Some were children."

"Father," said Beatriz, bowing politely, "we need your wisdom. We must escape the city. The king's army has it surrounded."

Father Tobias nodded. "The church of St. Martin's. We can seek asylum there. It'll be the safest place in the city. They'd never torch a house of Christ."

"Then take us there, Father," said Hann.

Father Tobias readied himself as he glanced over his small congregation of twenty-seven souls, those he was now responsible for. It hardened the man. A great wave of shame overcome Gilbert. This priest, who touched blood, who sinned against God, had more courage and resolve than Gilbert could ever dream of. Would his curse now damn this priest like it had to all those around him?

"Follow me," said Father Tobias. "Grab anything you can use for weapons, *but* only for self-protection! No heedless violence. There's been too much of that spilled on this terrible day. We'll gather anyone we can and head for St. Martin's. May God watch over us."

They spent the next few minutes scouring the Wareham docks. What they found were mostly fishing instruments: rods, hooks, tridents, nets. By the time they all trekked uphill to reach the church, only Father Tobias remained unarmed. Gilbert, for his part, had a small hammer he found buried beneath the ash of what used to be a forge.

Their flight up to St. Martin's Church was a blur; Gilbert, Hawk, Bartholomew, and Beatriz stayed close to one another while the large group of armed peasants plunged between buildings and houses, sneaking through alleyways and over fences, as they hid from the warring troops slaughtering the city. The priest became more and more aggravated. The destruction and horrors of battle intensified the farther they climbed. Dogs ate corpses on the streets. Livestock burned alive. Horses stampeded down the thoroughfares, trampling peasants beneath their hooves as they both fled from the hellfire.

The hearts of the inhabitants had turned to bitter ashes, and the loss of their homes turned their thoughts to wild fumes. Many other frenzied occupants joined along with them, and by the time they reached the base of the knoll that the church sat upon, they had gathered a small militia of fifty-plus peasants and newly forged vagabonds.

They froze when they saw the bodies of dead soldiers at the front entrance of St. Martin's Church. In the inflamed city surrounding their consecrated knoll, the shouts of men, women, children, and animals commingled into indistinguishable noise. If any sound of war came from within the church, it was impossible to separate it from all the other destruction.

Hann asked Father Tobias, "What do ye think?"

"We'll enter from the chancel," the priest answered. "Even if there are soldiers inside, they will not spill blood in the church. We'd best stay safe, though. Follow me, children!"

They rounded the church until they came upon a small wooden door that led into the apse. They pressed in with their weapons at the ready.

The inside of the church was a hellish red color. The smoke of the burning city wafted through the narrow windows, and the intensity of the heat made the interior feel uncomfortably warm. Gilbert and his friends followed closely behind Hann, his sons, and Father Tobias, when the priest stopped suddenly next to the altar. The rest of the peasants trailed in behind and filled the chancel. They covered their mouths and gasped in shock at what Father Tobias saw.

Multiple well-armed soldiers and knights fought in the center of the nave, with one knight being brutally assaulted by the others. Father Tobias wasn't glaring at them though; his eyes turned to a much more horrifying sight...

Two dead priests lay on the ground, their arms holding their disemboweled intestines.

Father Tobias's tears fell in a mighty storm as he touched the limp body of his fellow clergymen. The priest stood, his body shaking with rage.

The knight in the center of the nave raised his mace to crush the other knight.

"STOP THIS MADNESS!" yelled Father Tobias.

The knight and soldiers pivoted. They glared at the priest and the peasant army behind him. Father Tobias, looking intimidating in his blood-soaked habit, glared at the knight with all the fury of the divine. "Dare you defy God by spilling blood in His holy church?!"

"Leave here, Father," said the knight with a mace. "This is not your affair."

"It is now, my son! Look at what you've done. Begone at once!" The priest's voice shook the walls. God Himself spoke through him. The soldiers trembled.

The mace-wielding knight turned to his men, his voice shaking as he pointed to the other knight and said, "Bring him with us."

"NO!" Father Tobias's voice boomed. "You shall shed no more blood, lest you wish me to beg God that He banishes you to the deepest realms of Hell! You have dirtied this sacred ground and slain two shepherds of men. You've spat in His holy image. Leave now, and I will still pray for your salvation."

Father Tobias's plea was so sincere, so wrought with anger and sadness, that Gilbert felt himself moved terribly. His hand tightened around the hammer.

"I will not, Father."

Gilbert and the fifty peasants tensed. Then, glancing at one another and at their priest, their protector and liaison to the Almighty, they all stepped forward. They would *not* let this knight and his barbarians ruin more lives. They would *not* let the rich landowners who destroyed their homes with fire kill their religious fervor. They held aloft their weapons, their fishing instruments and tradesmen tools, and waited for the moment to use them.

"You will leave now," began Father Tobias slowly, "or I'll have the Lord smite thee where thou stands." The priest raised his arms into the air.

That was all it took. There were some things one wouldn't chance. From birth, everyone had the fear of God hammered into them, which the Church intensified until they only knew Christ and his Father's power. This was a God who would drown all beings in a flood because they turned away from Him; surely, He could stop all their hearts if a priest needed it to be done.

The soldiers ran out of the church, stumbling over each other.

"Begone," the priest said one last time.

The mace-wielding knight reluctantly stepped away from the one lying on the ground. That knight spat at the other and said, "I'll find you again," before he fled the church.

Father Tobias let out a vast sigh and fell to his knees. The peasants huddled around him. It took tremendous courage to do what he just did. The knight kneeling on the ground collapsed, his plated harness clanging out in the hollow, red-stained church. Some of the other peasants ran up to him and quickly stripped his armor. The knight moaned as they dressed his broken body and bandaged some superficial cuts along his arm and neck.

Today would be a day about helping those who needed it.

It felt good. They'd all survived. That felt terrific, actually. Gilbert smiled. Maybe, just maybe, he wasn't cursed after all. Through bravery and strength, there was still hope to be had in the world. His brother was still alive; he knew it in his soul.

It was time to keep searching.

CHAPTER XXIII
EMMA

WHEAT GREW IN COPIOUS amounts around Oxford; the city stood like an indomitable island, monumental and unmoving within the vast bronze sea of swaying barley. The pleasant summer breeze sent wave-like undulations through the crop fields until they crashed into the towers and ramparts, which would forever be sentries for the empress and all her denizens. The air was dense with grain particulates that reflected the sunlight, sparking in and out of existence—golden stars in a blue sky. These seeds of human labor, and God's fruitful bounty, rained upon the citizens of Oxford as they raised their voices, feasted, and danced in the streets (or sneezed constantly on account of the assailing wheat).

Today was Lammas, or better known as St. Peter's Day, and it celebrated the first harvest of the year. Over the last few days, and throughout the entire early morn, every able-bodied man, woman, and child had been harvesting their fields; but now, at midday, they partied. Every belfry in Oxford—from St. Martin to St. Mildred to St. Ehbe to whichever saint remained to be given a church—sounded their bells in divine unison to praise the Lord and His endless benevolence.

Emma followed Theresa and Madame Beatrice through the crowded streets. She was overwhelmed; there were visitors from every corner of every shire in southwestern England. Talk of war and the king's advancing army, which recently invaded Wiltshire, hung over every conversation like an evasive fog. But there was an unspoken agreement among the peasantry and nobility alike: on this day there would be no fearmongering or treachery. Today would be a day for celebration and enjoyment. War will reach them much like the inevitability of winter, but they'll have *this* day forever.

Unfortunately for Emma, she'd spend it doing work.

"T'would it be too much to ask for these dolt-festering imbeciles to stay off the middle of the road during their acts of recklessness?" Madame B huffed as she pushed away a group of kids who ran blindly into the three of them. "I can hardly take a step without trampling a dress. And it's too hot for this many people! I'm sweating a river."

"Have ye considered not wearing so much clothing, perhaps?" asked Emma.

Madame B scoffed. "Better to be dressed conservatively than be eyed as prey. While our empress is away, we must be her surrogates, in manner *and* discipline. We're handmaidens of the Roman queen. How the people see us is how they'll see her."

"We wouldn't need to worry if we had enjoyed the day in the castle like everyone else," muttered Theresa miserably.

"Empress Maud will return any day now. All must be impeccable for her arrival, lest—"

"Lest an assassin hide in her linen basket and slit her throat?" asked Emma.

"Precisely. But I could do without the attitude. This is serious."

Emma sighed. She was convinced Madame Beatrice couldn't be any less serious even if seven naked jesters tickled her simultaneously. The absurd image made her laugh.

"What's so funny?"

Emma rolled her eyes. "Nothin', madame."

Excitement rose in a nearby cluster of peculiar-looking people. A little girl screamed. Next to a townhouse on their street, a bright light flared up. Flames licked at the sky, turning the falling wheat alight. A long piece of decorative cloth that bore the crest of the Angevins had somehow caught fire, and the breeze raged it into a small bonfire. The crowd around the burning banner divided into two sides, one that was trying desperately to snuff the flames while the other adapted it into the festivities. Two men sang in a strange language, while a small group danced around the flames.

"What tongue is that?" asked Emma. Their lovely voices, even amidst all the grand turmoil around them, galvanized her toward merriment.

"Hebrew," Theresa answered. "They're Jews."

The Jews clapped along with the song, eventually rousing themselves into a sort of infectious frenzy. They dressed funny, Emma thought, and the men had long beards that hung to their chests. She had an overwhelming desire to join them. She glanced back to see if Madame Beatrice was immune even to jubilees such as this; the madame looked dreadfully afraid. Holding her hand over her heart and using a handkerchief to cover her mouth, her eyes reflected the flames of the pyre.

"Madame, are ye okay?" asked Emma.

"Belt it," said Madame B distantly. "I'm of no concern to you."

Emma looked at Theresa, who appeared content to let the madame suffer, but something inside her couldn't ignore this. Emma's mother had a similar fear of fire.

"Why don't ye sit down?" suggested Emma. "Maybe ye just need to 'ave some fun. Eat some food and have some wa—"

"You *stupid* girl!" Emma jumped at the ferocity in the madame's voice. The fire in Beatrice's eyes redirected at her. "Games and fun and all this bile nonsense will fix nothing. Nothing! You can prance around and lift your skirt and tempt yourself with sin all you like, but don't push your debauchery onto me. Your youth and beauty will wilt away just like everything else."

Emma stood back aghast. Theresa, bless her heart, placed her hand on Emma's shoulder for support against their madame's diatribe. Madame Beatrice blinked as if rising from a stupor, and the incandescent darkness seemed to leave her eyes. She gazed around as if confused. The madame took a breath. Emma had, beyond all reasoning, expected her to apologize, but instead she only said, "I must go. Finish shopping. Be back at the castle by nightfall."

Madame Beatrice fled into the stream of the crowd without looking back. Theresa patted Emma on the shoulder.

"Don't take it personally," she said. "That bitch hates anyone who enjoys living. Whatever soul she had, left her long ago. Go have fun. But be sure to be back in time. God be with you."

Theresa turned away and disappeared into the street. Emma's mind was scrambled; her thoughts were a dizzying array of confusion and anger. In her hand she held a few shillings meant for fresh eggs and other produce from the livestock outside the city walls. She was told to get some exotic vegetables, the kinds of food and sundries only available during large harvests such as this, when traveling merchants from all corners of the kingdom are drawn to one area. Emma pushed through the crowd toward the eastern gate. She did the calculations in her head.

Yes, it should work. And if I'm a little later, Madame Bitch will just have to take it.

Emma laughed. She didn't curse very often, but doing so felt right in this moment. She skipped down the street, her head full of profanities she could spit at the head handmaiden.

Let's finally have some fun!

She overflowed with ecstasy. Tom wrapped his arms around her, tucked up right underneath her breasts, as they galloped atop Noblefire—a steed that Tom "borrowed" from the king's army. They rode through Oxfordshire, letting the land pass by them in a vibrant haze. They flew through a lively meadow, and Noblefire trampled a great path in the tall, shimmering pasture; grasshoppers and other insects leaped away from the horse's thundering hooves. The rush of sultry air felt wonderful on her face. Noblefire breathed heavily from exertion, widening Emma's legs as its belly expanded with air. Her butt bounced up and down with the rhythm of the gallop, yet she harbored no fear, for Tom's firm and vascular arms kept her pinned securely on the saddle.

Emma laughed. For the length of her mission thus far, her mind had been a revolving tide of dark thoughts. She imagined the disappointment in her mother's eyes when she woke up, yet again, daughterless. Once the intensity of her anger toward the empress wore off, Emma's doubts doubled, and she felt terribly isolated and small.

Was she actually capable of being a spy for the king? Could she really avoid detection from one of the most powerful women in the world?

And what she had done to Isabella . . .

But Tom helped. Whenever she was with him, the dark thoughts drifted away, until they were only vaguely perceptible on the outer limits of her psyche. Everything was changing so rapidly. The world. The kings. The queens. Her emotions. Her body. Every day she discovered something new about life and about herself. It was scary, but also liberating.

Emma closed her eyes to it all and let the thrill wash over her. In this present moment, she was as beautiful and free as any of the many princesses she adored. Madame B was a fool to forget how to live. *This* was why God created life. Emma, so completely overwhelmed with this sudden stoking of her spirit, leaned over and kissed the inside of Tom's forearm.

That was all it took.

The next thing she knew, she was on her back with Tom mounting her. They created their own world within the blades of grass, blocking out the surrounding kingdom with a green curtain wall. Their kisses were impassioned, unrelenting, and slightly suffocating.

Okay, maybe largely so, thought Emma as she gasped for air. She'd never kissed like this before. The urge to part his lips and taste him was more important to her than her desire to breathe. Doubt, as it had many times in the last few weeks, threatened to ruin her time.

Am I doing this right? Does it feel good to him? Should I—

His tongue flicked against hers. It was so sudden and unexpected that it made her push away. Tom pressed on though, undaunted and unashamed.

"Relax," said Tom through a bright smile. It continued on, each new thing making Emma more self-conscious, more uncomfortable than before. The final straw was when he grasped her breasts. It jolted her body. Viscerally. Violently. She had barely acclimated to having breasts herself, and she did not know they could be *this* sensitive. She yelped.

"That hurt," she said, scrambling up and brushing the dirt off her dress. She felt like she had dodged a terrible mistake. It was as if she could feel the Lord's penetrating and disappointed gaze. Tom, looking annoyed and embarrassed, clicked his tongue so Noblefire would cross to them from where he grazed. "I'm sorry," said Emma softly.

"Don't fret," said Tom. "God clearly hasn't made you a woman yet."

They rode back to Oxford as the sun bolted toward the western horizon. They stopped near the Oxford mill and dismounted next to the water wheel. She and Tom sat down along the edge of Castle Mill Stream; the giant wheel churned endlessly in the restive waters, foaming the surface, the wood creaking and straining almost pleasantly. Eventide descended on the festivities of the day, and way up on its high hill, the castle's many windows glimmered with bright-orange warmth like a beacon of human strength above the chaos of the surrounding kingdom.

Within the quietness that the evening hours demanded, Emma asked, "What did it feel like to kill someone?"

"It felt good," said Tom. He tore a length of cured meat in half and handed it to her. She chewed on it while considering her next words.

"I killed someone. I didn't mean to. I should 'ave said somethin', but I was so scared." Her eyes burned red; tears ran hot down her cheeks. "It didn't feel good to me."

Tom watched her teardrops splash on the ground. He patted her on the knee. "You'll survive," he said. "Next time though, make sure ye learn something, huh? They aren't gonna be happy that you have no news."

"I'm sorry. I'm trying, Tom. But oft does the empress leave, and when she's here, she holds council behind closed doors. That damn madame won't let me near her. I fear she suspects me."

"Then kill her too."

Emma sneered, for at first, she believed it to be a poorly timed joke. Tom glared at her though, serious and unflinching. "Do what ye must, Emma. This is the second time I've come, and you've given me nothing worth our effort. This isn't a game. Ye ain't stealin' bread nor stalkin' some baron's fourth cousin. Remember our dream? This is how you become a princess. *This.* How do ye think nobles become so? They backstab, steal, murder. 'Tis all the same. You 'ave already done it once.

"So get into those closed councils. Get close. For the king's army approaches, and he would give a king's ransom for any information on how to avoid a siege. Ye hark? It could be mine. Do it for me. For *us*. I'm putting my honor on the line for ye. Please, Emma."

"Okay," she said shamefully. "I'll try harder."

Her gaze turned to the river. The many stars of the heavens reflected and sparkled on its surface. She asked him, "Do ye ever wonder what stars are?"

"They're stars," he said plainly. "Why care about them any more than that?"

From there, Tom updated Emma on her mother and Alice; the two lived in a small village named Sutton Courtenay, and it made her feel better knowing they weren't still on the roads where bandits, wild animals, or worse could get them. She then said goodbye to Tom and left for the main gates. After such a turbulent day, she was looking forward to the protection of the castle and getting some sleep.

The darkness of the outer city descended upon her, and only the large huddled shapes of men remained outside. Emma wrapped her brown cloak tighter around her and hurried onward. More than a few of those men leered at her from within dark doorways.

"Boo!"

Emma leaped into the air as two hands touched her. She spun and slapped down, clobbering Crispin in the face. The boy moaned and massaged his face.

"Ow! What was that for?" Crispin's face turned pink from the slap.

"Are ye daft?!" Emma asked, exasperated. Her heart was halfway up her throat. "Oft do ye scare folk?"

"Sorry," he said. "I didn't mean to scare ye."

"Didn't mean? Didn't mean?! Ye screamed *boo* and touched me." Emma nearly slapped him again. "What are ye doin' out here?"

"Enjoyin' the food. All kinds of delights to be tasted during feasts."

"Your mother lets ye roam about after dark?"

"I like lookin' at the stars, twinklin' and whatnot. What do ye think they are?"

Emma paused. She glanced the boy over while he scratched his chubby cheeks. Feeling annoyed and angry at him yet again, she stuck up her nose and said, "They're stars. Why care about 'em any more than that?"

Crispin shrugged. "Just curious. Me thinks they're angels. Mama says we live in God-forsaken times, but I think they're proof He's still here. What are *you* doin' out here after dark?"

Emma considered lying, but she was already tired of Crispin's company and thought the truth might make him leave. Or at least, a half-truth would. "I was bein' courted by a knight."

"Ye weren't being courted," he said.

"Was too," said Emma incredulously.

"Was not."

"Was too!"

"Was not!"

"How would ye know?!"

"Because," said Crispin, seeming very upset suddenly, "ye would seem happy if ye were being courted. But ye look sad, not happy."

"You're so annoying," said Emma. Feeling like a little girl, she turned around to storm away.

Four men surrounded her—strong peasant-farmer types.

Emma stepped back. They advanced on her. Without realizing it, she'd pinned herself between a food stall and a house. The four strangers maneuvered in such a way as to make escape impossible. She could smell the booze coming from them.

"God's blessing, fair woman," said one of them. He held a dagger in his hand.

Crispin pushed Emma behind him, squaring up to the four men as best he could. He was trying to become a shield, but unfortunately, he was a few inches shorter than her, so the men still had direct eyesight of Emma.

"Scram, boy."

Emma grabbed Crispin's arm, begging him to stay through her grasp. "We were about to leave," said Crispin, trying to will some command into his boy voice.

"Where to?" asked one of the other men.

"The castle," said Emma quickly. "We live in the castle."

One man scoffed at this. Another one of them spat on the ground. They all moved closer. Crispin tensed. "We do," he said. "She works for the empress. Wouldn't want to mess with her, would ye?"

"Think we care about what some foreign whore thinks?"

"We mean no trouble—"

"Never had royalty cunt before," said the third man. "Wonder what that feels like?"

Emma's body went stiff. She couldn't breathe. Crispin pushed her farther back and said, "Sir, I don't know what you're talkin' about, but I 'ave no cunt, and she's not royal, so . . ."

"Belt it, ye fatass pig. Quell your voice lest we fuck your ripe bum too."

"Hey! There you are!"

The men spun around. The one with a dagger hid it behind his back. Emma nearly cried in relief. Madame Beatrice sprinted down the street, her filthy work dress bouncing off her as she trucked past the peasants.

"Out of my way! *You*." She pointed at Emma. "You were supposed to be back by nightfall! And where is—? Where are the eggs and food you were to buy?"

"We're watching over them," said the first man. Madame B turned to face them. "We can help her get the food and bring her back—"

"You'll do nothin' of the sort," said the madam. "Get your foulness away from here before I report you to the earl and sheriff myself." When the men hesitated, she took a step forward and said, "BEGONE! I am in no mood to be tested by dickless swine! Go!"

The men vanished in a huff. Once they were out of sight, Emma collapsed onto Madame Beatrice, clinging to the madame's dress and burying her crying face into the cloth. To her surprise, the madame let her cry for a few seconds before she finally pushed her away.

"This is why I told you to return by sundown," said the madame. "Stupid girls die. Where are the coins I gave you?" Emma handed her the shillings. Madame Beatrice swiped them away and said, "Since you are incapable of even buying food, you are to remain inside the castle. Am I understood? Good. And *you*," she said to Crispin. "Don't think I won't tell your mother."

Crispin bowed his head. Madame Beatrice pivoted on her foot and motioned for them to follow. Emma hurried behind. She never knew she'd be so happy to see that terribly mean woman. Crispin walked alongside her. Emma reached out and tugged on the boy's arm.

"Thank you," mouthed Emma silently.

Crispin smiled. He reached out and took her hand in his. She let him. It felt good to be tethered to the earth through him. For the first time, Emma began to wonder if Tom wasn't the only one who could make her dark thoughts vanish.

Crispin, meanwhile, was simply glad that Emma didn't realize he'd pissed his trousers.

CHAPTER XXIV
GILBERT & WILLIAM

T HE WORST WAS THE waiting. William knew Eadric had survived the ambush, and it was only a matter of time before the Hellhound of Rutland came to kill him.

Days passed. He heard a rumor that the Hellhound was recovering from his injuries, that he was saved by priests and their angels, and the Lord had taken his side.

A fortnight passed. William dreaded every moment. Would this be the hour he came for him? Would this be the day his life ended?

To fill the endless void of time, he did nothing but think and dream. He dreamed of being with Gilbert and Beatriz and Hawk and Bart, lying with them beside the drizzling creeks of Normandy, and those dreams often mutated to salivating fantasies of banquets and feasts. During his dreadful waking hours, he'd imagine what he'd say to his brother if he ever saw him again, or what he'd plead to the Hellhound if he gave him a chance to speak.

After recovering from the siege of Wareham, the war camp eventually moved; a length of fabric was thrown over William's cell as the oxen pulled his prisoner cart. More rumors reached the ears of Alfwin the gaoler, and those eventually poured from his mouth within William's vicinity. Rumors that the Hellhound killed his own men. Rumors that he went mad with hate.

Was Duke Richard really that terrible? Was what his father did really worth all this carnage? William believed it was true. It had to be. No sane man would go to the lengths Eadric did for a false story.

Eventually, as the weeks turned into a month, each day passing on drearily to the next, equally hot, equally humid, William began to hope that today would be the day. He wanted to get it over with. He wished the Hellhound would finally come for him and set his mind at peace.

Nearly a week had passed since Gilbert and his friends escaped Wareham with a large group of refugees—around two hundred of them in total. Having banded together under the indomitable leadership of Father Tobias, they set their eyes on the safety of the sturdy walls of Bristol along the western coast, a city safely under the command of Empress Maud and her half-brother. The predominant sentiment for the distraught families who'd lost their homes in the fires of Stephen's army remained the same: head northwest, as far away from the disputed southern shires as possible.

"Now what?" asked Hawk.

"We find Will," said Gilbert miserably as the sky darkened above them. It had been a foreboding day, overcast from dawn till dusk, punctuated by occasional bouts of brief-passing rain. He kicked a rock, while the refugees formed a camp along the edge of an ancient wood.

"We should find shelter first," said Bartholomew. He glanced back worryingly at his wife, who had been praying unceasingly since they had arrived in England.

"You and Beatriz find a dry tree we can sleep under," said Gilbert. "Maybe now enough time has passed that me and Hawk can talk to Father Tobias, see if he knows anything about Stephen's army or the Hellhound."

Bartholomew nodded and led his wife away. Thunder rumbled distantly. Gilbert had a sinking feeling that he and the refugees were in for a long night. They had all set out in the morning hoping to reach Bristol by nightfall, but that had turned out to be far too ambitious. The migration turned grueling with the road dissolving to mud; the treacherous summer rain caused joint pain in the injured and elderly alike.

"Do you think Beatriz will be okay?" asked Hawk, pulling his floppy, bright-red Phrygian hat tighter around his temples as the sky began to drizzle on them again.

"She's tougher than the rest of us," said Gilbert. "I'm more concerned for Bart."

"Aye. Their marriage is odd, ain't it?"

Gilbert nodded. Their whole dynamic *was* strange. They rarely touched one another, acting as if they were newly courting and not as if they'd been friends for years; perhaps even stranger, at least as far as Gilbert and Hawk had noticed, they'd yet to have sex while on their journey. Where was the love? The passion?

"Maybe they don't want us to feel uncomfortable?"

"She always used to have these bouts," Hawk said with a smile, remembering all the adventures of their youth. "You know how she is. She focuses on one thing and naught else. Maybe that's what religion is to her right now."

"You think she'll give up on that too then?"

Hawk thought for a moment. "No. We're all good Christians—well, the good-ish kind that the Lord may let in with some proper begging—but she seems almost nun-like."

"I hope for Bart's sake that she doesn't treat him like a nun would."

They reached Father Tobias farther down along the tree line. Between the darkness of the trees, small smoldering flames sprouted up like blinking eyes; these families, both whole and fractured, clung desperately to these fires, their emotionally battered minds imprisoned somewhere harrowing between gratefulness and lamentation. The lucky ones escaped with heirlooms or cutlery to sell, but most fled with nothing but their tunics and their stolen lives. One family somehow escaped with their cow . . . Gilbert wondered how they managed that.

"Oi! There be my new friends! Come hither. Come hither!" Hann waved Gilbert and Hawk over to where he and his sons were aiding the priest.

Dressed in a fresh habit and no longer covered in blood and soot, Father Tobias appeared much more pious. The whole first night after the sacking, the priest could be heard muttering prayer after prayer, begging the Lord to forgive him for his sin of touching blood—an act forbidden for the clergy.

Hann slapped his sons on the back of their heads. They both seemed to be in their mid-teens, making them only a few winters younger than Gilbert and his company. "Edwin, Cedric," said Hann, "say hello to our new friends."

"Hello," they both said. "May God bless ye."

"We must speak with Father Tobias," said Gilbert.

"He's givin' spiritual guidance to the wounded," said Hann. "Though he owes ye both a great debt, so I will make him listen."

"Thank you, but we can wait if he's busy."

"Nay, nay. Ye helped us, we help you. Come on! Your ol' friend Hann has your backs."

Father Tobias was leaning over a woman with a festering wound on her shoulder when Hann stood over the poor woman to get the priest's attention.

"Father Tobias! My friends here need your help."

"I'm busy, Hann," said the priest, unable to keep the annoyance from his voice. Hann continued on as if he hadn't heard an ounce of resistance.

"They search far an' wide for someone. Please. They helped ye, yes? You help them in return."

"And why are *you* helping them?" said the priest, sounding almost accusatory.

Something like a smile crept upon Hann's face. "What? Lord Christ would want all Christians to help their fellow man. Would He not, Father?"

"I'm sorry about what happened to your wife, Hann. May God watch over her soul. But while Paradise may offer complete absolution and deliverance, the world of man does not. No sin goes unpunished here."

"No," Hann said sourly, "they do not. So why don't you be a righteous little priest and help these poor men, unlike what you did for mine."

Gilbert and Hawk glanced at one another. They were mightily uncomfortable. Never in his life had Gilbert heard a peasant talk to a man of God in such a manner. Father Tobias sighed and turned to them. "How can I help you, sons?"

"We don't wish to disturb you—" Gilbert began.

"You already have. Now, prithee hurry and tell."

Both Gilbert and Hawk shied away from Father Tobias's curt remark. Hann stood beside them, himself thoroughly unaffected by the stern words. Father Tobias seemed to realize the anger in his voice. He straightened his habit, took a deep breath, and said, "I'm sorry. I pray God gives me more strength and patience in the future. I've been overwhelmed with the task He's put before me. I'm a shepherd of men, not a leader. May you pardon my irritability."

"All is forgiven, Father," said Hawk, giving him a light pat on the shoulder.

"If that were only so," Hann cut in. "I'm sure God wouldn't want us to be patient in times such as these, would He? Hurry it up, Father, we have not all day."

Hawk gave him a sideways glare. A lifetime of friendship had taught Gilbert what that look was. Disgust. He decided to ease the tension and said, "We need your help to find my brother. He was taken hostage by the king's war constable, one they call the Hellhound of Rutland."

"I've heard of this beast," said Father Tobias. "Though I'm but a simple priest, son. I'm sorry. I know not where he is."

"We were hoping ye might point us in the right direction. You know the region. Maybe you know where their encampment could be?"

Father Tobias shook his head. "I've never desired to keep up with the movements of Maud and Stephen." The priest formed his hands into fists before hastily regaining his composure. He sighed. "I regret not having taken a greater interest in politics. I used to believe that too many of my brothers had soiled their hands with the filth of it. Now I see I was foolish to ignore it entirely."

The priest's hands shook, his mind envisioning the death and torment that he saw in Wareham. Hawk reached out. He held Father Tobias's hands until the man stopped shaking.

"I wish I could do more," he said. "But I may know some who could help."

"Whatever you can do, Father," said Gilbert gently.

"Yes, Father, out with it!" Hann slapped the priest on the back. Father Tobias stumbled from the man's blunt strength. Gilbert stuffed down his annoyance at Hann.

Is he trying to replicate Hawk? It hadn't slipped his notice that his slap on the back was eerily similar to how Hawk had tapped the priest on the shoulder. Gilbert glanced over at his childhood friend, and Hawk appeared to have made a similar connection.

"You see them over there?" Father Tobias pointed toward the far edge of the tree line. Despite the dim light and drizzling rain, a group of cloaked figures scurried around a fire. "Those are friars of Carmel. They've traveled all about the kingdom, tending to soldiers as well as the refugees they conjure. If anyone would know the whereabouts of Stephen's bivouacs, t'would be them."

"Wonderful," Gilbert said. "Thank you for your help, Father."

"God be with the lot of you," said Father Tobias, giving a discerning glance at Hann.

It wasn't until they got closer to the Carmelite friars that Gilbert could discern their conspicuous white habits. The Carmelites were a nascent mendicant order in this corner of the world; it was said that during the recent Crusades, the Carmelites fled the holy Kingdom of Jerusalem and migrated to France to escape the wrath of the Muslims. Most nobles and peasants weren't aware there even *was* a new order of Catholic hermits in the region, as the pope had yet to acknowledge them. Gilbert only knew of them because the same order of friars had visited Geoffrey's army in the early days of his enrollment. Like most mendicant orders, the friars of Carmel lived an eremitic lifestyle; they had no earthly possessions and only visited the most deprived paupers, blessing those affected by war and human greed. They survived on the pure, benevolent graces of the rich, who'd gift them alms for "fixing" the impoverished peasants in their cities and towns.

Gilbert also knew, much as Father Tobias did, that they stopped by army encampments regularly when out in their travels. It was as good a place as any to give prayer and receive alms.

"Pardon me," began Gilbert as they approached the friars, "and may God forgive us for our intrusion so late into the day."

"Peace, my son," said one friar. He was a tall fellow with extremely pale skin. "We're here at the behest of Jesus Christ and his blessed Virgin Mother to tend to all the unfortunate of the world. What is it you require of us?"

"We—"

"We seek the nearby encampment of King Stephen," Hann said, interrupting Gilbert and pushing Hawk back.

The tall friar frowned. "I could tell you where it is. But I must ask, why on God's heavenly earth would you want to go there? Weren't you just attacked by their forces?"

"We were, but—" Hann yelped as Hawk pulled him away and covered his mouth in one swift movement.

Gilbert spoke up before he decided to interrupt them again. "Someone very dear to us is in that army. We believe he had nothin' to do with their assault. We wish only to find him."

"I can tell you where they're camped," began the friar, "but I'm afraid you won't be able to enter. They're on an active campaign. Only the clergy or messengers with military information are allowed entry."

Gilbert knew the man was right. They would have trouble even entering the camp, let alone discovering if William was even there.

And if William isn't there?

Gilbert shuddered. The degree to which this task daunted him became magnified in that moment. He suddenly realized how difficult it might be to find his brother in the war camp of a king. Better not to think of it at all.

"Please," begged Gilbert. "We mean no trouble. I want only my kid brother."

The friar looked between him and his companions with a sad expression. "Before they assaulted Wareham, the army had settled but a half-league southeast of the city. I imagine they'd be posted there for a while yet. They'll wish to maintain the port in case Empress Maud tries to retake it."

"Thank you," said Hawk, keeping his hand firmly over Hann's mouth. Gilbert thanked the friar as well. The three of them returned to Bartholomew and Beatriz. The pair had finished arranging their sleeping spot under a high-canopied oak tree.

"How'd it go?" asked Bartholomew.

"Some Carmelite friars told us that the king's army was staying in a camp southeast of the city," said Hawk.

"And ye think we can find Will there?" asked Beatriz, finally taking a break from her prayers.

"Probably not," Gilbert said. "But we know the Hellhound is in his army. The best chance we have of finding someone who knows that big bastard would be in Stephen's camp. It's a lead."

"Issue is gettin' in," said Hann. The group faced the outsider, who seemed oddly content in ignoring his teenage sons. Hann continued onward, undaunted by their stares. "That's an active encampment. They won't let any strays in."

Gilbert sighed. Annoyed and exhausted, he turned to the peasant and put his hands up gently to ease the remarks he was about to make. "Hann, we appreciate your help in getting us out of the city. We really do. But we don't need your help anymore."

"Sure ye do."

"No," Hawk stated. "We sure as Hell do not."

"Don't know about that. Seems to me you're pretty stuck at where you're at, it does."

"Thank ye for everything," said Gilbert. "But this is a private affair. Please, under God's gracious name, respect that."

Hann stood there for a second, not saying anything, and Gilbert became worried that he might do something unexpected. He reluctantly bowed his head and said, "T'was my pleasure. God bless ye all. God blessed!"

They all smiled politely and watched the strange man saunter away. Beatriz, finding strength once again to talk, asked Gilbert, "How do ye plan on gettin' in?"

Gilbert could tell she was trying to get back in control. He appreciated that about her, how she actively fought against the woman she was a mere year ago.

"I 'ave an idea," he said. It was a stupid, terrible idea . . . but then again, all their best scams had the same idiotic origin.

"I don't like that look," said Bartholomew; the slight curve at the edge of his lips betrayed how he really felt.

Looking into the eyes of Bart, Beatriz, and Hawk just then, Gilbert realized they'd all been secretly awaiting a moment like this. The truth was both quite sad and quite beautiful. They *did* miss their old shenanigans; they *did* miss the people they used to be before the war.

Gilbert had to clear his throat as emotion prodded at him from within. "The friar said that only military messengers or clergy can get in. We can't pretend to be in Stephen's army, but—"

"But we can feign holiness," Hawk said with a grin.

"Oh no," Beatriz moaned.

"We don't need to do anythin' that'll send us to Hell," Gilbert reassured her. "But if we steal a few habits and cowls . . ."

"I can't do that," she said. "I told ye I was religious now."

"That's why it'll just be me and Hawk goin'. We sneak into the friars' camp early in the morn, borrow a bit of their clothing, and then sneak into Stephen's encampment."

"I hate this idea."

"'Tis the best plan I got."

"Then let's get to bed!" Hawk said excitedly. "Looks like our thieving days have yet to fade into memory."

A dank, gloomy mist settled beneath the groaning boughs of that tenebrous forest, with only the faint sound of a distant quacking duck being heard. The moon had already hidden itself beneath the horizon, leaving the earth exposed to the unrelenting watch of the sparkling firmament—God's own keen eyes judging the sins of man.

Gilbert and Hawk wound their way through the trees, eventually reaching where the Carmelite friars had been camped earlier that night.

"Fuck me."

The friars were gone. Anxious and worried, they investigated the ground, but the inky blackness of night made it nigh on impossible to spot anything amiss or suggestive of the holy order's whereabouts.

"They've vanished. As has the priest."

Gilbert and Hawk spun around to see the bastard himself, Hann, standing patronizingly tall and proud by one of the slender trees. He had a hunting dagger in his hand. It glistened in the moonlight. He slid it into a scabbard. Gilbert sighed. He knew where this was going.

"Did you see where they were heading?" Gilbert asked.

Hann nodded his head. "But first, I believe, some people owe me an apology."

CHAPTER XXV
EMMA

"MY LOVE, I FEAR the winds of war blow your way. My knight tells me Oxford is circled on the king's map. We've burnt much of her wretchedness away, re-seizing village after village. Rest assured, King Stephen *will* win the war. But he needs your aid."

Emma's heart fluttered in her chest. It was the earliest hours of dawn, when the first pale light shimmered ever so slightly above the distant eastern hills. She and Tom were alone in the dilapidated shack they'd first met Mildritha and Crispin in.

"What can I do to help?" Emma asked.

"There is more I must tell ye," said Tom with a frown, "something most dreadful. Your mother has taken ill. Alice and I do our best to care for her, but we both have duties that keep us away from easing your mother's aches. Even worse, Alice has now caught the same illness. But do not fret, love, for I've found a way to save them . . . forgive me, my star, for I betrayed ye."

Emma wiped away stinging tears. "How can that be so?"

"I was granted an audience with the king's council, and to them I told of your existence. My darling love, a spy for us deep in Maud's trust. I told them ye could help seize the castle, but Stephen wants proof. In confidence, they told me that the enemy had smuggled a letter from across the strait, written by the empress's half-brother. It's imperative that you steal this, Emma. It should've arrived by now. Take it. Hide it under here." Tom lifted one edge of a fallen stone, revealing there to be a small gap beneath. "Another spy will transport it back. Do this, and we will have the favor of a king. A *king*. Imagine what that could do, Emma.

Your mother and Alice cannot receive the care they need without proper aid. Stephen can provide that for us *if* we prove our usefulness. This is our chance, our future. We can save your mother's life. *You* can save her."

Emma hugged Tom. Tears streaked down her face as she imagined her mother lying sickly and pale, the life draining from her eyes. The world darkened around her. Emma forced herself to remember the burning fires of Marlborough, the corpses turning to coals.

I hate Empress Maud. I hate her. I hate . . .

Her heart hurt, for the words lost weight in her mind. That was the most frustrating part. Despite all the pain and suffering they went through, she could not build up the hatred in her soul. It angered her. She could not despise the empress no matter how utterly hard she tried.

All she could find in her heart was sadness. She yearned for the warm summers of her youth, those spent chasing other kids and basking in sunlight. Where had that little girl gone? How far had she fallen that she wanted, now more than anything in the world, to be another person who hated the world?

The sun dipped westward. Oxford's curtain wall spread long shadows over the inner bailey. Crispin guided Emma past many clergy and noblemen who were beckoned to the castle. Empress Maud desperately wanted to find an edge in the war, as things were turning sour for her; King Stephen and William of Ypres were capturing all the surrounding shires, submitting castle after castle, slowly constricting around Oxford like some gigantic invisible hand readying to strangle them all.

Emma shook her head. She couldn't think of that now. Only her mother. Only Alice. She'd abandoned both of them to pursue this dream of a better life. *Or,* she thought less romantically, *for revenge against the madwoman who torched our home.*

"This way," said Crispin. He waved her down to where the battlements met the southeast tower. She could hear the moat splashing against the shore on the other side of the wall. Even in the middle of summer, those gushing currents would be frigidly cold. "There, do you see?"

She looked. A rat scurried across the ground, it and three others. They scampered away and disappeared into a small hole burrowed into the castle's tower.

"Does anyone else know they're here?" asked Emma.

"No, they'd kill them if they found 'em. They aren't hurtin' no one, and they haven't tried to eat our food yet, so . . ." He shrugged.

"Perfect. Thank ye, Crispin."

"Always." The boy stood behind her awkwardly. "And what do ye want with them?"

"You should leave now."

"Are ye goin' to hurt them?"

"Only two."

Crispin's color drained from his face. But despite his clear agitation, he asked, "Do you need help?"

That surprised her. She blushed in embarrassment. Emma had been too mean to him. Sometimes she forgot he wasn't an innocent boy; he *was* her age. He lived through this life as she did, through war and famine, through grief and pain.

"Would ye help me?"

"Like I said, *always*."

Emma became very grateful to have found a friend like him. She placed her hand on his arm, and he smiled. It disappeared entirely when she asked, "Did you bring the knives?"

Empress Maud covered her nose with a handkerchief. Madame B and Theresa's eyes watered from the stench. Emma stood by silently, trying to cover a self-satisfied smirk.

"Sheriff d'Oilli, Master de Vere, I want this room searched at once. Find the source of this hideous odor," said Empress Maud. She turned to Duke Richard, who stood in the doorframe afraid to enter the smelly chamber any further. "My duke, tell the council we will reconvene inside the hunting lodge."

"Is that where you wish to stay tonight?" asked Aubrey de Vere, steward of Oxfordshire.

"Would you ask me to take bed inside a pile of manure?"

"I'll have the chamber there readied at once," he said, practically sprinting away.

Emma was immensely pleased with how this was going. Earlier in the day, when the bedchamber was clear of any eyes, Emma hid the disemboweled rats deep within the packed feathers and straw inside Empress Maud's mattress. She had further spread the vermin's offal on multiple surfaces around the room, layered so thinly that the blood would blend into the dark wood finishing. The bedchamber, as Emma had hoped, stank something terrible.

"What would you like me to do, my queen?" asked Madame B.

"Grab my clothing only. Bring Lady Theresa and help ready my room at the lodge."

"What about her?" Madame Beatrice nodded at Emma. For the first time since the empress's arrival all those months ago, she looked Emma in the eyes and took her in.

"Emma is your name, correct?"

Emma bowed. "Yes, my empress."

"Help clear the room of my belongings. You'll stay here in the castle, so if I need something we forget, you can run it to us during the night."

"As you wish, my empress."

Empress Maud turned around and left the chamber with Duke Richard. Madame B, in an act unbecoming of a lady like her, gagged. She waved her hand in front of her nose. "Right," she said nasally. "Let's gather her things, quick-like."

It wasn't until a few hours into the moonless night later that evening that Emma arose from her sheepskin cot and slipped noiselessly out of the handmaiden servant chamber in only trousers and a dark tunic. Tiptoeing down the corridor and exiting through the door at the far end, she listened to the sound of snoring castle guards. The bedchambers were on the first floor of the guardhouse, which sat at the bottom of the motte inside the bailey. She descended the wooden stairs to the ground floor and rushed up the hill toward the keep.

As she hoped, Empress Maud brought many of the housecarls and visiting aristocrats with her to Beaumont Palace—her father's impressive hunting lodge on the northern outskirts of Oxford. There wasn't a single soul wandering the bailey except for the odd watchman patrolling atop the battlements, whom she could spot a mile away on account of the torches they carried. But she, both small and limber and with hair as black as pitch, could hide in the darkest shadows of night with no one noticing.

"Emma?"

Oh, God damn—

She spun on her heels. Crispin stood at the wooden door leading to the cellar below the keep. He held a small drum of alcohol in his arms, the candlelight of the cellar spilling out from below him like some ethereal halo.

"What are ye doin'?" she asked, annoyed.

"Duke Richard has been likin' to have ale brought to him nightly," said the boy. "Says he can't sleep without it. Has nightmares or somethin' like that."

"Well, carry on then," she said hastily in a hoarse whisper.

"What are *ye* doin'?"

"Crispin, why can't ye just stay out of my business? Huh? Do you enjoy following me or something?"

"I don't—"

"Don't think I don't notice you," she said. The fear she had been suppressing of thieving Earl Robert's letter was, unfortunately, spilling out of her in an instant. The intensity of it all made her tongue turn to venom. "I see you following me. I'm a grown woman. There are things I must do that ye have no place in. Now, if you'd please, get as far away from me as possible and stop asking me *stupid* questions."

"I'm . . . I'm sorry," he said, his face turning red as a tomato.

Emma couldn't stand looking at the damage she'd done any longer, so she turned and ran alongside the keep. She navigated to the wall the masons and carpenters were renovating, where a gigantic pile of stone awaited to replace the wooden keep. Emma scanned the scaffolding that hugged the steep side of the castle until she spotted the ladder the workers had left behind.

She climbed, careful not to slip and hoping her footing wouldn't fail her like it did in Marlborough. When she reached the top of the scaffolding, she lifted the ladder and placed it along the wall. She heard the whistling of the watchman first. The guard passed not more than thirty feet away. Luckily for her, soldiers who stood atop battlements tended to watch for movement *outside* the ramparts and not within. Once he passed, she began to climb.

Now for the terrible part.

About fifteen feet above her, a small alcove jutted out from the side of the keep. It was a unique feature that only a few castles had, and one that gave Emma a chance to sneak into the keep right next to the empress's bedchamber. It had a hole at the bottom.

What had Madame Beatrice called it again? A *garderobe*? Such a foreign, fancy-sounding name for something that was quite crude—an overhanging latrine.

Emma steeled herself; she had to be honest about what she was doing. She was going to climb into a *fucking toilet*. There were streaks along the walls of the keep, places where the wood would be permanently stained white and brown from . . . from . . .

Emma held back her vomit. The *garderobe* had been hastily built a year back to allow the aristocrats who visited Empress Maud a private place to relieve themselves without leaving the protection of the castle. It had been closed down for the past few weeks, however, as the masons were working directly below it to reinforce the castle.

That didn't mean it didn't stink.

Emma wafted away the smell and put on the gloves she'd stolen from the worksite earlier. Little did she know, the worst part was yet to come. Her fingers slipped on something as she gripped the opening above her. A liquid grime dripped out of the hole. This time, she couldn't keep it in. Emma vomited over the side of the ladder, adding to the foulness along the wall. She hardened herself.

Think of Mama. Think of Alice. You must steal it, Emma. Ye must.

She hoisted herself up. It made a suction noise as bits of goo sloshed between her fingers. When she stuck her head and torso into the toilet, the smell overtook her. Fighting with all the strength she could muster, she held back the vomit and pulled herself through the *garderobe*. She closed the curtain that covered the hanging latrine as she entered the keep's corridor. She ignored the putridity of her own stench. When she was certain no one was around, she sped over to Empress Maud's bedchamber and snuck inside, closing the bronze-reinforced door behind her.

The chamber was dark and musky, and the stench . . . actually, the stench wasn't that bad anymore. *Yeah*, thought Emma dourly, *somethin' is very wrong with my nose*.

The fire at the hearth was down to a smolder; the slight orange glow would be barely perceptible if not for the blackness that permeated everywhere else. Emma navigated to the beeswax candle atop the dresser and lit it with the hearth fire. Under its flickering light, she searched the first few traveling chests.

None contained the letter.

Empress Maud would be a right fool if she left an important letter from her brother unattended after what happened last time. Anticipating that, what Emma was really after were clues. The empress had brought most of her top advisors with her to the lodge, and thus she'd left the castle attended by only a skeleton crew of peasant-workers and militiamen. All of whom, in Maud's probable estimation, couldn't read.

And that was Emma's greatest secret. No one expected a lowborn peasant *girl* of all people to read. A typical spy, even if sent to retrieve a letter, would become confused if it were hidden with many others. How could they possibly know which one it was?

Another wave of nauseating guilt came after her, while she thought of her mother and what her last words to her had been. What a stupid, selfish girl she was.

Eventually, Emma found a small receipt written on a piece of stained parchment. From what she could decipher from its text, it was a confirmation of a copy made by the library scribes. Emma winced. Of course! It made too much sense. An important document, like a letter sent by the leader of your army, would be too valuable to risk losing, regardless if it's stolen or destroyed. The empress would obviously like a copy transcribed word-for-word and kept somewhere secure, somewhere like the Oxford Castle library.

Emma groaned. That was going to be a problem.

Voices.

She jumped. They became more distinguishable: men. Emma panicked. She blew out the candle, submerged herself back into the pitch black of night, and dived under the bedframe. She pulled her legs under the bed right as the chamber door swung open. All Emma could see were their boots.

"Be quick about it," said one of them. He had a thin, reedy voice, which seemed hollow, as if he struggled to talk and breathe simultaneously. There was something in his voice that was familiar. One of Empress Maud's close confidants?

"I'm moving as fast as I can," said the other man with a deeper, more menacing tone. They closed the door behind them. Emma covered her mouth, scared to make the slightest sound.

"God, the smell is horrid," said Reedy Voice. "What a stroke of fortune."

"Let's hope it stays vacant a while yet," said Deep Voice.

"She keeps them in the chests."

"I know, I know."

"Check that one."

After a few seconds of shuffling through the chest, he stood up suddenly. "What is it?" asked Reedy Voice.

"Someone's been here."

"Impossible. I've kept watch on the stairs."

"You must have let someone slip by."

"How dare you. You're under *my* command. Now I tell thee, I have let no one by."

"Well, unless the empress-bitch has suddenly stopped caring about organizing her papers, she wasn't the last one in here."

The men stood still for a moment. Emma screamed internally. Her heart thundered in her chest, screeched in her ears.

"It must be *him*," said Reedy Voice. Dread pummeled outward from him, almost as if the Devil had entered the room at the uttering of *him*.

"My lord," said Deep Voice, "heed my words: he is not here."

"He hounds me, Braxton. He's no longer a man. I know he's spoken to Satan, schemed with the Deceiver. Do you know what they say of him on the battlefield?"

"Don't listen to peasant lies. I nearly killed him myself."

"They say his eyes glow red. Swords and pikes go right through him without spewing blood. They say he's a living corpse, and his only wish is to reach me. *Me!*"

"Reach us," said Braxton. "Which he will not."

"Stephen promised me!"

"Quiet, my lord. Prithee, peace. I am pledged to serve you."

"Then serve me, Sir Commander. How much more must I prove to that insolent boy for him to chain his dog?"

"He'll listen, my lord, if we help him capture the empress. Stay calm and focused."

"The Hellhound will kill me first."

"Not if we act quickly."

"I need more time then. Go to Bampton Parish, Sir Commander."

That froze Braxton. "Is that your wish, my lord? For me to die in battle? Fortified defenses did not keep him from slaughtering Hurst, nor two of my best men in Wareham. I fear he is unstoppable."

"In battle, maybe. But if the king were to imprison him . . ."

"Why would he do that? He's won countless battles for Stephen. Why would he betray one of his best warriors?"

"What if he were to learn the truth?"

The room went silent. "You'd have me tell him?"

"If it came to it."

"But, my lord—"

"Go to Bampton. He'll find you first, but you *must* buy me time. I'll do everything in my power to find that letter and give Stephen proof of my loyalty. But if that does not work, then our only chance is for you to tell him the truth."

"You're telling me to unleash chaos."

"Yes. With chaos comes opportunity. A hound is still a dog, no matter how well trained. Go at once. Stephen has multiple spies here and is pitting us against one another. He's a betting man, but only if the game is stacked in his favor. I intend to find this other spy and kill him. I won't let him reach me. God be damned."

"I won't let him reach you, my lord."

"You were always my favorite, Braxton. Your knighthood deserves more honor than I can bestow."

"What of your bastard son held hostage?"

"That boy has been a hostage his entire life. First from his whore mother, and now by the Hellhound. What do I care of him? His mother may finally convalesce in her extortion efforts now. I'll be happy to be rid of him."

"Richard—"

"Go. We have work to do."

Emma didn't take a breath until both men had left the chamber and closed the door behind them. She stared ahead, horrified and disgusted. Duke Richard was the other spy for King Stephen, and she was now in a race to find Earl Robert's letter.

CHAPTER XXVI
GILBERT & WILLIAM

WHERE THE FUCK WAS the Hellhound of Rutland?

William ticked. He was getting worse. It had been months since the assault on Wareham. Every sound was Eadric coming for him. Every guard was a masked phantom, waiting to lead William further astray. He knew now that the spirit had to be a devil, an agent of the Great Adversary. It doomed him. It led him to believe that his only way out was to kill his captor.

He'd got it all wrong. He must have. Lord Eadric was only doing what he believed to be right. Christ had saved him, after all. If a priest and his angels had blessed his damaged body, and if they'd bestowed upon him a full recovery, then those wanting to kill him must be equally—although perversely—divine.

As the months stretched on and the summer heat waxed to an unbearable pinnacle, William knew it was time for him to admit the truth: he'd wronged a venerated soul.

Eadric was not a hellhound, only a grieving father. In his lengthy days of thinking and dreaming, William began to admire his captor. This was a righteous man, a trustworthy man. How had he been so naïve? He was going to die because he betrayed a Christian; William deserved Hell.

Under the absolute darkness of pre-dawn, the stars shimmered at their purest; an owl hooted nearby, while a nightjar, out in the mire some countless leagues away, cackled its haunting yet serene dirge for the moonless night. It was only because of the flickering glow of torches within the monastery that Gilbert, Hawk, Hann, and his sons, Edwin and Cedric, could see the monastery at all. They crept up to the clearing.

The monastery resided in the glade of a large forest. They were about a six-hour hike from the refugee camp. A stockade with a hefty wooden gate surrounded the holy site, but it was in desperate disrepair. They could see right through the barrier.

"Why would nomadic friars have their own monastery?" Gilbert whispered.

"They don't," Hann said quietly. "This is the Glastonbury Priory of the Benedictines. But they take in friars when they've nowhere else to go, even those of other orders."

"What can we expect?"

"The usual ins-and-outs. Refectory. Dormitories. Chapel. Cloisters."

"Try the dormitories first," suggested Hawk. "That's where I'd store my clothes."

"Should be empty," Hann agreed.

"Why's that?" asked Gilbert.

"See those stars? That's Orion. Means dawn will be upon us soon. Means monks and friars should be about to hold morning mass. Means—"

"Dormitory should be empty."

"Smart lad." Hann elbowed him playfully. He pointed to his two sons, who had remained uncomfortably silent this whole trip. "My boys will keep watch at the chapel. If the monks, Prior Matthew, or that damnable *Circator Pius* leave mass early, they'll warn us."

The vehemence with which Hann spoke Circator Pius's name sent a chill down Gilbert's spine. It must have caught Hawk's attention too, for he glanced at him sideways and asked, "Who's this Circator Pius?"

"The circator of the priory. Big fellow with big arms, can't miss him."

"What's a circator?"

"A monk who makes sure the younger ones follow the rules. Bastard beats them too. He's second only to the prior, and Pius would argue he's above even him."

"Sounds like ye know this man," said Gilbert.

"Me, my wife, and my boys sought asylum here once. T'was winter, and we were starvin'. But! Best we not worry about it now. Come." Hann waved them onward as he and his sons moved for the stockade. "We must move fast before morning hymns."

They found the gate unlocked and pushed into the courtyard without issue. The monastery was roughly the shape of an "L"; the northwest corner housed the chapel, the southwest corner lodged the refectory, and the entire southern cloister, which spanned to the southeast corner, held the chapter house and dormitories.

Hann took the lead. He guided them across a well-tended vegetable garden until they reached a central well. They ducked behind it. Monks, appearing like dark spectres within the cloister's covered walkway, glided toward the chapel in an ominous procession. They waited until the monks disappeared into the chapel. After a few silent minutes, a haunting Latin chant seeped out of the chapel's venerated walls and drifted through the night air until it collided with the hooting owl and the wailing nightjar.

O! how he defiled the very consecrated ground he stood upon! How his paganistic birth doomed him so! Gilbert the Accursed prepared himself, for he believed God would strike him down at any moment for his sacrilegious blasphemy.

"Gilbert." Hawk shook him comfortingly. "Stay with me. You'll survive this."

"Thank you," said Gilbert, holding his arm for support.

"Right," said Hann, glancing back at them. "They've begun. Boys, to the chapel. Gilbert, Hawk, follow me to the dorms."

They split up, his sons moving to the northwest and them to the south. They waited outside the cloister's southern hall, listening for any sign of straggler monks, before they rushed into a far chamber secured by a locked door.

"What now?" Hawk whispered.

"We enter." Hann produced a pouch from under his robes. He pulled out an iron key that fit the lock exactly.

"You stole from the clergy?" asked Gilbert, aghast.

"No. I stole from the men who wronged me." Hann winked at them, unsheathed his hunting dagger, and opened the door before they could ask anything further. The dormitory was a long rectangular room with twelve simple beds stuffed with hay and straw. There were another dozen goatskin blankets spread on the ground—makeshift beds for the visiting Carmelites. Next to the beds were trunks, chests, and sacks holding their only earthly possessions.

"There's so many of them," said Hawk.

"Best be quick then."

The dormitory was dark except for the faint light of a sconce outside the chamber door; thus, Gilbert and Hawk had to slowly feel their way through the possessions of the holy men. Hann stood watch like a sentinel at the doorway, keeping an eye out across the cloister where his sons were spying on the mass. Occasionally, Gilbert would hear their holy chants echo through the thin walls. It filled him with such dread and shame that he had to close his eyes, take a calming breath, and remind himself why he was doing this.

For William, Gilbert. You're doin' this for Will.

But then a warm breeze would flow across the monastery, unsettling the wick within the sconce and causing the light to flicker in the room. The Matins chant would explode around him, loud and intimidating. Dust rose from surfaces uncleaned. And appearing like sorcery within the glinting dust, Gilbert saw the huddled form of his baby sister, her tunic ravished to scraps, while the dancing light plagued him with memories of the approaching torchbearers.

Gilbert forced himself to look away. His temples sweated.

That's not real. She's dead. It's not my fault. It's not my fault. It's not my—

"I'm not seeing the friars' habits," said Hawk. "Only the monks'."

Gilbert regained control of his breathing. They needed the friars' clothing. Stephen's army would be suspicious of why two Benedictine monks would appear so far from their priory, but the friars of Carmel were known to travel and give spiritual aid personally.

"What now?" asked Hann.

Gilbert thought hard and ignored the shunned misdeeds emerging from the darkest corners of his mind; he ignored the way the sanctified ground rumbled beneath his depraved feet.

This was why he always hated going to church. It roused fear and anger. The glorious cathedrals of Normandy were a stern reminder of the saintly heights he was denied at birth. Everyone, from the moment he was born, has told him of his wickedness. His mother. The other villagers. His parish priest. They all burned him with their devout virtues, scalding his spirit until all that was left was the ashes of his own depraved honor: cravenness, thievery, blasphemy.

Who was he to stand in a house of God?

It doesn't matter, he thought defiantly. *What matters is my brother needs me.*

"Gilbert?" Hawk watched him closely. Gilbert lifted the monk's black habits out of the crate. He held it up for them to see.

"Hann, I take it that ye know this circator pretty well?" asked Gilbert.

Something flashed in the peasant's eye. "Aye. Ye can say that."

"Tell me, what would he think about the Carmelites staying here?"

Gilbert, Hawk, and Hann, dressed in the dark habits of the Benedictine monks, approached the archway leading into the chapel. They passed Edwin and Cedric, who hid behind a neatly kept shrub. Latin chanting drifted to them. The monks and friars sang Matins—the first mass of the day, done just before sunrise—and their voices lifted the souls of all but Gilbert; the words echoed lifelessly in the hollowed space of his soul. They chanted:

"Kyrie eleison, Christe eleison. Kyrie Eleison.

Domine Jesu Christe, Rex gloriae!"

The three thieves entered the chapel. Gilbert clenched as his foot stepped into the church. No lightning struck him from the Lord. Maybe

God approved of the theft if it meant saving his kin? Gilbert pulled the cowl farther over his head, hiding his face in shadow.

"Defunctorum de poenis inferni et de profundo lacu."

The monks and friars were lined up in four rows. At the head of them all stood an altar with a thickly bound tome upon it. Prior Matthew, his face and features obscured by the darkness of the night, stood behind the altar leading the chant. Hann pulled on their habits and pointed to a monk at the rear of the congregation who stood taller than the rest. Circator Pius.

"Requiem aeternam dona eis, Domine ..."

Gilbert's plan was simple: cause a rift between the monks and friars, escort four friars into a private chamber while masquerading as monks, make them strip down, then extort them for their white habits. Hann vowed to create the initial distraction with Circator Pius. Gilbert believed it best not to ask about his obvious history with the religious man.

"Et lux perpetua luceat eis."

Relativus, Gilbert smiled to himself, *just as William used to save me in Boulogne.* Create a distraction big enough, and no one will notice the extra commotion going on besides it. And then, unbidden, another thought came to Gilbert.

Does God not punish the wicked because He's distracted with worse anarchy elsewhere? Are Christ and His angels not asleep, but simply preoccupied?

"Qui audis orationem ..."

They approached Circator Pius. Standing directly next to the monk, Gilbert realized how tall and imposing the circator really was. He was large in stature, with massive legs, shoulders, and arms. He tensed as they approached. There was no greater sin against a priory than causing a ruckus during mass. The Psalms were law, and betraying them meant betraying God.

"How *dare*—" Circator Pius began, gripping his large hands into hammers.

Hann held out a large silver cross with inlaid jewels, while Hawk held out a text full of some kind of gibberish; none of them knew how to read, but they assumed it must be filled with something religiously important... probably?

"What's this?" the circator whispered coarsely.

"AD TE OMNIS CARO VENIET PROPTER INIQUITATEM."

"I found these divine tokens in the belongings of the friars," said Hann conspiratorially.

Gilbert and Hawk braced. This was the weakest part of his plan. Even if the circator didn't recognize Hann's voice somehow, he might become alerted to the fact that they were imposters. Hann did well to lower his tone and strain it. Hopefully sleep deprivation, the absolute darkness, and the overlapping voices of the Matins chant would all combine to make the plan work.

Hann had promised them that Circator Pius, a traditional zealot even among the most religious of men, would be none too pleased with an unorthodox monastic order like the white-cloaked Carmelites. He'd promised Pius would be waiting for an excuse to throw them out.

"Which ones?" asked Circator Pius, his eyes turning hard.

Hann pointed. Gilbert smiled. It was working.

"REQUIEM AETERNAM DONA EIS, DOMINE..."

Circator Pius gathered the four friars they pointed out, placing his meaty hands on their necks, and urged them none-too-gently to exit through the archway. Some of the surrounding Carmelites turned to confront the monk, but Hann, Gilbert, and Hawk blocked them, acting as if they were also in a powerful position like the circator. They exited the chapel, none gladder than Gilbert, as the haunting words of the clergy were vibrating his innards. Their chants drifted out to them even as they entered the refectory.

"Et lux perpetua luceat eis."

Circator Pius locked the refectory behind them. A giant table with long benches took up most of the rectangular chamber. An ornately carved lectern stood at the end, a place where Prior Matthew could read scripture even when the monks ate.

"How DARE you steal within a house of God!" Circator Pius raised his fists.

The Carmelites cowered back from the hulking man. They fell against the table and benches. The bravest among them, a smaller man with thin, graying eyebrows, put up his hands and cried, "What do you speak of, Brother? We have stolen no goods!"

"Show them!"

Circator Pius stepped aside. That was when Hann took the jeweled cross, an enormous silver instrument of immense mass, and swung it at the circator's head.

"Etsi prævaluerunt super nos

impietates nostræ..."

The circator's skull cracked with a spine-shuddering *snap*! Blood splattered. The Carmelite friars screamed. Gilbert and Hawk jumped back in stunned terror. Hann yelled maniacally. The door to the refectory broke open; his sons rushed in with raised knives.

"Tu propitiaberis eis."

"Stop!" Circator Pius commanded. "God sees all!"

Hann bashed him on the head again. *Crack!* The tip of the cross pried off bits of his skull. Chunks of shredded brain landed around Gilbert in an awful crescent.

Hawk grabbed Gilbert's arm. "We have to save him!" he yelled. "They'll damn us both!"

Around Circator Pius's shriveled frame, Gilbert saw demons reaching up. The shadows in the chamber deepened. He saw the Lord vanish from the earth and flee to the Heavens. Gilbert's knees wobbled. His stomach convulsed; vomit ejected from his mouth.

"Requiem aeternam dona eis, Domine..."

The Carmelite friars froze in place. The barbarity of it all locked them to the floor.

Hann dropped the silver cross and stepped back, his breath ragged. Edwin and Cedric stabbed into the monk with their daggers.

Circator Pius turned on his side, his eyes locking onto Gilbert. He raised his hand toward him. His mouth muttered silently, *help me. Save me, son... dear Lord, please have him save me!*

"Et lux perpetua luceat eis."

Gilbert took a step forward...

... into the crescent of brain matter. He collapsed in on himself. Rather than seeing the splatter of the monk's head, Gilbert saw a dark crimson moon, waxing from crescent to full. His throat closed off. His fingers curled. A shrill, motherly voice berated him:

His love is a poison that'll bury ye into the deepest pits of oblivion. Beware ye!

It was all his fault.

Circator Pius's eyes turned as red as the accursed moon, while blood spilled from his eyelids and foamed from his mouth. In a desperate attempt to avoid the butchering, the monk curled his body into a ball.

Then, to Gilbert's horror, his body *changed*.

"Kyrie eleison."

Circator Pius turned into Olive, Gilbert's baby sister. Her sweet, gentle, three-year-old body lay broken and lifeless. Another victim of his curse, his calamity. She cried out, her body morphing and disfiguring her until she became the two stillborn twins that his mother had painfully torn from her womb. Their bodies lay half-created, like fleshy mounds of clay that God forgot to give shape.

Then, the monk turned into William, crying, bleeding on the floor of some dungeon. His mother screamed at him:

He will corrupt ye and beget your deaths, as he has to all his family!

"Christe eleison."

To hellfire he will bring ye!

Gilbert saw the dead bodies of his friends. Bartholomew. Beatriz. Hawk. They all bled; they all cursed his sinister name. Gilbert's tears ran hot.

"Kyrie Eleison."

The corpse lay crumbled on the floor of the refectory, its head split open in two places, and its body stabbed over twenty times. Hann spat on the cadaver.

"Domine Jesu Christe, Rex gloriae!"

"What the Hell?!" Hawk yelled at them.

Hann and his sons glanced back at them. Hann shrugged, nudged the corpse with his foot, and said, "Revenge. My family would have lived happy lives like all these fat, religious pigs. But this one caught me stealing their goods. Huh?! What did you need them for?!" He kicked Pius's body. "How do ye like that, ye stupid fuck?! My wife starved because ye threw us out! She died that winter because of ye! I'll kill all of ye! Prior Matthew. Father Tobias. All of ye who gave us this grief!"

"You murdered a man of God," said Hawk. "I ought to kill ye where you stand!"

"Not with that one helping ye." Hann pointed at Gilbert's cowering form and laughed. "Never trust a craven. Go on. Get your damn robes and begone. I'll be taking these myself."

He and his sons gathered the bloodied cross and the other valuable trinkets from the refectory. Hawk looked at Gilbert, shook his head, and ordered the Carmelite friars to remove their white habits. They did so without commotion, their eyes never leaving the gore.

Gilbert and Hawk fled as the first rays of dawn shone through the glade. For the duration of their six-hour hike back to the refugee camp, they didn't speak to each other once.

CHAPTER XXVII
EADRIC

"**D**on't lie to me. I can see it plainly on your face that you're not well of mind. What's wrong? Is it Commander Braxton still?" Eleanor leaned against the chestnut tree that both she and Eadric sat beneath. The massive trunk smelled of sweet pine and attracted numerous woodpeckers.

"He almost had me killed. Why wouldn't he be on my mind?" asked Eadric.

"I thought death was what you were after?"

Eadric picked at a wild primrose with a lovely and serene scent that reminded him of fresh bread. The petals were bright-white and soft, almost fuzzy to the touch. He snapped them off the vibrant yellow center. "What else needs fixing back home?" he asked.

"Along with bracing the trusses and adding shingles, we need to discuss the usage of the outer land. It isn't fertile enough to grow vegetables, but I still think we can get away with a lovely flower garden. It'll give it some prestige among the other estates." Eleanor had an endless list of issues that their Rockingham estate needed fixed. Eadric hadn't seen the halls his father built in over two years, and he wasn't keen on visiting it in the near future. In fact, his future seemed pretty sedentary at the moment given his physical condition.

"Very well. As you wish."

"Damnit, Eadric. What's the point of this if you won't be honest?"

"I don't understand. What's the matter?"

"The matter is you're *never* this agreeable. And when you are, it means you want to be rid of me. Do you wish me to leave?"

"No," he said. He sighed and immediately regretted it. The movement sent a sharp pain through his ribs, causing him to wince. It had been two months since the attack on Wareham, and he still didn't know how he managed to survive, outside that Sir Álvaro had found him inside the church with his wounds cleaned and tended to. But most of the damage was internal . . . or rather, *is* internal. It still hurt to breathe, he couldn't walk without a considerable limp, and his right shoulder felt like two plates of metal scraping together any time he moved, making his right arm near useless. After the battle, it had taken almost an entire month to recover from his fever alone. Eleanor had stayed with him every night, watching him carefully.

"Well, if you don't want to be rid of me," Eleanor began, "and you don't actually care about Rockingham, then why did you persist in coming out here with me?"

"I suppose I needed to get away from the camp. I've been holed up, babied by my superiors, gazed at with suspicion by my fellow soldiers. I rarely felt the sun while bedridden."

"I could've dragged your bed outside if all you wanted was to feel the damn sun."

"Prithee, peace. Perhaps I wanted to get away from the noise and enjoy the quiet."

"Then why the Hell did you bring me along? You know I'm never quiet." Eleanor smirked. Eadric begrudgingly smiled.

But she did indeed go silent for a bit, and the two of them listened to the chatter of insects and birds. There was a constant ringing that Eadric could always hear now; another casualty from the fight that he may never recover from. He inhaled the warm breeze as it shook the canopy above them and glanced at his wife. She wore a yellow dress, one that the tailor hemmed so it wouldn't hang lower than the middle of her calf. Made of nettle and lined with silk, it was a dress designed for walks like this, both stiff enough to survive getting plucked at by twigs and bushes, yet wide enough to allow her chest to breathe if she got winded. It was simple and elegant and suited her very well.

She looks pretty, Eadric admitted. Now, he, with his arm and chest and leg and head bandaged, with his insides feeling like sloshing water filled with poison, and with his nausea always bubbling at the base of his throat...

"I appreciate you," he said. Those words tasted strange spewing from his mouth, almost like a different kind of bile. "I mean to say, I appreciate that you care for my estate. I know it isn't easy to manage on your lonesome."

"What in Hell has got a hold of you?" Eleanor asked incredulously.

"What?"

"Six years into our marriage and *now* you decide to become pleasant? You're not allowed to do that. No, my lord, you aren't. Now come on."

"What?"

"Stop saying that blasted word and give it to me. Come on, insult me." She jutted out her chin as if he were going to punch her in the face. "I know you want to. Give it here."

"I have nothing to say."

"Of course you don't, because you've been too chickenshit to do anything since your injury. The only good thing to come of it is you finally lost some damn weight."

"I'm sorry for trying to be considerate."

"Eadric, I don't need you to be considerate. I didn't agree to having a *kind* husband. We both knew why Stephen had wedded our houses, and it wasn't so we could live happily ever after. This sudden change of heart is sweet and all, and I like compliments like the next maiden, but this isn't us. I don't need you to feel bad for treating me like a misbegotten. And trust me, I certainly don't need to feel awful for stealing your estate. Now what I would like is for you to agree, full-heartedly, to plant this flower garden inside Rockingham, because I think that would be really lovely. And for whatever stupid fucking reason, I would really, really like for you to be a part of that process."

Eleanor took a deep breath after finishing her rant. Eadric watched her wide-eyed. He had never heard her speak like that, and God be damned if she didn't scare him.

Eadric looked his wife in the eyes and said, "I want to plant that flower garden."

"Thank you," she said. "And thank you again."

"For what?"

"For finally appreciating all the work I do, you ungrateful bastard."

She smiled, and he smiled back. They both knew it. Now *this* was them.

Beneath the cool shade of the timeworn chestnut, which blocked the sweltering sun as it reached its zenith and blazed upon the wide, green pastures of southern England, a wife gently tucked her shoulder into the crevasse of her husband's arms. He allowed it; she allowed it. And together they watched grasshoppers hop from blade to blade in the meadow, while sparrows and goldfinches sang and feasted on the breadth of summer insects.

"I reluctantly apologize for disturbing your afternoon."

Eleanor and Eadric jumped in surprise. King Stephen stood behind them with a small entourage. They were only a quarter mile from camp, but this was the first time Eadric had properly seen the king outside a few visits to his sickbed.

"My king." They bowed.

"Lady Eleanor, would it pain you if I were to rob your lord husband of your presence, if but only for a short while?"

"It would not, my king. We'd both be honored." Eleanor nudged Eadric. He bowed his head despite the dread he felt.

"I thank you, my lady," said the king.

Eadric and King Stephen, leaving behind his entourage, took a leisurely stroll through the hilly mounds, and the king, graciously, made his pace slow enough that Eadric could keep up with his limp. Stephen watched his underling with his deep blue eyes. There was so much cunning and suspicion in them, it made Eadric shy away.

"I want to discuss what happened in Wareham," said the king. "I've had many meetings with Commander William and have had his counsel. He has, quite extensively and severely, informed me of your recent perfidiousness. What say you of this?"

"I don't deny it, my king. I have done what I believe is right."

"I can respect you for following your heart, but this isn't a matter of right versus wrong. We're at war."

"I'm aware, my king."

"Do you? Because from what I've been told, you have been outright manipulative, and nearly treacherous, in your newfound authority. Explain to me how I can allow someone who abandons their post and leaves their men to die to remain a constable? Explain how I'm to uphold the laws of my kingdom if one of my most trusted lords blatantly disregards them? God forgive Eadric, but I've even been told you aren't attending mast."

"My king, I'm afraid I don't know what to say. The truth is, I only have one thing on my mind, and it has rotted away all else in my brain."

"And it has made you weak of spirit," said Stephen. He pulled irritatingly at his silk clothes. "Blast it! I hate these confounded garments. They're too hot to wear during the summer." Cicadas chirped endlessly around them as the king stopped a moment to take in the countryside. He at least had the decency to sigh before he said, "Eadric, I'm going to have to punish you. It was foolish of me to believe you could forsake your vengeance. I now understand that you'd allow it to endanger my people, and my army."

"I was in the wrong," said Eadric. He struggled to maintain eye contact with Stephen's keen stare. "I know it. I swear to the Lord Almighty, I never thought I'd get this bad."

"Tell me, what have you learned concerning Duke Richard? Tell me this treason hasn't been for naught."

"I'm still unsure of his direct whereabouts, but I know where to find his second-in-command."

"Is it this Commander Braxton you speak of?"

"Yes, my king. We questioned the soldiers I injured in the church before they died. Their words were jumbled though, like a drunkard, and they only said he fled north. When we asked them to be more specific, they only spoke one more slurred word."

"Which was?"

"Bampton, or so we think. But they could have said Rampton too."

"And doubtless you're aware that the next stage of my plan was to assault both those towns simultaneously?"

"Yes, my liege. But we know not whether he fled to the castle or the parish."

"I'm sorry that's as far as you got," said King Stephen. His sorrow appeared authentic; this wasn't mock-pitying. "It pains me to say this, but you've left me no choice. You won't be going to either assault."

"My king?"

"I am relieving you of duty. You may keep your Rockingham estate, but you are no longer in my military command. Your actions have been unacceptable, and in truth, I should have you sequestered or worse."

Eadric's heart jumped into his throat. He dashed forward as fast as his lame leg could take him. "Please, my liege."

"I won't hear it."

"Please, Stephen! I need to find him. I can't do it by myself."

"Is that so? Because you're rather intent on disregarding me the second you have a chance."

"You're right. I have been. Look where it's gotten me." Eadric dropped to his knees, kicking up a cloud of dirt. "I'll do whatever you ask."

"I cannot trust your loyalty. You have proven to be treasonous."

"Please, Stephen, my king. I've won countless battles for you—"

"Commander William—"

"Goddamn the fucking commander!"

"Don't use the Lord's name in vain."

"I'm sorry, my king, but William would've failed you time and time again if it weren't for me. My loyalty is to *you*, not that worthless man."

"You have a devil's tongue."

"Satan would never beg like this! Stephen, please, just promise me I can have my vengeance. Even if I'm not the one to find Duke Richard or Commander Braxton, promise me you'll capture them for me. Tell me that, my liege, my king, and I will be yours forevermore. I'll kill whomever you need. I'll bear any sin."

"If we sack Bampton Parish and Castle Rampton, regardless if you find this commander or not, you'll still keep your pledge never to desert your post again?"

"Yes, my king. *If* you promise me."

King Stephen smiled as if he had accomplished some remarkable feat. He held out his hand to Eadric. "You have my oath. Should they locate Commander Braxton in any town, they will imprison him until you've had your way with him."

Eadric kissed the king's hand. Stephen helped him stand.

"Do not let this quest ruin your favor in my eyes again," warned the king. "I will put down a rabid dog before I let it destroy me. Am I clear?"

"Yes, my liege."

"Good. I would have you with me during this campaign. The end is nigh. Empress Maud won't elude me for long, not with the Hellhound by my side. Now, let's find this bitch and the walls she cowers behind."

***

Eadric advanced with purpose down the narrow corridors of Wareham's dungeon, an axe in hand and a decision all but set in his mind. Will had betrayed him. Now he must lose his head.

He still didn't know how the boy hostage had managed such a treacherous move while imprisoned. The only logical conclusion he could come to was that Commander Braxton or Duke Richard had a spy deep within their army, perhaps even a high-ranking officer—someone who could get past the gaoler and talk directly to the hostage. Who it was, or how they did it, was something he hoped to learn before he executed the boy. It took him months to come to this decision. He wanted to hold on to the boy a little longer, to see if Richard would finally hear word of his bastard being held hostage, but now that the army was finally moving forward again, he couldn't delay it any longer.

Will was waiting for him, his face pressed up against the small iron bars that made a window through the wooden door. Eadric saw fear in his eyes as he spotted him, but also something else . . . something like relief. The wait must've been torturous, knowing for months that his scheme to ambush the Hellhound had failed, knowing his comeuppance would come. But Eadric wasn't in any hurry to serve justice; rather, he forced Will to wait, and starve, and wait again until the spotting of his harbinger of death became an ironic release of tension.

Gaoler Alfwin unlocked the door for him and excused himself. Eadric slipped into the cell and closed the door. With the two of them alone at long last, he stared at the boy hostage and asked, "Why? Why would you choose this fate?"

"Because who would trust the Hellhound to keep his word?" Will's voice was frail and destitute of any remorse—a broken man who made a desperate gamble. "Oft I've heard of your insatiable vengeance. How many hundreds have ye killed? They swore to me that, succeed or fail, ye would forget my freedom. Was it not true that you would've taken your own life after my father was slaughtered? Is it not true that you would've killed yourself trying? The oath of a dead man means naught."

"Who told you this?"

"A phantom."

"Hark!" Eadric lunged after him. The boy stumbled back and crashed into the wall. He held the axe aloft over Will's cowering body. "Speak the truth and the truth alone, and I will end your life with a painless blow."

"I speak the truth!" screamed the boy, glaring up at him with teary eyes. "A vile messenger with black clothes and an animal's face came for me in the dark of night."

"They concealed their face?"

"Yes, with a mask that looked like an owl. But they were not a man, for a man couldn't curse us as thoroughly as they. They tried to doom us both. A fool they made me."

Eadric studied his countenance with scrutiny, yet the quiet sincerity with which the boy told all this, the apt dejection and humility, was enough to make Eadric believe the Devil himself had come down and paid the hostage a visit.

"Did you recognize the voice?" asked Eadric. "What did this phantom sound like?"

"It was deep, but not unnaturally so. T'was forced, me believes. Strained almost."

"And his height? How did he keep his countenance? What did he bargain with you?"

"I don't know, my lord. T'was so dark."

He slammed the frail boy against the wall. He brought the blade of the axe only a few inches from Will's neck. "Do you not know anything?!"

"No!"

"Satan speaks with your tongue!"

"No, my lord."

"Can you not tell me anything?! Can you say nothing that would spare your life?! You claim a man in ghoul's clothing visited you. Can you not also say he guided your hand?"

"His hand did not. My choice was my own."

Will's response angered him and churned something deep inside his soul. A few months ago, he would've killed Will without a second thought, but something was staying his hand.

Why is this so hard now?! Kill him!

"Give me a reason not to do this," said Eadric. "Tell me where Commander Braxton fled to. Is it Bampton or Rampton Castle? Or tell me where your father is. Where can I find him?! How can I draw him out?! Tell me you're still useful."

Will tilted his head. The axe blade cut off the edges of his patchy beard.

"Bampton."

"What?"

"He'd be at Bampton Priory." The boy hostage laughed. The turmoil of emotions that had built up inside him had released in one exasperated cackle. "Me knows where he is! My father would place him at Bampton!"

"How do you know this? If you're lying—"

"Then what? Ye'd kill me? When I studied under my father and Earl Robert, he told me of Bampton. It was the parish he grew up in. It's where he learned the ways of writing and lordship. He and his knights know its layout. He even taught me its interior."

Will laughed so hard that tears launched from his eyes. The incredulity of it all, of how fate seemed to keep colliding him and his captor together, was enough to drive any man mad. After a few seconds of lunatic-like laughter from Will, Eadric joined in. They laughed together with only the cold iron blade of an axe separating them.

I suppose this is a day for forgiveness, thought Eadric. *A day of second chances.*

"Well," said Eadric at long last, after their laughter dissipated in the cell's void, "I hope you're ready."

"Ready for what?" the boy hostage asked.

"I'm going to sack Bampton Parish, and you're coming with me."

CHAPTER XXVIII
GILBERT & WILLIAM

He wasn't sure when it happened exactly, but he started to care deeply about Eadric. He *wanted* him to kill Richard, *wanted* him to slaughter his father.

Other than the gaoler, the Hellhound was the only person who could free him from the humdrum destitute of each day. It got to the point where William forgot the faces of all those he loved. Gilbert. Hawk. Bartholomew. Beatriz.

They all faded away; everyone but the Hellhound of Rutland.

His stomach growled something fierce, and his body thirsted for more water. But he was alive. He was alive all thanks to the generosity of Baron Eadric of Rockingham.

He heard the voice of Gaoler Alfwin outside, talking to someone. William listened intently. Yes! It was his friend. Eadric lifted the canvas that covered Will's wagon cell. The sun shone, and the faint breeze felt lovely compared to the rank humidity under the linen tarp. Eadric looked down at him.

William couldn't help himself; he smiled with glee at seeing his captor.

Gilbert and Hawk placed the Carmelite friar habits on the ground. Beatriz and Bartholomew inspected them.

"What's this?" asked Beatriz, finding blood splatter on hers.

"Ignore it," said Gilbert. She glared at him, but he said no more.

They all tried on the habits, but none fit Hawk nor Bartholomew, for they were both too tall and too lanky. Beatriz grumbled as she realized she would be the one forced to dress as a nun and enter King Stephen's camp. She spent some time after that praying to God, hoping he wouldn't banish her to Hell for pretending to be a woman of the cloth.

They left by mid-afternoon, traveling southeast to reach the bivouac Father Tobias had told them of. After a few days' travel, they reached the spot and found, much to their dismay, that the army had left some time ago. Charcoal burners, who had stopped by the River Sherford as they navigated their way east toward London, told them that the army had headed directly north to continue their campaign. From there, the four friends started a long journey of following lead after lead, passing many small towns and villages that claimed the army had raided them or stolen their provisions to "support the king from the dangerous Angevin foreigners." It took two long weeks of nonstop travel, eating what fruit and bugs they could, until they reached the army just east of Devizes.

Bartholomew and Beatriz had a tender goodbye that made Gilbert and Hawk rather uncomfortable. They both shied away from the lovers' embrace and stood together awkwardly a few paces away. Gilbert looked at his friend. They hadn't spoken to one another since the night Hann took the circator's life on the floor of the refectory.

"I'm sorry I didn't try to save him," said Gilbert. "I don't know what's wrong with me. I think Ma Maman is right. I have inherited her cravenness."

Hawk shook his head and said, "Nay. I think you simply think yourself a coward, so you are one. Think clearly, and you'll find you're very brave indeed."

Gilbert and Beatriz arrived at the army encampment under a vibrant azure sky dotted with white fluffy clouds with flat gray bottoms; it was as if a shepherd sheared his sheep and scattered the wool to the wind, allowing the fur to go where it pleased until it found a spot up in that endless blue. The sun shimmered and boiled above them like a bright-yellow stew. Heat waves undulated over the horizon, and Gilbert had to stop every few hundred paces to wipe the sweat from his eyes. It was mid-August and by far the hottest day of the year. Their long white habits did little to alleviate the celestial warmth.

They approached the entrance that the guards had erected on the perimeter of the camp. Beatriz glanced at Gilbert sideways, her own pores seeping with sweat, both from nervousness and from the oppressing heat. He took a deep breath.

Beware ye, his mother said from the pits of his heart, *for if he drags you to that war-torn kingdom, he will corrupt ye and beget your deaths*.

Gilbert squinted away her wicked words. "If we get through," he said to Beatriz, "split up. Do what ye can to learn where they keep the prisoners or where the Hellhound is."

"And how do I do that? Do I just go up to 'em and ask?" she asked sarcastically.

"I don't know. Tell them they're doing their Christian duty."

With that useless exchange said, they walked up to the guards. Gilbert clasped his hands together and bowed his head as if in reverence to the Lord's benevolence for giving them such a beautiful day, when in reality he wanted to cover the mixture of shame and embarrassment that washed over his face. The circator's mutilated corpse—another victim of Gilbert's lifelong curse—had been disturbing his dreams.

The guards paid them no mind as they passed. Beatriz muttered a prayer next to him before she wiped more sweat off her face.

The encampment was massive, much bigger than Gilbert had expected—a city of tents for miles on end. Soldiers flocked between the newly erected civilization with zeal and purpose; morale seemed high, and that could be both a gift and a curse. High morale meant they'd be less likely to pick on two innocent friars, but they'd also be more likely to honor their duties, like protecting the prisoners' block or their captain's quarters.

"Meet back here at sundown," said Gilbert.

Beatriz sighed and muttered, "May God give me strength."

They separated. The intensity of the sun beamed down on Gilbert's trepid courage, and he became lost in the city of arms. The primary thoroughfares were clogged with supply carts and wagons drawn by horses, oxen, and donkeys, making passage near inaccessible, while the dirt tracks between tents became muddy alleyways beneath the labored boots of the men-at-arms. Foot soldiers drunkenly staggered between impromptu alehouses, sneakily wagering games of dice behind hidden tent flaps; meanwhile, beyond that, the normal activities expected in a city carried on: men made love with their wives, the wounded aided the cooks and smiths, children chased butterflies and beetles, women carried fresh water, commanders held meetings, traveling merchants bartered, soldiers trained, animals grazed. And Gilbert, in the midst of it all, remained ignored.

Even after spending much of the afternoon eavesdropping on conversations, he was no closer to finding the prisoners or the infamous Hellhound of Rutland. Any discussions he heard regarding the latter were quickly shut down, usually by another soldier telling them to "shut their mouths lest they wish for the big, burly bastard to bash in their heads and hurl them into the sea." Gilbert was about to abandon the day when a timid voice asked, "Father?"

He twisted around to find a peasant-soldier who had his entire upper torso bandaged. A large scar ran down his right cheek and cut his coarse, untrimmed beard in two. His skin looked sickly, and his hair was a wanton mess.

"Yes?" Gilbert asked, then quickly followed with, "My son?"

That's what a friar would say, right? Or was it only priests who say 'my son?'

"Me needs to confess," said the broken soldier.

"I don't—"

"Please, Father. I have little time left."

Gilbert shook his head. He had to refuse if this man actually needed one final confession before death. Gilbert, born under the Devil's red moon, couldn't save this man from damnation nor cleanse his soul for eternal salvation.

He was just . . . a man.

"Please, Father."

Looking into his begging eyes, tears leaking from his soul, Gilbert knew he couldn't refuse. It couldn't hurt anything, could it?

"What's your name?" Gilbert asked.

"Wihtred."

"Very well, Wihtred. Go ahead."

"Right here?"

"Why not?"

"Oh . . . um, bless me, Father, for I have sinned . . ."

The false friar listened patiently while he learned way more about Wihtred than he ever wished to know about any man. He heard his deepest and most profound thoughts, becoming intimate with his regrets, his pains, his desires; they were all given to Gilbert's open ears. When he finished, Gilbert awkwardly blessed him and gave him a few repentance prayers to do.

"Is that all, Father? Much I 'ave sinned."

Not wanting to drag out this blasphemy much longer, Gilbert simply said, "Yes."

"Thank ye, Father. The Lord has lightened my load." Wihtred smiled a broad, gummy smile, and Gilbert felt good. He finally did something that helped someone.

He turned around and frowned. Five more peasant-soldiers, all equally bandaged, scarred, and sinful, awaited their turns to give penance.

The sun plunged behind the western trees and absconded to the land of shadow, which lengthened and widened until it corrupted the entire expanse of Wiltshire, overrunning the glistening stars and half-moon with streaking clouds as gray and forlorn as winter's bite. It was in these twilit hours that Gilbert finally returned to Beatriz after a long evening of listening to the sins of man. She stormed up to him, vapors of anger steaming off her white habit. Gilbert opened his mouth to apologize—

Beatriz swung up her finger to silence him. "How DARE you! How *DARE* you, Gil! I have waited for hours believin' ye to be dead!"

He glanced around anxiously as nearby peasant-soldiers and ranked commanders bemusedly watched the arguing friars. Gilbert tried to shush her.

"Don't ye dare!" she screamed, even angrier than before. "What would I 'ave done if ye were deceased? Or better yet, trapped with your brother?"

"Beatriz, please."

"Don't *please* me, ye damn selfish, no-good, prick-sucking motherfuck—" She stomped her feet. "GOD FUCKIN' DAMNIT! YE MADE ME CUSS *AGAIN!*"

"Beatriz!"

"No, no, no. For almost one year I've been proper, with a saint's mouth and proper morals. If I'm goin' to Hell for t'night, then I'm goin' to get my soul's worth." She took a deep breath. "Fuck you, ye churl knave whoreson shite-eating, bugger-loving, daft, bloody-arse cock-headed swine!" She finished her rampage with a long series of heavy breaths.

"Are ye done?"

"No. No, I am not."

A small contingent of onlookers had formed around them. Gilbert shooed them away. He wondered how far the gossip of a swearing nun would make it in the drinking rounds tonight. "That felt good," said Beatriz. "Dear Lord Christ, I'm sorry. But that felt good."

"I'm sorry for not being on time," said Gilbert. "Did ye find anything on Will?"

"Nay. I spent all day soaking in my sweat and didn't hear a word."

"Me neither, but I learned much listenin' to damn near two dozen confessions."

"What do ye mean?"

"Well . . . I may have allowed a man to confess his sins. Then, a few more showed up. Then, a crowd."

"Gilbert! Ye can't be takin' confessions!" She lowered her voice. "You are *not* a priest. You can't absolve their sins."

"But don't ye see, Beatriz? We wasted a whole day wandering this camp learnin' nothing. Men aren't open with their secrets, but to a priest . . ."

"We aren't priests."

"If we hear enough confessions, maybe one of them will say something about William, or this Hellhound. If he's half as evil as people say, then those who follow him will have dire sins to get off their chests."

Beatriz shook her head. "I can't do this."

"Why?"

"Because I'm not here to go to Hell. I came here to save my soul. To do a truly virtuous deed and save William. *This*? Gilbert, this is *blasphemy*. We are not righteous people. We're thieves, charlatans. I told ye, me and Bartholomew were turnin' our lives around."

"But don't ye see—"

"I see. It's a good plan, really. But one I can't do. I'll still listen around the camp, but I will not look faithful Christians in the eyes and tell them I can absolve them. Don't ye see? You aren't damning only yourself, but all of them too. I beg of you, don't do this."

A light wind blew across the world. The trees ruffled. Some strange bird shrieked.

"I have to do anything I can to save him," said Gilbert.

The clouds parted, and the half-moon reflected in Beatriz's eyes. "Then I'll pray for ye."

The next two weeks passed in a blur of vices and transgressions. Word of a holy man who was hearing confessions spread like wildfire throughout Stephen's encampment, and many came to divulge their immorality to the false friar. Gilbert heard so many tales of murder, rape, and pillaging that he became numb to the details. Pride, greed, envy, wrath, lust, gluttony, sloth; tales of their strangulation on the lives of men, and their interwoven vileness, swam through Gilbert's head like a vexing headache, his mind throbbing with the trespasses of the impure. And through it all, man after man after woman after man, Gilbert was constantly reminded of himself. He heard his own faults in their confessions. He relived his own sins, his own failings. When he gazed around the camp, what he saw wasn't a place of productive and proud men full of honor, but a city made for men like him; this was a place for those looking to distract themselves from the heavy sin they carried inside—a city for the cursed.

Every night, when he and Beatriz returned to Hawk and Bartholomew and gave them updates, he'd look up to the sky and expect the blood moon of his birth to reappear.

Another fortnight of scavenging for any signs of William or the Hellhound passed, yet they heard nothing. It was as if they'd disappeared from the earth. Rumors spread that they were about to move camp again, and that King Stephen had a plot of how to attack the empress. One morning, they started striking the bivouac. Gilbert was worried that they'd lose their chance to learn anything about his brother.

It wasn't until the next day, when the tent city was almost completely stripped, that he finally learned something useful. A knight in black armor and a long drooping mustache approached him.

"What's your name, son?" asked Gilbert.

"Señor Álvaro de León," said the black knight. "Forgive me, Father, for I have sinned."

"Speak then, son, for I and the Lord shall listen."

Gilbert tuned out the knight as he went on a lengthy and rambling diatribe about the multitude of sins he'd committed. He'd learned early on how to separate his mind from his feelings during these confessions, for the darkness of the world would swallow him up if he listened to them with the whole of his heart. Honestly, he only listened for a few keywords—words like *prisoner*, or *hostage*, or—

"... Hellhound's accursed persistence."

"Wait." Gilbert nearly screamed. The knight jumped at the friar's sudden interruption. "Say that again."

"I'm sorry, Father. Say *what* again?"

"That part. Repeat it, please."

"I said I'm losing my patience with the Hellhound's accursed persistence. Every time I think of him, he makes me want to—"

"Many soldiers speak of this Hellhound," said Gilbert, trying to steer the confessional. "Is he pulling you into another one of his shameful war expeditions?"

"Father, I don't mean to anger God, but I cannot speak of war plans."

Gilbert's mind swam. He couldn't afford to lose this chance. "But if he were to lead you into more sin, it is best you tell me now. I can absolve you ahead of time, if need be, so that your heart may feel lighter going into such Hell."

Gilbert hesitated at his own statement. *Can a priest absolve people before they've sinned?* Then, he reasoned, *if they could do it after, why couldn't they do it before?*

"Can you really do that, Father? I've never heard such a thing."

Shit. Well, might as well commit now.

"Yes." Gilbert waited dumbly.

The black knight lowered his head and began, "He wishes to bring me and my squire to attack the parish. It shames me to admit that I, too, have a part in this plan."

"Which parish?" asked Gilbert excitedly.

Elated to hear that Bampton Parish was only a little over ten leagues away, Gilbert and his friends gathered their necessities and left that very night. With any luck, they'd reach Oxfordshire within two days and beat the Hellhound of Rutland and his invading force to the religious community.

The group talked little on the way there. Beatriz gave Gilbert some harsh looks as she whispered to her husband occasionally. Every time she did so, a burning flame would rear up inside his cheeks. How dare she think herself better than him? He did what he had to do to learn the Hellhound's location. *This* was how they would find William.

His soul had been damned since birth anyway. Why should he care now?

Gilbert glanced over at his lifelong best friend, and Hawk, like he'd been doing often since they fled the Glastonbury Priory, avoided his eyes.

Well, damn him too, thought Gilbert, hardening his resolve. If his friends believed him cursed, so be it. No matter what, he would save his brother; no sacrifice was too great.

His love is a poison that'll bury ye into the deepest pits of oblivion.

And she was right. Buried deep within the darkness of his heart, Gilbert knew his mother told the truth.

It was his fault his baby sister had been killed.

It was his fault his family had been tarnished.

It was his fault William had been captured.

But it was his friends' fault for not being wise enough to realize he'd do the same to them. Gilbert was only being what he was born to be. A depraved craven.

CHAPTER XXIX
EMMA

A*hhhhhhhhhhhhhhhhhhh!*

"A *ball?!*" Emma covered her mouth, realizing she had shouted the words at the same volume as the screaming in her head. Madame Beatrice grimaced and covered her ears.

"Yes, now if you'd please." She handed Emma a stack of vibrantly colored garments.

"Is this—?!"

"A gown? Yes. *Please!* Don't scream again. Jesus Christ, help me. Tonight, we must be as eloquent as the empress herself, and you certainly can't be wearing . . . well, that."

The colors were gorgeous—golden yellow with light turquoise threads woven within. It almost made her cry. "I don't know what to say."

"I suggest you say nothing and instead put on the dress. We don't have all day."

"Who's the guest Theresa will attend to?"

"Only worry about yours. Lady Ansfride. Her mother was Juliane de Fontevrault, the empress's half-sister. After the death of her parents, she now controls a large abbey in Anjou that could be decisive for Geoffrey's war in France. And please, Emma, whatever you do, do not mention her condition."

"Condition?" Emma was woefully ignorant of the gossip of life overseas in the kingdom of France. She knew there was some juicy intrigue and steamy relationships that happened over there, but she rarely got foreign visitors in Cudworth or Marlborough.

"Her face is terribly scarred," said Madame B, "and she doesn't take kindly to people mentioning it. She has full clearance to anything she wants in the castle, so please see to her every need."

Emma perked up. *An opportunity*, she thought. Tom was to arrive within the next fortnight to retrieve Robert's letter, and she was running out of time. Perhaps she could convince Lady Ansfride to visit the library if she were to give her a tour of the keep?

Madame Beatrice waved Emma on to take off her dress. Red-orange sunlight spilled into the handmaid bedchamber through the narrow slits of the window slats, creating lines of radiance along the ground. Emma stood atop the light, letting the warmth spread across her toes while she stripped down. Madame Beatrice politely turned away and remade her bed for the third time today. It was a curious habit. The madame often repeated the same chores multiple times a day.

Layering out the garments before her, Emma startled. Suddenly apprehensive, she realized she'd never dressed herself in such fancy clothes before. Was there a certain order she was supposed to put these on? A certain way to fluff them?

Madame B seemed to notice her hesitation, and asked with a bite of mockery, "You don't know how to wear clothes?"

"I know how to wear *clothes*. But a dress like this . . . I've never—"

"Must I do everything for you? Here. Raise your arms."

Emma shivered, her skin goosefleshing, as Madame Beatrice's fingers grazed over her bare skin like tiny icicles, deftly fastening and layering the dress so that it hung perfectly around her. The madame hummed to herself. This was the closest she'd ever been to Beatrice. *Her eyes are gorgeous*, thought Emma. They were youthful, though not exactly childlike; there was certainly maturity to them, a way Emma could tell that Beatrice had seen some terrible things . . . but they didn't *feel* old.

Then, as the process of dressing her went on, Emma's mind wandered to other things. Things like her mother. Like Alice. She thought of the life she had left behind at the behest of Tom. Like a monsoon storm that devours the countryside in an instant, her mood radically changed. Darkness and doubt roiled within her chest, choking her airways, hammering her ribs. Her mother had fallen ill, and *she* was the only thing that could save her. Shame grasped Emma, and all thoughts of the ball or of being a princess felt like a foolish, wistful fantasy.

Madame Beatrice must have sensed the tension in Emma's body, for her expression softened as she fluffed the golden dress. She asked gently, "Did your mother teach you proper etiquette?"

Emma nodded.

"Then remember those lessons well. These aren't ordinary guests tonight. It may seem a room full of girls and women to you, but they're essential for our lady's plans. What they're doing is brave. Many of the men they serve, for all outward purposes, are sworn to Stephen."

"Why would they send their daughters and wives if they're sworn to the king?"

"There's one thing you should know about barons and lords: they don't choose sides. They choose the winner, or they die. The only way to be right is to support both positions. But then, when they must seek counsel with their sworn 'enemy,' who do you suppose they oft send as commissary?"

"They send their women?"

"Aye. Our empress taught me this years ago. While men are trained to lead and battle, women are taught to conciliate and bargain. How women feel, what they *think*, is what they report to their men, who are out doing harm. If you win over their women, you win over their fiefdoms. Do you understand?"

"I think so."

"Thus, my dear, none of your peasant-like shenanigans tonight. This is too important. We must impress the ladies of these enemy men. That is our task. *Not* dancing, or drinking, or anything of that nature."

Emma nodded, but sadness crept over her. A month had passed since Madame B saved her and Crispin from those terrible men outside the city walls, and she'd hoped sharing that intimacy would make them friendlier; instead, it had only made the madame more forlorn.

"Do you hate me?" Emma asked, unable to contain the thought.

Madame Beatrice froze. She searched Emma's face. "No," she answered gently. "I only hate the way you make me feel."

Emma took a deep breath before rapping on the door and entering the bedchamber assigned to Lady Ansfride. She barely held her gasp; Lady Ansfride was ugly.

Her face was a husk, a skull with a thin layer of skin to masquerade it as alive. She had no eyes. The empty sockets were hollow, the surrounding red skin pulled taut and oozing a slight yellow-green mucus. Even more horrifying, the poor woman had no nose; or, better described as *half* a nose, for it was severed right in front of her face, with tendons and cartilage clearly visible. Her nostrils looked like the eyes of a demon, staring out wide and black in the midst of her face.

But then, Emma's eyes drifted to the rest of her; Lady Ansfride was beautiful.

Her skin was clear and pale and looked as soft as silk. Her brunette hair, braided into an elaborate pattern, was both eye-striking and natural. As for her dress, it mesmerized any who gazed upon it; it had a purple floral pattern sewn into the side, spiraling upward until it reached her bodice. Her figure was healthy and womanly, and she made Emma feel utterly envious.

"Are you the servant?" asked Lady Ansfride. She had a sweet, almost-melodic voice. It seemed entirely perverse that such a lovely voice could come from such a hideous face.

"Y—yes," stuttered Emma.

"Bring me my blindfold. It's inside my trunk over there."

Opening the trunk and ruffling through the clothing, she struggled to find the blindfold until Lady Ansfride clarified, "You're looking through the wrong side. A little further down on the other end."

Emma glanced back over her shoulder at the woman on the bed. How could she hear which side of the trunk she was searching through? Emma found the blindfold exactly where the lady had told her. She crossed to the bed and gave it to her.

"Took you long enough," said Lady Ansfride. "Are you blind?"

Emma hesitated. "Uh, no?"

"Good. They definitely don't need two of us tonight." She tied the blindfold around her face, covering her eye sockets and some of her missing nose. "You're young. How many winters have you seen?"

"Fourteen. Soon to be fifteen."

"How does a fourteen-year-old girl come into the service of a Roman queen?"

"By accident largely."

"Is your father a nobleman?"

"No," Emma said. And then, adding, "I didn't know my father."

"Don't sound so sad," the disfigured woman said. "Fathers can be real bastards. You're often better off not having one at all. Do you know what Maud wants from me tonight?"

"Something to do with your abbey in Anjou."

Lady Ansfride reached out and grasped Emma's arm. She jumped but forced herself not to rip her arm away. "Out so easily with that information," Lady Ansfride said skeptically. "You must be a new servant. A word of advice, love? Never be forthright about what your lady wants. Never."

Emma stayed silent. Her pulse was racing. She licked her chapped lips before her brain finally caught up to the moment. "Apologies, my lady," she said, gently prying Lady Ansfride's slender fingers off her arm. "But I was told to give you anythin' ye desire. I'm also to give you a tour of the castle, if ye wish."

"I wish not. Guide me immediately to the lodge. I wish to speak with Maud before all this nonsense begins."

"Are you sure? The library often impresses—"

"My dear, what on God's green earth would *I* need with a library?" She waved her hand in front of her blindfolded face.

Right, thought Emma, *I'm an idiot.*

"Now come," ordered Lady Ansfride. "Let's see what your mighty queen wants from a half-butchered woman."

"My brother wrote to me," said Empress Maud, wearing an eloquent dress of a deep ruby color. "As I predicted, my husband's largest concern remains with suppressing the duchy of Normandy under Angevin rule. Robert testifies my husband *laughed* at the prospect of sending more men-at-arms to England. You may think me concerned, but I have little desire to be more indebted to Geoffrey than necessary. We're on our own, but I cannot retake the crown without Robert's help."

Most of the men at the table nodded. The ball had technically started, but no one was dancing. Emma found the whole affair rather dull; there wasn't any music or mirth under the magnificent wooden archways that braced the very stone around them, nor was there any open floor to dance upon. A few large tables were put together to seat all the guests—including their housecarls, bannermen, and handmaidens—as well as a few of Empress Maud's most trusted advisors. Old-Codger Reginald, who Emma danced with when she first arrived at Oxford, stoked the hearth fire at the end of the hall. Candles flickered atop the table, which shone dancing light over partially eaten meals.

"That is why I need your help, ladies," Empress Maud continued. "Each of you can become a staunch ally of the magnificent Angevin dynasty. Imagine a world where the kingdoms of France and England were each ruled under one monarch. Imagine the commerce, the taxation, the *wealth* that could flow through our streets. Stephen would not allow you such a world. All I need from you is your help. Robert must make it back to me. He's the commander and chief lieutenant of my army, and without him, we can win no battle outright. Now that Stephen has taken Wareham, Robert remains stranded in Normandy. Each of your families owns land from here to France or has access to resources that can help. Sneak my brother back to Oxford, and I will guarantee you and your families will have the utmost priority in the new world I'll create—the one my father and his father before him believed in."

Emma thought her words were rousing, but the other women seemed less enthused. Empress Maud waited for any response, but when none came, she waved for Madame Beatrice, and the two privately corresponded with each other. Madame B then stepped away, and Empress Maud turned back to the table of guests. "If the men in attendance could please do me a courtesy. I'd like to have a few minutes alone with my fair maidens."

That brought out quite a few disgruntled moans. At the additional behest of Steward Aubrey de Vere and Lord Miles FitzWalter, the men were placated and ushered from the chamber. If the need for a man's agreement for them to listen angered the empress, she did a fine job masking it. Once the chamber housed only women, Empress Maud sat upright a little straighter.

"You can be frank with me, my ladies," said the empress. "I've made mistakes, as any ruler would. Please tell me how you feel, so I may offer recompense."

"I've been to funerals with more cheer than this," said Lady Ansfride. She licked her fingers clean. "Maud, I'm disappointed. Oft you frame yourself as superior to your male counterparts, yet this meeting has more arrogance than a comely man."

A gasp went through the chamber. Empress Maud didn't react at all. "From what I've heard, Lady Ansfride, it seems your tongue matches your temper. Do not mock me with the same propaganda my cousin uses. If I act masculine, know it's because I must. This is a world ruled by cocks, and we all know those aren't good for long."

Emma glanced around the table at the other women. Besides Lady Ansfride, there were six dignitaries who arrived at the ball—all powerful women of various lords. They all seemed less-than-pleased with the route this conversation had taken.

Lady Ansfride smiled and waved toward Emma. "Servant girl?"

"Yes?" Emma asked.

"Untie my blindfold. I wish for the women here to see me as God intended."

Discomfort spread around the table as she undid the fabric around Lady Ansfride's face. Everyone had the decency to resist gasping. Ansfride drank from her tankard of wine, coating her throat with intoxicating wetness, before she began:

"In ages past, my sister and I used to have these dolls made of straw. I remember envying the other girls. Their dolls had small dresses with eyes sewn into them by artisans. Ours were nude and crude, and I was forced to use small black pebbles for its eyes. I'd play with it until the pebbles fell out, and I was rudely reminded it was just a bundle of thatch. We were playing with those dolls when *they* came. There were birds chirping outside the window.

"And with them was Granddad, the one you know as King Henry—God rest his soul, and so on and so forth. I recognized the guards he entered with, so I believed everything normal. I was seven, I think.

Sybil only five. Granddad told us to come with him, that he was taking us on a trip. He had already packed for us, so we left, eager, excited to spend time with him. He took us to the Chateau d'Ivry. At the time I didn't know that was a direct affront to our parents. They went and placed us in a small bedchamber with only one narrow window and a few sheepskins for a bed. Granddad told us we were staying a while, and then he introduced us to a man by the name of Ralph Harnec, who was the constable of d'Ivry. Granddad left us with that strange man in that odd bedchamber with our eyeless thatch dolls and locked the door behind him.

"I never saw him again. If you want to know the legacy your father left for my sister and me, Maud, it's of a grandfather who hated his bastard daughter and banished his granddaughters because of it. It's a miracle he loved you at all."

She waited as if expecting a biting remark from the empress; rather, Maud didn't flinch. She remained muted, listening to the words of her niece. Lady Ansfride continued:

"We lived in that tiny bedchamber for months. And the heat that summer . . . it was hard to breathe. We could rarely bathe, were barely given enough water. I mean, the *heat*, the *stench*. It was horrid. Sybil and I would stand on our tiptoes and press ourselves against the window, desperate to feel fresh air. Any time we felt a faint breeze, and it'd push our sweat away . . . those were the best days. My sister cried constantly. Most of the time I couldn't stop her. Sometimes I lost my temper and slapped her. Did she think I knew where our parents were? Stupid girl. No, I don't know why they won't come and save us. I don't know.

"I couldn't cry, lest that would make her worse. Only she could. I had to wait. Only when Sybil was asleep, or when she was lost in her daydreams, could I openly weep.

"Finally, Ralph returned for us. Our door was unbarred, and we were carried, emancipated as we were, by guards who no longer recognized us. I could tell the constable was angry. He swore with words I had never heard before. He spat twice at my sister and me. We were taken to a cellar of some kind, and a tall man was there. I was glad. I remember that. I was glad Sybil was too young to know what it meant when they called him executioner.

"There was a lit brazier with a metal poker. They held me down first. I could hear my sister crying behind me, but this time I couldn't soothe her. I screamed. Begged them for our parents. Promised I'd do anything. In return, Ralph Harnec placed a rag in my mouth, laughing at me, glaring at me. Then he started crying. His tears hit my face. Cold, wet tears, which evaporated when the poker wreathed in hellish flames was lifted before my eyes. I tried to running, fighting. But they had me pinned.

"Then I heard Granddad. *Heard*, never saw. Can you guess what your father told the executioner, Maud? I remember it. Word-for-word. *Don't dirty her face*, he said. *Her dowry won't be worth much, but we might still get a small castle for it*."

The table of women were stunned silent, with only the faint, timid sounds of the flickering flames atop the beeswax candles making noise.

"When it was done, they'd taken both my eyes and the tip of my nose. It's funny. Granddad was wrong. I'd never be worth a castle after that." She froze for a moment before continuing, "The worst part was hearing my sister thereafter. The world is never louder than the moment you lose your sight. And the first thing I heard was my sister's wails as they gouged her. It was too much. It rang in my ears for what seemed an eternity. Finally, they took her tongue . . .

"That was the last time I ever heard Sybil cry. I was so *fucking* happy about it. Thank God I couldn't listen to her tears, her wails again. Thank God . . .

"Ralph released us four months later, and I was left wondering why Granddad would want this for us, wondering why our parents never saved us. But I soon found out. My mother, an illegitimate daughter cast off by her king father, was gifted to the highest bidder. Our father had the best castle to give, and so Granddad married her to him. I've no doubt King Henry was proud of his work. He had many bastard children. A strategic number, I'd say, for he used them all to gain further land and titles, marrying them off one by one. In time though, my mother was forgotten, and my father's ambition disregarded. He expected so much more after he wed a king's daughter. So, they rebelled, with the aim of capturing the Chateau d'Ivry from Ralph Harnec and

Granddad. Unfortunately, the only thing our parents won from that accursed upheaval was Ralph's fury. And their children's disfigurement."

"Why did you tell us all of that?" Empress Maud asked after an extended silence. Even she seemed exhausted from the story told to them. Lady Ansfride tied the blindfold back on.

"Let's pretend it's a fable, and *not* real, dearest aunt. What lesson did you learn of it?"

As Empress Maud thought for a long second, Emma came up with her own answer. It thrummed deep within her heart; an impulse palpitated through her veins. She couldn't quite put it into words yet, but like most things seemed to nowadays, it all connected back to her mother and the life she'd left behind.

"What is the moral to you, dearest niece?" Empress Maud asked.

Lady Ansfride laughed. "The moral is that the world is *fucked*. For a time, I believed it to be only men who ruined the world, but now I see women are truly their perfect partners. You ask for vengeance, just as my mother asked for vengeance, just as Ralph asked your father for vengeance. My world was destroyed long ago by your family, Maud, just as many of the other women here. There's nothing you can offer us to save the lives we've already lost."

Dancing! Music!

The words came to Emma all at once. She needed a way to quickly gain access to either the library *or* Empress Maud herself. She'd forever be her third handmaiden behind Madame B and Theresa ... unless she did something bold. She didn't know why, but she thought she knew what Lady Ansfride wanted. Looking around the table, all Emma saw were tired, broken women; for once, maybe they needed to feel like the princesses they were.

"Excuse me, empress," said Emma, her voice shaking.

"Emma!" Madame B gasped, glaring at her. "My apologies, my lady. I'll escort—"

"No," said Lady Ansfride. "If I may, Maud, I'd like to hear what she has to say."

Madame Beatrice glanced back at her mistress. The empress thought for a moment, and then said, "Go on, Emma. What were you going to say?"

"I thought, maybe, perhaps, everyone would prefer to dance and hear some music before we continue talks? I know Lady Ansfride has traveled a long way to get here, and she has yet to have any time to convalesce."

Empress Maud frowned. She looked around the table at her guests, then back to Emma. "I don't believe we know anyone capable of playing instruments," she said.

"Jory!" Emma suggested excitedly.

Empress Maud looked at Madame B. "Who's Jory?"

"He was a cook," said Madame Beatrice.

"Is he no longer a cook?"

"I..." Madame Beatrice hesitated. She scratched at the scarf around her neck. "I let him go. And his mandolin broke in the process."

"I know where he is," said Emma. "I can go get him. He has other," and here Emma glared at Madame B, "*non-smashed* instruments."

Empress Maud considered this. She glanced at Lady Ansfride, who seemed to *feel* her glare somehow, for she sat up a little straighter and stretched. "I would like to hear music," said Ansfride. "T'would make for a better night than all this dour nonsense."

Within the next hour, Emma, with the help of Mildritha and Crispin, found Jory drinking at a tavern in the scholarly quarter of Oxford. He agreed wholeheartedly to return—as it turned out, intellectual vagabonds didn't pay well for musical talent. It wasn't much later that they were back inside Beaumont Palace, with Jory's stringed notes bouncing rhythmically off the beamed ceiling. The dining chamber warmed with the splendor of wine, music, and good company. Tensions relieved. The hearth popped comfortably at the far end. The women chatted about things other than war or allegiances or corruption.

Meanwhile, Madame Beatrice stood in the corner and watched it all gloomily.

Lady Ansfride was the only one bold enough to dance. So unafraid she seemed, and so unbothered by what others thought of her, that Emma found it terribly difficult to keep her eyes off of her... and her disfigurement. The hollowed eyes, permanently red as if always in pain from trying to see once more; the half-nose, the cartilage and bone visible through the opening. It was a miracle she hadn't died yet.

"Dance with me," Lady Ansfride said, pointing almost exactly at her.

Emma took her hand and was immediately taken into rhythm with the woman, staying silent, simply feeling each other's movements and swaying to the plucked strings. Ansfride smiled, a large homely smile that would've been truly lovely had it not made Emma think of a skeleton grinning from the grave.

"Are you staring?" asked Ansfride.

She thought about lying, but no matter how many times she tried to rephrase her words, it felt *wrong* to do so now. "Yes," Emma said. "I'm sorry."

"I want to thank you for this suggestion. Oft do I forget how to enjoy my other senses so thoroughly. They become a tool, you see, something I need to use rather than enjoy."

"Did the king—sorry. Did your granddad really do that to you?"

"He knew what Ralph would do to us, even if he was too cowardly to get his own hands bloodied. That makes him complicit. 'Tis the same thing in my heart." Finally, Ansfride added, "As was my father and mother's part. They're equally guilty."

"I'm sorry."

"Don't be. It was not you who forced their hands. Tell me, do your parents love you?"

"I never knew my father, but my mother . . . she does."

"It is a blessed thing to have parents who truly love you. That's seldom the case in courtly life. Not in times like these."

It came all at once, passionate and unrelenting. Tears. Emma let them fall freely down her cheeks. She looked at this poor woman, missing eyes and a nose; a life of pain caused by royal politics. It was too much to bear, and it made her feel incredibly stupid. As if Ansfride could read her mind, she reached her hand up and brushed the tears off Emma's cheek.

"Why do you cry?" she asked. "Do my words cause you harm?"

"No," Emma answered. "I've always wanted to be a princess. I thought my life would be better. I dreamed of it, of flowers and castles and servants and . . . and . . ."

And here was a woman who was a princess, the granddaughter of a king. Look at what it had done to her.

"Now I see how foolish I've been. My mother loved me. She was always there when I needed her. She taught me to be a good Christian, to care for others—to patch roofs and tend to gardens. And all that time, all I wished for was to be elsewhere, in one of my fantasies, being courted by knights and pampered with admiration."

"Ah," said Lady Ansfride. "How easy it is to want a life other than yours. But you forget, dear Emma, that you were always a princess to your mother. She admired you. Pampered you. She'd have given you flowers and castles and servants if she could. You chase a dream you've already achieved. Don't be so harsh on yourself, young one. The world is already hard enough."

The tears turned into sobs. Emma saw her mother's face, so clear and perfect. She *was* her mother's princess. Her Emma. Ansfride pulled Emma close to her, and they embraced in the center of the lovely tunes that the bard spun around them. From the corner of the chamber, Empress Maud, Madame B, and the others watched as two princesses danced.

CHAPTER XXX
EADRIC

BAMPTON WAS A PARISH community about fourteen miles west of Oxford—a community of God formed in a flatland of abundant trees and arable soil. It held all the basic Catholic compound needs: a central church, a ministry ward, a housing wing, and a multi-use shop for cooks, stable hands, carpenters, masons, and more. Empress Maud chose this thriving community, home to hundreds of priests, monks, and workers, as one of her last lines of defense outside Oxford.

Eadric and Will watched it all die.

A fantastic ring of turbulent flames was all that remained of the palisade that the empress's army had constructed before their arrival. The narrowly dug ditch behind the palisade—which Eadric loathed to call a moat—was being filled with dirt by King Stephen's infantry. They weren't in any hurry, though. In a morbid twist of fate, the palisade that the empress had built to protect the parish community had ultimately become their demise; they were ensnared by their own defenses, engulfed in a fiery inferno.

It was a good thing too, since Eadric was still getting used to this new life of his. He had a permanent limp, as well as a bum shoulder and arm that'd never be strong again. He now had to rely on his nondominant left hand and use a short sword to fight, both of which made him feel mightily uncomfortable. Not to mention, he had Will tethered to him by a length of rope. Eadric ignored the bemused looks that the two of them got from the surrounding peasant-soldiers.

"You believe him to be in the ministry ward?" he asked the boy hostage.

"It's the most defensible position," Will said.

Billowing smoke from the palisade obscured some of the view, but Eadric could still see the front line of Stephen's army fighting through a blockade that Maud's troops defended at the entrances to the ministry ward. Across the courtyard from there, a separate legion of the king's army set fire to the multi-use shop. Eadric shook his head. King Stephen's flair for the dramatic had caused him to become partial to the cleansing might of fire. It had become a sort of emblem of his. The ruin of ash they've left in their wake was a message, not only to the empress, but to all those who thought about rebelling in the future.

A twinge of anxiety buried inside Eadric's gut. It would do him no good if Commander Braxton was cooked alive inside the king's flames of ambition.

"Are you certain?" asked Eadric.

"'Tis what my father would command," said Will.

"Let's introduce ourselves then."

He pulled Will along with him; the boy grew wide-eyed as they pinched through the smothered gap in the ring of fire. Soldiers separated for them. Word spread of the betrayal during the invasion of Wareham, and King Stephen was forced to execute the soldiers that betrayed Eadric. Ever since then, the peasant-soldiers have kept a wide berth from the Hellhound of Rutland.

"Shan't I have a weapon?" asked Will. He twitched nervously.

"No. Live or die, you'll be relying on me. I recommend you don't lead me astray."

"That's supposed to make me feel better?"

He and Will crossed the courtyard for the ministry ward. The boy hostage almost tripped when he became distracted by the screams coming from the burning multi-use building. The horrific noises of warfare had become second nature to Eadric, to where he was blunt to all such sounds of misery.

He grabbed the rope that connected him to Will and yanked the boy toward one of the ministry's side doors. The enormous building stood three floors tall, with multiple shuttered windows overlooking the surrounding grounds. The exterior of the building was whitewashed evenly throughout, and its bulky square shape was intimidating to look upon.

As if the fear of God wasn't horrifying enough, the buildings have to portray that as well. Eadric shook his head. *Hubris*, he thought. *Only humans can believe giant spires dotting nature's skyline are a holy thing.*

"Where would he be inside?" asked Eadric. Will thought for a moment.

"First floor. Probably a chamber in the northeast hall. T'would give him a view of the battle, plus a quick escape if needed."

"It won't be."

Eadric unsheathed his short sword with his good left hand. He studied its weight. He wasn't completely impotent while fighting with his nondominant hand, but he wasn't nearly as effective either. Eadric bent into a fighting stance. His knees creaked, and his spine stiffened. His body revolted against him. Eadric cursed to himself. He felt naked in his lack of plated armor. Eleanor and he had an awkward twenty-minute tussle earlier today where they tried to place the plate and armguards on him, but it was impossible around all the bandages. The only protection he wore today was the standard-issue foot soldier garb—coif, helm, mittens, and a thin gambeson.

For today's fight, the Hellhound of Rutland was on equal footing with everyone else.

The battle was fought fiercest at the blockades. These blockades at the entrances to the ministry ward were, much like a gatehouse, death funnels for the besieging army. Wielding pikes and polearms, Maud's soldiers thrust their weapons and speared any opposing soldier who came near. Eadric watched the turmoil of battle unfold around him, their army slowly advancing against the empress's, the fight turning thick and hot with the hemorrhaging lifeblood of the many. Will stepped closer to him, ticking more rapidly. It was an instinctive human reaction, the need to pull close to someone of flesh and blood and dreams and hopes as the world collapsed around them. Eadric stuffed down the retching sensation that erupted up his gullet.

My God, what's wrong with me?

He couldn't remember the last time gore and carnage had caused him to vomit. Years? Decades? He shook his head; he was losing his grip.

The apathetic reality he'd forged for himself since losing his daughter was slipping away. But there was no going back from the things he'd done. No repentance. This was the thing about guilt Eleanor couldn't understand; he must keep marching forward, step after step, slain person after slain person, until he held the corpse of Duke Richard before him. He had to succeed, or else all those he ... he ...

Killed. Say it, you fucking bastard. All those you killed, *that you* murdered. *All the fathers and sons you've taken. All the memories you've robbed. Every act of evil you've begotten was yours and yours alone.*

Eadric strengthened his resolve. Yes, this was the way it must be. This was what Eleanor attempted to tell him during their date under the boughs of the chestnut tree. For him to grow a conscience now, after all the suffering he'd caused, would be the ultimate disrespect for those families he ruined. It would be his final wound. In a way, he'd sensed this pressure for a while. His vengeance had transmuted from being about Lucia to being about vengeance itself. If he failed, all the lives he took, all the pain he caused, would be for nothing. In a strange and perverted way, he could create one last act of kindness by following through with his blood feud.

"Not like this," whispered Eadric. He pulled Will closer and said to him, "The king said I couldn't lead, but I'm not waiting around while everyone dies. Stay close! Don't trip!"

Eadric charged into the death funnel. In his left hand, he gripped his sword; in his right, he held his kite shield, for his injury made it useless to do much else. Eadric screamed, stirring his lust for violence. It was time for him to become the Hellhound of Rutland once more, and if not for himself, nor for Lucia, then for all those he'd slain before.

"Their deaths won't be in vain!" yelled Eadric. "Hell can't have me until I've earned my place!"

The Hellhound raised his shield in front of him, braced, and pummeled into Empress Maud's front line. Her soldiers screamed; they stabbed at him. Eadric knocked the first pike aside. He jumped from his left foot to his right, using his own momentum to close the gap. A sharp pain fired up from his ankle. He bit through it, swinging his shield across just as a second polearm pierced at him. He deflected it, his shield rattling, his muscles straining. A whirlwind of wood, steel, and iron,

Eadric whipped the sword back across his body, blocked a third strike, pivoted, avoided yet another deathly blow, and danced himself into the center of the blockade.

Five enemy soldiers surrounded him. But he'd closed the gap, meaning all their polearms were useless. In his extensive warfare experience, he'd learned there were two ways to even out every battlefield. Rise to their level or force them down to yours.

Eadric was a fan of the latter.

He rammed his shield into one soldier, crushing him against the corridor wall. Eadric's shoulder popped against its socket. Another enemy soldier swung a dagger. Eadric ducked; the slash grazed his helm, peeling off steel. He stabbed his sword and punctured through the soldier's *maille*, but the gambeson underneath stopped the point.

Fucking Hell, I'm not as strong as I once was.

That soldier bashed his elbows down, connecting with the back of Eadric's hand, causing his short sword to fall from his grip. A yell erupted from behind him. Eadric's armor suddenly felt too heavy. He tried to spin on his heels and block the blow, but his bulky shield bounced off the tight corridors, making him freeze for just a second. But a second was all one needed amid battle. Eadric glanced up; a soldier's blade pierced at his head—

An axe embedded in the soldier's nose. Eadric and the enemy soldiers halted in surprise as Will tore the axe from the dead soldier's face. Eadric had forgotten that a length of rope still tied him to the hostage. He nodded his thanks to the boy and kicked away the furniture that had been used to barricade the corridor. King Stephen's army flooded in behind them, causing Maud's soldiers to retreat deeper within the ministry building.

"Which way to the first floor?" asked Eadric.

"Down this corridor," said Will, needing only a second to recall his memory. "There's a chamber at the far end with stairs."

Chaos unfolded around them as they sprinted down the hall. Soldiers fought contested battles in narrow corridors. Priests, monks, and almsgivers fled in any direction they could. Desperate peasants stole goods in the turmoil.

"Left. Into there."

Eadric followed Will's instructions, and sure enough they found a room with a staircase. They raced up it into an alcove that split off into two halls. Down both corridors, Eadric spotted a mesh of bodies fighting against bodies. It was impossible to tell who was on which side.

Even more alarming was the smoke; it drifted across the ceilings of both halls.

"Where now?!"

"Down that way."

The first floor was full of bedchambers where the parish and all its clergy residents slept. Will continued to lead them down one corridor to another, and Eadric was certain that he'd have become lost in the maze of corridors and chambers without Will. Every corner of the ministry ward sang with the clamor of battle, while the spreading flames leaped from room to room.

Damn Stephen and his yearning for fire!

"He should be around 'ere," said Will. Eadric pivoted and glanced down the nearest corridor. He spotted a man bearing a surcoat with Duke Richard's emblem, the red splotch on an azure sky. They stormed into the chamber at the far end of their corridor. And the last one to enter was someone he knew well. Commander Braxton.

"You were right, lad!"

Fleeting was Eadric's joy, for he knew this fight would differ from the last. Commander Braxton looked resplendent in plate and *maille*, yet Eadric wore only a simple gambeson and a shield. This time, however, it was the Hellhound of Rutland who sprung the trap. He pounced, using all his turmoil to will his muscles past their point of exhaustion.

"Eadric!"

Will's shout came too late.

The first thought that came to Eadric's mind, stupidly, was that Will had used his Christian name for the first time.

The second thing he thought was, *oh shite*.

Adjacent to Commander Braxton's chamber was a room consumed by flames; light shone out of the room like an orange furnace, and the heat was near unbearable.

Then it imploded.

The ceiling crumbled with the combined weight of the floor above it, bringing down bodies and prayer tomes and trusses and thatch. The entire wall and half the floor of Commander Braxton's chamber collapsed. All of Richard's soldiers but Braxton fell into the blazing inferno below, which erupted with its newly fed flames. A flurry of sparks sprang into the corridor.

God brings me luck again, thought Eadric. He and Will hurdled past the licking flames and stumbled into the room. Commander Braxton glanced back at them in surprise.

"You're a fool, Eadric," he said. "You're a damned fool. You doggedly pursue this abominable quest."

"Get on with it! I wish not to hear your voice, but to see your eyes turn red."

"Hark! Lest my words fall on deaf ears. You follow your king, yet you question not how he rose to such power?"

"My king, your empress . . . it matters little to me who rules."

"Aye, but it is *your king* who ordered the death of your daughter," said Commander Braxton with such fervent conviction that Eadric wavered on his feet.

"It was no highborn," said Eadric with a shaky voice. "The peasants ordered it. Your duke was the only man who knew in advance, yet he did nothing! *You* did nothing to protect the men and women you were sworn to defend!"

"No, my lord. It was Commander Hurst and I who knew of the plot. It was *us* who intercepted the message from one of Rowan's knights."

"My brother's knights would never divulge information to you. Rowan and his guards hated Richard. Hated you."

"I know. That's why I squashed the knight's head with my mace."

His anger boiled over. Eadric took up the rope that tethered him to Will and severed it in half. He didn't care if the boy hostage ran away. All he wanted was the commander's life.

Eadric lunged at him. Commander Braxton lifted a shield that lay on the ground, its wooden front burning with embers, and knocked aside the piercing blow. The commander continued his momentum, punching forward with the shield and ramming it into Eadric's stomach. His gut convulsed, sending shockwaves through his body that buckled his knees. Braxton yelled, swung his mace, and almost backed Eadric into the fiery hole next to them. Eadric raised his shield. *Thud! Crack!* He blocked two more swings of the mace. He grunted. His liver and shoulder ached from the blows.

"Tell me where your lord is," said Eadric, wincing.

"You're in no position to give me commands, Eadric."

Commander Braxton, screaming, heaving, wound back his mace and flung it down on Eadric with all his might. Something snapped in Eadric's arm as he blocked the blunt force of the attack. But he used the pain to his advantage, stepping into the blow to grapple the commander low around the waist. They fell to the ground, both losing their shields. They rolled over each other, nearly toppling off the precipice into the inferno. Eadric threw off the commander's helm. His eyes landed on Braxton's ear; he bit down, tearing the ear clean off, cartilage and all. He grinned at the knight's vicious screams. They pushed each other off, but not before the Hellhound got one last slice with his claws. His fingernails cleaved a trail of four parallel marks through the commander's face.

"Where is Duke Richard?!" yelled Eadric.

"You still don't realize it, do you?" asked the commander between ragged breaths. "The peasant revolt . . ."

"What of it?!"

"Do you really think the *lowborn* could've schemed such villainy?"

"T'was them! Peasants!" Eadric's eyes burned with passion as embers showered around them. He wouldn't let Braxton spit these vile lies at him. "Do you proclaim conspiracies?! If anything, Empress Maud curated it, just like she did at Reading. She uses the peasants and their fury against her enemies."

"No, you fuckin' dolt! She fights fire with fire. T'was Stephen who deployed that first peasant assault. He knew Duke Rowan was siding with the empress."

Eadric shook his head.

"He was your brother! Surely, you knew he was against the usurper Stephen? Remember back when King Henry was still alive, and his son had died, and he'd chosen Maud as heir. The king had too many allies, too many friends. Stephen knew he couldn't directly threaten the throne, so he started his plot in secret, scheming how to undermine those who followed the king's declaration. Those like your brother."

"You lie!"

"Did you really believe a movement as large as that peasant revolt was kept secret?" Commander Braxton gnashed his teeth together. "Do you believe an uprising in the thousands could be without rumor? Think for yourself, Eadric."

"Enough!" Eadric picked up his sword and sliced at Commander Braxton. The commander bounced back and slid a dagger from a small scabbard on his belt.

"Don't die a fool!" shouted the commander. "Of course the nobility had heard of that feeble uprising! Every drunk peasant in every tavern in the southern shires was speaking of the damn thing. *The Bloody Wedding. The Royal Massacre.* Whatever they called it, inevitably, we'd catch wind. And Stephen did. He did, Eadric. He knew about it, yet did nothing."

"He would've told me."

"Would he? I wonder . . . Stephen is overly ambitious, but he's not an idiot. He loves making a scene, does he not?" Commander Braxton spread his arms wide, alluding to the whole military campaign, taking castle by castle and burning everything in between. "He saw an opportunity. If he fed the flames of revolution, if he kept Duke Rowan distracted by his rivalry with Duke Richard, then he could wipe out one of King Henry's supporters without starting a war himself. Your daughter's death was a tragedy plotted by the man you now serve."

"Silence!" Eadric fought off tears throbbing at him. "For the last time, where is your lord?!"

Commander Braxton let out a sigh. Finally, at long last, he revealed it.

"He's in Oxford, with the Holy Roman bitch herself. And they're doing their best to save this land from a king who'd coordinate the slaughtering of hundreds of highborn, and then ask those same people to support him!"

Eadric rammed into Commander Braxton. The commander's head whipped into the wall, splattering out blood. Braxton's arms and fingers sprawled outward in a visceral, spasmodic reaction. Eadric pulled

Braxton away from the wall and slammed his head against it again, leaving a second bloodstain. The Hellhound pulled back—

Commander Braxton stabbed with his dagger. Eadric grabbed his wrist right before the blade entered into his gut. He twisted the commander's hand, loosening his grip, and in a flash of motion, he disarmed the commander and plunged the dagger deep into Braxton's neck.

And within that brief moment, when he pierced the blade through the soft flesh of his enemy's throat, Eadric envisioned he was doing it to King Stephen instead.

Blood gurgled out. It was over, just like that. Battles and brawls, they often ended that way. A lot of buildup for a quick, brutal end. Commander Braxton smiled, showing a mouth full of red blood, and grabbed the back of Eadric's head.

"I see it in your face," said Commander Braxton with his final breath, "... the truth."

CHAPTER XXXI
GILBERT & WILLIAM

His captor cut the bonds that tied them together. He threw the discarded rope onto the ground. William's lip quivered. Commander Braxton seemed so much stronger than Eadric. He had full armor, while the Hellhound only had a broken body like William's. Eadric roared and charged at the knight. Fire bubbled up from the massive hole in the ground and shot sparks of embers around the two men as they crashed into each other.

Now's your chance, thought William. *Run, you idiot! Flee!*

But what if I protect him? What if I help him kill Richard? If my father is as evil as he claims, then I don't want his wealth or titles.

A tic overwhelmed him, then it was over. He had never been so sure of anything in his life. It was time for him to leave. He gave his captor one last glance as he and the knight fought to the death. This wasn't a good man, but he was once a great one. An angel fallen from grace. William would miss him.

He turned and ran out of the chamber, down the hall, past the inferno room and past the countless chambers of fighting and death, and straight into the stairwell. Tears streamed from his eyes. William hated how confused the world had become. He wanted the simple life he had with his brother. He prayed for nothing more than to see Ma Maman and Mon Papa and meet his baby brother. How he would love it if he could go back to the house of learning, slowly deciphering the scrolls and tomes of ancient times, and understanding battle strategies with his father and Earl Robert and the other fantastic people he'd met in Rouen.

He wished to be with the people who quieted his mind, or with those who challenged the complexity of his thoughts. He wanted the world to be something he could control.

William ran down the staircase to the bottom floor—

Someone grabbed his tunic and yanked him down.

Sir Álvaro stood over him, his black armor covered in blood and viscera. His mustache peeked out over his *maille* coif. "Where're you going, prisoner?"

William was about to respond when he heard someone scream his name.

He and the knight turned, and there, at the bottom of the stairwell, armed with a hand axe and a polearm, were his older brother and his friend, Bartholomew. William had never felt such longing as he did in that moment, seeing his brother alive. William knew he wasn't a coward! He knew he'd come and save him.

"Gilbert!" screamed William, joy resounding from his voice.

That was when Sir Álvaro, the black knight, dropped William and unsheathed his longsword, leveling it at his brother.

It was another painfully hot, dry day beneath the smoldering summer sun, and some way, somehow—to the infinite amusement of Hawk, to the extensive admiration of Bartholomew, and to the exasperating annoyance of Gilbert—Beatriz had talked the priors into giving them a *tour* of Bampton Parish, even despite the fact they were preparing for a siege. Soldiers bearing the surcoats of the Angevins were hastily erecting a palisade of sharpened tree trunks around the perimeter of the parish, while others were working long, extensive hours digging a shallow ditch just beyond that. The impending battle made Gilbert queasy just to think about.

Beatriz and Hawk walked in front of Bartholomew and Gilbert as a friendly man named Prior Leónel guided them through the multi-use shop—one of the few places that the non-clergy could enter. Probably because of his unrelenting nerves, Gilbert found himself in a humorous mood today. He couldn't stop laughing at how well Bartholomew appeared to blend in with the bald and humbly dressed religious men. Although he was used to his friend's new appearance now, there were still times when he saw Bart and it took his brain a few seconds to remember who he was. There was a time not too long ago when Bartholomew and Hawk used to be two crows of the same feather, each outdoing the other with how outlandish they could dress.

They stopped at a first-floor storage chamber where Prior Leónel pointed out some artifacts from the local church. Beatriz gasped and held her arm out to it reverently. She smiled broadly, tears making her eyes sparkle. Bartholomew grinned at her.

"I can't believe this is the same girl we pulled cons with," Gilbert whispered to Bart.

"She's changed," said Bartholomew. "For the better, I believe. This journey has been good for us."

"What? How so?"

"I fell in love with her craziness, and she fell in love with my . . ." He trailed off as he searched for the word.

"Non-crazy?" suggested Gilbert.

"I guess so. But then she found she needed the Church, while I found I needed the feistiness of our prior life. It strained us both."

"We could tell. Hawk and me have never heard ye so muted before. We thought she had you whipped."

"I wish she had me whipped." Bartholomew chuckled, and that made Gilbert happy. Despite his growing anxiety about his curse and his mother's omen, especially in how they related to his friends, it thrilled him that Bartholomew was finally beginning to open up. He had been largely stoic and unvocal since they reunited months ago.

"We were both growing apart, I think," Bartholomew said in confidence. He glanced at his wife ahead of him, her fingers tracing the timeless artifacts. He smiled and said, "We needed to embrace both religion *and* tomfoolery. And we needed to do good."

"I'm sorry it had to be because of me and Will."

"Don't be. We love you both. I would die for you both, as I would for her."

A sharp horn blew a single vociferous note from outside the flimsy walls of the multi-use building. At once, the multitude of carpenters, cooks, porters, servants, masons, farmers, couriers, and all else who worked within the parish rushed to the windows and swung open the shutters. The horn cried again, from beyond the perimeter palisade and beyond the shallow ditch, past even the farmlands turned dry from the invasive summer sun. It resounded all the way from the trumpet of a herald dressed in bright-blue livery; about him stormed a cavalry of armed knights and men-at-arms, and to their flank ran a legion of foot soldiers bearing torches and cauldrons which sloshed with oil.

Empress Maud's army scrambled to organize a counteroffensive, but as they lined up archers to pin down the approaching torchbearers and oil slickers, the king's cavalry punctured through the openings in the unfinished palisade. A second and third wave of soldiers screamed behind the first, shouting in triumph as they saw their men bust through the fortifications so easily, finally believing that they would not die on this mucky summer day.

By the time Gilbert and the rest of the civilian inhabitants got their wits about them, the king's foot soldiers started a fire so sweeping—in no small part because of the summer's treacherous heat—that the entire palisade sparked aflame. So monstrous was this circle of fire that entrapped them all within the parish, that the thick fumes formed an immense black dome around them all, as if they were under an imposing vault dedicated to the Great Archangel. In the courtyard between the multi-use complex, the church, and the ministry ward, the cavalry crashed into the uneven lines of Maud's soldiers. They butchered through them; many were trampled under the stampeding horses, while many more had their torsos and arms severed.

The twisting barrel of black smoke pressed against the window and made Gilbert's eyes burn. The barbarous smell of sulfur incinerated his nostrils. But if what he heard from the black knight near Devizes was correct, then this battle meant the Hellhound of Rutland was here.

"Gilbert, come on!" Bartholomew pulled him away from the window. Hawk seethed with nervous excitement, while Beatriz held the fear of God in her eyes. Bartholomew moved to comfort her.

"I take it that's the army?" asked Hawk.

"Aye," Gilbert said. "He must be here."

A stream of workers flooded around them to escape the building. Gilbert had seen the carnage outside, however, and he knew flames trapped them.

There was no escape. Only survival.

"We need to get out!" Beatriz said, clutching her self-made cross.

"Which way?" asked Bart. They glanced around for Prior Leónel, but he had already vanished within the swath of panicking civilians.

"Does anyone remember the way out?"

"Aye," said Hawk. "Thisaway!"

They followed him into the frenzy. The corridors were a funnel of screaming, crazed people; they had to fight through them all. There were only two stairwells in the building, and each was at opposite ends of long corridors that connected to dozens of independent chambers. They were all squished together, the air thickly moist and pungent with the perspiration of fear. Gilbert felt as if they'd be crushed from the press of bodies. He held onto Bartholomew's hand, who held onto Beatriz's. Hawk had disappeared a little ahead of them in the throng of bodies; but luckily for them all, Hawk's insistence on wearing his stupid red cap made him easily recognizable among the fray. It bobbled like a rooster's crown above the crowd.

Gilbert glanced through the chambers they passed, trying to espy the battleground out some window. He hoped, despite the improbability of it, to spot the man he was searching for.

"We need to stay near the window!" Gilbert said.

"What?!" Beatriz screamed at him. "Are ye crazy?!"

"We need to find the Hellhound!"

"We'll look once we're outside," said Bartholomew.

Gilbert grimaced but didn't argue further. When they reached the stairwell, the screams became shrieks, the loudest of which came from below them. Suddenly the current of bodies shifted, and the crowd rushed back into them. Why were they running upstairs?

"Fire!" someone shouted. "The buildin' is on fire!"

Terror pierced through the thin veneer of Gilbert's resolve. The crowd evolved from panic to pure hysteria. Hawk, Gilbert, Beatriz, and Bart sprinted back, trying to get to the other stairwell before everyone else. The crowd surged. People shoved. Stomped. Battered. Spat. Cursed. Black smoke filtered up through the minuscule cracks in the floorboards. Bartholomew gagged. Gilbert coughed up blazing fumes.

It took everything in him not to be tripped or knocked over. He could feel the weight of the mob behind him; he could feel their force pressed against his back, compressing his chest, threatening his breath. All around him, people coughed for air that was no longer fresh. His hand lost Bartholomew's grip, and the small gap between them immediately filled with two bodies. Gilbert couldn't see much, and the world turned dark around him. Finally, a hand pressed reassuringly on his back. He peeked behind him. Hawk held onto him, shoving men and women away from them.

"Keep going!" he mouthed—his words lost in the cacophony of screams.

They spilled out of the second stairwell that led into the stables. The stable hands and farriers were desperately trying to rein the horses out of the collapsing building, but the beasts neighed and stomped and kicked at anyone near them. Beneath their feet, the ground became soot. Everyone slipped on the sludge, falling into the same foulness they were inhaling.

Gilbert and Hawk caught up with Beatriz and Bartholomew outside. A large section of the building collapsed behind them. The harrowing last screams of multiple inhabitants clashed with the thunder of crumbling rubble. The implosion sent up a pile of cinders nearly as high as the building itself, covering many in gray ash. More men, women, and children crawled from the collapsing wreckage. Beatriz grabbed Bartholomew and Gilbert's arms.

"We need to help 'em," she cried.

"Don't be foolish," said her husband. "We must escape."

The others fleeing with them had found a small gap in the flames of the palisade. They jumped through it to the safety on the other side. King Stephen's soldiers barely gave them a glance; they weren't interested in the peasants or clerics, it seemed, only Maud's soldiers.

"Please!" Beatriz begged them. "Do ye not feel the importance of what our mission is here? 'Tis to do good! To repent of the sins of our past. Please help me! We can save them."

More screams. More cries. More pain came from the burning building.

"I'll help," said Bart, placing his palm gently on his wife's cheek.

"As will I," said Hawk.

They all looked at Gilbert, who glanced toward the soldiers fighting in the massive courtyard. Empress Maud's forces had retreated into the church and ministry ward. Stephen's soldiers were attempting to break their lines and bust through their barricades. Then, as if divinely provoked, Gilbert remembered how good it had felt to help ease the mind of the soldiers at the encampment, and he remembered how light the air had been after he and Hawk eased the tensions, albeit through violence, at Denier's Treatise way back in Rouen.

Despite the fear and panic that flowed through him, he always gained courage thanks to the bravery of his friends.

I have time, Gilbert thought sternly.

It took only a few glances between the group to form a plan and get to work. Hawk and Bartholomew, being the largest and strongest of them, ran into the building and helped haul people out. Beatriz and Gilbert took those who had trouble walking, either from age or injury or fear or all three, and guided them to the gap in the palisade. They worked efficiently together, as they always did and always would, managing to save dozens of lives. Unknown time had passed in this state, the world around Gilbert becoming the blackened faces of the thankful, before he felt Bartholomew tapping him on the shoulder.

"Gilbert!" he shouted. "Gil! Is that—?"

Gilbert had already spotted him. William, his kid half-brother. He was being towed by a length of rope, leashed like a dog to a large man holding a short sword and shield.

What the hell are ye doin' here, Will?

"Gilbert, is that—?"

"Yes," said Gilbert. He saw the armored man pull his brother up to a defended entryway to the ministry ward. They fought their way in and vanished inside. His heart leaped into his throat. He did not come this far to watch William die in front of him!

"Where are Hawk and Beatriz?"

They appraised the chaos unfolding around them, but they couldn't spot them. Gilbert then looked Bartholomew in the eye, and he in his, and they both came to an understanding.

"Thank ye," Gilbert said to his friend. He stifled a tear that threatened to descend his cheek, for he had truly convinced himself that his friends secretly hated him, and that the Lord had forsaken him. But in the middle of a smoldering parish on the way to Hell, Gilbert changed.

Maybe, just maybe, he wasn't forsaken, cursed, or broken.

And so, for the first time in Gilbert's life, he ran toward the danger; and Bartholomew, like the loyal friend he was, ran with him.

They approached the ministry ward at the entrance that William and the Hellhound had busted through. From inside the building, they heard the fighting at its most hectic. There were a plethora of dead bodies and weapons discarded at the barricade. Bartholomew grabbed a long polearm; Gilbert reached for a bloodied hand axe. They glanced at each other, nodded, and then charged toward the sounds of fighting.

Somehow, by the grace of God, it didn't take long for Gilbert to find his brother. William stood halfway up the staircase, pinned to the wall by a tall knight whom Gilbert immediately recognized—the one who had finally confessed to him about the battle here. The knight's black-dyed armor opaquely reflected the flickering flurry of embers around them. He yanked William off the ground as if he weighed the same as a pillow. Up close, Gilbert could see how scrawny his brother had got. His bones protruded from his skin, his long hair hung damply to his face, and his right ear was cleft partially off.

"William!" Gilbert screamed as if the sound of his voice could dash the knight against the staircase and save his brother.

William and the black knight turned to face him. The glow of fire coming from the corridor above them must have lit Gilbert's face well, for his brother's face glowed like he'd seen Christ Himself. His smile was broad, and his eyes flooded with tears.

"Gilbert!"

The knight dropped William, unsheathed his longsword, and pointed it at Bartholomew and Gilbert. His armor was immaculate; the way the hauberk, gambeson, *maille* coif, nasal helm, splinted armguards, and chausses all tied together made him look invulnerable. It was like staring at one of the ancient demigods brought to life. How could they possibly damage something like this, all steel and no skin outside his narrowly visible face?

"Gilbert! Help me!"

Gilbert, with a layman's hand axe in one hand, glanced at Bartholomew, with a polearm held shakily in his own hand. Bartholomew glared back at him with the same fateful smile.

Would ye have him butchered, Gilbert? Would ye make certain your curse damns him as it did her?

Bartholomew nodded. Gilbert almost laughed.

All my life, I've hurt the people I've loved with my feebleness, thought Gilbert. *But not again.*

NOT AGAIN!

Bartholomew ran up the stairs. Gilbert yelled, hefted the hand axe, glared up at the knight—

And hesitated.

If he drags you to that war-torn kingdom . . .

Bartholomew pierced forward.

. . . he will corrupt ye . . .

The black knight sidestepped and parried the polearm. Bartholomew screamed. He pulled back the weapon. But he was too slow.

. . . and beget your deaths.

Gilbert watched, eyes watering, mouth yelling; he was, and always will be, a coward.

The black knight pierced his sword into Bartholomew's midsection. The tip sliced through the side of stomach, cleaving a chasm across his obliques. Bartholomew collapsed, and the knight kicked him into the floorboards. The wood exploded into splinters under his force. Bartholomew yelled, spitting blood, and Gilbert . . .

Gilbert watched.

Then, he didn't. Fury found his courage, and he hefted his hand axe.

"Gilbert, no!"

It was William. Gilbert froze again. William grabbed the black knight desperately and pulled him away. "Bring me back!" begged his half-brother. "Sir Knight, bring me back to Baron Eadric. I want to go back."

The black knight moved for Gilbert.

"NO!" William screamed, pulling back the knight. "He's in danger! Eadric will die! You must save him!"

Gilbert saw the lust for violence disappear from the knight's eyes. He turned, grabbed William, and hauled him up the stairs into the blazing light of the corridor. William glanced back once, and only once, and mouthed a single word to Gilbert: *relativus*.

Knowing that to follow would only beget death, Gilbert helped Bartholomew stagger to his feet, and he pulled his blanching friend out of the ruins of the ministry ward.

CHAPTER XXXII
EADRIC

THE AIR BLEW PAST Eadric and Eleanor in a cold burst. There wasn't a single thread of blue sky visible behind the dark gray clouds that rolled over the realm; voluptuous and low-riding, they suppressed any feeling of warmth and hopefulness. The stiff breeze flapped at Eleanor's dark-green dress, making her hold on to her wimple so it wouldn't fly off.

"Prithee stay, Eadric," Eleanor shouted while she tried to catch up. "Don't do something you'll regret."

"I have to know the truth," he said without looking back, continuing to cross the short hill that separated the war camp from the king's quarters. The River Thames passed them to their east, and beyond the coursing waters, visible over some tall willow trees, the roof of Oxford Castle could be seen, appearing cold and militaristic under the gloomy sky.

"Are you so asinine as not to see past your own idiocy? King Stephen will not take this accusation lightly."

"'Tis not an accusation from me."

"Implied accusation, then. Eadric, please slow down!"

He stopped. His wife caught up with him and needed to catch her breath for a second. She glared at him, her eyes straining for him to discover reason—well, her reason.

Eadric began, "If what Commander Braxton said is true—"

"Then what? Huh? Then what, Eadric? How does it change anything?"

"You know damn well what it means. It means *he* murdered my daughter. It means he used me from the start. He knew, and yet he twisted my pain to serve him, dangling Duke Richard in front of me like I'm some kind of . . . some kind of . . ." Eadric searched desperately for the word he wanted, but his frustration fumed quicker than he could think.

"Like you're some kind of hound?" Eleanor said with a sorrowful smile.

"God, I fucking hate that moniker." Eadric massaged his eyes. "I need to know, Eleanor. I have to."

"And what if he did? What would you do if Stephen openly admitted that he was the man you believed Duke Richard to be? Would you kill him on the spot? Is regicide the solution to Lucia's death?"

"Belt it! I won't take such chastisement from my wife."

"You will, by God, you will! Because I'm the only person in the world who will have your back when this ship sinks!" For the first time ever, Eadric saw Eleanor cry. The wind whisked her weeping tears back toward her ears. She said to him, "You don't get to stand there and pretend like you're doing something noble. You want them to kill you. You want to die, but you don't have the courage to do it yourself. Your spirit never left Rowan's castle."

"How dare you use my grief against me! This shame will be upon you."

"Not I, but you! If you do this, the shame will follow you for all of eternity. What of mothers who miscarriage? Of children eaten by wild beasts? What of the fathers, daughters, wives of all those you've slaughtered? Everyone who lives on this accursed earth grieves. The Lord didn't create this world for those who succumb, but for those who persevere."

"Do you have any idea how strong I have to be to do this?"

"I don't want you to be strong; I want you to be my husband."

Eadric stared at the ground and said, "Eleanor . . . you don't want to know me. For if you truly did, you'd lose belief in God. Leave me to die, for pity's sake. I don't need you here."

Eleanor paced up to him. Eadric's legs locked. He knew what he said wasn't true. He relied on her so much more than he let on. Eleanor took his hands into her own, and he instinctively touched his forehead to hers. The frigid breeze swirled between and around them; the warmth from the other's breath was the only thing keeping their faces warm.

"Hark my words, Eadric," said Eleanor intensely. "I despise how much I care about you. The way you sulk and brood, how you manage your temperament, that forlorn glare in your eyes . . . I hate all of it so much that I've begun to cherish it." She took a deep breath that trembled out of her. They stepped closer so the rest of their bodies touched, their lips only inches apart. "If what Braxton claims about Stephen is true, then I too wish for the king to fall from grace. Let God smite him down and have Empress Maud rule over us for generations. For as much as I pray that I could detest you and all you've done, I fear it's impossible to be near you and not care for Lucia too, nor for your quest to avenge her. I pray every day that she'd come back from the dead, and I could see you for the man you were then."

"That man is so long forgotten it feels like a dream."

"I know, as is the woman I was before I lost my son and husband."

Eadric opened his eyes and looked into Eleanor's beautiful blue irises. She rarely spoke about her former family. The two of them were complete opposites in how they handled the deaths of their children. In a way, it was a swap of what most people would expect. Eleanor handled it in a traditionally masculine way, stoic and without tears, but Eadric let it seep into every fabric of his being. His grief, his despair, his anger—it had become fully his own.

"But we're here now," she said softly. "You and me. We hated our ordained marriage, but perhaps we both needed it. It was always us against the world. So I'll ask you again, if King Stephen gave that peasant revolt succor, how does it change anything now?"

"He can't get away with it." Eadric's voice was gentle. His wife had completely purged any anger inside him, wisping all his temptations of violence away with the wind.

"Oh, Eadric. If Lucia even had a semblance of your dedication and passion, then she could've ruled the world. All I'm asking of you is to be smart about this. Don't put Stephen in a position where he feels he has to do something drastic to save his pride, not now when you're so close to finally succeeding."

Eadric nodded, enjoying the friction of their skin pulling against each other. At long last, he allowed his mind to wander. He thought about the softness of her skin, the tenderness of her wrinkled hands, the smell of her body. He thought of her, and then of nothing at all.

For the first time in over a decade, he thought of absolutely nothing.

"Baron Eadric of Rockingham would like to hold counsel with you, my king," said Wilkin the guardsman.

King Stephen was inside the war tent surrounded by his entourage, including William of Ypres, Bishop Henry of Winchester, Sir Álvaro, and other trusted dukes and knights, as they made final preparations for the siege of Oxford.

This was precisely why Eadric planned on interrupting Stephen now, on the eve of battle and potentially his crowning moment.

"I have no time for private correspondence," King Stephen replied.

"My king," said Eadric before Wilkin could shove him away, "I have no desire for this to be private. Ten years ago . . ."

"For God's sake, Eadric."

". . . a peasant revolt started here. Just south of us."

"I know plenty of it."

"It started small, but it grew."

"Wilkin, escort this man—"

"It grew so large and so vast that it was spoken of in the streets of London." The guardsman reached for Eadric, but he shrugged him off and stepped closer to the king. The knights around the room reached for their weapons. "Empress Maud wasn't within a hundred leagues of our kingdom in those days. Was she not?"

"Eadric, this is *my* council chamber," King Stephen said louder.

"King Henry was still alive then. Yet we knew. We earls, dukes, barons, and lords. We knew you had your eye on the throne, and that *you* saw yourself as a better successor than the king's appointed daughter."

"Sir León. Remove Eadric at once before he commits further slander."

Sir Álvaro moved. Eadric stuck out his hand, giving the knight a brief but trusting look that said, *I know what I'm doing.*

"And you were right," said Eadric. "You are so much greater than Maud could ever be. You kept us together through years of turmoil. Even though barons and dukes and priests switched sides every new season, you held strong. Even when imprisoned, your lovely, elegant wife was a force to be reckoned with. Taking London back. Taking you back."

"Can you get to the point, Eadric? I'm in no mood for speeches."

"I never, not once, stopped believing in you. Believing what you told me. Believing in the future of England you fought to attain. Every step of the way, you were always in charge. Were you not?"

He waited for a response. The war tent was silent.

"I was," said King Stephen.

"You spent years trampling a path to the throne. Yes? You're cunning. You didn't decide the night King Henry died that the kingdom was yours to take. God didn't ordain it to you in some manifested dream."

"No. I spent my life preparing for this honor."

"As you should, because your greatness will flourish once you expunge the rot Empress Maud has bequeathed on our green country," said Eadric. The guardsman looked between him and King Stephen, yet everyone in the room seemed frozen in time. Even Eleanor, who stopped at the opening, seemed perplexed.

"Thank you," the king said stupidly.

"What King Henry didn't know was that you already had dozens of barons and dukes swear allegiance to you, did you not?"

An ugly pause passed between them. Stephen nodded. "I did. We all knew Henry, may God rest his soul, chose a woman as heir."

"You offered those barons and dukes great things if they backed you. Land. Estate. Wives. Wealth."

King Stephen didn't bother responding. He studied Eadric, trying to read between his words. Eadric continued, "And you knew who was against you. Which barons, which dukes?"

"Yes."

"You knew my brother had sworn an oath to the empress then? Don't bother feigning ignorance; you just proclaimed you knew all those who opposed you."

King Stephen glared at him. He responded, "Not all, apparently. But yes, I knew Duke Rowan wasn't fond of my aspirations."

"Then you knew why the king wanted my nephew to wed Duke Richard's daughter? He was attempting to bring Duke Richard to *his* side. He wanted another southern duke to vow to defend Maud after his death."

"You've wasted enough of my time. What is it you want me to admit?"

Eadric stood up straight. He glanced back and caught his wife's eyes. She begged him not to. He peeked at Sir Álvaro, and the knight nodded for him to continue. "I wonder," Eadric began, "now that we're on the cusp of achieving your ultimate victory, did you know whose side *I* was on? Back in those days, when we all prayed no war would come, did you know who I wanted for the crown?"

King Stephen stuck up his chin, making him look down on Eadric. "You were on nobody's side. You wished to remain neutral, to hole up in your Rockingham estate with your daughter. Or am I wrong in my assessment?"

"No," said Eadric, his voice catching in his throat.

He now knew the truth.

"You would have let your vast military might go to waste, withering up as age caught hold of you," said King Stephen. "It would've been a pity. I wouldn't be standing here, about to take Oxford, if it weren't for you."

"You're right, my king. It's a good thing I'm on your side."

"It is. It's a very good thing." King Stephen waited for Eadric to say something more, but then, sensing no immediate response, he asked, "Is that all?"

"Yes, my king. You've lifted a great burden from my mind."

Eadric and Eleanor stood on the western side of the River Thames, shivering beneath the onslaught of northern rain and air. The trees were beginning their yearly transformation, shifting into the gold, red, and brown coloration that marked the decline of summer. The River Thames, while not mightily wide here, had choppy waters now, its whitecaps spraying wildly.

Will stood behind them, his arms bound and connected to a horse. Will's imprisonment was more of a formality now than anything. Ever since Sir Álvaro had recaptured him in Bampton, Eadric had made sure that Will was properly fed and housed. Will still had to be a hostage, at least in perception, for Eadric already had enough scrutiny against him. If he were to release a war hostage, the speculation of possible treason might grow too loud. William didn't seem to mind, though, as he appeared to be somewhat committed to helping Eadric complete his vengeance. He shook his head. Was he starting to feel something for the boy? In another life, a life where his nephew married Lady Lorena and the houses of Duke Richard and Duke Rowan were joined, William would've been a distant relative of Eadric. It was ironic. They were only destined to meet because they were destined to *not* be family.

"Make way for the king and queen! Make way for the king!" The herald blew his trumpet, and the shrill sound cleaved the wind.

The massive army next to them, comprising all the reinforcements that King Stephen and William could muster, split down the middle to create an aisle. King Stephen and Queen Matilda strutted down it atop their magnificent steeds. The army stood dormant but attentive, waiting for the order to pillage and kill. King Stephen and Queen Matilda passed to the front of the army and waited for their twelve-year-old son, Prince Eustace, and his eighteen-year-old wife, Constance of France, Countess of Toulouse and daughter of King Louis, to ride up behind them.

King Stephen satisfied himself by gazing out at all of it: his kingdom, his royal family, his army of dukes, knights, and mercenaries. He dismounted his horse and handed the reins to Prince Eustace. Eadric had only seen the prince and princess a handful of times, and those times were during the dark ages of the war, back when Stephen had been captured by Maud, and the queen and prince had to stabilize the kingdom themselves. It was, and still is, an impressive feat, especially considering that Eustace was only ten and the queen was . . . well, a woman.

King Stephen spread his arms wide to his legions. Today, Stephen had omitted the typical ornamentation and splendor of his outfits, instead opting for a practical uniform which proudly displayed the crest of Boulogne—three red circles in front of a bright-yellow shield. Even in the dim gray weather, the red and yellow colors appeared vivid and pristine.

"Not even a rainy day can keep Stephen from glowing like the sun," said Eleanor with a bite of sarcasm.

"Hark, my dear," said Eadric. "I believe he's about to shine on us yet again,"

Anger flowed through him as he watched the king; he was certain now that Stephen knew, at the very least, *something* about the peasant uprising. And more importantly, King Stephen knew Eadric would never have joined the war . . . unless something drastic happened to him. Something like losing a daughter.

And if everyone in the realm knew only one thing, it was how dearly Baron Eadric of Rockingham loved his daughter.

"My vassals!" shouted King Stephen over the rumbling river behind him. The entire army, all thousands of them, hung to every word their king spoke. "My brothers! Today we end this abominable insurrection begotten by Maud and Geoffrey. Our kingdom has suffered because of the war she brought! Her father the king, God bless his loving soul, had changed his mind on his deathbed. By his decree, he left *me* the English throne! All this death, these long years of starvation and butchering, should've been avoided. Today we say, no more! No more death! No more starvation! No more wickedness shall plague us from the foreign empress! Today, and however many days it takes to capture Oxford, we fight for our friends, our family, our kingdom." King Stephen paused for dramatic effect. Even from a distance, Eadric could see the king smiling to himself. "Today we save our realm! With me, brothers! With me!"

And King Stephen, in the dramatic fashion known to him, pivoted away from the army and charged into the frenetic River Thames. The water swelled up to his chest, but no higher, and he held up the ceremonial sword of his forefathers so it glinted resiliently above the storming waves. William of Ypres raised up his own family sword and yelled out a terrifying war cry. He sped forward, and soon enough, the thousands of soldiers, knights, dukes, and mercenaries followed after their king. It was a glorious sight, seeing an army cross a trembling river during a storm on the eve of autumn.

This moment would become a symbol of King Stephen and Queen Matilda's tenacity, as was intended. King Stephen was intentional in every action. *Every one*, thought Eadric coldly.

"Are you ready?" Eleanor asked him.

He watched the oxen and horses pull their siege weapons across the river. The trebuchets rocked back and forth in the high winds. Their scope and size were impressive; the minds of the engineers behind their design must be perverse indeed.

Eadric could get along with them pretty well.

The army forded the river and navigated through a sparse wood, eventually coming out onto an open field that surrounded Oxford. Eadric saw the city's walls, and the reinforced stonework of the keep. It was smaller than he had imagined. Gazing across the field and taking in the city that housed his greatest enemy, Eadric could only think of one thing:

I have you now, you bastard. You've evaded me for ten years, but I've finally found you. Oh Lord, oh God above, please give me this last strength. Let me finish what I've started. Let him die by my hand. Let him know that no sin goes unpunished.

Even God, in all His glorious knowledge, didn't know if Eadric prayed for the death of Duke Richard, or for the death of Stephen of Blois, usurper king of England.

CHAPTER XXXIII
EMMA

How long can a chicken run without its head? Does it depend on how long it takes for the blood to gush from its unclogged throat, splashing out in all directions, drenching the world in red?

Emma swung down the hatchet onto the fleeing hen. It fluttered away just in time, letting loose a feather that spiraled in the air. Crispin dived for it. His hands grasped its thin legs, but the chicken contorted its claw and slipped out, causing the large boy to flip end over end, chicken-less, until he smashed into the trestle table in the center of the kitchen. The table lurched, shuddering, and his mother desperately tried to keep the bowls of vegetables, herbs, and spices from flying off it. She couldn't save it all. Fresh eggs rolled off the table and cracked on the hard floor; a bowl of flour flipped over, exploding a puff of white powder, which sprinkled down on Crispin like a million snowflakes.

"Crispin, you idiot!" shrieked Mildritha. "Get that damned bird!"

"Sorry, Mama," he said, rubbing his tenderly bruised elbows. He looked white as a ghost, covered in the spilled flour as he was.

"Out of the way!" yelled Emma. It took all her strength, but she shoved Crispin over so she could clamber over him. He gasped, puffing out flour, as she smothered his belly. "You're so fat," she commented.

"Sorry," he said.

The chicken balked at Mildritha and scampered between her legs. The lead cook lifted her skirt and jumped in the air. Emma was impressed. She didn't think the older woman could get her knees that high. Emma and Crispin shoved, flung, and wrestled themselves in between the chaos, until they eventually captured the little bugger and handed it to Mildritha. They laughed. Emma enjoyed the feeling of being young and stupid and silly again. Her eyes lingered on Crispin. He was the only one who could make her feel that way anymore.

Cool air blew in from the darkness outside the kitchen window, a grim reminder that summer was fleeting—only a brief respite from the winter that came before and the one hereafter. No matter how dearly she dreamed not to be, Emma was a peasant; and for the lowborn, winter was the true unavoidable war. Kings and queens and princes and usurpers all could fight at each other's throats, dismantling the kingdom piece by piece until only the ruins of their wrath remained. But then winter would come. It would come, and it would douse the ruin they wrought with blistering snow, covering all the destruction, all the bloodshed and butchering, all the senseless loss and endless suffering, until it lay frozen beneath the white fury of God.

All peasants knew this. All nobility knew this. But the highborn had houses without holes and hearths with endless fuel, and thus they had the luxury to fight wars over pride and glory during the warmer months. For as long as the peasantry do their diligent farming, the feudal lords always have more food to take, even when their sturdy homes and hungry flames go cold.

"Do ye hear that?" asked Emma, listening to the wind.

Jory, who was tuning his lute, and Old-Codger Reginald, who was peeling away at a mountain of potatoes, humored her and listened out the open window. Faintly over the harsh breeze, they could hear the wails of a large host. A soft crying sound. It droned over the castle walls and carried up the Oxford hill until it hit their ears unsolicited.

"Yes, I hear them," Jory said sadly. "Oft I pride myself on the ability to bring joy to the pitiful. I fear *I* could not even help them. Has the war reached you yet, young lady Emma?"

"'Course it has."

"Not truly if you don't recognize their sorrowful dirge. What you hear are the cries of refugees. King Stephen—"

"Hush thee," Mildritha hissed. "Watch your tongue. The walls have ears, and to call him king is dangerous indeed."

"Well, he is king, by title alone perhaps. But if songs will call him such, I will too. Hark, young Emma. Stephen, current king under certain subjective perspectives, is winning. I'm sure you wouldn't hear Her Highness admit such a thing, but his army is slowly surrounding us. They've cut off her access to the sea, and therefore access to her husband."

"More importantly," said Old-Codger Reginald, "from the goodly Earl Robert."

"Indeed. Sir Robert was her entire army, the best fighter in all of this kingdom and the rest. But now he's trapped in Normandy with the empress's petulant baron husband. The point being, Stephen's already sacked multiple castles. They say he burns each town he passes, raping the land, raping the crops, raping the women, ruining the value of Maud's domain. These cries you hear are from the piteous few who've survived. Women and children mostly. Alone. With winter fast approaching, and no home to take shelter in, I fear their chances of survival are slim."

"Must ye be so dour!" said Mildritha. She bundled herself up in the corner next to the pot of boiling stew. They were all crammed in the kitchen, exhausted and hungry after a long day of servitude. Over the last few months, Emma had drawn close to the small group she ran into way back when she first entered Oxford. She looked at them all with a pleasant smile.

It almost dispelled the darkness looming inside her. Tom was coming tomorrow, and she only had one more night to find that letter and save her mother and her friend.

A knock came from the open doorway. They turned and found Madame Beatrice standing there. She had a runny nose, which she kept plugging with her handkerchief and scarf. Over the week a sickness had taken hold of her, so it had been Emma and Theresa who'd been taking care of Empress Maud most recently. Madame B sniffled.

"You're needed," the madame said to her.

Emma said her goodbyes and followed Madame Beatrice through the keep to the empress's bedchamber. Empress Maud had decided, after living a few long weeks at Beaumont Palace outside the city, to have all of her bedding and furniture tossed out of her castle bedchamber. After the smell from the quartered rats finally dispersed, she returned to the castle.

"Theresa caught the illness too," said Madame B. "Our lady has specifically requested you for tonight. Her bath is already heated, so all you'll need to do is keep it stoked and see to the rest of her bathing needs. Make sure she doesn't get too drunk."

Emma nodded.

"I mean it." Madame Beatrice stopped her in the hall. "She isn't doing well with Robert stuck across the sea. Don't let her drink too much. Please. If she asks for more, tell her we ran out of her favorite vintage."

Emma couldn't help but smile. "You love her, don't you?"

Madame B didn't respond. She didn't need to. Emma could see in her eyes that she did.

"More wine."

Emma filled Empress Maud's tankard up to the rim. The empress lay naked in the largest tub she'd ever seen, hot sea coals simmering beneath, heating the water to a comfortable temperature. Sweet-smelling flowers filled the perimeter of the room, as if the empress was holding on desperately to the final scent of summer. Outside in the darkness of night, only the death of winter awaited.

"Where are you from?" asked Empress Maud.

"A small land far to the north. You probably haven't heard of it."

The empress took a sip of her wine. Her words slurred as she spoke. "You're like all the others. You think because I was sent to Rome when I was young, that I don't know my father's kingdom, the land I was born in. Tell me where you're from. I promise I'm not some foreign invader. I know England."

Emma made up something on the spot. "The Sherwin family from western Cumberland."

". . . Huh." Empress Maud laughed. "I guess they were right. Well, Emma from the mostly unremarkable shire of Cumberland, I wanted to thank you. Your idea to bring in music did wonders for opening those dastardly closed-off women. Lady Ansfride and two others even decided to linger longer."

"I know," said Emma. She tried to hold back a laugh of her own. Empress Maud must have been drunker than she suspected. Never had her lady said anything so obvious before.

"What do they say of this war up in faraway Cumberland?"

"I don't know, my lady."

"Don't call me *my lady*. You're not Beatrice. Refer to me as *my empress* only."

"Apologies, my empress."

"Fill it." Empress Maud held out the tankard. Emma indulged her. Maybe if she got her drunk enough, she'd be willing to give up something Emma could tell Tom. Something that'll convince the king to save her mother. "Do you hear them?" asked the empress, listening to the refugees far outside. "They want entry to the city. Do you think I should let them?"

"Yes?"

"If I do that, they'll eat through our provisions, and we'll all starve come winter. But if I leave them out, then only most of us will starve. It's a tricky thing to be hated so much. To be a woman is to be despised, but to be a queen is *aspiring* to be despised. No doubt you've heard my cousin's army surrounds us, capturing the countryside one town at a time. I was a fool to send Robert for Geoffrey. Do you know what my husband would choose in this predicament? He'd choose the third option: leave them out, starve everyone else, and flee with all the food."

Emma saw her chance to rein the conversation. It seemed the thing Stephen feared most was Robert arriving back in England. *Get information on that*, she thought.

"And what does your brother think of Geoffrey?"

"He doesn't. He cares only for me and my wellbeing. My husband is just an overseas distraction. Stephen is the *real* bastard."

Well, that didn't work. Let's try . . . "He doesn't hate your husband too?"

"Hate?" Empress Maud twisted in her bath, appraising Emma with her bright eyes. "Do I hate my husband?"

"It seems like it."

"Does Cumberland typically produce girls of such insolence?"

"Am I wrong?"

". . . No." Empress Maud chuckled. "No, you're not. He severed any chance we had when he sent Robert away empty-handed."

"What will your brother do now?"

"He'll find his way back to me. He always has." The empress sighed. She waved at the water in her bath, watching the ripples bounce off the tub, off each other, off her. "What a mess I've made of all this. I've let him surround me. I'm no tactician. I'm an empress. I was born to rule, not warmonger. Stephen's torching my kingdom to cinders, and all I can do is pray the ash doesn't suffocate me. Are you a devout Christian, Emma?"

"Yes."

"The Church has decided I am more of a Christian than Stephen. Poor cousin. Even his brother has abandoned him. Now he'll singe England to embers just to spite us all. The men following him are all useless. They'll allow it to happen. The only one with any sense over there is Matilda. I underestimated her before, but I shan't again."

"My empress," said Emma, desperate to change the conversation back to her goal before Maud got too melancholic, "would you like me to retrieve something of your brother's? Perhaps if you had a memento of his, you'd feel less lonely."

"I'm not lonely," said Empress Maud harshly. "I'm not. But I do miss him. He sent a letter."

Emma's heart hammered in her chest. "Did he?"

"My damn husband . . ."

"Would you like me to retrieve it for you?"

"No."

"Maybe if it helps you feel better?"

"Nay, girl! You've spoken out of turn twice before. Do not do so a third time." Empress Maud stood up in the tub. "I've wallowed in self-pity for long enough."

Emma retrieved a fresh robe for her as the empress dumped the remainder of her wine into the tub. Empress Maud watched the red liquid spread through the steaming water like a hellish storm cloud.

"I will not let you destroy me," Empress Maud whispered to herself, the red water reflecting in her pupils. She glared up at Emma. "Go find

Madame Beatrice. Tell her I'm calling a council. I want nobody in or out of the keep. Have her grab the letter from Robert. I'll need it."

"Is something the matter?" asked Emma, feeling as if she might vomit. How would she get the letter and escape the castle now?

"Yes," said Empress Maud, Countess of Anjou, Princess of England and Queen Dowager of the Holy Roman Empire. "I wish to call upon God. It's time for Him to choose a side."

The piercing-cold wind blasted Oxford Castle with a turbulent frenzy, as if it were determined to knock down the keep and drown its inhabitants in the treacherous River Mill Stream. Madame Beatrice riffled through the empress's private chest. The surrounding air was impossibly still, a stark contrast to the mighty uproar of nature outside. Through the closed window slats, the world brightened ever so slightly. Emma was out of time. Daybreak was upon them. She needed to meet Tom soon. She felt stifled, like the feverish repose of the bedchamber was suffocating her. A distant thunderclap did little to calm her nerves.

"There you are," said Madame B. She stood up, holding Robert's letter in her hand. She covered her mouth while another bout of sneezes erupted from her.

"I'll carry it for ye." Emma stepped up to grab the letter. Madame B recoiled.

"Nay. This is far too important. I'll hold on—" Madame Beatrice keeled over and coughed. She used her scarf to wipe saliva from the corner of her lips. "I'll hold on to it."

The sky continued to brighten.

"Ye can't go near the empress," Emma said, "lest ye get her sick."

"No, Emma. She entrusted it to me." Madame B slid the letter into her dress.

She barely heard the madame over the ringing in her ears. Everything but the rising sun seemed frozen in time. Madame Beatrice coughed again, and as she did, all Emma could see was her poor mother. She saw her bent over some dusty old bed, hacking out her last breath, dying because her daughter wasn't brave enough to save her.

Emma took a deep, exhausted, trembling breath, and with it, she let go of everything her life had been this past summer. With that last exhalation, she said goodbye to Mildritha, to Crispin, to Madame B and Old-Codger Reginald and Empress Maud and Jory and everyone else who gave her a taste of what being highborn was like. She was going to throw it all away. She knew now, at long last, that she'd never be a princess. She'd always be what she always was.

A street rat. A thief. A spy.

"Give me the letter," demanded Emma, mustering as much authority as she could.

Madame B glared at her incredulously. "How dare you," she said.

Emma blocked her as the madame tried to pass around her. They froze. Emma wobbled. Her nerves were on fire. Madame B stood up straighter.

Wind slammed against the window shutters. The wooden slats cracked.

The sun rose.

"Emma," Madame B said sternly, "I'll give you one chance to leave the keep. I won't call the guards. I won't tell the empress. But you must leave and never return."

"No, madame. I need that letter."

Madame Beatrice's eyes widened as understanding and rage covered her face. "I knew it. T'was you that got poor Isabella killed, was it not?"

The overwhelming nerves and fear swirling within Emma turned to anger of her own. "Give me the letter," Emma said again.

"How long have you been a spy for him?"

Be strong, Emma. Be like Tom.

She stepped toward the madame. That was a mistake. Madame Beatrice reached under her dress and pulled out a short dagger. Emma gasped. Beatrice sliced at her. The nascent sunlight glistened off the blade. Emma jumped back.

"Don't come near me!"

Madame Beatrice coughed, hunching forward from the force of it. That was when Emma moved. She sprinted forward and rammed into the older woman. The madame reeled backward. Emma gripped Madame B's wrist and twisted. The dagger dropped to the floor. Beatrice tried to push back, but a cough erupted deep within her again. It weakened her, if only for a second, and Emma took advantage. She shoved herself on top of the madame and sent them both crashing. Beatrice's head bounced off the floorboards. She screamed.

The wooden shutters cracked apart, and the frigid wind pierced into the bedchamber. Thunder clapped. The dawning light spilled into the room.

Madame Beatrice shrieked, but her voice went hoarse. She was too sick to yell for help. Emma reached her hand into the madame's dress and ripped the letter out. Beatrice yanked on Emma's dress, shredding the fabric. Emma whipped her arm up. It collided with the underside of the madame's chin. They shoved and clawed and punched at one another until the madame finally released. Emma pulled away with Robert's letter and a handful of fabric from the madame's dress.

Emma ran to the door, only stopping when she heard Madame Beatrice coughing next to the bed. Emma glanced back. The madame looked terrified; her eyes were wide in shock, and she was hyperventilating. But not because of Emma. The madame gazed into the sunlight, her hands clasped around her exposed neck.

Emma had thrown off the madame's scarf during their tussle. Looking down at the fabric she'd ripped from the madame's clothing, Emma realized she had also stolen her handkerchief. Beatrice's hands shook fiercely as she lowered them from her neck. Emma gasped.

A long, grisly scar ran across the length of her neck, protruding from her skin like an ugly mountain range. Emma saw why she wore the scarf all the time. The madame was truly a beautiful woman without that horrendous wound.

The handmaiden glared at her. She opened her mouth and did something Emma didn't expect; she started crying. The hideous scar bobbed on her neck as she sobbed and hyperventilated and sobbed some more. Blood dribbled from an open wound on the back of her head. Beatrice prodded at the gash there.

"I remember," she muttered to herself. "I remember . . ."

"You remember what?" asked Emma, the suspense of it all making her stay. She glanced down at the handkerchief. It was embroidered with red thread, spelling a name. "Who are you?"

Ever-so-softly, during the quiet hiccups between her thunderous sobs, the madame said, "Lucia . . . my name was Lucia. Please, please. Don't make me say more. Don't make me say more or he'll hurt me . . . he'll hurt me."

Emma didn't push her. Her heart burning a hole through her chest, she turned and ran out of Empress Maud's bedchamber with Robert's letter in hand. She fled from the keep, her feet rushing her down the long hill to the gatehouse before the watchmen heard word that they were to shut the gates.

Meanwhile, abandoned in the empress's bedchamber, the older handmaiden wailed as her past trauma overtook her all at once.

"I remember . . . I remember . . ."

And it was true. Lady Lucia of Rockingham, at long last, remembered who she was.

INTERLUDE
A WOMAN'S LOT

1132 A.D.-1140 A.D.

CHAPTER XXXIV
LUCIA

I N THE VOID OF Lucia's existence, crisp and clear in her head, she heard her father's voice. Tame and measured, he asked her, "What did dying feel like?"

Terrible, she responded. *I was scared and cold. I saw your face, frozen with horror, stuck behind the latticework of Uncle's gate. I felt the knife slicing me open; again and again and again. I thought, this can't be. This can't be.*

"That you're dying?"

No. I thought, this can't be my father. This can't be his jovial face wrought with such horror, grieving with such pain.

"Let my daughter go! Please take me! Take me!"

"Daddy, don't cry."

"LET HER GO! GOD, PLEASE LET HER GO!"

"I am sorry."

"Lucia!"

"Your lot did this to us . . ."

"Lucia!"

". . . and it is ye who must pay."

"LUCIA!"

Anna leaned down and whispered into Lucia's ear, "I'll try to save ye, but I need to make it look real."

The bridge to the inner bailey raised up. Her father screeched and thrashed and bellowed as the edge of the blade sliced across Lucia's throat. Her chest became soaked with the spouting of her own blood. The gate closed; she forever lost sight of her father.

Her vision blurred. Anna's hands closed around her neck. Everything went black. Lady Lucia of Rockingham was lost to the world.

"What does death feel like?" her father asked her.

Like a billion particles of light, expanding forever and ever, splitting and smashing into each other—eternal fire crystallized from compressed darkness, hardened to a single point of existence. Like the heat of a lover's breath. Like the softness of a mother's touch. Like the provocative mirage of a beautiful dream. It was like watching the world slip away far below, drifting into the firmament—falling, falling, until it became a single point in the darkness below your feet. And, adrift within the frozen night between the stars, you take in that single point which was your everything; that single world which held everything: a billion lives, expanding forever and ever, splitting and smashing into each other—eternal love and hate crystallized from compressed passion, hardened into a single point of existence. Your *existence.* Their *existence.* Our *existence. And there was an overwhelming sense of understanding, complete and immutable, that you would, forevermore, only be an outsider to that point; an acceptance that you are no longer a part of that everything.*

And that it was okay. It was okay not to be part of that everything.

She awoke briefly to hands pushing dank, soiled rags against her throat. She was somewhere dark. Anna stood above her, looking down at her with a worried expression. Lucia managed to lift her eyes just enough to see two elderly women staunching the bleeding.

"Did I kill her?" asked Anna. "Fuck. I tried not to cut too deeply."

"She's lost a lot of blood," said one of the elderly women. "So much, but ye avoided her artery. She needed to get here quicker, much quicker."

"Please save her."

There were six hard rasps from a door somewhere else in the chamber.

"They're here," said the second elderly woman.

"We can't let them find her," said Anna. "They'll want to parade her. Do unspeakable things."

"Grab that blanket. *Quick.*"

Lucia passed out as they threw the blanket over her unmoving form.

"Did you feel I betrayed you?" her father asked bluntly.

Yes. Why didn't you save me? Why didn't you come back for me? I was left all alone, abandoned. My fear turned to pain, and the pain to anger; my anger begot loathing, and the loathing begot apathy.

Clip-clop. Clip-clop. Clip-clop. Clip-clop.

Lucia moaned. She pried her eyes open, wincing immediately at the sunlight sparkling down at her. Her body shuddered. Her head rolled side-to-side. She moaned again from the pain of it. She felt around her. Her fingers traced unshaved wood.

Clip-clop. Clip-clop. Clip-clop.

Hooves? Her body rocked again, and she heard the strain of an axle. The sunlight glittered and then died out. In the shade of the tall trees above her, Lucia finally realized that she was on a cart drawn by two ponies. They moved through a muddy pathway that slithered through a dense forest full of ivy-infested foliage. It was hot and humid out, and as Lucia came out of her near-death stupor, she heard the sounds of life: birds, insects, the wind between the boughs and shrubs.

She reached for her breast and was relieved to find that her mother's handkerchief was still there. She then touched her neck. An immense wave of pain shuddered through her as her fingers grazed a protruding scar right below her chin.

"Don't move. Your scab could reopen."

Lucia glanced back and up. Her eyes fell upon an older peasant woman walking next to the cart. She held a long stick in her hand, which she periodically swatted the ponies with.

"Where am I?" asked Lucia hoarsely.

"South of Bristol," the woman responded.

"Who're you?"

"Call me Madame Beatrice."

"How long was I asleep?"

"In and out of fevers for weeks. Anna snuck ye out, she did, for savin' her maidenhead. Good lady. Didn't want ye to be slaughtered and humiliated."

Lucia scanned the green leaves glistening in the wind. She tried to sit up, but her arms were too weak to stir with such vigor.

"Where's my father?" Lucia asked.

"You 'ave no father."

"Yes, I do. He is the baron of Rockingham."

"Your father is dead," said Madame Beatrice.

"That's . . . that's not true. It can't be."

"Forget your past, little one. It is no longer yours."

"I am Lucia of Rockingham. Lady daughter of Eadric of Rockingham."

"Not anymore, ye hark? Ye be a peasant woman lookin' for work."

"*Fuck* you. I am not! I am Lucia of—"

Madame Beatrice smacked Lucia square across the cheek with her swatting stick. Her head rebounded off the cart, making her ears ring.

"We stopped the men lookin' for a Lucia. 'Tis true. We stopped them from havin' her, whether she were alive or dead. But we don't know what happened to her since. Now, dare ye speak your true name around here again, ye will be tortured and assaulted in the ways known to men. You are *not* Lucia. Henceforth, ye will be known as Beatrice. Do ye understand?"

"I am Lucia—"

This time she was quick enough to react, but her arms were still too weak to block anything. Madame Beatrice's slap stung the side of her face.

"You are a Beatrice!" The madame hit the ponies with her stick. "I am sorry about your father, but we are givin' you the best life we can. Don't waste it."

Lucia lay in the cart and cried.

"What did you miss the most about living?"

Everything:

The way the sun filtered through trees; my blood rushing as I ran through grass; the way our dresses twirled during a dance; the heat of the blacksmith's son inside of me, touching me, kissing me; my father's stupid lessons on castle fortifications, and the way his face lit up when he talked about me. I missed the boring moments too. Moments of waiting, sitting, thinking, dreaming. I missed being able to cry, to feel. And the sounds . . . the sound of the ocean lapping on a beach; of birds singing at dawn; of children playing outside. Even the smells . . . the smell of fresh bread from the baker; of flowers plucked by my admirers; of the fresh dirt on my mother's grave. I missed animals: dogs cuddling against my legs, cats sleeping in the setting sun, pigs gorging on fresh slop, sheep grazing in the countryside, fish swimming in a stream, tadpoles turning into frogs.

I missed it all. Everything and everyone. Lord Christ, I missed living.

It was the first day of December, in the eleven hundredth and thirty-fifth day of the Lord Jesus Christ, when Henry Beauclerc, king of England, died without an heir. On the far southwest side of the kingdom, in a swelling port town named Bristol, the Master and his three sons saw their chance to become earls.

Lucia was scrubbing floors when the first dirge-bells rang. She lifted her head in confusion. The Master shoved her with his foot as he passed. She quickly went on scrubbing. The Master's home was a villa that survived the Roman occupation in the late third century, as well as the Viking invasion thereafter. It was now owned by a baron from Brittany named Lord Raoul—who preferred to be called Master—and his wife, Lady Hawisa, who was the second daughter of Robert FitzHamon, Seigneur of Cruelly and founder of Bristol Castle. In the three years since Lucia had been "given" to the lord and lady as a handmaid, she had learned many disturbing details about the foreign baron.

Lord Raoul despised Robert Fitzroy, Earl of Gloucester and half-brother to Empress Maud. He despised that Robert's wife, Lady Mabel, was the chosen favorite of FitzHamon's daughters. As far as the Master was concerned—from what Lucia understood of the many, many rants she'd heard from Lord Raoul's diseased mouth—*he* and his wife should've been given the earldom, and *they* should be the ones living in Bristol Castle. It certainly shouldn't be his father-in-law's eldest daughter; not the daughter that constantly travels abroad with her husband while they gather support for the king's daughter, a *woman* of all people.

Sure, Robert Fitzroy was an illegitimate son of the king. Sure, Mabel was the late lord's eldest daughter, and not Hawisa. And sure, Lord Raoul and Lady Hawisa sat around in their magnificent Roman villa and did naught but let their three sons run amok and harass the daughters of Bristol. But they were *clearly* better suited for the castle than Lady Mabel and Lord Robert Fitzroy.

For three years, Lucia lived under their roof and stayed silent, listening carefully to Madame Beatrice's instructions. For three years, she ignored the misogynistic ramblings of the liege lord and his sons. And for three years, although she'd become known as Beatrice, Lucia repeated her name to herself so she'd never forget it.

Lady Lucia of Rockingham. Lady Lucia of Rockingham. Lady Lucia of...

She always listened for news of her father: if he was alive, if her estate still stood, if he searched for her. She heard nothing. Tidings came slowly to the town on the edge of the kingdom, and most of it that ventured to them were foreign affairs. Many ships came into their plentiful wharves; ships from Wales, from Ireland, from France, from Spain. One of the darker secrets of the lord and lady of the villa was that they transported slaves through the port. Slaves were forbidden under the rulership of King Henry, but Lord Raoul and Lady Hawisa saw that as an opportunity to gain further capital. They needed to be rich if they were to stand up against Earl Robert, Lady Mabel, and their family.

Lucia wasn't allowed to leave the estate, and it had been over a year since she last stood under an open sky; thus, it was a special opportunity indeed when a young redheaded courier from Lincoln spent the night at their villa. She wasn't about to let this chance slip from her grasp. In the middle of the night, when the moon still shone low in the eastern sky, Lucia crept out of her servant quarters, past the light-sleeping Madame Beatrice, and strode through the opulent villa until she reached the guest bedchamber.

She startled the teenage courier when she entered. She knew from seeing her reflection in still water that she'd grown ugly. Her scar had festered and scabbed over so many times it would seem her head had been stitched onto her torso, and her eyes were permanently bloodshot from being hounded with nightmares on so many sleepless nights—dreams of Yvette dead on the floor and her father screaming while the knife sliced her throat again and again and again. She calmed the boy, however, and with a little convincing, she even persuaded him to carry a letter for her all the way to Rockingham when he returned to Lincoln.

She went to bed that night and slept more peacefully than she had in years.

In the void of Lucia's existence, crisp and clear in her head, she heard a voice. She was unsure of who it was, as the voice had grown unfamiliar to her over the years. Tame and measured, it asked her, "Who are you?"

I am Lucia of Rockingham, proud daughter of Baron Eadric of Rockingham.

And I will *return home.*

Lady Hawisa and Madame Beatrice yanked Lucia out of bed in the middle of the night. By the hair they dragged her, kicking and screaming, to the Master's bedchamber. Once inside, they threw her onto the ground. Lucia gasped for air. She clasped her hands around her neck, a soothing effect she'd adopted since that fateful night. She glanced up through her disheveled hair. Lord Raoul and his three sons stared down at her.

In the corner of the chamber, the courier boy stood with her letter in his hands.

"Who are you?" asked Lord Raoul, his voice rank with the smell of mead.

The fire of her youth, which she'd been suppressing for the better part of three years, hurled back through Lucia in an instant.

"Lucia of Rockingham," she said proudly. "I am Lady Lucia, first and only daughter of Baron Eadric of Rockingham, and I demand to be set free."

Lord Raoul kicked her in the stomach. She yelped, keeling over, coughing up spit and blood. The Master placed his foot on her back and smothered her to the ground. Lucia growled. She clawed back at him. He kicked her again, and that blunt strike broke something inside her. She cried out. No one in the chamber moved to save her.

"Who are you?" the Master asked more sternly.

"Lady Lucia of—"

He slammed her head into the ground. The *thud* would echo eternally in her memory. Lucia screamed. She wrapped her arms around her head to protect it from the onslaught.

"Now this, sons, is what happens when they're given too much power, too much freedom. They forget who they are. They forget their place!"

Another kick. Another scream. Another cry for help.

"*This* is what your uncle wants leading the kingdom. A slobbering, weak whore. Do you think a woman could really lead the realm? We'd be ruled by her husband, a foreign baron who can't even stop uprisings in his own damn land!" Lord Raoul stood over Lucia. The flickering sconce silhouetted his colossal frame. "Who are you?"

Lucia breathed heavily. Blood seeped from her nose and from a cut on her head. Her eyes, fierce with hatred and dread, stared through her hair at the man wobbling above her.

"My name is Lucia of Rockingham. And if you touch me again, my father will bring the wrath of divinity down upon you. I swear it."

The wetness of her hate made her eyes glossy. The pain in her stomach was immense. She knew she couldn't stand, but what else was there for her to do? If she was going to die, she would do so with a big *fuck you* and *see you in Hell*.

Lord Raoul took out his cock.

Lucia twisted and looked for Lady Hawisa and Madame Beatrice. Were the other women just going to watch? Was his wife just going to stand there and fucking cheer him on?!

The piss hit her face.

Lucia winced. It smelled rotten, like month-old cheese and moldy cabbage. The Master struggled. His piss came out harsh and forceful for a second and then died off in a little trickle. He pushed. It came harsh again, then died. Harsh, then died. Harsh, then—

"That fucker Robert thinks he can own *my* town because he's the foreign bitch's brother?" Lord Raoul scoffed, stuffing his penis back into his trousers. "He thinks he can live in *my* castle? *My* home?! And whores like this think they can rule because their idiotic fathers were king? They think they know power?!"

The Master waved away the women and the courier. "Get out. I must teach my sons another lesson about power. Give the boy something for his loyalty."

Lady Hawisa and the courier boy left. Madame Beatrice stooped down next to Lucia and said, "I warned ye to never say your name. Ye've done this to yourself."

She closed the door to the bedchamber behind her, abandoning Lucia inside with the Master and his three sons. Lord Raoul stood over her. He smiled. "I'll ask again, who are you?"

"Who are you?"

I am Beatrice. A whore and a handmaid.
I am nobody, just as it was meant to be.

Years passed. Her distrust of men grew; her hatred and fear compounded. Madame Beatrice died in the autumn. She fell ill on a Tuesday, and she was dead by Friday. Beatrice—who had another name in another life—became the new Madame B of Lord Raoul's Roman villa. As the new head handmaiden, the lady of the house granted her new privileges. One of which? Lord Raoul and his sons couldn't touch or harm her without "proper reason."

Madame B soon learned that there were many "proper reasons" to be harassed.

But Madame B appreciated one new freedom. She bundled herself up, covering the wounds and bruises given to her in her past life (as well as those given to her within her servitude), and finally exited out into the vast world. It had changed so much. It'd grown cold; it'd grown gray; it'd grown hostile.

"What did you miss the most about living?"

There was nothing I missed. I hated living. The bliss of no longer waking to pain, to agony . . . it was everything I could want. Why would I ever wish to live in a world like this? Why would God wish for us to live an existence like this?

Madame B lost track of the years, the months, the days. Time passed, and that was all she knew. Sometimes news would trickle into Bristol. "Stephen of Blois had declared himself king, can you believe such a thing?!" "Empress Maud had entered England. Yes! The late king's very daughter!" "My cousin in London sent word that King Stephen and Queen Matilda had taken control of the city." "Did you hear? Foreign mercenaries from across the strait have entered the kingdom." "Knights, bandits, and soldiers destroy village after village, town after town. No woman is safe. No child is safe. No man can protect them!"

Madame B ignored it all. She hated men, so what did she care if they died in battle? She distrusted women, so what did she care if they got raped and pillaged? She despised the world, so what if its children were slaughtered?

It was a better fate than having to live in such a terrible, God-forsaken place.

"Did you feel I betrayed you?"

Who are you? You converse with me nightly, yet you never show yourself. Are you a demon? Have you come to reclaim my soul? You can't. It's already gone. I lost it long ago. Kill me, if you have grace. Take me far away from here. You can only betray me by keeping me alive.

Madame Beatrice started to get horrible headaches. Ever since that night when the courier betrayed her, and Lord Raoul banged her head against the ground, she'd been assaulted with terrible, long-lasting headaches. The pain was unbearable. She'd hide in a dark room so the lord and lady wouldn't hear her crying and punish her for not working.

Lady Hawisa became cruel. She hated how much attention Madame Beatrice got from her husband, and how many looks she got from her sons. She would throw things at Beatrice, assault her with words and grating remarks. Each day, another part of Madame Beatrice's soul would chip away, the fragments scattering away with the wind.

Maybe someday soon she'd die, and she'd appear wherever her soul fled to.

Lord Raoul became more irritable by the day. Whenever news arrived that his brother-in-law, Earl Robert Fitzroy, and the empress had gained leverage over the usurper king, he became angrier. More than a few handmaidens came through the household working under Madame B. She tried to be kind to them. She tried to teach them how to clean properly, fold properly, brush properly.

All of them failed eventually. And when that happened, they were punished. Madame B begged. She begged and begged that they'd assault her and not the young woman who had the most minor of infractions. It was her fault! Hers! She was the one who taught them wrong. But then the girls would be brought to the Master's bedchamber, where he and his sons awaited, and Madame Beatrice's heart would harden as another chip of her soul would blow away with the wind.

She taught herself how to be sterner and harsher with the young girls. She realized she had to be mean and cold, sometimes outright hostile. It was better than seeing them called to the bedchamber at night. It was better than losing another piece of her soul. It was better.

"What does death feel like?"
Like happiness.

It was early spring in the year eleven-hundred and forty of their Lord Jesus Christ, when Lord Raoul and Lady Hawisa hosted their in-laws, Countess Mabel and Earl Robert Fitzroy. They were to have a lengthy conversation over supper about the political leanings of Gloucester, as well as discussing Bristol's earnings from its active trade routes with

France and Ireland. Madame B, now a servant at the Roman villa for almost eight years, was the only one trusted enough to take care of such esteemed guests. The cook prepared the meals, and she attended to the lord and lady's wills, until the sharp ringing of a bell announced an unexpected guest.

If there was any change in Madame Beatrice's countenance when Empress Maud entered, then it would've only been in the slight widening of her eyes.

Earl Robert stood and embraced his sister warmly. Madame Beatrice always wondered what it was about certain people that made others bow to them, but she understood it the moment she saw the two siblings together. Empress Maud's presence overwhelmed the room; she was as elegant and beautiful as she was keenly aware of all activity inside the chamber. Earl Robert seemed, as hard as it was for Madame B to believe, taller and even more authoritative when he stood next to his older sister. She gave him strength, and that strength redoubled within his already imposing and astute character.

A hint of doubt crawled into Madame Beatrice's heart. Could this be a man and woman she could finally trust? Could these two aristocrats be the salvation for her withering spirit?

Madame Beatrice watched from the dark corner of the main hall, appraising the empress and earl as they spoke. She studied the way they moved, the way they walked, the way they deftly navigated Lord Raoul's presumptuous suggestions and Lady Hawisa's scornful stubbornness. Each moment the empress spoke, Madame B felt herself draw closer and closer to her. Empress Maud's confidence became her own; her impassive resolve bolstered hers. Eventually, the political discussions died down, and the hearth simmered to a faint blaze, and the deep red wine from the kingdom of France was drunk generously by the hosts. Madame Beatrice noticed that while the lord and lady of the villa had been thoroughly soused by drinking their spite away, the empress and her brother had hardly touched their own goblets. And while she refilled her master's cup, Empress Maud, for the first time that night, seemed to notice Madame B. It made Beatrice's heart stop. Lady Hawisa stretched her arms and yawned dramatically—a poor attempt at trying to draw the empress's attention.

"Late grows the evening," said the lady. "My lord and lady, my *queen*, might I request we finalize our agreement so that my husband and I may get some much-needed rest? I'm sure you're equally tempted by the allure of tranquil slumber."

"Certainly," said Earl Robert with his even-keeled voice. "We'd like to send out a herald tomorrow to announce that you two will take up occupancy at Bristol Castle while my wife and I follow my sister to London. If you swear allegiance to Maud, we'll allow you to stay at the castle and gain all taxation rights until our campaign ends."

Lord Raoul and Lady Hawisa were practically licking their lips at such a prospect. Their sons, who sat silently at the table all night, were equally ecstatic. This was all they had ever wanted. *This* was their chance to become earls. Madame Beatrice knew as well as they did that once they lived inside the castle, they would never give it up again. The lord and lady of the "lowly" Roman villa had been planning this for years. They'd betray the empress and her half-brother, and if they must, they'd even slaughter their sister, Countess Mabel. They were determined to become the earl and countess of Gloucester by year's end.

"And as a reward," began Empress Maud, "for protecting my brother's castle and estate while we subdue the usurper, we will grant you new titles and holdings in your home kingdom, once my husband finishes his campaign in Normandy and Brittany. You'll become one of the wealthiest families in your duchy."

"Then send word for the heralds at once!" Lord Raoul said. "Let them say it with pride in every tavern and every hall in the realm: the lord and lady of Bristol swear fealty to the empress! Here, here!"

"Excellent," said Empress Maud. She stood up, and everyone else followed. "It was a pleasure meeting you and your family. May God bless you all."

"God bless you," said Lady Hawisa, curtseying as deeply as she could.

"Our queen *and* empress, God bless." Lord Raoul and his sons bowed.

Empress Maud, Earl Robert, and Countess Mabel moved for the exit. Madame Beatrice's heart sank. The coldness of the chamber overwhelmed her. She caught the eye of one of Lord Raoul's sons. He winked at her, smiling degradingly. That was it. All her pain and suffering and anger rose inside of her. Her head throbbed. She took a deep breath, gathering her bravery. What did she care if they killed her for this? There'd be no greater mercy to Madame B.

"My empress!" screamed Madame Beatrice.

Lady Hawisa gasped. Lord Raoul pushed aside the chairs to grab her. Empress Maud and her brother spun around to face the handmaiden.

"Who are you?" asked the empress.

The empress's eyes met hers, and in them Beatrice saw solace, safety, and comfort; she saw the woman she wished to become. In the eyes of Empress Maud, Madame Beatrice saw a life worth living again.

"They plan to betray you." Madame Beatrice's heart thundered in her chest. Lord Raoul sprinted toward her, ready to grab her by the hair and do unspeakable things.

"How dare you!" Lord Raoul growled.

"You dirty whore!" shrieked Lady Hawisa.

Fuck all of them, she thought, cursing to herself for the first time in years.

"They've spoken with Archbishop Henry," said Madame B. "They plan to side with Stephen once you've given them the castle!"

Lord Raoul reached her. His large hand grasped her shoulder and pushed down. Madame B yelped. He shoved her onto her knees.

"Don't listen to her, my empress," said Lord Raoul. "She's a rotten peasant-wench of Welsh descent. She's no better than a slave!"

"I am not!" screamed Beatrice. The lord's sons ran up and held her down. One of them clamped his hand over her mouth. She bit down, gnawing her teeth through his fingers. Skin shredded from muscle. He squealed.

"I am not!" Beatrice screeched again. "I've heard what they plan! They'll betray you all!"

Lord Raoul hit Beatrice across the back of her head. Her world went black. She awoke half a second later; stars filled her vision.

"Shut your cocksucking mouth," said the Master, "or I'll—"

He froze as Earl Robert raised his sword to the lord's neck. His sons went silent. Earl Robert's hand was steady. He held the point of the sword beneath the fat man's gullet. In an act of strength astounding to even the most battle-hardened knights, the earl kept his longsword lifted with one hand as he used his other to lift Beatrice up.

"You will not touch her again," said Earl Robert to Raoul and his sons. Madame Beatrice leaned against him for support. "Are you well, my lady?"

She nodded.

"Is what you say true, madame?" asked Empress Maud.

Beatrice nodded again.

"She's a lying snake!" shouted Lord Raoul. "She's a spy trying to turn the family against each other!"

"Earl Robert?"

"Yes, my empress?"

"Please keep the lord, lady, and their sons confined to this hall. No one leaves until I've learned the truth."

"Sister!" pleaded Lady Hawisa to Countess Mabel. "Sister, we would never betray you."

Countess Mabel gave her a stern glance before turning her attention to Beatrice.

"Sister? Mabel?!"

"She's a liar!" screamed Lord Raoul. "She'll betray you in the end!"

Empress Maud and Countess Mabel led Madame Beatrice out of the chamber and into a long corridor. They stopped her under a fierce-burning sconce.

"Who are you?" asked the empress.

"My name is Beatrice."

"I trust, Beatrice, that you have evidence for such a serious accusation?"

Madame B nodded. Unbeknownst to her consciously, she'd been stockpiling evidence against the Master and Lady Hawisa for many years. She knew countless people who had private meetings with them, many of whom were known allies of Stephen.

"Then I will have you held in protection until this is settled. If you are truthful, then you have my word that they will never hurt you again."

Beatrice broke down. Her tears came freely and unhidden for the first time in forever. "Thank you," she sobbed. "Thank you, my empress."

"Take her to your castle," said the empress to Countess Mabel. "Give her food and warm bedding."

"Yes, my empress."

"Thank you," Beatrice muttered through her tears. "Thank you . . . thank you . . ."

Later that week, Empress Maud visited Madame B within Bristol Castle. The empress told her that Lord Raoul, Lady Hawisa, and their three sons were being tried for treason. She also invited Beatrice into her service. The madame didn't hesitate. She knew from that moment on that she'd give her life to serve the woman who saved her. She would let nothing hurt Empress Maud.

Her life would forevermore be about servitude, but this time, for a person she believed in.

In the void of Beatrice's dreams, crisp and clear in her head, she heard the mysterious voice. Tame and measured, it asked, "What did dying feel like?"

Terrible. I was scared and cold. I had abandoned Maud and left her to endure the challenges of the world alone. I saw her face, alone and destitute. I thought, this can't be. This can't be.

"That you're dying?"

No. I thought, this can't be what all my suffering was worth. It can't be for nothing.

PART THREE
SCARLET SNOW

AUTUMN & WINTER, 1142 A.D.

CHAPTER XXXV
EMMA & MADAME BEATRICE

Tom awaited Emma at the dilapidated shack outside Oxford. Her heart almost exploded with joy as she rounded the wall and saw her handsome knight—well, squire—sitting there. He had on his full armor: padded gambeson and chausses, steel helm, black surcoat. He also kept a mace tied to his belt.

"Oh, thank God you're here!" She ran up and embraced him. The feel of his strong arms around her body was glorious. All at once, her built-up tension and fear released under his firm body.

"Did ye get the letter?" he asked. She handed it to him. "Brilliant, my love. Absolutely brilliant."

"Give it here."

Emma jumped out of her skin at the unfamiliar voice. It was deep and had a strange accent that made her skin crawl. She twisted around in Tom's arms and saw a man sitting atop a stool in the corner. The soft overcast light lit the side of his face. His eyes looked like two penetrating white beacons, shining hellishly through the darkness of the shack. His bushy mustache covered the tops of his lips. He wore armor too, only it was dyed entirely black. Tom handed the letter to this man.

"Is that it?" asked Tom hesitantly.

The man read the letter. "Yes. This is very good Thomas. It seems that girl of yours is capable after all."

Tom smiled. It was a large, stupid smile, the biggest she'd ever seen on his face. Tom, perhaps finally realizing that she wouldn't know who this man was, introduced him. "Emma, this is my knight. Señor Álvaro de Leon. He's *Spanish*."

"God be with ye," said Emma.

"How did you get this from that whore?" Sir Álvaro asked.

"I got it from her handmaiden, Sir Knight."

"Humph. A girl did what an impotent duke could not. Richard deserves the hound." Sir Álvaro tucked the letter into a pouch on his belt. "Tell me, what else did you learn while with the empress?"

Tom nodded at her encouragingly. She admitted, "Not terribly much, I'm afraid. Her handmaiden wouldn't let me near her for a while."

Sir Álvaro gave Tom a harsh glance. "Do you have nothing else to report?" asked Sir Álvaro. "Our king will need more than this pittance."

Thunder sounded, both hollow and all-consuming. Soft rain began to pitter-patter off the sharp slope of the shack. Sir Álvaro and Tom shared a look, one that seemed fully unconcerned with Emma and the fate of her mother and her friend. Her panic doubled over.

"Maud worries about her brother," Emma blurted out. "He's trapped in Normandy. Her husband refuses to help her and won't send support. Please. I can tell you more. I can find more."

Sir Álvaro huffed. He stood up, stretching his back and long legs. "This was pointless, I see," he said finally. He glared at Tom. "Don't bother returning to me. I'll find a more suitable squire."

"No, please!" shouted Emma before Tom could beg for himself. "I know more. I—I—the keep is being improved to stone. I know where it is weak! Where it is only supported by rotted timber. And—and—the castle is low on food. The empress worries she cannot stave off a siege for long!"

Sir Álvaro moved toward the exit, and with him, Emma foresaw the undignified death of her mother, Alice, and the world she'd abandoned but so desperately wanted back. Emma thought back to every secret and every tidbit of information she could use.

"Her handmaiden's real name is Lucia! Archbishop Henry secretly met with the empress! Maud is allergic to chives! Please, Sir Knight! She—she—!"

He stopped at the open door and turned back to face her and Tom. Behind him, the world wept softly. Emma heard screams, screams that had become all too familiar. They were almost godlike in their symmetry . . . reverberations of a home that was sacked. Emma was a child no longer; she knew in her heart the music of war: yelling, screaming, suffering, dying.

Ding-ding-ding. The bells of Oxford tolled, warning all the world that King Stephen of Blois had arrived. *Ding-ding.*

"What did you say the handmaiden's name was?" The knight's expression changed. His eyes seemed demonic, staring like embers into her soul.

"Lucia."

"Describe her. What does she look like?"

Emma left out no details, even handing him the embroidered handkerchief. Sir Álvaro's expression never softened. The black knight hearkened to her words with the utmost attention as the city fell around them.

"It cannot be," he said. He went silent for a long second, clearly in deep reflection. Emma waited with bated breath, hoping, praying. "It could, if . . . Tom, you've done well. You've done very well."

Sir Álvaro smiled. It was a dastardly, huge grin that made Emma's legs wobble. This wasn't a knight standing before her; it wasn't even a human.

"Thank you," he said to her. "They can finally be avenged. Thomas, no one can know about this. Do you understand?"

"Yes," Tom said dryly, sweat running down the sides of his temples.

"Make it so," said Sir Álvaro, "and you'll finally earn your knighthood."

The black knight vanished into the rain-drenched outskirts. Emma ran to the hole in the wall. "Wait!" she screamed. "What of my Mama?! Of Alice? Will they be saved?"

"I'm sorry, my love," said Tom from behind her. "But they were never ill."

Emma faced him. The rain poured down behind her, rising in intensity, the water droplets splashing off the ground, off the roof, off the wall, and wetting her. A chillness blew in that made her shudder. Tom stood still within the shack, his head down.

"What do ye mean? Tom?"

"It was a lie. A horrific one. They are alive and well. Both of them."

She fell back against the wooden walls. Her fingernails scraped marks into the planks. She shook her head; she couldn't think, couldn't breathe.

"Why?" she asked, barely able to look at him. "Why would you lie about that?"

"It was my chance to become a knight. Finally. I knew you could never be a good spy, but I'd hoped you'd be better. I thought I had chosen the wrong girl. You were just too . . . normal."

"Tom." The chill air blew rain into the room. Suddenly, her entire world became the confines of the shack. The sound of the rain, the tolling bells, the screaming citizens, and the besieging army all disappeared. There was only her, Tom, and the awful truth.

"But we did it," he said excitedly, his eyes mutating. "I can finally become a *knight*! A fuckin' knight, Emma! All thanks to you. I picked the perfect girl after all." Tom reached out his hand and stroked her cheek. Despite herself, despite the anger and confusion and the cold stare in Tom's eyes, Emma succumbed to the warmth of his fingers as they molded the softness of her face.

"They're alive . . ." Her voice broke. Her heart ached. She wanted him to carry her far off, away from this horrid city and its putrid walls, and take her to see her mother and Alice.

"I'm sorry," he said instead. "I wish you could be there for it. I'll always remember you, Emma. May that give you some peace."

Her heart slammed against her chest, matching the thunder of the heavens. She moved his fingers off her face and searched his eyes for the man she fell in love with, her knight in shining armor. He was no longer there.

"Tom?" she dared to ask.

Tom never responded.

He moved with incredible speed, unbuckling his mace and swinging it up. Emma dived. The mace slammed into the wooden walls of the shack, cracking it asunder with brutal might. Tom roared. He reared around and swung it again at her head. She leaped to the side, but the weapon clipped the edge of her shoulder. She heard something explode; her shoulder obliterated into cracked fragments, shredding skin, flinging blood across the muddy ground.

She cried out, but Tom was already on her. He tackled her onto the dirt. She became enveloped in the earth's filth as her former lover straddled her.

"Tom, stop!"

"I'm sorry," he hissed through clenched teeth. "But I was born to be a knight!"

A pitchfork pierced through the back of Tom's head. It punctured through his face, spearing out an eyeball and popping it into a creamy-white string of gore. Emma screamed. Tom fell off of her, lifeless but twitching feverishly. A hand reached down and yanked her to her feet. Vaguely aware she was covered in Tom's blood, she wiped her face clean. The pain in her shoulder made everything hazy and discordant.

"Are ye okay?" asked a gentle voice. A pair of soft hands touched her face and turned it toward her savior.

Crispin stood before her. Even though his hands shook from the death he had just wrought, he glared at her with a determined expression. "We need to go," he said. "The king is attacking. C'mon, Emma. We need to get back before they close the gates."

Emma didn't have time to argue and tell the stupid boy that she was a traitor and would be hanged for going back. She didn't ask how he had found her, or how he knew she would be in trouble. Her world was one of pain and torment and hurt and loss and nothing more.

Crispin dragged her through the streets of the outer city. All around her, Maud's foot soldiers yelled for the citizens to clear the way as they sprinted to defend the city walls. She saw flames arise from the homes closest to the battlements, and she knew they had already lost the outer city. She had seen this all before. It was an ugly display of divine irony.

Mildritha found them outside the drawbridge. She embraced her son and scolded him for being so idiotic to flee from the keep during a siege. She shoved them back across the roaring moat. The frigid wind and biting rain made Emma's bones freeze.

Winter was early. Oxford had fallen. Tom lay dead.

And her life was forfeited.

Lucia wept.

The pain *hurt*. It hurt so badly. The fragmented memories of a decade both lived but forgotten swarmed through her like the tempestuous rapids of a springtime flood. The life before, the one she had previous to the cataclysm, pained her most of all. How had she ever been that girl at the wedding, the one who danced and loved and lived foolishly ignorant of divine tragedies?

How had she forgotten herself?

"Beatrice? Beatrice?!" Empress Maud kneeled down to her hunched form. On the outermost limits of her submerged consciousness, beyond the curtain of rain shimmering down over the precipice of the keep, Lucia became vaguely aware of the ringing church bells.

It isn't Sunday, so that must mean . . .

War. Siege. Death.

Lucia slapped at the empress as she tried to pull her into a consoling hug. Lucia scrambled back, slamming into the bed. Empress Maud followed her. "Beatrice, stop this foolishness!" the empress demanded. "We are under attack!"

"No!" she screamed, her hands clutching her neck. Were those clashing swords she heard? Heads rolling. Daggers slicing, again and again and again and—

Screams. Blood.

She saw him from her lofted position on the battlements. A dozen knives stabbed her uncle while his bloodied gaze turned heavenward; his life essence soaked the center of God's green earth. In the tenebrous darkness of the inner tower, she saw her dead friend, her dead aunt, her dead life. "No! No! Save me!"

The empress grabbed onto her shoulders, but that only made her feel more trapped. Like she was captured by the brute in the armory. Or pinned under the Master. Under his sons.

Never again!

Lucia fought. She slammed her fists into the empress. Maud yelped. The Roman empress took the full brunt of Lucia's panic, her skin bruising.

"Beatrice, stop this!"

"LET GO OF ME!"

Thunder shook the castle. The shouts of dying men surrounded them. Lucia knew she'd be next. She reached for her neck. Her fingers grazed that horrid scar, protruding and festering with the echoes of endless pain.

It was happening again. This time they'd finish her off. This time they'd—

Men rushed through the doorway. Lucia's eyes grew wide. They were here! She screamed again—a visceral, helpless wail. She felt sickly. Her skin was clammy. The world was a blur of bright lights. Enraptured by feebleness, her mind a vacuous haze of overwhelming fear, she punched and kicked and writhed at the woman who held her.

Unsheathing swords from their scabbards, the men moved to protect the Holy Roman Empress and throw off the attacker.

"Stay put!" Empress Maud ordered the charging men.

"My empress—"

"Don't come near!"

"Don't hurt me," she pleaded. "Don't hurt me."

"I won't," said Empress Maud softly. "I won't let them, Beatrice. I'm here. Look at me."

"No..."

"Look at me."

As Lucia finally focused on the face of the most powerful woman in England, the world became less bright. Her breathing relaxed. She sweated less. All the panic and turmoil and unrelenting fear was pushed away, and the world became a singular point: the benevolent care upon Empress Maud's face.

The empress seemed to understand this change. She reached out with her gentle hands and held Lucia's in them. "I'm here. I'm here, Beatrice. Hark my words. You are safe."

"My lady," said Lucia distantly, as she slowly resettled into the present with the tender aid of an empress. Her muscles ached, as if she'd been holding up the weight of a castle.

"Beatrice, I need you with me. You are *not* that woman I saved in Bristol. You are *not* that disposable wench. You're the handmaiden of a queen. You're the best friend of an empress. You *are* too important to me. Please come back to me. Come back."

"I'm so sorry," said Lucia, the tears streaking down her cheeks.

Empress Maud wiped them away without a single look of judgment in her eyes. It was incredible; Lucia's fondness for her, which she didn't imagine could grow any more, deepened twice as much. Empress Maud had been the one to pull her out of the darkest moment of her life. She'd given her a purpose for living after she'd forsaken it entirely. The empress was the greatest woman Lucia had ever known, and this was only further proof. Even when Maud's entire world was falling apart, when her cousin's mounted fury was toppling her empire, she still took the time to care for her handmaiden.

"There she is," said the empress with a genuine smile. "There's my friend. Gather yourself. I need your aid. We are besieged, and I must know *exactly* where we stand. Our food stock, troop numbers, workers available. I need to know it all. A count of all women and children who've taken refuge in the castle. Everything. Can you do that for me?"

Lucia nodded her head. She would do anything for this amazing woman.

"Thank you. We will survive this onslaught. They will never touch you; I swear it. My cousin will not best me, with or without my brother. This kingdom is *mine*, and it shall be."

With her handmaiden calmed, Empress Maud retreated with the men and hastily made plans for outlasting the siege with her advisors. Lucia stood up, brushing dust off her torn dress and picking up her discarded scarf, trying her best to block out the sounds of battle from beyond the castle gates. Thunder rumbled more distantly, and the rain lessened to only a faint drizzle.

What now? What's next?

Staying organized, mentally and physically, always helped her. The woman she was before would've hated being so exact with her every action. But she wasn't that woman any longer. She had a lifetime of trauma suppressing her now. Very well. She'd survive it. She *must*.

There was an empress who needed her, and that was reason enough.

Again, she thought, *What now? What's next?*

Put on the scarf. Put on a new dress. Fix your hair.

Her face ached something fierce from where Emma had hit her. *Damn that stupid girl*, she thought. She knew she shouldn't have trusted her. Something always felt off.

No matter. If that girl has any semblance of intelligence, she'll be far away from here by now.

She knew she'd have to tell the empress about the stolen letter, but that could wait. The letter was of little importance now that Stephen had them surrounded.

What now? What's next?

First, gather the workers and take their count. Ask Mildritha to give an exact inventory of our food surplus. Then ask Jory and Reginald to gather everyone at the servant quarters.

She knew, because of the teachings of a man who'd loved her in the distant past, that withstanding a siege was as much about the organization and mindfulness of the cornered inhabitants as it was about the strength of their walls. She must be the stern handmaiden once more if they were to survive this. If she wished to never again become a slave, if she wished to never again be slaughtered like a pig, she'd have to become what the last decade forged her to be.

Madame Beatrice took a deep breath. It was time to control the castle once more.

"Madame?" asked a voice from behind her. She turned and found the cook's boy, Crispin, covered in blood and panting beneath the doorframe. "We need your help."

"What is it?" asked Madame B, unable to keep the annoyance from her voice. "I have much to do. Can it not wait?"

"'Tis Emma. She's injured."

"She's here?"

"Please don't hurt her. She's my friend."

"She's a traitor."

Crispin didn't respond to this. Madame Beatrice pulled the scarf off her neck slightly, releasing the pressure there. She could at least hear the girl out and learn why she did it.

Madame B glanced out the window at the battle beyond and winced. A headache was coming on. She steeled herself. This was going to be a long day indeed.

CHAPTER XXXVI
GILBERT

He let his legs dangle over the edge of the loft while Beatriz stooped down and padded the sweat off Bartholomew's fever-stained face. Hawk watched them all from his perch atop a three-legged stool, wringing his red Phrygian cap in his hands. The sky, which Gilbert watched through the slits in the wall, was a combination of twilight-blue and stone-gray; it spat rain at them and wracked Gilbert with guilt. Two other families slept on the ground floor below them, having paid a farthing like them to sleep inside a family's barn. They all lay upon stiff, itchy hay, but Beatriz was desperate to find some place warm and dry for her husband to either die in or finally convalesce. And so, they remained here, far away from wherever William was.

Thunder shook the walls of the barn and vibrated the thin floor planks of the loft. The kind-hearted family who rented them the space only allowed a single candle inside the barn—lest it catches aflame—and one of the families below drew the longest straw to keep it near them; thus, candlelight only reached them up in the loft via the miniscule gaps between the floorboards, shining up in narrow, flickering, horizontal slits.

Looking through the drizzling rain and listening to the rumbling sky, all Gilbert could think of was that black knight towing away his brother. They were within feet of saving him. Repeatedly in his nightmares, he saw the edge of that long blade slicing through Bart's skin, shredding it, the blood groove running thick with its namesake. It had been weeks since then, and still Bartholomew fought for his life. Gilbert knew his curse had caused this. He knew he had failed him, and yet, all he could think about was moving onward. He wanted another chance to save William. Maybe this time he wouldn't be a coward.

"We should leave t'morrow," he said suddenly.

Hawk nodded from his stool, but Beatriz had other ideas. She dabbed away her husband's sweat and said, "Nay. This is as far as Bart and me go."

"What? Why? Will is here. We almost had him."

"And look what good that did to Bart. He's nearly dead."

"That wasn't because of Will."

"No. It was because of your rashness."

"We need to leave *now*," said Gilbert. "Each day we wait here, William is transported farther away. He'll be beyond our reach if we wait much longer."

"He's dying, Gil," Beatriz yelled quietly. She was doing her best not to wake the families below them. "He cannot go farther. What do ye suggest? That we leave him here?"

Hawk watched them both from his corner. Gilbert stood and paced the loft, thinking. "We find a wheelbarrow to push him in. Everyone knows the king heads for Oxford."

"I'm not putting Bart in a wheelbarrow."

"When we get there, we can find some lodgings."

"There'll be no lodgings, ye dolt. The fuckin' city will be under siege."

"We need to get Will."

"No! I need my husband *alive*." Beatriz's eyes watered. The rhythmic *pitter-patter* of rain droned out her voice. "I tire of this insufferable journey. And I tire of your dour company. We've gone through Hell for you and Will. We have. But he and I were building a life together, with God, back in Caen. Understand? T'was a life we left for ye."

"Then don't stop now. Let's finish this."

"It *is* finished. Gilbert, we're no match for an army."

"We can come up with a plan—"

"Enough plans. Look at where all our plans have led us." Bartholomew groaned behind her. She placed her hand on his belly, feeling it lift and settle with his breath. "I'm leavin' this forlorn country," she said. "It makes me sick. Bart is going to live, and we'll find honorable trades back home."

"Why did ye come here at all then? Why help if ye were just goin' to flee once it mattered most?"

"How dare you," she said coldly, her face turning red with spite. "We came because we love you. Because we love William. I came because I wanted to shove it up your mother's self-righteous ass. You dare imply we don't care when my husband lies between Heaven and Earth?"

"Just say it."

"Say what?"

"You think me cursed. You think I've killed Bart because of my birth."

Beatriz scoffed and shook her head. "I will not."

"Say it!" His voice caused the families below to stir. Hawk stood from his stool. Beatriz glared at Gilbert aghast. She stomped up to him, her intense stare backing him against the wall.

"You're a horrible devil creature," she said. "You're not a man, nay, but the seed of a fallen angel. Everything you've done, everything that's happened to us, is all your fuckin' fault. All of it! Your mother was right, and ye were mistaken, and the red moon shines wickedly behind your eyes. Is this what you wanted to hear? Is this what ye wanted, Gil? I came here not to save Will, but to crucify *you*. I ventured to this faraway kingdom to expunge that demon from ye. And if that fails, to see ye killed. I've begged every monk, nun, and fuckin' priest from here to Caen to perform an exorcism on you. But none would have ye, for you're too far gone for any man of God to save."

"Beatriz, that's enough," said Hawk from behind her.

"I knew it," said Gilbert. Beatriz shoved him against the wall.

"Fuck you, Gilbert," she said. "Want to know what I actually think? I think you're a whoring coward. I think all your life you've used your birth as an excuse for your own cravenness. Know what I foresee? I foresee Will and Hawk both dyin' because you're too much of a gutless bitch to take responsibility for your own inadequacies. Ye've let your mother's sanctimonious, rotten tongue ruin your life. You are *not* fuckin' cursed. But you are pathetic."

They stood quiet for a long moment. Hawk rubbed the bridge of his nose. Bartholomew breathed uneasily on the ground, perhaps somewhat aware of their faltering friend group.

"Then go," said Gilbert. His anger malformed into sadness. "Flee. Never come and see me or mine again. I'll save William on my own. I was wrong to bring ye both here. You're no friend of ours."

Beatriz shook her head. She brushed away a tear before it soiled her cheek. "God damn you," she said softly. She turned back to her husband, hushing his moans.

Hawk crossed over to Gilbert. His face was a menagerie of pain.

"Are ye still with me?" asked Gilbert.

Hawk sighed. "Always," he said.

"Then we leave in the morn," said Gilbert, giving one last glance at Bart and Beatriz.

Abingdon-on-Thames—or simply called *Abingdon* for the locals—was a decent-sized market town which was nestled along a gentle bend of the River Thames down in a valley between wide, sloping hills. The town was only two leagues from Oxford, and it was their last stop before they reached the city. It was ruled over by Abingdon Abbey, a Benedictine monastery erected many centuries ago, long before William the Conqueror and his Norman-Saxons invaded the island kingdom. This was one of the oldest towns in all of England, with its foundation said to date back to the ancient Romans, making it an alluring spot for merchants to trade and barter at while they traveled downriver to distant London.

It took a week's travel for Gilbert and Hawk to reach Abingdon-on-Thames, and they did so as the trees aged into a charming mural of yellows, reds, browns, and greens, littering the well-trodden road with those vibrant leaves. Around the perimeter of the town was a meager stockade made of planks, tree trunks, scrapped wood, and anything else they could bundle together in a hurry. Whichever garrison Empress Maud had left with the town had given up with little fuss; Abingdon-on-Thames, like most of Berkshire, was controlled by King Stephen now. Luckily for Gilbert and Hawk, the king's army had seemingly spared the town, for the only sign of any sacking was a few score marks along the stockade and the small remaining regiment of soldiers who bore the blue and white colors of Blois.

Gilbert and Hawk needed substantial food and warm lodgings after nights spent under the stars, and thus the two of them ventured through town in search of an inn or tavern. They found a quaint place on Abingdon Road called The Saint's Respite, which was opposite the stone arches that led to the abbey. They felt particularly comfortable here, as an exquisite, wood-carved statue depicting Saint Mary stood watch across the street, protecting all those nearby from violence or bloodshed.

The Saint's Respite had a cramped interior, but the cooks were famed for their brilliant stews, and the hearth was said to never go cold. Gilbert and Hawk were getting short on funds—Beatriz had taken back her share of coin—and they had to haggle the innkeep and his wife down to a reasonable sum for a night's stay. They then sat at a table and ordered a revitalizing pheasant broth, slurping it down contentedly while enjoying a fine tankard of honey ale. After letting the drinks and food warm their bellies, the pair discussed their next move.

They weren't five minutes into their conversation when they noticed a young man and woman watching them from a nearby table. They seemed close in age to themselves. The man was tall and lanky with a mess of brown hair. His head and face were marred by scars, and one grisly slash went through his patchy stubble, which grew more on his neck than on his cheeks. The woman who sat opposite him was quite pretty. She had a pale complexion, spotted with freckles, and ginger hair that peeked out beneath her wimple.

Eventually, at the behest of the woman, the man approached them. He wrung his right hand in his left. He sweated through his thin tunic.

"Excuse me, good sirs," he said. "But I—we ... Uh, pardon our intrusion and, uh, well, our eavesdropping, but we were wondering—well, we more so overheard ..."

"Jesus Christ, Roger," the woman cried. She stood up now and approached them. "I'm sorry. My husband here isn't the strongest with words."

Gilbert and Hawk glanced at each other. They were bewildered, amused, and a little concerned that these two were spies of some sort. Horrible spies, but spies nonetheless.

"What he's trying to say," continued the woman, "is that we overheard ye speaking of traveling to Oxford. We're also goin' there, ye see, but we've heard that the road is dangerous and unforgiving. The king's army has laid siege, and bandits and ruffians have taken to robbing those who flee the city."

"Great," bemoaned Hawk.

Gilbert only sighed. His friend didn't understand the extent of Gilbert's bewitchment. Nothing could be simple. Nothing.

"We have a third companion with us," said the woman. "She's a cripple and cannot travel swiftly, or easily. Two strong lads like ye—"

"I'm a strong lad," said the man under his breath.

The woman rolled her eyes and rubbed his arm. "I know, love. But we could certainly use two more hefty men." When the two of them hesitated, she added, "We'll pay for your trouble."

The friends glanced at each other. *This would solve one problem*, thought Gilbert. And despite himself, and despite his curse, he still wanted to have enough coin for a return journey, just in case.

"Where is this third companion?" he asked.

"Come. We're renting a room here. She's in there now."

The crippled woman was older than he expected. She had dark hair that was reminiscent of a raven's wings, and deep hazel, bloodshot eyes. Her demeanor made Gilbert anxious, as if she could hear every thought and emotion that resonated inside his head.

Maybe she's a witch.

"This is Edith. My name is Alice. You've met my husband, Roger."

"I'm Gilbert. My friend here is Hawk."

"God's blessing on you," Hawk said.

"Your accent," Edith began, the wrinkles on her face contorting with her voice, "'tis French, is it not? Are ye both Normans?"

"Was it that obvious?"

"I dealt with my fair share of Norman aristocrats."

"How so?"

"I was a barmaid once, and before that, I was raised as a kitchen wench for a baron in Sussex. Lots of Normans traveled through there on their way to the larger cities."

"Which baron?" asked Gilbert.

"Ye wouldn't know him. He chose the wrong side and was killed for it."

"How'd you hurt your leg?"

"Fire," she said. Gilbert could see the mixed coloring of her skin, which gave credence to that statement. It still didn't explain the nasty scar, however, which she had been treating with ointment when they walked in.

"She doesn't like speakin' of that," said Alice. "Why don't we keep our pasts where they belong?"

"Very well," said Hawk, "although there is one thing I'd like to know. Why do ye head for Oxford if it's under siege? Got a family there?"

"A daughter," said Edith.

"And a friend," Alice added.

"That's brave of ye," said Hawk. He glanced at Gilbert but decided on his own that he'd continue. "We're looking for a friend too."

"We can help each other then. If the city is under siege, we'll need to sneak into and out of it. We can cover more ground with the five of us."

"Aye, we could do that."

"How much will ye pay?" Gilbert asked. He ignored Hawk's disappointed frown.

"Sixpence," said Roger.

"Six? For protection into a besieged city?"

"Ten then."

"Don't be ridiculous."

"We're not goin' poor—"

"Stop this," said Edith. She shook her head and scratched her lame leg. "If you protect us until we reach Oxford, *and* if ye help us find my daughter, you'll get plenty of coin. You have my guarantee."

Gilbert and Hawk glanced at one another. "When would we leave?" Gilbert asked.

"T'morrow. I plan on holdin' my daughter before Stephen takes her head."

That settled things for the time being. Gilbert and Hawk said goodbye to the three of them and went back to their own chamber. Their room was barely any larger than the single straw bed inside of it; it had no windows, and a door which didn't lock. They lay down in bed, exhausted beyond measure.

As they both rested in the dark, their bodies touching in the narrow bed, Gilbert stirred and said quietly, "Thank ye for coming this far."

Hawk was silent for a long moment, and Gilbert wondered if he was still awake before he finally said, "There was nothing for me in Rouen. I'd follow you to the ends of the earth rather than remain alone in that city. But I fear I am losing you."

"What do ye mean?"

"After we left your parents' abode in Caen, before we boarded the sea vessel, there was a moment when it felt *right*. Us, I mean. You, me, Bart, Beatriz. We were all together again. We were all there for one another. The sun was setting over the River Orne, and we were eating bread on the shore. And I felt peace."

"You're mistaken. We were incomplete. We aren't whole without William."

"Yes. But look at us now."

"You didn't have to come with me."

"You didn't have to be so cruel to Beatriz." Hawk's rebuke was like a strike from God. Gilbert lay stunned on the bed. "Even after all this time together, I don't think you understood what she and Bartholomew meant to each other."

"It was us against the world, the same as it's always been."

"You're wrong. It *used* to be that way. But now it was them against the world, and we were only a happy addition to their lives. Bartholomew and Beatriz's world was each other."

Gilbert's head flooded with his mother's voice, with his father's apathy. He saw Beatriz and Bartholomew fleeing from him, abandoning him under the brightness of the moon.

With those thoughts came the terrible memories: the blisteringly cold air, the crying baby in the primordial woods.

Tears boiled up within him; a life of worthlessness and shame and sin stirred his soul. His voice cracked, and he said, "You should leave, Hawk, before I destroy you too."

"I won't let you push me away."

"I hate what she said to me," said Gilbert, thinking of his fight with Beatriz.

"But she was right to say it."

"I loathe what I said thereafter. But I'm glad, for it'll mean I can't hurt them further."

Hawk sighed. "These feelings won't go away once we save Will. You'll have to seek salvation from something higher."

"From God?"

"I don't know. I'm just a dolt who likes to fight and do stupid shit with his friends. What do I know of these things?"

Gilbert took a deep breath. His voice finally stabilized, and the threat of tears dissipated. "Thank you for being here."

"You've said that already." Hawk laughed.

"Yes. But I mean it even more."

Gilbert fell asleep listening to the footsteps of hidden faces outside their closed door. He dreamed of a white, snowy field, with a faint sun that wasn't more than a silver halo behind the gray clouds. He saw William and his friends waiting for him in the center of the snowfield. Suddenly, the snow melted, creating a cold and tempestuous river between them and Gilbert.

He watched his friends and his brother from afar as they reveled in this newfound meadow they stood in, the lively grass and exotic wildflowers blooming in glorious colors. They radiated complete and utter warmth.

And all Gilbert had to do to enjoy that life, to be with Bartholomew and Beatriz and Hawk and William forever, was cross those dangerous, frigid waters.

CHAPTER XXXVII
EADRIC

Eadric stood on the verge of fulfillment, less than a thousand feet from his enemy. But between them towered a mighty wall, mortared with enough skill to make him feel half a world away. Beyond those few feet of stone, Duke Richard cowered in defilement of his hellish rebuke. It was maddening; restlessness had seized him whole. At all times during this ongoing siege, Eadric paced from one of the king's outposts to the next. They had full command of the city. The three gates were theirs; the outer farmlands were theirs; the surrounding shires were theirs. King Stephen possessed Oxford in all aspects but its heart, of which it still bled the empress.

In a way, Eadric could sympathize with how Stephen felt. They had the city under control and the castle under siege, blocked from any and all supplies, but still the moment of triumph remained elusive. To be so near, yet never feel victorious . . . it was aggravating.

I'm so close to ending this pain.

His heart ached for the moment to be free of all his suffering, both that which he felt and that which he caused. For over a decade, suffering and emptiness were all he'd known. Death could free him of both.

The Hellhound navigated through a few patrols until he finally reached the castle's only gatehouse to the south. Despite whatever scouts and spies the empress had, King Stephen's sudden raid on Oxford had caught everyone off guard; and much to their surprise, Maud only had a few hundred soldiers stationed here to begin with. They had no choice but to retreat behind the castle's ramparts when the king's army arrived. So swift and mighty was their attack that the empress failed to destroy the bridge that crossed the moat, allowing King Stephen the opportunity to have full access across River Mill Stream and attack the gatehouse continuously.

And this wasn't the worst of the empress's problems either. As much as Eadric hated to admit it, King Stephen's strike here, at this precise moment, was both genius and destined. They'd captured the outer walls of Oxford without damaging them, meaning, amongst other things, that the empress was not only cornered behind the walls of Oxford Castle, but she was further trapped behind the expansive city walls. The two layers of battlements were meant to keep her protected from outsiders; however, when assaulted so thoroughly and unobtrusively, it became their own prison, like a tomb with two reinforced lids.

Damn the king and his craftiness, thought Eadric bitterly.

No matter. It gave him confidence that Duke Richard was indeed behind these castle walls. There was no chance he'd escaped, no way he could've fled during their raid. He, like the empress, was pinned behind two walls with an occupied, half-destroyed city in between. Their only possible chance of escape was to catapult over the castle walls, swim across the River Mill Stream, and eventually ford the River Thames. But those waters were so dastardly cold and tumultuous that it would be a death sentence for anyone to try so, especially as winter descended upon them.

That was, after all, why the original engineers had built the castle at this exact spot, on a mound next to the river-turned-moat and the near-impassable River Thames.

Eadric stopped at the far end of the bridge that crossed to the castle. Over the top of the thirty-foot gatehouse, Eadric could see the keep standing stoically atop a motte on the northern edge of the bailey.

Are you in there, Richard? Up on that little, insignificant hill? Is that where you've been hiding from me all these years?

He was thrown out of his self-musings as an arrow whizzed by his head. He ducked behind the bridge's parapets. Another arrow pierced the wooden floorboard next to him.

"Come across!" yelled a soldier across the bridge. He and his group waved the Hellhound over. They had a battering ram with a roof atop it that shielded them from the arrows and rocks the guards threw at them from above. "Hurry! They take aim from the hoard!"

Eadric risked a glance over the parapet. The wooden hoarding ran the length of the curtain wall over the gatehouse and connected to a stone tower about sixty feet westward. The tower's façade was sliced with narrow windows and arrow slits. From one slit, sunlight glinted off iron. He ducked. An arrow flew over his head.

"Quickly now! We'll cover ye!"

Staying low behind the cover of the parapet, Eadric raced across the bridge. The soldiers loosed two arrows up from the battering ram, giving him the shielding he needed to jump from the bridge opening to beneath the roof.

"The Hellhound," said the soldier in amazement. He bowed. "Milord, what is your need?"

"Seemed you needed help," said Eadric. "What's your name?"

"Perrington. This here are Olaf, Winston, and Samuel. Over there we have Percy and Benjamin."

"Tell me the situation, Perrington. I wish to get my hands dirty."

Perrington lay dead beneath his foot, his blood sticking to the bottom of his boots and creating a sloppy suctioning sound as he peeled his feet away. He and the other five soldiers heaved back on the battering ram. They were terrified. But they yelled nonetheless, shoving the war engine forward. It slammed the portcullis. Their bones rattled. The reinforced wooden door behind the gate shuddered.

"Pull!" yelled Eadric, yanking back the ram for another go.

The iron portcullis was indented inward from their blows, yet the great door behind it showed naught a rift. They heard a loud *crack* above them. A small boulder bounced off their protective roof and shattered into pieces on the ground next to them. Ever since he took command here and had them triple their rate of assault, the bannermen of Empress Maud had committed to an unceasing storm, raining rocks, arrows, and other heavy-laden objects on them from the battlements and hoarding far above. It was one of these boulders that ended Perrington.

"Push!"

They slammed into the gatehouse again. The portcullis rattled. The door trembled.

"Pull!"

Sweat beaded down Eadric's face and pooled beneath his gambeson. He tried to flex his muscles, but they strained from effort and soreness. A month had passed since he had faced Commander Braxton at Bampton Parish, and over four months since he was ambushed at Wareham, yet his body still refused to recuperate fully.

I've given everything for this, he glowered as his body fought desperately for him to stop. *We've given everything for this. We threw away our life to slit this bastard's throat like he did to her. We can't quit now.*

"Push!"

The men cried out as they careened into the portcullis. One of them—Eadric believed his name was Olaf—almost collapsed from exhaustion. The other men moaned. He saw the quit in their eyes as well. An irrational bout of anger flooded through him. How could these men consider giving up when they were so close? The end of the war was nigh, just on the other side of the dented latticework and splintered gate; there, beyond, where Lucia's killer sat.

"PULL!"

The men scrambled to keep up with him. Olaf stumbled to his knees, almost falling outside the safety of the roof. The Hellhound of Rutland wasn't waiting for a common peasant-soldier. He pulled power from the ground, shoving his weight into the bottom of his legs, twisting around his trunk. He tensed his back, readied his muscles, and stomped his feet into the earth so he could push the battering ram straight through the portcullis, straight through the door, straight across the bailey and up the motte and through the doors of the keep, obliterating all to smithereens, until he finally drove the war machine into Duke Richard's craven body, pinning him against the keep's wall, and crushed his skull into fragmented mush.

"PUSH!".

The battering ram fell apart, literally.

The support rope that held the stone ram to the roof snapped. It rolled to the side and flattened the toes of Percy and Samuel. They yelped in pain. The support beams sundered. The roof collapsed, shattering and snapping, leaving them vulnerable to harm. Half a dozen *twangs* came from above. They rolled behind the collapsed roof and fallen ram. The volley of arrows struck the ground around them.

"You fuckin' dolts! What 'ave ye done?!" A slew of King Stephen's men rushed across the bridge. They released arrows at the hoarding until they reached Eadric and the other distraught soldiers. Amongst them, much to Eadric's surprise, was Sir Álvaro, who threw Eadric's arm over his shoulder and helped him off the ground. They limped back across the bridge as more arrows showered around them. God had blessed them on this day, for none found their mark.

"What were you thinking?!" asked Sir Álvaro once they were safely in an alleyway across the moat.

Eadric, hunched over and catching his breath, said, "I thought I could break through."

"This is a siege, not a frontal assault. You'll get yourself killed."

"He's in there, León. He's so fucking close. Like a storm cloud that is ever present, I feel cursed under its presence. It's driving me mad." Eadric leaned his hands against the half-burned wall of the nearest building. Sir Álvaro placed his hand on Eadric's back. A rat suddenly scurried out of a nearby hole and hurried down the wet alleyway.

"The king's going to be furious when he learns one of his siege engines broke. I'll make sure he doesn't learn you were involved."

"I need to get in. This has been going on too long."

"You've worked yourself into a frenzy, friend. Look at you. Come, take a walk with me. I was in the middle of giving orders from command, and you could use some fresh air."

"I'm so tired, León," he responded. The truth of that statement lit something deep inside him. Every fiber of his being was transfused with unrelenting, insatiable fatigue. It was so much more than pure debilitation, something far beyond mere human lassitude, that it had become a core facet of his being. His soul, his spirit, was exhausted.

Perhaps it was because he had abandoned God long ago. Or, perchance, it was because he had vanquished his own humanity years prior. *Likely a combination of the two*, he thought. *Maybe a man can live while disconnected from humanity, or while distant from the divine, but he certainly can't live while isolated from both.*

"Yes," said Eadric at long last. "I think that's a good idea."

They maneuvered through the half-destroyed city, ignoring the sidelong glances from the citizens who stayed. Oxford remained in a weird purgatory during the siege; it teetered somewhere between occupied and free. Sieges usually had this effect, as everyone knew it wasn't a permanent change, yet it often restructured a city irreversibly. The local men were already repairing the damaged homes and storefronts, while the women worked extensively to keep any semblance of trade and commerce alive; children danced in the rubble of King Stephen's destructive path; soldiers and knights played Nine Man Morris atop scorched barrels; thieves and charlatans stalked in the shadows. Some people turned an eye toward the castle, waiting for a sign of capitulation, while others turned a wary gaze outside the city gates, uneasy about the rumors of bandits and brigands. Often displaced refugees or army deserters, the bandits were said to be following the warpath and ambushing those who fled from the destruction.

On their long walk, Sir Álvaro and Eadric ordered bannermen to reinforce and bolster some posts while they left others to their own devices. It was a tricky thing during a siege. They needed to find a balance with the common foot soldier; it was important for them to feel needed and involved, but also given ample time to relax and gather their strength.

"I'm getting worried about you, Eadric," said Sir Álvaro as they entered northern Oxford.

"You needn't be."

"But I am. Anyone with eyes and a fine grasp on self-preservation can sense you're about to snap. Don't think the king hasn't caught on either."

They shared a look. "Spit it out," said Eadric, growing impatient. "It wasn't a coincidence that you found me at the gate."

"No. Your wife asked me to speak with you. And I wanted to help you before salvation had fallen out of your reach."

"You both clearly have something you want me to know. Out with it then."

They stopped at the northern gate. Through the opening, and between the soldiers guarding it, they could see Beaumont Palace. The opulent, gilded, sprawling estate was meant as a convenient lodging for King Henry—God rest his soul—when he did business in Oxford or hunted at the royal lodge in nearby Woodstock. But now during the siege, Beaumont Palace was requisitioned by Stephen and converted into their temporary command center.

Sir Álvaro waited for a patrol to pass. He led Eadric to a more secluded spot and whispered, "King Stephen grows weary of you, Eadric. Your actions have become aggressive, in his royal opinion. And that's not something I think even you can deny. Boldness and aggressiveness may be suitable traits for a warrior, but they become weak links in an army—something exploitable by the enemy. He won't risk any deficiencies when he's this close to victory."

"He wouldn't be here without me."

"I know. And he knows. But the line between friend and foe has blurred, friend. More dukes have betrayed and supported and re-betrayed him than any king in history. If you think he can't possibly believe you'd do the same, then I'm afraid you're overvaluing his trust."

"Do you know the truth?" Eadric asked suddenly, his gut tightening. He reached out and gripped Sir Álvaro's arms, feeling the cloth of his cloak between his tensed fingers.

"What difference does it make if he did?"

"Now you sound like my wife."

"I'm trying to protect you from yourself."

"Protection isn't what I need. What I need is understanding. My brother *died*, my sister-in-law *died*, my nephew *died*, and I . . . I was a father. You were one of her suitors. Don't tell me there weren't genuine emotions you held for her."

"There were," he admitted. "There is."

"Then you must know *why* it matters. I know I'm an evil, selfish churl, but everything I've ever done was for my family. I don't support Stephen because I want lands or titles or riches. I gave him my allegiance because he didn't support the man who allowed my family to be butchered. Now I know that's not true. The truth is, I gave him my allegiance *because* my family was butchered. And he knew that. And *that* infuriates me."

"You can't preach his sins to his face. Please, Eadric, hearken to my words carefully. To say you're on thin ice is an understatement, and by all reasoning, you're already trapped beneath the surface. You insulted the king in front of his consort, his royal entourage, even his fucking brother. Lest ye forget, King Henry was still alive when Lucia died. Stephen's rise to the throne was built upon his legal declaration as heir by Henry. And you called him a traitor, a schemer, in front of the archbishop of all of England, the most influential man in the realm. How do you think he would respond to that? How would you react?"

Eadric held his tongue. The knight had a point. But it didn't change the fact that if King Stephen allowed the uprising to happen, and *if* he knew Lucia had to die for him to join his army, it meant the last ten years of Eadric's life had been a carefully manipulated cataclysm. It meant the damnation of his soul had been, ultimately, spurred by the king himself.

It was Eadric's fault for falling so far from grace; but the threads of fate were starting to show, clear and visible for all to witness.

"Do you know?" he asked, letting the rage simmer in the depths of his rumbling voice. "Do you know whether Stephen allowed the peasants to revolt against my brother?"

". . . I know not."

"Then I will keep going like he didn't."

When Sir Álvaro placed his hand on Eadric's shoulder, his gut response was to push the sentimentality away. But something visceral and wanting stayed his hand.

"I loved Lucia," Sir Álvaro admitted. "I wanted nothing more than to be her husband. And for that part, I care for you like I would my own father. I came from Spain with nothing, and I grew my honor from the ground up. It was you who finally gave me the chance to court a lovely maiden like her. I'll never forget it. It hurts me to see you like this, just as it hurts your wife. Let us repay the debt. Let us help you."

The knight's words washed over him. The relationship between him and the knight was complex, to say the least. When he was a young bachelor and courting his daughter, he despised the man; Eadric had carried that disdain through the first few years of the war, but as Sir Álvaro and himself went through battle after battle, and as he watched

Álvaro go from a prissy, foreign aristocrat to a knight of noble renown and honor, it had changed his opinion of him.

For the same reasons, it didn't seem surprising for Álvaro to call him a father. In the same way, it seemed right to think of Sir Álvaro as a son, if for no other reason than being the last living connection he had to his daughter.

"Thank you, Sir León," said Eadric. "You've made me see things in a new light today."

"Please," said the black knight, smiling broadly, "call me *son*."

CHAPTER XXXVIII
EMMA & MADAME BEATRICE

THE STONE WAITED. FOR millennia it rested and waited, for that was the will of God. It overlooked a teeming forest, full of Trees and Plants and curious Critters. The forest thrived around it, and the Stone was overjoyed. It didn't mind waiting with such constant beauty around it. Rain and Wind, gifted to the Earth by the Firmament, slowly sheared away at the Stone, but it held firm and paid it no mind.

The Stone had plenty of itself to give away; it was happy to be a part of God's plan.

The Stone waited. Then one day, they arrived. They chopped down Trees and towed them away. In the distance, they built homes out of the lumber. The Stone could be consoled, however; at least the woodland wasn't destroyed for naught. There were fewer Critters now. That was unfortunate. But the good, godly Stone did as it was destined to do.

It waited; it was happy to be a part of God's plan.

The Stone waited. The forest was gone. They had taken it all. Tents were erected where Trees once stood, and they hastened God's work. They chipped away at the Stone, using tools made of the very rock they chiseled. They collected the Stone into chunks, squared it, and carried it off to distant lands on carts made from the same timber that once gave the Stone so much joy to watch. They eroded it much quicker than the Rain and Wind of the Firmament ever could.

Well, the Stone still had plenty of itself to give; it was happy to be a part of God's plan.

The Stone waited. They had turned the once-forest into a quarry. A miner broke off the final section of Stone from the land it had rested upon since the dawn of time. The quarry master gave the signal, and the workers, grunting and grueling, hefted the Stone onto a cart with other quartered-off sections of itself.

The Stone was happy to have companions on this next step in God's plan.

The Stone waited. It was placed upon Jew's Mount—a trebuchet wheeled into position by over a hundred soldiers. The war machine towered over the barren farmlands. It took fifty men to lift the counterweight, twisting the arm around the axle, and to lower the sling into position. The rope strained, almost screaming with excitement. The lieutenant patted the Stone as it was placed inside the sling, encouraging it to find its mark—to achieve God's destined fate.

"RELEASE!"

The arm whipped around the axle with the force of an entire cavalry. The very air of the Earth came asunder by a man-made gust of wind, an act of God made possible by the schemes of frighteningly clever war engineers.

The Stone waited no longer; it flew from the sling, soaring into the Firmament. It careened through the fog, piercing a hole through the vapor and trailing behind it wisps of frozen destruction. But it missed its mark. The Stone flew over the castle's ramparts, into the inner bailey, where it smashed into a man walking up the motte.

Jory's head exploded, bursting into a violent spray of red mist. His body rag-dolled under the force of the trebuchet's payload. The man fell to the ground alongside the Stone, which left a crater in the Earth. The Stone and the headless bard rolled down the hill until they both came to a rest against the southern wall. Bits of bone and brain matter wetted the Stone's surface; next to it lay the headless corpse. The Stone finally, at long last, was content.

After millennia upon millennia of waiting, it finally achieved God's plan.

Emma sat against the inner wall of St. George's Church. The house of God was bursting with women, children, and the injured; they sent prayers of hope that the raining boulders wouldn't brutalize one of their loved ones. Crispin bit his fingernails nervously, while he watched Mildritha and Old-Codger Reginald attend to Emma's swelling shoulder, wrapping her arm in a sling.

"There," Mildritha said, "try moving your arm now."

Emma tried. It wouldn't budge.

Crispin reached out and rubbed her good shoulder. Her tears came hot and fast and unrelenting. Mildritha attempted to give her some hope, but she knew the truth. She was now the thing she always loathed her mother for being. A cripple.

Mama, I'm so sorry. Why did I treat ye so poorly?

It had been almost a week since the siege started, and Madame Beatrice—or Lucia, or whatever her name was—had yet to heed Crispin's call for help. Emma was both grateful and terrified. Why hadn't she come for her yet? Had she not told the empress of her betrayal? The only thing that distracted her from her impending doom were the horrid fevers that overtook her. She constantly shivered from them; sweat soaked her garments, and it was near impossible to breathe properly.

Am I dying?

She'd seen fevers like this before. Often they were the onset of an illness, and it was always questionable if one survived that. Was her life now a simple roll of the dice? And if she survived, would she live only to be hanged the very next day?

As if realizing she needed comfort, Crispin wrapped his arm gingerly around her and hugged her. He smelled funny and had sweat of his own that clung to him, but his warmth was an undeniable comfort. Emma discovered, as she let him embrace her, that she no longer cared about his height or age or higher-pitched voice, and that she actually yearned for his company, for no one else dared to touch her—the betrayer of an empress.

Entering through the wide doors of the church, Madame Beatrice sped down the nave. She wore a beautifully tailored beige dress with a white scarf wound tightly around her neck and over her scar. Emma held her breath. The madame's shadow loomed over her hunched form.

"What happened to you?" she asked Emma.

"Retribution," Emma answered, "for betraying a queen."

"No. Your due recompense for that will be much more severe." Madame Beatrice pointed to Emma's shoulder. "*That* was retribution for believing yourself to be above a common peasant. You are a fool to have lied to me."

"I'm sorry."

"Why did you do it?"

"The empress torched my village. Sacked it. I thought if I spied for the king, then I'd never see my home burned again." Fighting to keep her voice steady, she glared up through wet eyes at the uncaring gaze of Madame B.

The madame shook her head. "You're a fool, Emma. There's no escape from that. Not a single home goes unscathed in war. Its flames consume the rich and poor alike."

"So I've learned."

"Do you weep because you learn of your folly?"

"I weep because I'll now burn alone," said Emma softly. "I told them about ye. About your real name. I'm sorry."

Madame B went silent for a long moment, scratching at her sliced throat. "Who'd you tell?" she asked.

"A knight dressed in black. He said there's another spy here. That he's—"

"*Belt it!*" whispered Madame Beatrice harshly. "Are you truly so daft, girl? Did your mother birth you straight onto your head?"

Emma was confused. Crispin, Mildritha, and Reginald seemed similarly perplexed.

"Why would you tell me this *now*?" Madame B asked. "Save that. Don't mention their name. You will tell the empress herself, you hark? You will tell her, and you will do so in exchange for your life. Do you understand?"

Emma stuttered. Was the madame trying to save her?

"I'll get you extra food and medicine, as well, in exchange for the information you have."

"Yes," said Emma, too stunned to elaborate further.

"Good." Madame Beatrice turned on her heel and moved toward the church doors.

"Thank you, Lucia," said Emma.

Madame B stopped in her tracks. A cloud unseen dispersed somewhere above, and a sliver of sunlight shimmered through the windows of the church onto the madame. The ground shook as another boulder slammed into the castle's fortifications.

Madame Beatrice left, never glancing back, nor ever letting her hand leave her neck.

"Damn that stupid girl," said Madame Beatrice in a huff.

She covered her mouth and blushed. Did she just curse? She did, didn't she? It had been ages since she had last muttered a foul word, and the ancient memories made her head ache.

This was all Emma's fault, and Lucia—

No. Not Lucia. You're Beatrice. Madame Beatrice, handmaiden of Empress Maud.

She rubbed her temples. Her mind was a tempest in battle with itself—a siege within a siege. Over these ten cruel years, Madame B had masoned fortifications within her mind; mortared together stone-by-stone, day-by-day, she locked away who she was. As a young girl, she'd always questioned what the term "a woman's lot" meant. Now she understood it profoundly within her soul.

A woman's lot was to bury the truths of the world—the horror and fear and suffering—deep within the darkness of their conscience, never to let it see the light of day; a woman's lot was to bear the world, yet always make room to bear a little more.

Madame B knew when she looked into Emma's eyes that the girl had finally learned that same truth, just like all the other girls she couldn't save within the torment of the Roman villa.

And it broke her. It broke *Lucia*.

Even buried away as she was, deep behind the toiled ramparts erected in her soul, the terrible boulders of shame and dread thundered against her walls. She'd believed, foolishly, that she'd been tortured enough, to where no further pain could harm her. She thought it impossible.

She was mistaken. Her protective walls still felt the colossal rain of fire and brimstone.

A siege within a siege.

She prepared herself while she sloped up the motte, entered the keep, and sequestered what Emma had done to her behind her internal bulwarks. She entered the great hall of Oxford Castle not as Lucia, but as Madame B, the empress's chosen handmaiden.

Then she was grabbed from behind.

Duke Richard pushed her face-first against the wall, the wood straining and bending from his crushing weight crushed. Her breasts pinched uncomfortably, her face becoming squashed and smothered. She sensed it first deep within her chest, a pressure of extreme force pushing out against her ribcage. Panic.

"Let go of me!" she ordered.

"Commands of the empress and Sheriff D'Oilli," said the duke. He patted her down, using his hands to violate the creases of her body. "We're to search everyone."

When his hands slowed and his "search" came to a close, Madame B pushed him off and asked, "Are you done?!"

Duke Richard looked awful. His hair was too long and wantonly tangled; his quilted gambeson was askew with bits of his undertunic peeking out. His eyes were wild, frantic, and over-dilated. It appeared as if he hadn't slept in weeks, or perhaps months. He smelled of stale ale. "Empress Maud wants to speak to you."

She tucked her hair behind her coif, trying to control her simmering panic and anger. She dismissively waved at him to lead her on. They found Empress Maud and Aubrey de Vere, steward of Oxford, inside a small storage closet on the far end of the keep. They were appraising the remaining stockpile of food when the castle shook; another stone hit the curtain wall. Maybe they'd all get lucky, and the trebuchet would break down again.

"Madame B, there you are," said Empress Maud with a forced smile. "Thank you, Duke Richard. De Vere, please keep quiet about this. I don't need further turmoil."

"Yes, my empress." He bowed.

"Help the sheriff and Duke Richard find the deceivers. I must speak to my handmaiden privately."

"Of course. May God be with you." The two men left.

"Close the door, Beatrice."

She did so, enveloping them in pure stillness. Inside the storage closet, there were no sounds of singing birds, squeaking rats, nor screaming men. The only sound that penetrated through the rotting walls was the rumbling drone of the surging River Mill Stream out in the moat.

"How may I serve you, my lady?"

"Enough formalities. We're in dire need, Beatrice. I've prayed to the Lord that He may show me the true path, but He seems as distant from my heart as my brother." She paused for a moment, looking her handmaiden over. "What happened to you? You look a mess."

"I was searched. Thoroughly."

"I'm sorry. I should've been clearer with the sheriff about being gentle with you. I know you're not the traitor, *but* somebody is. More than one, I suspect, with how absolutely Stephen trounced us. Probably his brother. Archbishop Henry can never decide what he wants."

"How may I serve you?" Madame B asked again.

"Look around, what do you see? 'Tis not even enough food to last through autumn, let alone winter." Somewhere up above them, footsteps caused the ceiling to creak. Empress Maud jumped. She glanced up at the sound. Sweat drizzled down her face. "I'm being watched. Every move I make is being gifted to Stephen by some fiend. He'll know. He'll learn how low we are on food, and when that happens, I won't stand a chance. He'll wait for winter to come, and he'll starve us until he wins the war."

Madame B's mouth went dry. She had never seen Empress Maud like this before. "We can't let anyone but the cook know this," she suggested. "If the others in the castle find out..."

"I need to know who is trapped here with me. I must escape for the good of the kingdom. You are one of the few people I trust, Beatrice. You're my friend. *But* I cannot have you going through another breakdown. You must be strong. Search for strength in Jesus Christ, or do whatever else is needed."

"I will be," said Madame B shakily.

"What else is on your mind? You still seemed troubled."

Should she tell her about Emma? Beatrice questioned the decision, but the possibility of losing Maud forever was the worst fate she could imagine. Then she would only be . . . *not* Madame Beatrice.

Another boulder hit nearby. The battlements inside her cracked. A voice deep within her, tame and measured, cried out. Madame B stuffed it back down. "Emma, your handmaiden, has something to tell you."

"Let me see her then."

A few minutes later, Emma stood between the two of them, her head bowed and her arm bandaged. She gazed up at Madame Beatrice, who gave her an encouraging nod.

"I took Robert's letter," she admitted.

"Stephen sent a girl to betray me?" Empress Maud scoffed. "Ironic. Did he think me incapable of taking a girl's life? Oft his propaganda declares me to be weak because of my *womanly affection*. So much so, perchance, that he began to believe it himself? I wonder."

"It was not he who sent me."

"Then you are a dimwitted fool to betray a queen and not even get a king's reward. Was it his wife? Lord knows it to be Matilda who has all the brains."

"Nay."

"Then who, child?"

"A boy who was courting me. He was a squire sent by his knight."

Empress Maud laughed. "Lord Christ, you really do deserve death. It is best to put down a slow child as you would put down a newborn birthed under a red moon. It is irresponsible, sinful even, to let them live otherwise."

"Empress," Madame B stepped in, "there is more. She is a fool, yes, but she has learned more that she will tell, *if* you spare her life." Madame B further pleaded with her eyes.

"If this is true, may the Lord grant you haste, *and* a plainly spoken tongue."

"I am not the only spy," said Emma. "There is another in your close confidence. Duke Richard. He wanted Robert's letter, but I had stolen it first."

"Where is this letter now? With this squire boy?"

"He gave it to his knight."

"Who is?"

"He was heralded as Sir Álvaro de León."

Madame Beatrice collapsed, falling against the pews. Emma and Empress Maud reached for her before her head slammed against the dirt floor. Madame B's blood coursed through her body, every sense coming to the forefront as a name she'd long forgotten came back to her with the force of divine winds.

"Beatrice?" Empress Maud shook her. "Beatrice? *Lucia*?! Can you control yourself?"

The challenge from the empress was like a slap across Beatrice's face. Shame swarmed over her; her legs buckled. *No*, she thought, *I will be strong for Maud.*

"I'm sorry, my lady," Madame B said. "I'll survive."

Empress Maud turned back to Emma. "If what you say is true, and Duke Richard *is* a spy, then I have more to fear than that damnable letter." The empress thought for a long moment, playing idly with her crown. "What shall I do with you?"

"Let her live," said Madame Beatrice, even surprising herself with how desperately she wanted to save her and finally rescue one girl. "Please. She is too well liked with others in the castle. To kill her now would damage morale. If the castle turns against you, I fear the worst."

"It won't. I'd kill them all before they mutinied on me. But you're right; to kill a girl now who can't betray me any further is useless." She turned to Emma. "Why did you come back? Why are you telling me this now?"

Madame Beatrice watched the girl closely as she shrugged. Emma seemed despondent, almost entirely unattached to any earthly wants. It reminded her of . . .

"I thought my mum was sick," she said softly. "And that my friend was sick. They were goin' to starve come winter. I thought this could save them."

"What you did was abhorrently stupid," said the empress. "But it was brave. The world is fueled by stupidity and bravery. I believe those two traits are a concoction that more women should ingest."

Emma and Lucia stood still, awaiting the tyrannical decision of a queen.

"I'll let you live on *two* conditions. For one, you are to remain with Madame Beatrice. You may never leave her sight, nor she yours. Second, there will come a time during this siege where I'll need a person of your degree of stupidity and bravery. When that time comes, you will accept."

"Thank you, my empress."

"You're relieved of duty for the day," Empress Maud said to Beatrice. "I have much to ponder."

The empress left the church, strolling past multiple castle inhabitants who bowed to her, and a few more who dared glare at her. As she watched the empress vanish out the doors of St. George's Church, Madame Beatrice expected her heart to feel lightened. She saved Emma. She finally saved one of them. But her heart felt no lighter; rather, she shook as her fortifications tore asunder, struck from the divine stones of God's plan.

CHAPTER XXXIX
EADRIC

"Me don't think ye should be doin' that, milord," said Gaoler Alfwin.

Eadric shoved him away and said, "Mind your rank. I can do damn well what I please with my own hostages." That seemed to do the trick as Alfwin grumbled his way back to his post underneath the endless gray sky.

Eadric handed a tankard of warm ale through the wagon cell to Will. A breeze blew past them and wisped away the steam from their cups. "It's frightfully frigid already," said Eadric miserably. Will simply nodded and took a sip, not commenting on how Eadric, at least, had a dry bedchamber with a hearth inside Beaumont Palace, while he had to sleep outside in the barren elements. Eadric had tried to move the boy from their exterior prison yard to the indoor Oxford gaol, but the bailiff claimed it was full of prisoners already. "If we don't end the siege before winter comes, I'll see to moving you to a holding chamber inside Beaumont. This weather will kill you."

"'Tis not too bad," said Will, the lie obvious on his face. "They put up wood to block the wind, and we've been rationed extra blankets."

Eadric scratched his beard. His emotions toward Will were getting more and more confused each day. The boy had initially been a means to an end, but as Eadric lost his grasp on what this war meant to him, he found himself isolated. He chuckled. It served him right that the hostage he'd hunted down in a foreign kingdom would become one of the few people he could open up to. Eadric was fairly confident that the feeling wasn't mutual—a genuine friendship can't be founded upon slavery. But outside Eleanor and Sir Álvaro, it was all he had. The human soul would go to remarkable lengths to find meaningful connections when it falls to its most desolate.

"I'm sorry. For everything, Will."

"I don't know how to respond to that."

"Know I never expect forgiveness. But once I find your father, I'll make certain his wealth finds its way to you."

God, I'm terrible at this apologizing thing.

Awkwardly, they each took a sip of their ale. It tasted of earth and pure bitterness, but it smelled of nothing. Eadric sniveled. He was probably catching a cold.

"You and your wife, are things better now?" asked Will.

Eadric laughed. "I think I may actually leave my estate to her, damnable woman. It appears impossible to stave off a woman's influence for long. Do you have anyone awaiting you in Normandy?"

Will shook his head. Eadric believed that the boy wouldn't ever open up to him when he suddenly said, "I was too young when me and my brother joined Geoffrey's banner. Didn't think of girls much at all."

"Pray you find someone who'll set you straight. I fought against it best I could. T'was a damn good fight . . . but I find myself glad to be loved begrudgingly."

"So, she loves ye?"

The question shocked Eadric. If any other man, let alone a lowborn, had asked him that question a few months previously, he would've stuck his dagger so deeply into their gut that they would've been shitting steel in the afterlife. To question a man on his marriage was to question him on his authority, his dominance, his honor. But this was not a few months back, and at present, he found himself not caring much of virtue or perceived manhood. Only when a person became insouciant to the future could they become unbound by societal and cultural dogma.

"I . . ." Eadric stuttered. *Does she love me? Should she love me?*

"Eadric?"

"Speak of the devil." Eadric found himself thinking about Eleanor often today, and he was joyed with the prospect of finally seeing her. It was strange how quickly life could change one's admiration of another.

He turned around with a smile on his face, but his mood immediately soured. Eleanor's eyes appeared young and livid in her wrinkled face. Her hands balled into fist. He prepared for the worst. She stopped in front of him and said, "The king requires your presence."

Eadric stormed across the open farmland between the Oxford city walls and the towering trebuchet, which His Royal Majesty had lovingly hailed as Jew's Mount. All the trees on the northern outskirts of the city were felled and coppiced when they first erected their occupation; they needed wood for the army and the area cleared for siege weaponry.

King Stephen and his knights awaited the Hellhound of Rutland below Jew's Mount as it was prepped to hurl another stone at Oxford Castle.

Eadric gripped his sword. The knights around the king stiffened; all four of them had on harnesses. *Pierce the* maille, *don't slash*, Eadric reminded himself. *Aim for the front of the neck or the back of the knee.* He could take one with a surprise attack, piercing his sword right through their windpipe. The other three would attack at once. Eadric still had a limp, and his dominant hand was mostly useless, but he had learned how to put more power into his core and legs. He could close the distance, using the pommel of his sword to bash one of their faces, but then that would leave an opening. They could slice the back of Eadric's knee while he was distracted. He could use the bashed-face knight as a shield. Block the blow. He would grip his sword by the blade and run it through the fourth knight. Turn back to the third. Evade his attacks. Then, what? A punch to the face? A feint to the stomach? There were so many variables.

"You've summoned me, my king," said Eadric, his voice overflowing with visceral contempt.

King Stephen held up a sealed letter and absently said, "You have new orders."

The nearby soldiers loaded the trebuchet as Eadric ripped away the letter, crumbled it, and discarded it on the muddy ground. The four knights reached for their weapons. Eadric focused solely on the king in purple garments. "Why don't you tell me yourself?"

"You are to leave for Kent," said King Stephen, tightening his lips to a line. He didn't bother hiding his anger any longer. "My brother is there to greet a mercenary army from northern Flanders. You're to rendezvous with them and guide them to Oxford."

Eadric's throat dried up. His Adam's apple pressed outward like a parasite trying to burst through. "When will they arrive from Flanders?"

"We expect them in a month."

"In a month, the siege may very well be ended," Eadric roared.

"Think, you daft brute. Why would I summon a foreign army if I foresaw the end of the siege before they arrived?"

"To be rid of me."

"Mind your festering arrogance, Baron Eadric. I can assure you that you're nowhere near such importance to me. This war does not revolve around you, and neither do my intentions. You're commanded to go to Kent, and you *will* do so. Gather your pride and begone by the morrow."

The soldiers pulled on the rope. It went taut, adding tension to the beam as the counterweight lowered beneath the axle. The stone waited to be loosed.

"I can't do that," said Eadric. "You know I can't leave. Your orders come from malice and cruelty."

"My orders are *not* to be evaluated by a bloodthirsty animal!" King Stephen stepped up to him. It was easy to forget how tall he was, but the king towered over Eadric. "If it appeases you, let it be known to God above that my orders are done by chastisement. This outburst from you alone proves my wisdom in doing so."

"What of your oath?! You've promised me Richard's head. You've told me your triumph will be my own. For ten years I've waited. Ten years since you gave me that first vow on our hunt."

"Do you have any idea how many promises I've made over the past decade? I'm the king of a Godless realm. I've been imprisoned by my kin. Tens of thousands of deaths burden my conscience, yet you crumble under the weight of a single one."

"I refuse," said Eadric, staying his hand from punching Stephen. Behind the king and his band of knights, the trebuchet continuously tightened and tightened. The rope whipped and snapped itself center in a blur of erratic motion. It strained, crackled, ready to snap under its own tension. The counterweight dipped lower.

"Then you'll be banished from this kingdom," said the king. "Your estate, your wealth, it'll all be mine."

"You're a right cruel bastard."

"You are released, Eadric. Leave the camp at once. If you remain here by eventide, I will have you charged as a traitor to the crown."

As the king turned back to the war machine, Eadric sprang forward and yelled, "Did you do it?!" He couldn't keep the torment out of his voice. It cracked and betrayed his anguish, his fear that it could actually be true.

The soldiers grimaced and yelled as they dug heels into the earth and cranked the beam around the axle as far as it would rotate. The rope pulled taut to its breaking point. Each strand of fiber braced between suspense and release, between holding strong or snapping. If one broke, the rest would shred thereafter.

King Stephen glanced at Eadric. He had a coy, spiteful smile.

"Was the revolt *your* doing?!" asked Eadric desperately.

The wind fluttered the king's purple robes away from him. Grass and dead leaves and twigs swirled in the air between them, but piercing through it all was Stephen's bitter stare.

"I pray to God you go mad wondering if I did," yelled King Stephen. "Release!"

The tension-bound rope recoiled; the arm spun; from Jew's Mount flew the boulder, soaring through ferocious weather, careening into the keep somewhere behind the castle walls. An awesome and terrifying boom followed it, with a high-pitched scream echoing a few seconds later. Somewhere far into the city, a church bell rang.

"Please, my lady, you must make your husband reconsider."

Eadric groveled at Queen Matilda's feet. The queen wore a lovely red dress interwoven with green and gold threads; an ornate belt kept the dress close to her waistline, while a long fox-fur mantle hung off her shoulders to keep her warm in the late-autumn breeze.

"I can't change the dictations of my king," she said. "I'm sorry, Baron Eadric."

"I've served you faithfully, my queen, and I have served your husband honorably. I act foolish only because I'm so close to finally avenging those who've wronged me."

"I know, my dear. I know." She placed her hand on his shoulder. Her touch was warm and inviting. A face as pale and beautiful as the saints in holy murals looked down upon him. "I am deeply sorry this has happened to you."

"I've fought so hard for this. When your husband was inept and in prison—"

"Watch your tongue."

"My apologies, but I must speak my mind. When your husband failed us, and you had to take command—"

"I did so for my husband."

"I know, my queen, but *I* did so because you were a beacon that he was not."

"This is most suggestive," she said while looking worriedly toward the open door of her chamber. They were inside Beaumont Palace, and any noble could be within earshot.

"I knew you could get us to this moment. It's because of you that King Stephen has not yet failed. Now all I ask, all I beg and pray for, is that I should remain here to capture the man who stole my life from me."

"Don't be so scandalous. It is unseemly."

He glanced up at the queen. The pain in his chest was immense, like his heart might burst at any moment. He reached for her hands and held them in his own. They were soft and supportive. "Do this for me. Please. Your husband is mistaken."

Queen Matilda ripped her hands from Eadric's grasp and slapped him across the face. He touched the tender skin of his cheek. It burned red and hot. The sting only added to the throbbing pain inside him.

"Your presumptuousness does you discredit," she said. "My husband is right in his rule. I may have leaned on your guidance when he was imprisoned by Robert, but he will *always* be my husband. I fully support whatever he commands. Now leave my presence at once."

Eadric stood, and Queen Matilda turned away from him to stoke the fire in the nearby hearth. She didn't even give him the courtesy of watching him leave.

"What are we to do now?" asked Eleanor.

Her and Eadric's bedchamber was gray and stuffy and cold. Sir Álvaro entered and closed the door behind him. He pulled his black cloak tightly around him to keep warm.

"I came as quickly as I could," he said. "I tried to make Stephen reconsider, but he's standing firm for now."

"Jesus Christ, Eadric. I told you not to confront him in front of his entourage."

"If you leave now for Kent," began Sir Álvaro, "then I may be able to convince Stephen to let you keep your assets. Perhaps even maintain your rank. He knows you're prone to angry outbursts. Hell, I think everyone in the army could attest to that."

Desperation gleamed in Eleanor's eyes; it hurt him. Eadric had learned to embrace empathy with her, for he knew he had failed her as her husband, her protector, and her companion. He thought deeply about where to go from here. He moved to the wall and felt the frigidity permeating through it from the vastness outside.

"I can't leave," he said quietly. "Not now. Not after everything I've done."

"Eadric, we've lost everything," said Eleanor. "If you stay here, you'll be imprisoned."

"What would happen to Will if I left?"

"The boy?" asked Sir Álvaro. "Who gives a damn about the hostage?"

"I do! I've fucked up too much to let everything I've done fall apart. I have too many sins to flee."

"Then what are you planning to do?" asked Eleanor. "How the Hell do you expect to get out of this?"

"I leave," he said, speaking the idea aloud as quickly as it came to him. Sir Álvaro and Eleanor glanced at him with puzzled expressions. "Do you believe you can change Stephen's mind?"

Sir Álvaro nodded and said, "I do. I'm one of his most reliable knights. And more than that, I think I can get him to realize how badly he needs you."

Eadric patted the knight on the back. Who could have thought he would ever be so dependent on this young man? Warmth flooded through him, an immense appreciation for Sir Álvaro. Snapping together one by one, he could feel the pieces of his plan coming together.

"The king must believe I've left for Kent," said Eadric. "If he buys that, then Eleanor can stay here where it's safe and warm."

"I can help too," she said. "I can tempt the queen back into your favor."

"What are you going to do in the meantime?" the knight asked Eadric. "Do you plan on traveling all the way to Kent?"

"No. I'll hide outside Oxford, or maybe even inside the city somewhere. There're enough houses and shops that they'd never bother searching for me here."

"And even if they did," thought Sir Álvaro aloud, "the average foot soldier wouldn't know that Stephen banished you. He'll want to keep that private. Bad for his public image if it's discovered he sent away his war constable. This siege will only get more strenuous as winter arrives. The king is loathed to admit it, but this army has as great a chance of starving as anyone behind those castle walls. They'll want to do everything they can to keep morale up."

"Then that's where we'll attack," said Eadric.

"What do you mean?" asked Eleanor, frightened of the vengeful look creeping up on her husband's face.

"I won't sit idly for months while Stephen tries to starve out the empress."

"What's your plan?" asked Sir Álvaro.

"Dissent. We turn the army against the king."

"Hah!" Eleanor laughed. "You are a crazed old bugger. Are you trying to get us tortured to death?"

"He knew about the coup, Eleanor." Eadric held back his emotions as best he could. "I know it in my soul. He might not have started it, but he let it happen."

"There's no proof of that," said Sir Álvaro.

"The proof is in his eyes. Like you said, the winter months will get bad, maybe the worst we've ever had if this early storm is a sign from God. Empress Maud will have to surrender sooner rather than later. But if we attack this smartly, we can turn the army against King Stephen during that same time. They're going to be starving, cold. You can already feel that sentiment, and we've only been at this siege for a few weeks. Imagine what another few months will do?"

"I don't like this," said Eleanor.

"I know it's risky, and it's certainly stupid. But half the suffering in this kingdom is because of that man. He *wanted* a succession war to happen. If he's going to take us out, then let us go out with a fucking fight."

Eleanor and Sir Álvaro glanced at one another.

"You two are the only people I have left in the world," Eadric admitted. "I need your help. I can't do this alone, not any longer."

Eleanor sighed. She chuckled to herself before glancing up and smiling at her husband. "Very well, darling," she said. "Where do we start?"

CHAPTER XL
GILBERT

GILBERT EXHALED, HIS BREATH visible and his flesh goosebumped, as he, Hawk, Edith, Alice, and Roger all left Abingdon-on-Thames in the wee hours of the morning; the day seemed twice as cold as the day before, and they suspected the next day would continue that trend. The rest of the town seemed cognizant of this, for many of the homes and storefronts remained closed as the sun rose over the vale, the townsfolk desperate to stay warm for as long as possible before they had to work the fields or fish the river. All of God's creations were destined for a short autumn.

It was only a seven-mile trek to Oxford, a half-day's trip by most, yet it took them most of the day to traverse the distance because of the older woman's limp. Edith was clearly in a lot of pain, but she pushed on nonetheless, hobbled step after hobbled step, until they crested a hill near the late afternoon and saw the besieged city.

Little pillars of smoke—some blacker, some whiter—plumed into the sky from various spots both within and outside the city walls. As opposed to the pure destruction they'd seen in Wareham and Bampton, the city here remained mostly intact. The outer palisade was burned to a pile of ash in multiple sections, but most of the sharpened wood spikes remained; the part-stone, part-wood fortifications that surrounded the city proper were marred with scorch marks and indentations, but they remained defensible. Distant blobs of people still stooped in the River Thames; the southern and eastern gates, as far as they could see, had activity around them.

When Gilbert imagined a siege, he imagined a city destroyed and a castle being assailed. But Oxford Castle, which stood gloriously unscathed upon a mound alongside a wide coursing stream, gleamed triumphantly under the setting sun, and it resonated in Gilbert's soul. *Indomitable*, it said to him. *Unassailable*. There were no ladders hooked onto its ramparts. There were no military men breaking into its bailey. Oxford Castle radiated comfort and stability.

"We need to hurry," said Edith.

"Why?" asked Hawk. "The castle looks amply protected to me."

"That's how ye know they ain't winning. There's no counterattack, no revolt. They have the city totally occupied, and that takes time. We got here too late."

Gilbert glanced over the city again, his perspective of it mutating.

"The king has taken the crop fields, the roads, the river. The city has fallen. All he needs to do is starve 'em from the castle."

"How do ye know all this?" asked Gilbert.

"I've been with military men," she said.

"You were a whore," said Hawk. Roger and Alice glared at him in disbelief, but Gilbert knew his friend well enough to discern the nonjudgmental tone under the brashness of his remark. Hawk couldn't care less if a person was a courtesan or a beggar or the damn pope; all he cared for was mutual respect.

Edith could apparently recognize this too, for she replied, "Yes. I learned many things from knowing these men."

Hawk smiled and said, "I'll remember that in case I must learn something in the future."

"Look!" Alice said, pointing. "Over there."

A scuffle erupted along the road about a mile away. Brigands pounced out of the obscurity of the shrubs. They attacked a wagon with four guards defending it. The fight ended quickly. There were close to twenty bandits, and they battled confidently against whichever unfortunate merchant this was. From their relatively safe distance, Gilbert and his company watched the bandits kill two of the guards, disarm the others, and loot the wares.

"May He punish them for their cruelty," Edith prayed under her breath.

"Let's go," suggested Gilbert, wanting to get off the main road as soon as possible.

"Aye," said Hawk. "And let's stay away from any trees or shrubs."

Luck graced them with her capricious favor, for they traveled the last few miles without being ambushed by armed ruffians. They entered the outer city from the southeast, and now that they were closer, they could see that the king's army was encamped on the northern side of Oxford. Hundreds of soldiers patrolled the streets. They stalked through the outer city; like flies, they harassed those who dared navigate the streets and invaded the homes of those who dared not; like crows, they plagued the small gardens of the citizens, plucking their fruits and vegetables until all that was left were spoiled plants and tainted soil; like ticks, they leeched on to the warm-blooded bodies of women, touching and molesting them unprovoked; like locusts, they buzzed with laughter and merriment as they swarmed through the city and fouled the very essence of the air, always searching insatiably for what they could defile next.

Seeing the outer city of Oxford thusly, and unwilling to be similarly ravished by flies and crows and ticks and locusts, they steered clear of that unfolding insidiousness. They found instead a discarded mill in utter disrepair along the shore of the River Thames. Long, groping tendrils of moss surrounded the mildewed wood like an ever-growing parasite, while the overgrown underbrush and crowded trees disguised it from any prying eyes. The water wheel didn't spin in the river's current, for the lower half of it had deteriorated away and was poked full of holes. Gilbert, Hawk, and Roger pried off a few wooden planks for them to enter inside, only to find out the interior was equally destroyed.

It was a perfect hiding spot.

The nights were becoming conspicuously bitter and cold, and seeing how none of them knew for how long they'd have to hide, they determined it to be imperative to find dry straw and grass to insulate the ground and to scrounge refuse to patch the holes in the roof and walls. They separated and scouted the city for anything they could use. A growing feeling of dread had been building inside Gilbert ever since he had laid eyes on Oxford. He wanted no part of his natural vileness to spread to the others, so he offered to go alone on this search. After some dissent from Hawk, his friend finally conceded and left with Roger. Edith and Alice, meanwhile, made their own group to scour the surrounding woods.

Gilbert took a deep breath as he was left alone in the dilapidated mill. He started when a loud, shrill caw erupted from above him. He glanced up. From a hole in the top corner of the mill, a crow appraised him with its black, beady eye. A chill came over him. The Devil was here.

The soldiers and military men ignored Gilbert when he wandered into the city proper. It appeared they were more interested in the women than the men today. Gilbert also suspected that he looked as terrible as he smelled; what would some soldiers want with a dirty vagabond?

The inner city was in ruins. Lining the well-trodden streets, townhomes and storefronts were blotted with scorch marks and broken facades. From within the darkness of those busted doors and windows, terrifyingly hollowed faces watched him trek through the streets; few dared brave them with Gilbert. The streets of Oxford remained as vacant as a diseased brothel. Patrols of the occupying army regularly sauntered down the main thoroughfares, but the few citizens who suffered the streets were yoked women carrying buckets of sloshing water from the nearest well or risk-taking opportunists who carried coin and other valuables to trade with the merchants who dared sell wares in a besieged city. Gilbert's stomach growled something fierce as he walked by one of these stalls. He glanced at what they were selling. Bread, already a week stale; thin cuts of fish meat, maggot infested; cabbage, dark green and rotten.

Gilbert winced. Suddenly those darkened, hollowed faces reflected differently in his soul. Starvation would run rampant this winter, and few within the city would survive it. Hopefully he, Hawk, and William could stay clear of the city come winter.

He exited through the northern gate and found himself surrounded by the king's encampment. At the center of the bivouac a half-mile away, towering above the hundreds of tents flapping in the wind, was Beaumont Palace. The largest and most extravagant tents were erected around that massive house. A large open field, devoid of any signs of life, wrapped around the castle and moat to the northwest. To Gilbert's surprise, there was little activity out here. It was strangely quiet, with the howling breeze carrying very few voices with it. Even under the midday sun, an abundance of braziers flickered their flames throughout the camp. Many of the soldiers who weren't on patrol were sleeping on the ground or within their tents; others were doing menial tasks to pass the time.

Are all sieges like this? Endless waiting. Quiet reflection.

Then, finally, something of particular interest caught his eye: a man bound by rope. A soldier yanked the man into a stumble. He led the prisoner through the dormant maze of tents.

A thought popped into Gilbert's mind.

His gaze drifted to the edge of the road. As of yet, he hadn't stepped off the main streets leading to and fro and through the city. The occupying force seemed to pay little heed to the few who trudged through the main thoroughfares, but would they become hostile if those same few drifted off the main path? Were the flies, crows, ticks, and locusts a deadly swarm waiting to be stirred to vicious violence, similar to a beehive which, seemingly abandoned, suddenly rouses to deadly life once disturbed by a heedless wanderer?

The thought corrupted Gilbert. It twisted the last of his sensibilities, malformed them into rancorous hubris. Distantly above them all, the castle watched.

What if I'm invincible? he thought.

The reality of his world became clear. The devilry. The pain. It always happened to those *around* him, but never directly *to* him. He had traveled into a war-ravaged kingdom with nothing but spare food and a few friends; yet here he stood, unharmed and untouched by the throes of death. *What if I'm protected by the Devil?*

What if . . .

Gilbert stepped off the main street. And he followed the prisoner. And no one stopped him.

The gaoler and his property filtered through the narrow confines of the encampment. Gilbert stayed close behind. With each stride, he believed his foul curse with more fervent faith. He blinked; a tear fell.

The path before him drenched into the rust-hued shadows of that terrible moon. But it scared him naught, for the tears cleansed the terrible ichor within him. He gained not so much as one queer glance from the hundreds of soldiers they passed.

What was an agent of Hell to insects and fowl? What was a hound from Rutland compared to Satan's own kin? Why should Gilbert fear at all, when his destiny was consummated at birth?

Near the opulence of Beaumont Palace, the prison yard held the captives inside small wooden cages that sat exposed to the elements. A lone gaoler patrolled the clearing in the middle of the encampment. Gilbert smiled and wiped away the wetness of his surrendered tears. Never before had he felt so whole and so empty, so bound yet so boundless. The world was beautiful; the world was cruel. His soul may have been forfeited at birth, but his life was truly his own. And while he remained on this terrible, terrible earth, he planned to take advantage of his fiendish luck and his accursed omen.

Legs and arms bound with rope, William shivered inside his cage. Gilbert moved straight for him. It was here, finally, that one soldier decided to say something. The gaoler stuck out his spear, blocking his path.

"Halt!" he ordered. "By decree of the king, announce your purpose."

Embrace it. Embrace the truth.

Gilbert stood up straight and announced, "Stand aside, for I am *corruption*—a soul tainted by Satan's blazing moon—ventured from a far-off realm to reclaim what is his. I am damned, and all those who step before me shall know the same fate. Stand aside. Begone. Your own salvation begs it. I shall siphon away all the love and joy you've known and cherished."

The gaoler bent into a low stance. "Bugger off, peasant! I tire of all these strange fuckin' visitors at all strange fuckin' hours."

Be what you were born to become, Gilbert. Become what your mother always knew you were.

A devil.

"Dare ye stand before Hell?" asked Gilbert with a low growl. The gaoler's arms trembled at this, the tip of the spear dancing before him. "Dare ye lose your sacred pilgrimage to Heavenly Paradise for a meager war prisoner? Please, I beg of thee, do not interfere. It is not worth it. It is my curse to watch all those around me perish."

"I'll gut ye where you stand!"

At this threat, the prisoners stood up within the confines of their caravan cells. William, glancing over the gaoler, spotted his older brother, and cried out as the guard took a step forward to impale him.

"Gilbert!"

Instinct and showmanship took over; a life of conning and thievery, of learning to embrace his curse, had trained him for this moment. He pulled his dagger from his belt, held it up to his left hand, and sliced his palm in two. The gaoler hesitated. Bright-red blood streamed down the crooks of Gilbert's hand. He wiped the wetness over his forehead, letting the warmth cascade over his eyebrows and drip to the dirt. It was like he sustained the wounds of Christ, and an invisible crown of thorns was hammered onto his head, leaking his life essence. Gilbert watched himself from some distant place.

"Take one more step, and thou shalt be banished henceforth to the deepest depths of Hell."

"Witchcraft..."

"More treacherous than that. I swear it by the epochal oath that eternally binds the tension between Heaven and Hell: ruin shall rain upon your life in such vast numbers, and in such mighty strength, that you'll beckon your everlasting torment to come forthwith."

William watched his brother exclaim all of this with astonishment.

The gaoler, having seen this display and exclamation, and knowing that no one would aid the defense of the Hellhound's war prisoner, shook his head, laughed an incredulous spittle of a smile that showed his broken and jagged teeth, and glanced back at the boy hostage he'd been tasked to watch since sailing through the Strait. To the boy within the cage, he asked, "Why is it always you who get the crazed visitors? Damn ye! And damn that accursed Hellhound for fraternizing with ye! I'm sick of this damn shift." He turned back to Gilbert, staring at his bleeding hand and crimson-drenched face. "Go ahead, ye fiendish lunatic. Satan can have both ye fucks! I tire of this shite."

The gaoler sat down on his stool at the edge of the prison carts and pulled his sheepskin cloak over him to stay warm. Gilbert ran up to William's cage. His brother reached through the wooden bars and grasped his older brother. Feeling his kid brother's touch at long last, Gilbert's eyes ran wet, the tears intermingling with the blood drying on his cheeks. He could feel every bone in William's body. His spine, ribs, and shoulders seemed to poke through the skin. William's own eyes were twice as wet as his own; his arms grasped at Gilbert and pulled him as close to the bars as possible. And in that brief moment in time, overwhelmed with the warmth of their love, Gilbert forgot he was cursed to doom them all.

"I knew you'd come for me," William said through his sobs.

Within Gilbert, the darkness diminished a little at hearing his brother's voice. He held William until his tics subsided and his anxious breaths mellowed to a steady crawl. William grabbed Gilbert's hand and glanced at his cut palm.

"I'll survive," said Gilbert.

"There's somethin' different about ye." William shuddered. He wiped the blood from Gilbert's eyes and stared into them. "What—what happened to ye?"

"Don't worry about me. I'm goin' to get you out of here."

But his words didn't seem to temper the concern on William's face. His kid brother let go of his arm and scooted back a few feet within his cage. "I fear my brother hasn't found me after all."

"Don't be an idiot. 'Tis me."

Gilbert glanced about the small clearing. Around them, Stephen's chaotically dormant camp lay in wait; there were quite a few soldiers who eyed them wearily. They may have been content enough to let Gilbert talk to a prisoner in their camp, especially the personal prisoner of a captain they despised, but allowing them to flee and escape was something else entirely.

"We need to get ye out of here."

"'Tis impossible," said William. A gust blew across the camp, and it made the two shiver. William's skin turned red from the cold.

"What are the patrols like? Is there any way we can sneak in?"

"Nay. They may let ye walk in, but there's no way back out. And—and—I never know when Eadric shows up."

Gilbert scrunched his eyes at his brother. Was that admiration he saw when he said the name of his captor?

"And Gilbert, my father is in there."

"In the castle?" Gilbert turned toward Oxford keep, where it stood erected behind the deep moat. William's real father was in Oxford Castle?

"He's huntin' him, Gilbert. He wants to kill my father. Says he will make sure we get his fortune when he does."

"That's foolish. What would your captor care for a couple of boys from a disowned family?"

"... I think he likes me."

Gilbert was stunned. The two brothers stared at each other, and they might as well have been leagues away. Neither of them knew who they were looking at.

"You've lost your mind," said Gilbert. "Being held captive by him has made you crazed."

William ticked, then he said, "I'm not the only one who seems crazed."

Anger boiled up inside Gilbert. He did not come all this way to have his kid brother turn against him at the very end.

"We can worry about what the Hellhound wants later. First, we need to free you. Hawk is here too. He'll help. You remember what I taught you on the beach?"

"*Relativus.*"

"Exactly. And I have two diversions in mind."

"Which are?"

"What is the one thing that could distract an entire army?"

His brother thought for a moment. "The end of the siege?"

"Aye, the exact moment they break through the walls. Who'd be paying attention to simple prisoners when they need to capture a holy empress?"

"And the second?"

A crisp wind blew through again. Gilbert and William shivered; the gaoler curled up in his cloak; the nearby soldiers huddled inside their tents; the cooks ducked close to their fires; frost shone brightly upon the sparse grass in the prison yard.

"Whenever winter comes," said Gilbert. "The first blizzard. No one will be out except your poor lot."

Pure terror overtook William's face. "A blizzard would kill me."

"Not if we get you out first."

"I don't like that plan."

"Me neither. That's why we hope they break through the walls first."

CHAPTER XLI
EMMA & MADAME BEATRICE

As did all souls ensnared behind the curtain walls, Emma waited.

Each minute, each hour, stretched endlessly on and on. Every eternal moment induced another question. When will the next boulder plummet from the sky? When will the gate be breached? When will the food run out? When? When? When?

And for Emma, the questions didn't stop there.

When will Empress Maud call upon me? When will I finally have the chance to apologize to Mama? When will my arm get better? When? When? When?

The lingering warmth of summer faded as the tail-end of autumn slithered closer. Dark and voluptuous clouds billowed over the top of the stone parapets, sprinkling rain that imbued a frigidity down to the bone—an invasive chill that spread its roots through the body like an icy, parasitic fungus. September passed to October; October approached November. The food stock dropped, and the people complained of hunger, and the food stock dropped more, and the dead multiplied until the stench of shallowly dug graves plagued the inner bailey. Jory was one of them. Emma had placed his lyre atop his grave. It only remained there for a day until it went missing; they suspected someone had burned it for warmth. Old-Codger Reginald had also died, though he did so in his sleep. They all hoped he went peacefully. So few of them ever did.

Crispin knocked Emma out of her dark thoughts by asking, "Are ye okay?"

She blinked twice as if awakening from a deep dream. "Do I not look so?" she asked miserably.

The boy shrugged. He, like everyone else, had lost a lot of weight since the siege started. He wrapped himself up tighter and smiled at her, and she, despite herself, smiled back.

"I can take care of myself," she said in a more playful tone.

"Me knows it."

Emma reached out, placing her hand on his thigh. "Thank ye for asking."

"You're welcome."

They sat on the outer steps of the keep, both she and Crispin wrapped in cloaks and blankets made of sturdy hide. But the tendrils of frost remained painfully frozen between their joints, and her inflamed right shoulder felt as if it was constantly burning. A breeze fluttered up the stairs and swept up to Madame Beatrice, who stood above the shivering children. She overlooked the chaos of the world around them. Men screamed by the gatehouse, where arrows constantly rained from the sky; and meanwhile, an angry mob formed around the doors to the kitchen. Crispin looked upon this nervously. Four guards were posted outside the chamber to protect his mother, but there was little anyone could do to placate a hungry mob. The crowd of trapped denizens demanded more food and greater rations, but the guards glared at them viciously with halberds held at the ready.

"He gives me nightmares," said Crispin suddenly. And then, clarifying, he added, "The man I killed. I see him in my nightmares. I'm always covered in blood. Mother tries to get me clean, but the water never washes it off."

Emma saw the nightmares on his face. His expression told every dream, every thought. She rubbed his back. "Maybe next time, I'll be the one to save ye," she said.

A guard whispered something into Madame Beatrice's ear. She straightened up and glanced down at Emma.

"It's time," said the madame. The waiting was over.

Theresa poured wine into Empress Maud's cup. The empress took a large sip that colored the edges of her lips. Her eyes never left Madame B and Emma.

"Does that sound possible?" the sheriff asked.

Madame B glanced at Emma nervously. Theresa poured wine into Empress Maud's tankard. The empress took a large sip that colored the edges of her lips.

No, Emma answered in her head, *it's not possible. But the empress knows I must attempt it; she'd have me executed otherwise.*

"Very well," the sheriff said. "We'll make sure the prayer room is cleared out so you may relieve your sins first. Madame B, if you could be so kind, lead us to this hidden postern you speak of."

Empress Maud put down her cup. "And one last thing," she said before they left. "Bring Duke Richard with you. I would like him to be your lookout."

The empress smiled at them, revealing stained teeth.

Madame Beatrice pushed open a rotted door whose hinges had turned rusty and brown. Cold air, which spun endlessly in the cavern beyond the door, blasted at them. Emma could hear the surge of River Mill Stream on the other side, and her gut twisted inside her at the prospect of falling into that horrid temptress.

"This is ridiculous!" Duke Richard protested. "Why on God's earth would the empress want to send us to certain doom?"

"'Tis not certain," said Emma, surprised by her own volition. Now was not the time to be hesitant; now was the time to become her own knight in shining armor. "Thieves steal food every day," she reasoned. "This is no different."

"Not from a fuckin' army! Nor when they're surrounded by watchmen and knights!"

"Duke Richard," said the madame, "I suggest you belt it and keep muted. The time for bravery has come."

The duke huffed. "I will be having a stern rebuke with Maud after this. Who does she think she is?"

"An empress," said Emma, enjoying the bright-red shame that crossed the older man's face. She glanced at Madame Beatrice. She was hiding it better than the duke, but she seemed equally disturbed and horrified by the task they were given.

In that moment, it struck Emma suddenly and overwhelmingly that she understood something very fundamental about herself. As she stood between the chosen confidant of an empress and the hand-picked spy of a king, she learned *she* was the steady torch that lit the way. Brave and resilient, she alone was chosen by kings and empresses alike.

Emma led Madame B and Duke Richard out of the postern into a natural cavern underneath the castle. A rivulet slunk down from a hidden fissure in the rock; it wound past them and through some tightly packed, leafless bushes. Emma and Madame Beatrice crunched the bushes downwards, their twigs snapping and flicking away. They separated them just enough to gaze through the opening of the cavern.

River Mill Stream thundered around them. They were beneath the western curtain wall of the castle. Here, based on what Madame B had told them, was where the river was at its narrowest and shallowest. They *should* be able to cross the river without swimming, but the thought of doing so made Emma shudder. Border ice had already fastened along the waterline, extending outward a few feet from the shore. Within a month or two, the entire river would be frozen over. Luckily for the empress and all those within the castle, the sheet of river ice will remain too thin to allow Stephen's army to cross and reach the battlements.

Emma glanced at Madame B, who glanced back at Duke Richard. The idea was somewhat thought through: as the sun rose into the northeast horizon, thereby allowing the fortifications to cast shadows over the western shore, they would be completely shrouded in darkness. And while a few watchmen from the king's army always circled the castle, it was unlikely they would expect anyone to cross the river during these frigid temperatures. Probably.

The three of them waited for a scouting party of five soldiers to pass on the opposite bank. The militia men continued southward until they rounded back to the city gates. According to their castle watchmen's intel, they would have another ten minutes before another patrol came through. A sound like the caw of a crow came from above them—a signal by the soldiers atop the wall that the way was clear.

I am brave. I am resilient. I am chosen.

Emma took a deep breath. She tried to rub her injured arm to rouse it, but it remained lame and dormant. She prepared herself as best she could.

Then she submerged herself in the torrential river.

Stepping into River Mill Stream was one of the worst things Madame Beatrice had ever experienced, and *that* was saying quite a bit. When her foot cracked through the ice, the air went out of her all at once. Her warmth fled down the stream, swiftly and horrifyingly, until all she had left deep within her core was a singular rod of heat, like a hearth resisting despondently while it was suffocated on all sides. She gasped and immediately regretted it. She'd need that air. Ice formed in her hair and on her garments. The strength of the river pushed against her, threatening to sweep her away to a frosty death. In a desperate attempt to distract herself from the harrowing cold, Beatrice mentally recited the teachings from her past life. Much to her amazement, she remembered most of the things she had learned.

The walls of Oxford were built in (Jesus Christ, the cold) ... Oxford Castle ... built in 1066 by Robert D'Oyly ... St. George's Tower was constructed with wood but reconstructed using limestone ... it's so fucking *cold ... a ditch and moat were built, allowing the river to naturally protect the south, east, and north ... a small postern near St. George's Tower can let occupants escape in desperate situations ...*

Beatrice exited the river, and her mind came back to her in a flash. It must have taken a few strenuous minutes to cross the entire river, but her mind and the thoughts of ancient learning had made it seem like mere moments. She was amazed; her mind's ability to transport her away from trauma had saved her sanity yet again.

But now she was dying.

The cold gripped her like an icy hand, the heat deep within her disappearing completely. Her clothes were soaked through and rimmed with frost. The mist from the river was almost worse than the water itself, creating snowflakes on her hair that sparkled in the rising sun.

Get to the tree line.

Beyond the river was an open field—about two hundred meters in length—that stretched to the surrounding forest. Beatrice glanced toward the king's encampment around Beaumont Palace to the north. No one seemed to appraise their direction. Emma had exited River Mill Stream first, and she was halfway through the open field when Duke Richard finally exited the river.

Ding-ding. Ding-ding. The many churches of Oxford rang as the sun rose and peeked over the east. Madame B could tell which bell came from which church based on its specific timbre.

Ding-ding-ding. St. Aldate's near the south gate. *Ding-ding.* St. Michael's to the north. *Ding. Ding. Ding.* St. Peter's Church to the far east. *Ding-ding. Ding.* All Saints Church in the—

Madame Beatrice shook her head. She growled at herself. The cold was making her lose control of her thoughts. She could barely keep her mind on track.

Take charge, Beatrice. Be strong for our empress. Don't fail her.

Beatrice ignored Richard's incessant babbling, ran up to where Emma was, and helped her reach the forest; the girl felt as if she were made of ice, a glacier brought to treacherous life by the frigid hands of God. Despite worrying they'd be spotted or frozen atop the tundra, they reached the tree line without any surprises. And much to their eternal joy, they found the stash of hidden clothes buried beneath an ancient birch tree, just as Empress Maud had promised.

They threw off their clothes and changed without so much as a care of any leering glances from the older duke. They huddled together and rekindled their warmth that nearly evaporated in the pit of their chests.

"What next?" asked Emma, appearing aloof and serious, her face ghostly blank. What happened to the life-loving girl Beatrice hated only a few months ago? And why did she hate this version of Emma even more?

"They should arrive down the road shortly," said Beatrice. She turned to the duke. "Will you be ready?"

Duke Richard grimaced and gripped the short sword that was buried with their new clothes. "Don't doubt me," he replied.

"Then don't give me a reason to."

The duke snuck toward the northern road leading to Beaumont Palace. The task Empress Maud bestowed upon them had multiple goals, as they oft did: to gain food they desperately needed, to have Emma prove her trustworthiness, to receive word from her supporters, and to tempt the duke into revealing his true nature. Duke Richard had been one of Empress Maud's most important allies in the southwestern shires of the kingdom. If he were truly a spy, as Emma suggested, he'd be unwilling to attack Stephen directly when he was on the precipice of victory.

Half an hour passed. The three of them hid deeper in the woods as patrols continually ambled down the road protecting ox-yoked carts that carried stones for the king's war machines. Lucia shivered thinking of how one of those could be the instrument of her demise. Finally, a wagon led by a donkey and five soldiers came down the road. A red scarf tied about the spokes of the wheel signaled that this was their designated target.

Emma nodded to her. Beatrice was amazed at the confidence in the young girl's eyes, but perhaps she shouldn't be. This was the same girl who entered the direct confidence of a queen to spy right under her nose. This girl had more courage than most.

Duke Richard seemed much less brave. He strangled the hilt of his sword, sweat seeping between his fingers. His eyes twitched between the approaching soldiers.

"Are you able?" Beatrice asked him.

"Yes," he said. "There are just some . . . *fighters* in Stephen's army who want me dead. Very, very dead." Somewhere in the forest behind them, a twig snapped. Duke Richard spun his head around like an owl, flinging sweat off his thinning hairline.

"Focus, my lord."

Past the forest and the roaring river behind them, the belfries sounded once more.

Ding-ding-ding. Ding-ding.

"How can one focus when being hunted incessantly?" the duke asked himself.

Ding-ding. Ding.

"We need to go," said Emma.

Ding-ding. Ding-ding-ding. Unrelentingly, the bells tolled for the dead.

Beatrice jumped in front of the donkey, pulling on her dress, acting as if she were being stung by a hundred bees. The men stopped in their tracks, their breath pluming beneath their iron helms. Much to their unfortunate detriment, it was the immediate reaction of men to wonder at and save women when they flailed before them. Back in a time before time didn't matter, Beatrice had used this power to make men blush and flounder; but today, as a grown woman transmuted by the hands of suffering, she used it to kill them instead.

Emma pounced from the underbrush. She pulled the pin, dislodging the wheel and tumbling it off the axle. Half-frozen vegetables and stale meat rolled off the wagon. Duke Richard roared. He sprang up and gutted his sword through one soldier's neck. His blood sprayed sideways, covering the face of the other. A soldier wearing a red scarf that matched the one tied about the spoke, lowered his spear and skewered the soldier next to him. Within a few moments, four of King Stephen's militiamen lay dead on the road. They were victorious.

"Lord FitzCount gives his regards," said the red-scarfed soldier.

Beatrice curtsied to the man. Empress Maud was right, like she always was. They were told they would meet a knight disguised as a soldier who was secretly in allegiance with Brian FitzCount; he'd make himself known by wearing a red piece of clothing. They were told he went by Sir Winston.

"I'm glad it went according to plan," said Duke Richard, gripping the knight's forearm. "Any information from Lord FitzCount?"

Lucia squinted at him. Was the duke trying to pry further information for the king?

"He's overcome with shame, my lord. He and Lord FitzWalter feel they've abandoned their oaths to Earl Robert, those to protect his sister while he's away in Caen. They are amassing a mighty force in Wallingford to strike back at the traitor king."

"How long will that take?" asked Beatrice.

"Another two full moons, my lady."

"That's too slow. We'll never hold out that long."

"My lords express their regrets. But the usurper king has turned your ramparts against you, and the city now serves as his own fortifications. If Lords FitzCount and FitzWalter attacked now, it would turn into another siege. An army is needed to counterattack Stephen."

"How many provisions did you bring us?" Duke Richard asked.

"Not much," Emma answered. She threw one of the sacks she gathered from the back of the wagon onto the ground. "Only a few weeks' worth at most."

"Regrettably," said Sir Winston. "T'was a tough harvest. There's not much food stored in the southern shires. We fear many will starve come winter. I'm sorry, my lady."

"Don't be," said Beatrice, remembering what she told Emma all those months ago. It was the job of a handmaiden to be a surrogate for their lady. "Empress Maud thanks you for your courage and for the help of Lord Brian and Lord Miles. Where did you say they resided?"

"Wallingford, currently."

"Wallingford. Can they hold the city?"

"Yes, my lady. My lords won't fail the empress again. I bring tidings of further news, if you can spare the moment. Earl Robert has learned of his sister's entrapment. He refuses to wait for Geoffrey's benevolence to blossom and has decided he would venture back across the channel alone."

"When did you hear this?"

"A little less than a fortnight back. We still await word if he's arrived."

"If he's here," said Beatrice with wide-eyed amazement, "that shifts the tides of war. There's not a single person Stephen fears more than him."

Now that's information we can test him on, thought Madame Beatrice while glancing at Duke Richard. If he were truly a spy, he cannot keep this information to himself. He'd have to report it to the usurper.

"Come," she said. "Let's move before they realize they have a missing transport."

The three of them, with further assistance from Sir Winston, collected the stolen provisions and headed back through the forest. God must have been watching over them, for they crossed the open field and back through River Mill Stream without a single patrol spotting them. They fled back inside the postern while the tower of St. George protected them overhead.

Within the city of Oxford, the church bells tolled endlessly.

CHAPTER XLII
EADRIC

On the first night that Eadric vacated the warmth of Beaumont Palace, he saw an eerie orange light dancing along the tree line. The light floated alluringly off the ground like those woodland fire faeries from children's fables. The immense darkness of the night sky, mixed with the haunting depths of those woods, made the light appear mischievous and bewitching. Eadric, of course, ignored it; he searched for his first hiding hole inside the city. After settling on an abandoned townhome that appeared secure from any roaming patrols, he tried his best to get some sleep. His dreams were assailed, however, by the flickering light in the dark Oxford woods.

Ding-ding. Ding. The multiple church bells of Oxford sang day-in, day-out—a siege tactic to drive the trapped inhabitants of Oxford Castle mad.

The only downside was it made everyone else go crazy too.

Every night, Eadric hid in a different house or store or barn or shed. October drifted into November, and any remembrance of their warm, gentle summer faded into a distant memory. The temperature dropped precipitously. It wasn't long before the occupied peasants who stayed in Oxford started spouting evil tidings. Eadric heard them whispering, claiming God was trying to cover them in a blanket of ice to suspend the war; the proof, obviously, was in how the holy bells of the church rang unrelentingly.

Ding-ding-ding.

Throughout all hours of the day and night, the belfries cried out. There was no such thing as peaceful sleep during a siege.

Eadric ventured amongst the populace sometimes, covering himself with layers of clothes, a cowl, and a vagabond's cloak. He had yet to be spotted by peasant or soldier alike, and he discovered a simple comfort in being able to blend into a crowd. Within the few open taverns and markets, Eadric spied on the complaints of the lower infantry.

"Freezing me to death is what they want. They 'ave me sittin' on me arse, watchin' the damn walls like the empress will float down over the side of 'em."

"Me hears our food is running low. What's that? Aye, the king *has* been lookin' fine fed. Fat as swine! Ye reckon they storin' a mighty load in that palace of theirs?"

"Don't be callin' me a friend, ye pissant. I'm in no mood to compare pricks."

They seemed to be the same issues every time, albeit disguised under different contexts. Food supply. Frigid temps. Tension amongst ranks. Idleness. Those damn church bells.

Ding-ding-ding. Ding-ding-ding-ding. Ding.

All of it, much to his luck, was exploitable. His plan started small. He began by talking with the drunken soldiers, playing the part of a wandering charlatan who had the remarkable misfortune to settle inside Oxford the day before Stephen's army arrived. He paid for their drinks with the little coin he had left. They thanked him and, in turn, allowed him to sit at their table while they gossiped of peasant matters: how bad the crops were this year, the last words they heard from their families, the horrid weather that wanted to turn England into a tundra bereft of life.

One night, a soldier by the name of Rudd mentioned the glowing orange spectre out in the woods. Eadric listened intently. Some believed it to be a witch, while others, a refugee camp. A middle-aged woman by the name of Alvina, whose house burned down in the initial attack, thought it to be a forest sprite who patiently waited for the rest of the city to burn down so it could reclaim the land that was taken from it. Whatever it was, Eadric once again dreamed of that dancing fire until he was rudely woken up by—

Ding-ding. Ding-ding. Ding. Ding. Ding.

Eleanor and Sir Álvaro reconvened with him in secret. He divulged to them all the rumors and griefs that the soldiers complained of, and then they went to work finding new ways to stoke those flames. There were many ways they accomplished this; for example, when around lower infantry, Sir Álvaro gloated about how the lords were given steady food at the palace. He'd openly discuss the luxury and comfort given there. Then at night, when those same soldiers were drunk and brazen and cold to the bone, Eadric goaded them further.

"Why is it we should starve when the king's belly remains full?!" he asked the soldiers. "There's naught to be gained if we win this siege. What happens then? The king and queen get to remain warm inside the castle and their lofty palace, while we're still left in the cold. Without food. Only to suffer."

Each day and every night, the three of them worked on widening the rift between the highborn and lowborn; the irony of what he was doing wasn't lost on him.

One day when he was snooping about, Eadric overheard guards wishing harm and damnation on the Hellhound of Rutland. They spat vitriol about his having abandoned his men. How he killed peasants for sport. How he beat his wife and sucked off the king—sometimes both simultaneously. He had often heard secondhand about what the foot soldiers thought of him, but it was a different thing entirely to hear it directly. It didn't shock him. He knew he had brought this on himself. But it still damaged something inside of him, a part of himself he didn't know was still alive.

When November neared the end of its first week, the weather already believed it to be February. Eadric had known cold in his life, yet he discovered that meant very little when he didn't have thick wooden walls and boundless bundles of firewood to keep the hearth fueled. The best nights were when Eleanor visited him. They sat together, covered in furs and blankets, and they talked into the deep hours of the night. They rarely spoke of their coup; rather, she told him stories of her life back in Rome, when she had a son and husband. In return, Eadric spoke freely of his life with and before Lucia. Some nights they made love—a softer, more delicate kind than before. Not violent and combative, but gentle and intentional. Maybe something in them had changed. Or maybe they were simply tired. When Eleanor visited, she looked much like he must appear: endlessly fatigued with matted hair and drooping skin. But under the stillness of the pale stars, she looked to him as beautiful and elegant as ever. On the nights when she lay naked next to him, Eadric's hands would sweat, and his heart would flutter. He was in absolute awe of his wife. This never used to happen before.

Other evenings they simply lay under the layers of blankets and embraced one another tightly to keep out the cold. But it never worked, no matter how many animal furs they stacked on. Regardless of how hot Eleanor's skin felt on his, nor of how many stockings or trousers or mittens or hats or shirts they wore, the bitter weather always found a way to freeze every joint in their body. So instead of sleeping, they shivered together while listening to the tolling bells.

Eadric woke up. His body shuddered from the inhalation of pure air. Ice crystals seemed to form inside his lungs. It burned. Eadric grimaced as he leaned up. A sharp pain stabbed through him, starting at his lower back and firing up—another symptom of sleeping in such wretched conditions.

What time is it?

Glancing around, he remembered he was in the upper loft of a barn that he'd snuck in the night before. A cow used to live here, probably some family's prized possession. It was dead. Its shriveled body lay on the ground, frozen over to delay the decaying process until next spring. The house next to the barn was now a giant ash pile. It was a miracle the flames did not devour the barn. The poor creature must have collapsed during the initial raid and starved to death.

Snowflakes fluttered in through the window. And Lucia stood next to it.

Ding-ding-ding. Ding-ding.

Lucia didn't breathe; no visible exhaust came from her nose nor mouth. Her skin was white and pure, without imperfections. Eadric couldn't decipher her age. She looked both young and ancient, like an angel that had been purified through death to have the everlasting beauty of youth. Eadric tried to speak her name, to tell her **DING-DING-DING.** His voice wouldn't let him. The ice crystals in his lungs clumped together, blocking his airways, making the inside of his throat feel as brittle as an **DING-**. He wanted to reach out to her, to bring her closer so he could **DING-** with her love. It didn't work. His muscles were too stiff to move. **DING.** She vanished, and Eadric tumbled to the ground.

He smashed backwards into powdered snow. He was on an open snowfield. A blizzard flung snow particles around him, yet he couldn't feel the tempest. Couldn't hear it. Mind jumbled. Only bells. Ringing. And He. Moaning. Agonizing. Twisting onto his side. Seeing it. A body. Through the blizzard. Barely visible. Yet he. Crawling toward it. A trail in the snow.

The body. Lucia. Dead. Exposed. Nude. Expanding blood from her body. White powder pooling a deep scarlet. Devastation.

Cradling her. Wanted. But his hands wouldn't open. Looking down at them. Fingers frozen together. Back of his hand. A fist glazed with ice. Reflecting himself. A longsword sliced down. At his neck. Through his neck. An executioner doing his duty. He saw his head fall.

Eadric awoke to Eleanor shushing him. She placed her hand on his chest. He glanced out the barn window and saw that it was sunny. The first snow had yet to hit the countryside. He lay on his back, panting and soaked in his own sweat. Eleanor tried to say something to him, but all he heard coming out of her mouth was *ding-ding. Ding-ding-ding.*

Am I going mad?
Ding-ding-ding-ding-ding-ding.

Eadric watched foot soldiers tear each other apart. He smiled at his work. This was the culmination of weeks of meticulous labor. Every night he ventured to various alehouses and taverns, sowing doubt and discord, turning them on each other, making them believe those in other posts were getting fed more, or gifted warmer clothes, or allowed to have women, or given extra time off duty. As he'd hoped, this led to countless fights among the different posts.

Often he glanced over at the distant castle walls. They were halfway through November, closing in on their third full month of the siege, yet Empress Maud had refused to fly the white flag and raise the gates. She stood firm. And with each passing day, King Stephen was rendered more and more incompetent.

Ding-ding-ding.

"Damn these fuckin' bells all to Hell!" screamed one of the nearby guards. Peasants and soldiers and Eadric alike nodded their heads in agreement.

Eleanor told Eadric that King Stephen would allow him back. Sir Álvaro told Eadric that the unrest was filtering up to the top. Everyone was on edge. His stomach growled. He rubbed it. When was the last time he ate? The days blended together. When was he told that unrest had reached Beaumont Palace? Today? A week ago? Or did he dream that too?

The passing patrols gave Eadric dirty glances, perhaps because he was one of the few people who ventured outside. Everyone else stayed in their homes where they could attempt to stay warm, and where they could avoid the bandits who attacked the city with more desperation. The king and his army were struggling to fight back against the marauders *and* the empress.

Eadric didn't care for either. He couldn't stand being trapped inside any longer. He'd been holed up in various burned shacks for months. Most of his time was spent watching water freeze over or his breath flutter out before him like he was smoking a pipe. He needed to be around people. It was the only way to tether himself to God's kingdom. Everything felt surreal. Ethereal. He wasn't sure if it was the cold, the loneliness, the hunger, or the despair that had him feeling adrift. Every day, he risked walking up to the castle's curtain walls. They were scuffed from where the king's war engines plowed their sides. But the trebuchets hadn't loosed in over a week; he overheard they broke down more often than they worked. What a shame. This siege seemed like it would go on forever, destined for an eternal winter standoff.

Eadric went mad just thinking about it. He sensed Lucia's stare even now. She watched him from the top of the Oxford battlements, gracing him with her presence from Heaven.

Don't worry, honey. Daddy will be with you soon enough. He needs to dirty his hands only once more.

Eadric finished his walk to the western gate. Dusk settled across the land. The clouds parted long enough for the crystal-clear stars to sparkle down on them. Out past the gate and the guards, across the River Thames, and over the patch of shivering grass, Eadric spotted that spectral orange glow wavering in the tree line.

It beckoned him.

Advent arrived in late November, and it was a miracle it hadn't snowed yet. The people braced for it, yet God refused, for whatever reason, to break the tension and cover the world in white. It felt painfully wrong, like a lover who worked up their partner with no release.

The church bells echoed distantly as the Hellhound of Rutland breached the edge of the Oxford woods. The orange light guided him onward. He reached for his sword at his side, comforting himself with the reminder that it was there. The night was dark. No moonlight glimmered through the leafless boughs. They stood silent, unmoving. There was no wind. Only still, perpetual, primordial frost.

The light led him farther and farther into the wood until he reached a small clearing. A campfire. The smoke arose from it in an array of colors: black, green, orange, blue. On the far side of the flames, a hut stood erect; animal skeletons adorned its front face. A boar skull. The jaw of a dog. Deer antlers. A collection of bird beaks.

"For thou, me'ave been waitin'," said a wretched voice—harsh and grating to the ears.

Eadric spotted an old woman with a bowl in her hands. Her wrinkled skin made her look like a newborn bird, with folds upon folds covering each other up. She had long white hair, and a crown made of rodent bones. She wore a necklace of feathers. Rings adorned every finger.

"Are you a witch?" asked Eadric.

"Oft doth your kindred giveth such names to us. Crone. Hag. Witch."

"Speak plainly. You are one, yes?"

"Yes." Her voice vanished into silence as quickly as it sprang forth. The only sound was the faint popping of the campfire. It erupted sparks into the air like frenzied fireflies.

"Did the devil send you? Are you here to collect my soul at long last? Has the notoriety of my evil finally breached his foul interest?"

"Sit." The crone pointed to a large rock next to the campfire, where a small tankard warmed itself. "Thou must consume of thine own volition."

He hesitated. Unable to flee or sit, he stood unmoving in the face of this ancient being. How long had she walked this world? Was she from the days of Christ? Even older? Was she a child of Cain, ignored and forgotten by scripture?

"What's in it?" he asked dryly, his throat feeling swollen.

"A concoction for thine inhibitions. A nectar so sweet, t'would render thy senses poignant, make visible the snuffing flames wrought by thine hands. A remedy for thy malady."

"Which one?"

"All of them. Confront thyself, so thou canst keepeth purity of mind. Thy soul has long passed into obscurity, but thou canst reclaim humanity for a brief respite. Drink from the vessel willingly, and meditate on thy need for admonishment. Thou wilt find clarity anew."

"I suspect if I do as you say, you will rob me of my things. Take from me all I have left."

The witch tilted her head crooked. Her black pupils glared at him under the hood of her hanging flesh. She stretched out her bony finger, pointing a coiled, overgrown nail at the stone.

Ding-ding-ding. Ding-ding-ding. Eadric sat. ***Ding-ding. Ding.*** Eadric drank. ***Ding.*** Warm. ***Ding.*** Bitter. ***Ding.*** Earthy. ***DING. DING. DING.***

Time passed unknowingly. Music played from deep below *middanearde*, the beat in rhythm with the church bells. The boughs of the tree danced. Mouths formed in the campfire, singing sparks of light. The crone cackled. A gust of wind, sudden and overwhelming, almost blew Eadric over.

It scared him. He must become a tree; he needed to be firm and strong against this impending maelstrom. The witch's laughter floated around him and disappeared far up into the night sky. He glanced down and realized he *had* turned into a tree. He could feel his roots planted in the earth meters below him. A monstrous weight pulled on his many branches. He gazed around him. Bodies, far too many to count, hung from ropes on each bough. Their necks were broken; tongues protruded from their purple faces. Some of them were skeletons. Others were newly deceased, their skin slowly melting off the bone. Eadric recognized one as the soldier he killed in Boulogne, the one he told to remind God to damn him.

A crow landed on Eadric. It cawed, ruffling its feathers. Right as it took off, it shat down the side of his face. He could feel the shit steaming on his bark. The crow gripped its claws onto one of the corpses. He focused on the victim this black death chose, and to his amazement, he saw it to be Sir Álvaro. The knight hung from the rope; his eyes popped from their sockets. The crow pecked at the dead man's stomach, picking apart his rotting flesh. His intestines spilled out, black and infested with maggots. Eadric forced himself to look away.

Lucia stood on the ground far below him. She was very little. Maybe four or five. The grizzly sight of what her father had become plagued her innocent face with horror. He'd killed nearly a hundred people for vengeance. For her. He wanted to banish this illusion, to break free and cover her eyes. But his roots were too deep and his branches too heavy from the weight of death. He watched with unrelenting regret as tears fell from his daughter's eyes.

"How could you do this, Daddy?" she asked, her voice broken and razor sharp. "I don't mean this much. You did this for yourself. Not me."

Eadric wanted to scream. He wanted to uproot and tear himself from the ground. The witch came up next to his daughter and handed her a lit torch. Lucia thanked her.

"Some things the Lord can't forgive. Some things *I* can't forgive . . . I have to burn you, Daddy. I must kill the monster you've become. You were everything a daughter could want, but now even Satan would be loathed to claim you."

He willed himself to speak, to beg her not to do this, but his mouth had gone extinct. Ants, maggots, and insects crawled through his trunk. The infestation traveled from the corpses of his victims to the inside of his being. There were millions of bugs inside him, devouring him from the inside out—a billion legs flaying every inch of his soul.

"I'm sorry, Daddy, but only the flames can cleanse your spirit."

She set him on fire. The pain was immense. Every root wanted to curl and topple his burning trunk to the ground. But life didn't work that way. A tree couldn't uproot because a storm approached. Nature couldn't avoid the causation of man. It must only endure.

Lucia watched her father, and all the many bodies hanging from his boughs, burn to ash. Her father howled. Roared. Cried. Begged. But no human could hear the screams of nature, the death rattle of trees.

Could even God?

Eadric woke up next to the campfire. He was near death. The sweat on his body had turned into crystals, and he could no longer feel his fingers or toes. He wheezed onto the hard dirt ground, trying to look around the clearing. The crone was gone, and her demonic tent was nowhere to be found.

"Baron Eadric, what's happened to you?"

With the last of his strength, Eadric rolled onto his back. A large company surrounded him. Ten, maybe twenty armed guards. King Stephen and Queen Matilda were among them. And before them all, leading the arrest party, stood Sir Álvaro.

"I've waited a long time for this," said the black knight, an elated smile on his face.

CHAPTER XLIII
GILBERT

*D*ING—DING—DING.

"Has it been an hour already?" asked Roger.

"No, my love," said Alice. "We told ye. They ring it to disturb the peace. It hasn't been an hour."

"Oh. Well, 'tis damn annoying."

"That's the point, love."

Gilbert, Edith, Alice, and Roger sat inside the forgotten mill. The walls rattled while strong winds and hail assaulted the countryside. In the five weeks since they approached Oxford, they've done their best to reinforce the mill and retain the little warmth they had. They set straw and dried branches on the dirt floor; they patched the holes with timber; they dug a fire pit and kept it fed as best they could. But the roofing was still poked with holes, allowing the torment of the sky to drizzle down upon the poor inhabitants. The storm came so suddenly and so intensely that they could not recover their fuel from the firepit before the rain drenched it. Now they sat miserably in the icy darkness, with only the faint trembling of their breaths audible, as more hail the size of eyeballs slammed through the roof and bounced off them, before finally melting into a muddy puddle on the dirt floor.

Gilbert had never been so cold in all his life.

Except, that was a lie. As he pressed his arms and cloak closer to himself, bones shivering and teeth rattling, he remembered a time when he *had* been so frightfully chilled.

That dark night...that frozen forest...those angry torchbearers and those terrible wails of a child—of a sister lost.

Hawk cracked open the door and entered. Gilbert shook his mind clear of that forlorn remembrance. His friend kneeled next to him. His cloak was saturated with rain that was transmuting into ice. He pulled his red hat down taut over his head, reached within his cloak, and pulled out two corked wineskins.

"Is that—?"

"Ha ha!" Hawk laughed. "It is indeed, friend. Come around. Let's get drunk and warm ourselves from within. We can best this accursed storm, raining water and ice, together!"

They heard a branch snap outside. They went silent and listened intently, but all they heard was the *pat-pat-pat-pat-pat-pat-pat* of the rain and hail. Wind shook the walls again. *Pat-pat-pat-pat-pat. Ding–ding–ding. Pat-pat-pat-pat-pat.*

"I think we're safe," said Edith. The older woman had been the first to hear the strange noises in the night. They had worried that it was those brigands they'd seen along the roads leading to Oxford. Just like everyone else, when winter arrived, the marauders would become more desperate for food and warmth. Their thieving and scoundrel ways could lead them to invade homes closer to the large cities. Especially cities that made easy targets, like the besieged Oxford.

Hawk uncorked a wineskin. And with its satisfying *pop*, all their tension equally dispersed. "Good. Let's drink, then. Quiet-like."

Roger snored in the corner, where he and Alice slept bundled under their cloaks and a pile of straw. Hawk sat near the door, glancing out the small crack into the forest beyond. Edith had her eyes closed but was still awake. Gilbert took a deep breath and sipped from the wineskin. The worst of the storm had passed, and only a faint rain remained. The world seemed like it was in a reprieve from some cataclysm. Muted. Lonely. Frozen in time.

"Are we clear to start the fire again?" asked Gilbert.

"Should be," said Hawk, glancing up at the sky above them. As Gilbert sorted through their kindling to find out if they had any dry sticks left, Hawk scooted over to Edith.

"Does the cold help or hurt your injured leg?" he asked her.

"Nothin' helps it," she replied, rubbing her lame knee gingerly.

"Do you trust us enough to tell us what happened?"

She gave Gilbert a sideways glance. Hawk laughed and asked, "Trust me, at least?"

"A roof collapsed on top of me," she said. "I was standing under a hole inside an inferno. A beam pierced me through the leg."

Hawk whistled. "Shit. Is that really what happened?"

"Would make for a fantastic story, wouldn't it?"

"It would indeed! Y'know, we're big on creating stories ourselves."

"Thieves?"

"What?"

The older woman glanced at them both. "Ye say you're big on creatin' stories. Sounds like somethin' a charlatan would claim. Means ye must be a good liar."

"You can say that."

"I do say that. And a good liar knows how to spot a lie. Do you think that's how I really injured my leg? Do I lie or am I truthful?"

Hawk clapped. "Oh, I like this game!" He handed the wineskin to her. "You sure you don't want some?"

Edith considered it for a moment, then took it from his hand and drank. She grimaced. "What in blazing Hell is that?!"

"No clue! I stole it from one of the king's wagons."

"Go on, then. Is it a truth or a falsehood?"

"What do ye think, Gil?"

"Seems as if you're bein' purposefully vague," Gilbert said to Edith.

"Cause I am," she retorted. "Do ye insist on more detail?"

"I do." Gilbert struck a rock against an iron dagger above the kindling. Sparks flew out.

"The roof fell on me because I was savin' a man who was bein' hunted by my daughter's father. I was tryin' to escape, but then the inn caught aflame." At this, the kindling finally caught alight. Edith watched the fire grow from its inception, the sparks glittering in the dark of her irises. "And it crumbled on top of me."

"Never mind," said Hawk, "I'm changing my answer. False! It has to be a falsehood."

"Why is that?"

"'Tis too fanciful! It's just a story, *has* to be."

Edith chuckled and said, "Very well. You go, then."

Hawk tossed the wineskin over the flames to Gilbert and stretched his limbs toward the fire, letting its warmth consume him. Gilbert, however, found little joy in the dancing light. The vacuous eternity that consumed him seemed to originate entirely from those sparks he nurtured to life. It seemed to him . . . hollow. Bereft of all purpose.

"Fear not, Edith, for though he is involved in the story," Hawk said, pointing to Gilbert, "he does not know the truth of it. He cannot cheat. T'was a night of celebration for him and William. In the morn, they were to leave to join the fray of battle, to obtain honor for themselves and our duchy. But then *he* got arrested."

"I was thrown in a gaol that night?" Gilbert racked his brain to remember back, but all he could recall to memory was the vehement vomiting that followed the next morning.

"Indeed. Disgusting behavior, they called it."

"On account of my birth?" asked Gilbert bitterly.

"No, on account of your disturbing drunkenness! The point being that you cannot attest to the story set during your time in detention."

"Are *you* able to attest to it? Weren't ye equally drunk?"

"Yes, and that is what'll make it particularly hard for you to guess the truth from falsehood." He turned to Edith to bring her into the story. "Now I will tell you about the time we rescued this man from a public flogging. It was late, and we were all afraid Gilbert would be detained too long to leave with the army. His brother had come up with a plan. T'was a stupid plan, but a plan nonetheless. We dressed Beatriz and William in filthy garbs and covered Bartholomew real dirty-like. I put on my fanciest clothes, and we stormed the gaol."

"*Stormed* the gaol?"

"In a way. We convinced the gaoler that he was possessed. You see, that was William's doing. Said he was a misbegotten of the red moon, just as Gilbert was. Told the gaoler that the two of them would put a mighty hex on him if he didn't release him from the cell. Said you and Will's deviltry was widely known and abhorred."

A smile almost cracked on Gilbert's lips. His brother was always braver than he was. Always smarter. Always better. Only William could find a use for his baneful misery.

"And that worked?" asked Edith with a raised eyebrow.

"Not at all!" Hawk laughed. He ripped the wineskin from Gilbert's hand and took a long gulp. "Nay, not one bit. That's where me, Beatriz, and Bartholomew enter. Beatriz and Bartholomew were pretending to be afflicted by the same curse being placed on the guard. They were thoroughly soused at the time and unable to form words in any language known to God or man, and thus they were doubly believable as hexed paupers. And I, as a nobleman who had perceived the whole altercation, spirit-gifted with a silver tongue even when overcome with spirits, could convince any fellow countryman that I, too, was a trustworthy, learned fellow. We put on quite a performance, only for the gaoler to be so terrified that he called forth the local sheriff and towns' guards.

"Within moments we were surrounded by men with their pointy pikes and swords. In such a precarious circumstance such as we were, I had determined that all hope was forsaken. God blessed, William saw things differently. He confronted them. Said they and all their begotten offspring would be poisoned from now to the end of eternity. Claimed endless misfortune would find them and all those they loved. And he did it all with a foaming mouth and chanting Latin like a crazed lunatic. T'was fuckin' awesome. We had Gilbert out moments later, drunken and sloberin', and all of us amazed William could scare off ten armed guards with nothin' but his own cleverness."

"Smart bugger," said Gilbert quietly. He glanced into the dancing flames, but they seemed to be coyly avoiding his stare. All he could see was his brother out there in the treacherous cold, shivering and waiting for his older brother to rescue him for once.

"So," said Hawk, "there's the story. Do I lie or remain a saint?"

"T'was very specific," said Edith. "Although ye have a sharp tongue, so perhaps you are skilled as an orator too? I hear there are plenty of minstrels in France."

"What say you?"

"Ye speak the truth."

Hawk smiled. He turned to Gilbert, waiting expectantly.

"'Tis true," said Gilbert. "That's a plan only William could conjure."

Hawk clapped. It was so loud and unexpected that Edith and Gilbert jumped. The sleeping couple even awoke briefly before moaning and turning back over.

"Got ye!" said Hawk. "T'was false. Ah, ye should've known better, Gilbert."

"Why? What was falsified?"

"You really have no memory of that night?"

A wind blew through the gaps in the mill. It provoked the fire, rousing it to a flurry of sparks. It crackled and popped, and the smoke filtered between Gilbert and his childhood friend.

"It was *you*," said Hawk. "You were the one who came up with the plan. William was the one the gaoler imprisoned."

Gilbert's heart pounded in his throat. He could feel his blood racing through his veins. "It couldn't be. You lie."

"William was the one throwing up on every citizen, and it was you who wanted to use your curse as a distraction."

"I'm not brave. Nor smart nor capable enough—"

"Why not?"

"Because I'm a craven."

"You're not. Not for him. Not for your brother."

Anger and confusion and madness and turmoil all boiled inside of him. Between the licking flames, he saw his mother's face. The darkness outside the mill turned a deathly red.

"I killed Olive, my baby sister," said Gilbert as he stared into the disturbed flames emitting a chilly heat. "Truth? Or dare you claim that as a lie?"

"Fuck you," said Hawk. "False. Lie. T'wasn't your fault, and you know it."

Studying and eyeing Gilbert in the keen way known to her, Edith took longer to answer. Immutable and unrelenting, she used the talents gifted to her by her past until at long last she read the expression of his soul as if he'd spoken it aloud. "'Tis true," she said. "Or at least, you believe it to be true. And if you believe it so, then it might as well be fact."

"True or false?" Hawk's voice was drenched with frustration and anger. "I knew a boy once, stupid and shy. All his life, he was told he was a sinner. For all his days, he was reared as if he was wrong; wrong for being born, wrong for being him. The corruption of his parents became the corruption of his mind, which became the corruption of all the world. True or false: he was loved still yet, despite believing himself wrong, despite every sin of the earth being his own, despite his own cravenness. He was loved by many. Is that a falsehood?"

Gilbert's eyes remained on the fire that gave no warmth.

"True or false?!"

"Ma Maman," Gilbert began slowly, deliberately, "was intoxicated by grief. Mon Papa worked late into the evening, not comin' home until the moon shone overhead. Back then we lived on the outskirts of the outskirts of Sées. Nearby was a wood as ancient as the monsters of fabled lore. We fancied we could hear them prowling deep within those boughs. William was warned never to enter; Olive was warned never to enter. But I? I was never warned. Know why? Because prowling deep within the dark secrets of Ma Maman's breast, she hoped that I would enter that forest and be lost forever." Gilbert glanced up from the flames, tears burning in his eyes. His voice came out in a whisper, strained like a lute tuned too tightly. "True or false?"

Hawk didn't respond. Edith only watched.

In his mind, the woods came alive. The darkness. The wailing. The torchlight. He *forced* himself to remember. Gilbert confronted his biggest act of cowardice: refusing to accept the truth of that wintry night.

"They came at dusk with scythes and sickles and pitchforks and axes. They came to burn us alive, seeking us out because the devil lived there. Because *I* did. T'was a horrendous harvest that summer. The soil had dried up, and the monsoons flooded anything that still grew. Insects came and devoured all else. The game in the forest died out. They say the animals went mad, foaming at the mouth and acting erratic without cause or reason. Meat was always infested with maggots. The children got sick. The lords pestered everyone for more taxes. And after all this ruin, they finally found the cause to be me.

"William saw them coming first. Ma Maman was crying in her bed. Oft did she spend the evenings wailing in grief after her miscarriages. He was unable to get her attention, so he ran to me. I tried to rouse her, but she wouldn't listen. So I grabbed Baby Olive, and I told Will to find Mon Papa and bring him here. The mob spotted us and came running; must've been half the village all told. I couldn't recognize their faces. All I saw was the blazing light of their torches. They screamed and hollered, throwing their weapons. Baby Olive was crying in my arms, and I thought our only chance was to escape into the forest. I ran through that ill-begotten wood until our tunics were soaked with the falling snow. T'was every bit as dark and cold as fabled yore."

At that moment, while Hawk and Edith were enraptured by the recounting of his greatest woe, the wind blew forth a flurry of snowflakes, the first of the year; they fluttered about in the brief, heavenly current, glistering above the white fire, until the gust dispersed and they floated gently to the earth—as all things without souls must; and as he continued his story, the snowflakes fell about him in a silent dirge while the wooden frame of the mill shook in fervent lamentation. The watchers of his testimony reserved their judgements, for the mill became darker, and the air more chill, as they transported to that same blackness, and that same iciness, as recounted and restored from the deep recesses of Gilbert's imprisoned memories. His pain saw the fires of day at long last.

"They were still coming. I could hear them shouting and screaming and cussing right behind. All I could focus on was Olive holding on to me, crying into my ear. The mob was catching up. I knew they only wanted me, so I forced her arms off my neck. I placed her on the ground, covered her with as much clothing as I could, hushed her, told her to be quiet, then I made as much noise as I could muster. And I ran. I ran until the darkness swallowed me, and the faceless mob wasn't even an echo in the night. After I escaped, I stood there for a long time listening, making sure they were gone. Then I heard the beasts. Their hellish roars. I panicked, thinking of how I had left little Olive all alone. I tried to retrace my steps, but I've never been so exhausted. I ran as fast as I could, but the fuckin' snow . . . I kept slipping and imagining them tearing her apart, hearing her insufferable cries. Finally, I found the spot that I left her at . . .

"She wasn't there. She wasn't fuckin' there. There was nothing, nothing except a torn tunic. No blood. No trails in the snow. Nothing.

"When I got back home, it was burning. The mob had set fire to it. William, Ma Maman, and Mon Papa were all watching. My mother's face when she saw I had come back without my sister . . . the smell of our home dissolving to ash . . ."

Hawk shook his head. "'Tis not your fault," he said. "You were eight. You were *not* responsible."

"For the rest of the week we searched through those accursed woods, never to find her body, never to find a trace. Never to find forgiveness. You claim it was not my fault. But it was me the mob wanted. It was my sins that brought the town to shame. It was my existence that conjured such evil."

Hawk threw the wineskin at him. In the immense cold of the freshly snowed air, the gourd felt like a dense rock. Gilbert yelped and rubbed his fresh bruise.

"Go on then!" said Hawk. "Drink yourself to death. Give in to your falsities." He glanced over at Edith. "What is it you said earlier? If ye believe it, it might as well be fact? Well, there you have it. If you believe yourself cursed, it might as well be fucking true!"

Gilbert glared at his friend aghast. Hawk's face was bright red, veins bulging out of his neck. He had never been so furious with him before.

"What curse do ye speak of?" asked Edith with concern.

"This fool believes every wicked thing that has happened to him is because he was damned at birth."

"Bad things happen to decent people all the time," she said looking at Gilbert, "not just the wicked. Trust me, I know it."

"And besides," said Hawk, "we were all cursed at birth. Did you even bother to listen to our stories? Did the hex of the moon also make you a fucking imbecile? Did it make you blind? Deaf? Have you not seen what we've all seen since we coming here? Have you not heard the sermons given at Mass? By Beatriz during any of her million prayers or holy rambles?"

Hawk's eyes pierced over the precipice of the dwindling fire. No matter how badly Gilbert wanted to, no matter how desperately he wished to disappear into the sublime acceptance of his foulness, he couldn't drown himself to damnation while Hawk was around. No, his friend would never let him do such a stupid thing as that.

"We are *all* damned," said Hawk. "All of us since birth have been damned to this accursed world. We are *all* born with sin, with pain, with the fate of suffering that long predates us and will long remain after us. To live is to be cursed. *That* is God's will. You are not special in your agony." He pulled his red Phrygian cap over his eyes and curled up beneath his cloak. "Now I am going to bed, and I don't want to hear anything else about this curse until we rescue your brother, and we're back in our home kingdom."

"Hawk—"

"Nor before ye apologize to Beatriz and Bartholomew. Not a moment sooner, you dumb churl!"

Gilbert and Edith sat silently for a long time after that. The flame, so cold and empty, continued to burn and eat itself alive until it was nearly extinct. Watching the fire do so, and hearing the words of his friend haunt him even long after he fell asleep, Gilbert crumbled. In the inevitableness of the blaze, he foresaw his own eternity; his soul eternally devoured...

But not by the Great Adversary; nor by a curse, nor the moon, nor a mother's scorn.

He saw that he alone had caused his life to be bereft of warmth.

The white fire collapsed to a pile of smoldering ash, and Gilbert, at long last, felt the heat of the flames.

CHAPTER XLIV
EADRIC

T HE CELLAR COLLECTED THE moisture of blood and sweat like a bathhouse, filling the air with the toxic fumes of human deterioration. Fecal matter and piss, both of the same wet consistency, settled in the far back corner. The rest of the dank cellar was splotched with bright blood, as if Duke Richard's banner had come to life in this torture chamber.

Sir Álvaro kicked him in the stomach. Eadric keeled over and dry-heaved. He had no more blood left to spit out, and he could barely muster a whimper. His injuries were strategically superficial, but also plentiful. Two of his left fingers were misshapen. They stopped feeling pain long ago and were now numb reminders of the suffering Sir Álvaro could inflict. A short flight of stone steps led up to a wooden door with a rounded top. King Stephen watched the beatings from there, standing high and mighty over the violence of his fury.

"Are you finished?" asked the king.

"With your permission, my king, I'd like to have more time," said Sir Álvaro.

"Take as long as you desire. I request only that you dispose of him out the back. I don't want the women and children seeing him. T'would give them nightmares." King Stephen gave his hellhound one final, expectant look, as if waiting for the crippled dog to give one last bark. When none came, he smiled and said, "I'm glad my prayers were answered, Baron Eadric. You have indeed gone mad."

"Fuck you," wheezed Eadric. Sir Álvaro bowed as King Stephen exited through the cellar door. Eadric rolled over into his own blood-speckled vomit. The stench was revolting.

"It was foolish to believe you could hide what you were doing from the king," said Sir Álvaro, circling Eadric like a predator. The black knight stomped down onto Eadric's hip; something snapped. His body tried to spasm, but the cold locked him in place. Around him, the room spun. His mind and body were disconnecting from each other.

"Why . . . ?"

"Because you're a blight upon this land. You and your daughter were a rotting infestation on my life. The two of you schemed to have me ruined." Sir Álvaro moved toward his toolkit, where a hammer, saw, pliers, and scissors lay in a grisly pool of clotted blood. The black knight chose the pliers.

"What did I do?" Each word felt like a rough brush being scraped along his throat. Eadric grimaced. "To what do you refer?"

"My family in León is ruined. I doubt you knew this when you picked me as a suitor for your daughter. León must have seemed very foreign to you and very exotic to Lucia, no doubt. I gathered that the most anyone here knew about my home was the immense wealth it developed. Allow me to teach you a thing about Spain. My people are a private sort, so few know it in these cold, miserable lands, but my realm has been ravished with war, much like this one. I was of a middling house, not as high as King Ferdinand and his council, but not a simple fief either. It was our great misfortune to be just north of the Caliphates.

"Your priests speak of them as if they're apparitions. I can attest that they're very real. They invaded swiftly from the southern lands of the Iberian, laying ruin to my family's holdings. I fled with the hopes of ten generations on my shoulders, a hope that I should bring back prosperity to my tarnished family; that one day soon, before the Muslims had seized our kingdom forever, I might stand again in that glorious valley under a Spanish sun and reclaim the land taken from us. All I needed was to return promptly, wed into a family of wealth and esteem. I needed coin, lots of it. Only an exceptional dowry would do. And I was willing to give everything for it."

"You've never spoken of this," said Eadric, his vision blurring as he drifted to the boundaries of consciousness.

"Would you have made me a suitor had you known my family was in shambles? Lucia despised me as it was. Do you think she'd have been allured by the prospect of dismantling Islam in my home country? No, I should expect not."

Delirious from loss of blood, or maybe mental degradation, Eadric imagined himself in northern Spain. His heart jumped at the prospect of standing under a brilliant sun, the breeze warm and alluring. It all seemed impossibly distant in this horrid cellar—the ground hard and frozen over, the walls stone-etched and unwavering. What would it feel like to be in a Spanish villa, surrounded by ornate wooden panels and the smell of spicy, exotic foods?

"By the night of Lord Merek's wedding," Sir Álvaro began again, "the fate of my family was nearly sealed. Word came that morning from home. A herald told me that my uncle had perished in a reckless battle against a Caliphate castle; my father had succumbed to alcoholism and abandoned my sisters and mother; my youngest sister, Marabella, only nine, turned to prostitution to help feed them, and the mark of a whore is near impossible to expunge from a bloodline."

Eadric remained quiet on the ground. He wondered why Sir Álvaro continued on with this diatribe; however, the prospect of avoiding torture for another few minutes kept him from asking. The knight appeared to be getting to the point anyways.

"That wedding was my last chance to win over your daughter. I had no time to dally, no time to spare if I was to take my newfound dowry and return to León to save them. I tried to swoon many other maidens, but Lucia was my final *real* chance." Sir Álvaro glowered as he imagined the wedding ten years ago. His hand white-knuckled around the pliers. "Then she spat in my face, and you embarrassed me in Rowan's great hall. Your putrid words dashed all my hopes. I knew at that moment there was no saving them. I was stuck here, in this frozen wasteland, doomed to know that my dream of waking under that Spanish sun was never to be." Sir Álvaro stood still a long moment after that, staring out as if he could see past the boundaries of the cellar. "I learned four years later that they had all died. My sisters, mother, father, cousins, nephews, aunts, uncles. All scattered. All dead. All lost."

"I'm sorry, Álvaro."

"After all these years, and *now* you finally respect me enough to use my Christian name? Come now. You don't need to lie, Eadric. We can finally let our hatred of one another be known. There's no return from this. No salvation. It took eight years and endless battles won for me to recoup the dignity that your rebuke had cost me. I had to be knighted to even be glanced at as more than a womanizing, foreign aristocrat. And even then, it was already six years too late for my slaughtered family."

"Some things can never be forgiven."

"Some things indeed. I'll never forget what you and Lucia cost me." Álvaro grinned. "It's funny. As someone with a similar taste for unquenchable vengeance, you may be the only man alive who understands why *this* will feel so damn good."

Eadric almost laughed. Sir Álvaro's triad appeared so carefully rehearsed, so absolute, that his minor slip was laugh-inducing. The knight didn't seem to get the joke.

"'Tis a shame you'll only achieve half your vengeance then," said Eadric.

"No. My retribution will be fully realized, unlike yourself."

Eadric finally laughed. His intestines twisted into a knot. The guffaws hurt his chest, but he couldn't hold back from the outlandishness of it all. "Have we both gone mad?"

"She's alive."

"You're insane," said Eadric, unable to continue his laughter.

Sir Álvaro glared at him, his eyes like burning coals. "She's alive, Eadric. Some angel must have protected her, for her veins were not severed when they sliced her throat."

Eadric's laughs turned to heavy breathing, which transformed into a shallow growl. "I'll wring your fucking neck if you speak of her."

Sir Álvaro hammered him with a heavy kick. Eadric yelped and spun onto his stomach. The knight buried his foot into Eadric's spine, pinning him to the hard floor. His blood-splattered face stuck to the ground. The pain was astounding.

"You spent a decade slaughtering peasants and nobles alike for her, yet you never investigated if she survived."

"How dare you! I did! I fucking did. I asked everyone I could, but they—"

"They had burnt the bodies, right? Not even a mass grave was erected so they could be placed in consecrated ground." Sir Álvaro lowered himself, pinching his knee into Eadric's back. "Did that eat you up, believing Lucia to be in Hell because she wasn't guided to the afterlife? A shame it was, all those years you wasted."

"Enough! Release me or have me killed. I tire of your detestable voice."

"Lucia is alive, Eadric."

"She's dead." The words were sour in his mouth, but it was the truth. "She died."

"You want to know the best part?" The black knight had the largest smile Eadric had ever seen. "She's here. In Oxford."

Eadric's heart shuddered in his chest. The swirl of emotions was too terrible to describe. Mental torture. It had to be. "Break my body," begged Eadric. "Do with me whatever you wish. Just leave my daughter out of this. Her soul doesn't deserve to be thrashed so."

"Oh, I intend to break every bone you have. *Eventually*. But that's just the thing, Eadric. This involves your daughter. And like I said, the best part is she's alive and well inside that beautiful fucking castle."

"Álvaro!"

"Belt it!" He dug his knee into the base of Eadric's spine. Eadric shouted, weathering the sensation of a hundred daggers twisting into his back. "Call me Álvaro once more, and I'll burn out your tongue. I speak the truth. Lucia is behind those walls. Hell, she's done well for herself. The empress's own handmaiden, going by the name Beatrice."

"You lie." Tears pooled under Eadric's eyes. He didn't know what to think, what to feel. Anger? Confusion? Exhaustion, pain, overwhelming despair? This was worse than torture. It was cruel beyond measure to have his own dead daughter dangled before him like this.

"You've always been a halfwit, Eadric. A strong, brutish one, but a halfwit nonetheless. I will say it one last time. Lucia is alive." Sir Álvaro waited for him to process the possibility that it could be true, to drink in the tears flowing down Eadric's face. "Imagine," he whispered, "what it must have been like for her? How long do you think she lived as those peasants you so despised? How much rape and violence she endured?"

"She would've found me. Lucia wouldn't abandon me."

"You're an idiot! She became a peasant. Do you know how hard it is for one of them to travel across the kingdom with bandits, storms, and raids ravaging every fucking corner? Have you spent any time outside the war?"

He realized he hadn't. Every moment, every action of his over the past ten years was done for war and vengeance. Everything.

"You are that daft. I don't believe it. Were you not aware that most people think you're dead? Most people believed you took your own life after your beloved daughter died. You're never at your estate. You're rarely at council. A select few people know who the Hellhound of Rutland really is, perhaps only us generals and Duke Richard. For anyone else, for the soldiers and common folk, the hellhound could be anyone, even an apparition."

"She's dead, León. Lucia's dead." Eadric's voice wavered. He couldn't let it be true, because if it was, that meant—it meant—*Jesus Christ, that would mean—*

"Did you know I have a spy inside the castle? It's a man you might know. Duke Richard."

"You fucking whore!"

Sir Álvaro smashed the iron pliers into Eadric's hand, shattering bones, rupturing knuckles and tendons. Eadric cried out. He could feel the bits of bone rattling inside his hand like loose dice and scattered sand.

"Duke Richard is my spy," he said. "You two are destined for one another. He's every bit of a single-minded, paranoid lout as you are. He has no idea he's been next to your daughter for years now, and I have it on good authority from him that the empress will attempt an escape soon, *with* her prized handmaiden. I'll bring Lucia back so you can see for yourself."

"If what you say is true, then I will tear you apart the moment you lay hands on . . ." Eadric's heart skipped a beat. His brain lost function for the briefest of moments as he forced himself to say it. "... if you lay hands on her."

"There's the insufferable bastard I want. I want that fire in you when I snuff it out."

Eadric's mind flooded with thoughts.

Lucia can't be alive. But if she is?

Don't be a dolt; he's torturing you.

Was everything we've done for naught? Did we kill all those people for a hollow vengeance? Was there ever an excuse for our carnage?

Lucia is alive? Jesus, she can't be. Make her dead! Please, God, make her dead.

Eadric couldn't see through all his tears.

God, if she's alive, kill me now. If she's alive, kill me.

No. Wait. Let me see her. What were those dreams if not glimpses of a future?

What the Hell is happening to me?!

"León, please," begged Eadric. "We've had our differences. Don't torture me with this anymore. Is what you tell me the truth? Is my baby girl truly alive?"

Sir Álvaro grabbed a handkerchief from beneath his padded armor. "I was given this as proof." It was small, delicate, and covered in blood. On one corner though, on the lower edge where Eadric's entire sanity lay on the fringe of speculation, was the threaded word: *Anabel*. The name of his first wife; the embroidery of Lucia's mother.

Sobbing like he never had before, Eadric crumbled. Each cry made his body jolt. He spasmed on the ground, overcome with remorse and jubilation and everything those two emotions meant. He wept and accepted in his soul that it *could* be true. He may, miraculously, be only a few thousand feet from his daughter. And he may die here without ever seeing her again.

"You're not the only one who can hold a grudge for ten years," said Sir Álvaro. "When she escapes with Empress Maud, I'm going to collect her. I'll ravage your daughter out there on the cold ground. But don't you fret. I'll drag her mangled body before you and enjoy her again, so that you may savor her form succumbing to mine. And then when I see you reliving all the suffering you've gone through, I'll slit Lucia's throat again. I can't imagine a greater joy than seeing you experience her death twice."

Eadric had never known fury like this. There was no limit to the many ways he imagined shredding Álvaro apart limb from limb. The black knight laughed. His vindictive grin showed razor-sharp teeth, and his eyes were pure with intense satisfaction, like a predator after fulfilling its bloodlust. His breath was hot and wet against Eadric's face.

"I can see you're furious," he said. "I wonder what emotion will appear when I bring Lucia before you. Imagine what she must look like now. A full woman, with a full body." Sir Álvaro licked his lips, moistening his mustache. He picked up the pliers again. "Imagine how plump, how soft... how wet. I wonder what I'll see in your eyes when I'm inside her."

Eadric spat out some more blood. He used the last of his strength to breathe in new air. "You know what I see in your eyes?" he asked the knight.

"What do you see?"

"I see fear," said the Hellhound of Rutland. "Fear, because you've never known an enemy like me." He let the blood seep out of his mouth and cover his teeth in the redness of his own pain. "Do not think my death can save you from me. I'll wreak so much havoc in Hell that Satan himself will come to fear me. I'll slaughter every demon, every angel, until the Great Adversary begs God to release me from damnation. I'll haunt you until your dying breath. And when you too finally arrive in Hell, you'll find it to be *my* domain."

Sir Álvaro's prideful smile dropped for the briefest of moments. But Eadric saw the flash of terror, the dread of horror. Sir Álvaro recovered himself quickly and yanked Eadric's head forward, gripping his earlobe with the pliers.

"Let's continue, shall we?"

Eadric was tossed into the prison yard wagon cell with Will. The lad's eyes widened as if he'd seen a ghost. Covered in his own blood, Eadric was missing multiple fingernails and an earlobe, while his entire body was sickly blue with bruising. The frigid air turned his sweat and blood into crystals on his shredded clothes.

"Eadric," shouted Will, his voice trailing off into the wind.

Eadric forced his swollen eyes open. Sir Álvaro disappear into the surrounding camp.

Lucia . . . if you're out there, Daddy's coming. Daddy's here.

He passed out soon after.

So intense was the winter cold that Eadric could not feel the pains of his tortured body. His broken fingers felt like icicles. The only indication that he had broken ribs was how difficult it was to breathe, but even the blistering winds or frigid nights that made his heart stop could be causing that. If it weren't for the possibility that Lucia was alive, that she *might* be inside those impenetrable castle walls, he would've laid on the ground and welcomed his final breath.

Now more than ever, Eadric was determined to get his vigor up. He had Will lift him onto his feet so that he could get strong enough to support himself. It hurt. It hurt like Hell. But all Eadric saw every moment of every day was Lucia's face and Sir Álvaro standing over her.

In the second week of his captivity, Eleanor finally stormed up to the prison yard. Snow fell down around her, and the softness of the dawning light made her look heavenly. The gaoler stopped his wife from getting too close.

"Milady, I 'ave strict orders to bar you from visiting."

"Come now, Alfwin," said Eleanor. "What trouble can a little 'ole wife cause? He's locked up good, and you're a strong man. Here, I brought you some food. How horrid that my husband causes you suffering, keeping you out in the cold like this. Please, 'tis the season of the Lord's birthday. Let me visit my husband. I wish to please the Lord and to be a good wife. It's only bread and stew. Everyone, lords and prisoners alike, deserves warm food on this most holy of holidays, wouldn't you say?"

Gaoler Alfwin was taken aback, mainly because of the steaming bowl of stew that Eleanor had brought for him. "Very well, milady. But only for a few minutes."

"How sweet you are, Alfwin. Enjoy it, and may God be with you."

She slinked past him as he enjoyed his warm food. Her lighthearted smile faded the instant he couldn't see her face. "I should smash that guard into the fucking earth for freezing you both to death," she said. Eadric laughed at her and reached through the bars for her body. The zap of warmth from her touch was wondrous beyond words. "My poor husband. Look what's happened to the both of you. Have your stew."

Eadric and Will ate it heartedly. Eleanor, even with her giant fur pelt on, warmed her arms by rubbing them. "We need to get you out of here before you turn into a frigid corpse."

"I 'ave a plan," said Will suddenly.

"You do?" asked Eadric and Eleanor together.

"My brother visited me a week ago. He's waiting for there to be a storm, and when there is, he's going to break me out. He can free the two of us."

"Why would you help me?" asked Eadric, a tidal wave of affection for Will overcoming him, further drowning him in his own guilt.

"We're both hostages," said Will simply.

"What can I do?" asked Eleanor. "You may catch a sickness and die during a blizzard."

"My brother will bring animal skins. Blankets. Extra coverings."

"We can still use your help," Eadric said to his wife. "We'll need supplies. I'll need a new sword and some proper boots. I'll also need food before I head out into the snow."

"Why on God's earth would you venture back into the blizzard?" asked Eleanor.

"My daughter's alive." He waited for his sentence to sink in. Her face was unreadable, but she knew as well as Eadric what that meant. "Look at me," he said gently.

"No," Eleanor said, pushing herself away. Eadric reached out and held her arm tight.

"Look at me, *please*." She blinked away a tear, maybe the first she ever shed for him. "She survived, Eleanor. I know it in my heart. Álvaro is going after her. I can't let her down a second time."

"What do you mean León is—"

"He claims I'm the reason his family is dead. That because I didn't wed him to Lucia, and that I cursed his name on the night of my nephew's wedding, he couldn't return to his kingdom and rescue them from the Caliphates."

"That's foolish! You don't have that power over his life. He searches for someone to blame his woes on. He doesn't want to claim responsibility for fleeing from his family as they were attacked."

"He's going after her."

"She's dead. Didn't you see them cut her throat yourself? Does he have proof?"

"He had my wife's handkerchief. Lucia always kept it with her. She would never give it up. Never."

"What if he stole it from her ten years back? What if he grabbed it from her corpse?"

"Eleanor!" Eadric nearly toppled over. His wife softened as she saw his tears fall. "If there's a chance... if there's the thinnest chance she's still alive, I need must risk it. I have to know. If I had spent all this time, all these years, killing so many instead of hunting her down. If I've abandoned her..."

"Oh, Eadric."

"Please, Eleanor. Please help me. I'll give you everything. The estate. The land. Just help me save my daughter. Help me redeem myself as a father."

"You're a real whoreson," she said. "You're a real whoreson for making me like you so much. I would've helped you rescue her for nothing."

"I know," he said. If he had any tears left, anything after weeping for Lucia and the dozens he killed for a hollow vendetta, he would have surely done so now.

"Tell me what to do. Tell me the plan."

CHAPTER XLV
EMMA & MADAME BEATRICE

Emma was dying the same slow, painful death that generations of humans have died before her: starvation.

Every day inside St. George's Church, after morning prayers, Emma, Crispin, and the other poor souls that still lived half-lives trudged up the motte—which was cratered inwards at a dozen spots, like the inner alveoli of freshly cut bread, and smoldering from months of trebuchet bombardment—and went into the kitchen to get their daily allotment of a quarter of a cabbage, a slice of bread with some butter, and half a turnip. While enjoying these starved meals, Emma thought back to happier times. She thought of spring days when the sun dazzled aglow with warm yellow light, and the earth reflected that same enjoyable heat; when bees buzzed around blooming foxgloves, primroses, and daffodils; when the soil was softened by temperate air and came alive, full of worms and insects; when robins and goldfinches and tits flew above the world, singing lovely songs that heralded warmer days, longer days, lovelier days. She missed the breeze, and how it would carry with it the smell of fresh-baked bread, or the sweet fragrance of perfumes sold by traveling merchants, or the earthy scents of ripening crops.

Homesickness struck Emma so overwhelmingly that tears welled up at the corners of her eyes. Her heart dimmed to an imperceptible stillness in her chest while the grief piled up on top of her—grief for her mother, for Alice, for Roger, for Tom, for Isabella, for Ansfride, for all of Marlborough.

Most of all, as selfish and shameful as it was, Emma grieved for the girl she was a year ago. Her laughter, her dreams, her insatiable appetite for life... all of it was tarnished and burned to cinders. Another casualty of the war.

Now the sun sat distantly in the sky, a silver halo that never brought warmth, and the earth remained firm and bereft of life. Emma was acutely aware of how closely her mind and heart matched the woes of winter. The smell in the air was of burned things: burned buildings, burned possessions, burned bodies. Occasionally as part of their siege tactics, Stephen's army would have massive cookouts upwind and let the delicious smell of roasted game, fish, and pork drift over the ramparts and drive them all to madness.

Emma was thin; her ribs showed through her skin. She found it difficult to muster even the faintest energy. The nights went on forever and ever, and she and Crispin were forced to huddle together under blankets that did little to keep out the nippy air.

Every moment was another moment closer to death, or another second closer to King Stephen breaking through the gates and his knights and militiamen having their way with them. Emma knew what that meant for girls like her, but she lacked the capacity to worry about it much.

She and Madame Beatrice had snuck out of the castle through the postern two more times, but the second time the knight, Sir Winston, was caught before they reached him. His body was hung from a nearby tree, his armor stripped, his penis cut off, and his orifices oozing a black liquid.

It came as a surprise to Emma to learn they were only a few weeks away from Christmas. Her days had been a blur of praying, eating, praying, suffering, praying, and sleeping. She rarely focused during church, and the Latin spoken by the priest jittered around her like discordant notes. One day, Empress Maud decided to hold a miniature festival. After morning prayers, the procession of starved Christians moved to the kitchen, where a smiling and relieved Mildritha served them stew of such magnificent variety that the multitude of them took immense joy in burning the roof of their mouths with the hot broth. Because of this celebration, wine, beer, and ale were served in copious amounts, and the chambers within the keep and servant quarters became filled with laughter. Their spirits rose briefly as the food and drinks sat comfortably in their bellies. But as quickly as the pain faded on the roof of their mouths, so too did the direness of their situation fade back to the forefront of their minds. The rest of the quasi-festival passed uneventfully. Soldiers continued to walk the walls, unwilling to loose anymore arrows, as they had long since run out of spare timber and stones. The nights came even sooner, and frothing storm clouds continually approached from the west, as if a wicked darkness was spreading across the kingdom to claim them.

Emma took a meandering stroll along the bottom of the battlements, while the last bit of sunlight disappeared beyond the horrendous storm. She saw the spot where Jory's head had rolled to. She saw the area they had buried their dead. She saw the section of the keep she had climbed to steal Robert's note. She saw men and women huddled, discussing when to raid the kitchen. She saw soldiers covering their tears. She saw the priest praying over workers who clutched crosses and rubbed rosaries. She saw the reality of God's world.

Here, atop a small mound in England, where the world and war stood still, was where the fates of many would come to a resounding frozen finale.

"This is foolish, my empress! Madness!" claimed Aubrey de Vere, earl of a shire currently under control by a usurper king. Beatrice looked at him with a distant gaze. This was a man who was deemed an earl by a dead king; this was a man ordained as steward of a castle that was on the brink of collapse. What power did he think he held against a woman like Maud?

"It'll never work," said Robert d'Oilli. "As your marshal deigned, I forbid it."

"I cannot stand it any longer!" Empress Maud stepped away from her retinue and placed her hand upon the narrow window overlooking

Beaumont Palace and her father's kingdom beyond. "I have brought enough suffering to this city."

"Then surrender," urged Duke Richard.

Beatrice hated him most of all. Within a few days of stealing the wagon of provisions, Stephen had redoubled his efforts of attacking the castle. *And* he sent scouts to Wallingford. It was obvious now that the duke had betrayed them. He was just like the other cowardly barons, flipping sides any time they pleased. First Stephen, then Empress Maud, and now Stephen again, always trying to finagle themselves to the winning side. They didn't care about glory. They didn't fight for what they believed.

They didn't truly love the empress like Beatrice did.

"If I were to surrender and let my brother save me again," said Empress Maud, "the realm would never accept me. It would only be further proof that a man is needed to rule. It would prove that I need my husband here, and I would rather be killed than see Geoffrey take my father's kingdom. My *son's* kingdom."

"But to sneak out the postern would be immediate defeat," said Sheriff d'Olli. "Stephen is watching the castle more closely now than ever. Even if you somehow snuck past his lines, then you'd have to trek all the way to Wallingford. Past patrols and beasts and untamed wilds. You'd freeze before you got within ten leagues."

"Then protect me!" Empress Maud spun toward them. The last bit of daylight shone through the window and sparked the dust around her. She looked truly regal, as if haloed by God Himself. "Look at the approaching storm. The time is nigh! Come with me, dressed as me. His scouts and patrols could not spot more whiteness in a blizzard."

Her plan was not as foolish as they made it seem. Beatrice believed it to be quite ingenious, if not wholly romantic. A little less than two dozen of Maud's most trusted companions, men and women alike, were to be covered from head-to-toe in white cloaks and sneak out the postern when the first blizzard hit. If timed right, River Mill Stream *should* be frozen over, and Stephen's army *should* be hunkered down for the storm.

The logic was mostly sound. Who'd expect someone to flee during the most dangerous conditions that God could throw at them?

"Be with me," pleaded the empress. "The castle must be forsaken. I cannot watch anyone else starve, and I refuse to bury another crushed child. This is the only way to save them all."

And at that moment, the empress cried. Beatrice was shocked; she'd never seen the empress express such emotion before, and most certainly not in front of men. The tears fell down her cheek, and the empress flung them away with a disgusted expression, like she was appalled at doing something as human as crying.

"I want to see my brother again," she said. "I want to end this suffering once and for all. I'm exhausted seeing the kingdom my father, and my father's father, built be destroyed because of this obscene betrayal. The kingdom is mine by right, and I will not stay put as it falls."

One by one, all those in her retinue nodded their heads, some of them brought to tears themselves. They all agreed they'd flee with the empress into the first blizzard of the season. Empress Maud excused them all for the night, and Madame Beatrice, overwhelmed with the turmoil of it all, took a walk along the bottom of the battlements.

As she strolled along, she saw not the inner bailey, but the flamboyant courtyard of Duke Rowan's castle. Beatrice saw the corpses of Lady Yvette and Aunt Adeline lying dead inside a dark tower. She saw Uncle Rowan being stabbed with a dozen knives. She saw the grave of Anabel, her mother, forever enshrined behind their home in Rockingham. And lastly, despite avoiding it during her many cruel and traumatic years, she dared to see her father, Baron Eadric, the only man who ever loved her.

In imagining his face, all the emotions of the life she had lost came back to her. She saw his compassionate eyes while he looked at her. She saw his infectious grin when he told a joke about her. She saw his horrified despair as Anna slit her throat.

The weight of the world seemed to double above her. Her legs shook, and her breath trembled. But this time, as her thoughts and feelings and the greater world toppled over, she stayed firm, standing against it all. For the first time, Beatrice braved the harrowing tide of her past.

"Madame Beatrice?"

She turned to find Emma behind her. The last light of eventide disappeared as the storm clouds approached overhead, swallowing the firmament star-by-star. The color in Emma's face turned a muddled gray. They both stood in a forlorn section of the inner bailey, away from the keep and the constant fighting by the gatehouse. Near them was only a ruined section of wall where one of the king's war engines had hit its mark. A pebble tumbled down through the crack in the rampart. Their breath plumed in front of them, commingling and dispersing under the remaining starlight.

"What are you doing here?" asked Madame B.

"I was goin' for a walk. You?"

"Quite the same. Did you enjoy the feast?"

"It was nice. May I ask ye a question? Why don't you go by Lucia anymore?"

"It was the name my father gave me," she said in a trance, feeling the cracks deepen, the fissure elongate. *A siege within a siege. A battlement for the mind and ramparts for the soul.* "My mother died in childbirth. Usually, a father would disown a baby girl who did something so cruel. Mine loved me deeper instead."

"What happened to him?"

"Only God knows. After I was taken, I was adrift without knowledge of most things. I knew nothing of the world around me. My goal was survival. Survive until the next winter, the next spring. I never heard his name, saw no one with a resemblance . . . and he never found me. Perhaps he thought me good and dead. I'm not sure. Maybe he died in battle. But survival was all I knew, on and on. Until eventually, *she* found me. Empress Maud remade me, and in doing so, I accepted the name she met me by. I worked my way from her cupbearer to her handmaiden. I love her, so I can be Beatrice for her."

"I never knew my father," said Emma. "I was told he was despicable, the worst type of man." The girl went quiet. One by one, the stars reflecting in her eyes disappeared. "I think that's why I'm a bad person. His blood flows in mine."

"We are not our parents."

A siege within a—

"You once said you didn't hate me, but you hated how I made you feel. How am I not a terrible person then?"

Beatrice's gut felt as if it were made of iron. It sat uncomfortably inside her, a pain pushing outward. "No. I hated the way you make me feel, because..."

"Because why?"

"...because you reminded me of myself."

The fissure split the rampart in half, and her soul escaped. It was enough to collapse the battlement whole. It crumpled apart, stone and mortar cracking in two, into a pile of suffocating dust. The weight lifted off her gut.

Beatrice breathed in fresh air and exhaled debris and realized that her keep had turned to ruin long ago; all that remained of her tattered fortifications was the refuse of a life she'd chosen to abandon out of fear it could still hurt her.

But it couldn't.

She no longer feared it. All that remained inside of her was gratitude and longing for the girl she'd lost ten years ago.

"You reminded me of myself when I was young," Lucia explained. "You were happy, enjoyed all things, loved music and dancing. It scared me. I feared those feelings would betray me again."

"I feel those feelings no longer," she said. Her eyes were downcast, dark and starless.

"I know," said Lucia, "and I hate it. I know if my father saw me now, he'd think me a stranger. How could his little girl know so much pain? How could she have survived so much?"

Emma reached out and grabbed her hands.

It was the only thing that felt right to Emma. She grabbed Lucia's hands. She held to them as if they'd both tumble off into the abyss of stars if she let go. The madame's hands were warm and inviting, and she felt the woman trembling through them.

The truth came out suddenly, and releasing it tasted as sweet as honey. "I want to die," Emma said.

"I did too. Every day, for so long. This is no world for women."

"Is this what I must look forward to for the rest of my life?"

The older woman paused. Emma couldn't read her expression in the darkness of the storm-infested night. "It doesn't have to be," she said finally.

Emma wondered at this. How could that be the case? How could she choose not to have pain and suffering? How was this not the life allotted to peasants or women, to a thief and murderer and everything else Emma was?

Lucia looked at her, tears falling from her eyes, and said, "Maybe the bravest thing we can do is to never lose who we were before the pain."

"It'll be hard," Emma whispered.

"Yes, but think of how beautiful we'll be when we embrace them again."

The madame pulled Emma into a hug, and the warmth between them burst into a bonfire that could light all of England. From the rolling clouds far above, a single snowflake twisted and twirled and spun all the way to the ground.

"Mother Mary, give us strength," said Emma.

A flurry of snowflakes fell around them. The ground turned white.

"Mother Mary, give us strength," Lucia repeated.

It would not stop snowing for the rest of the night.

The blizzard raged beyond postern's dilapidated door. The cracks in the wood were frozen over with ice. Lucia stood next to Empress Maud. Behind them waited Duke Richard, Sheriff d'Oilli, handmaid Theresa, and seven armed guards—the best fighters in the empress's garrison. Twelve of them in total braced themselves below St. George's Tower. They all wore matching white garments, including white cowls and white scarves to wrap around their faces.

The plan from here was simple; they were to split into two groups. Lucia, who looked almost exactly like Empress Maud, was to lead one group off to the north while Empress Maud remained protected by her best fighters; she'd take them straight across the frozen river to the west.

It was unlikely that anyone in the horrendous conditions outside would spot them. But in case they were, they would have to decide which group to go after. The hope was that if they'd choose, they'd go after Lucia's.

Empress Maud pulled her into a hug. Beneath the thick fabric of her scarf, the empress said to her, "May God be with you, Beatrice. May He give you strength and protection. May He bless me with the same grace and courage He's bestowed upon you."

"Thank you, my lady," Lucia responded reverently. Empress Maud cupped her face between her hands. She looked her in the eye.

"With God's guidance, I'll lead my group to Abingdon-on-Thames, where I can then ride for Wallingford. The road will be hard and treacherous, but I believe in my heart I will find you again. There'll always be a place for you at my side."

Lucia wiped away her tears before they could freeze on her cheek. "Thank you, my lady. I will."

Empress Maud, forever the one to make the first move, opened the postern door. Snow blasted in, blowing through the doorway and launching a breeze so ferociously cold that the exposed skin around Lucia's eyes felt like it would burn off.

Empress Maud gasped, overtaken by the subzero conditions. Then, undaunted, she pushed onward like she always did.

Lucia followed her. Then, Sheriff d'Oilli. Then, Theresa. Then, the rest of the guards. Then, taking up the rear, was Duke Richard, who'd requested to be taken with them. He was clearly terrified of being found by someone in Stephen's army. Who he feared so deeply remained a mystery, but Empress Maud decided that it was better to keep a spy within eyesight rather than leave them behind to release all kinds of information.

The two groups pushed through the thin protection of the brambles that covered the postern cave and entered God's glacial wrath. The brilliant whiteness of the storm made her believe she'd gone blind.

As Lucia and her group of five guards stumbled away from Empress Maud's and stepped onto the frozen River Mill Stream, her mind turned to the small girl in the keep who broke down her walls.

Emma, may God protect you. Do not fear, child, for you will become a lady much greater than I.

CHAPTER XLVI
GILBERT

T HE BLIZZARD ARRIVED BRISKLY in the early parts of the morning; the initial gale shook the dilapidated mill to its dubious foundations. Then the wind tripled in strength. The storm-side of the mill leaned inward, and lengths of wood were shredded from their larger partitions. The air screamed around them, loud and horrifying, as if it were the screams of Christ and all His angels.

Alice, Roger, and Edith all huddled in the corner. They held each other close, shuddering from the iciness of their own breath. While they were pressed into the warmest pocket of the mill they could find, Gilbert and Hawk layered on every bit of clothing that survived the adventure from Rouen. It wasn't much. Before they left, they gave their travel companions the last few bundles of faggots, as well as the remaining grouse they'd hunted.

"God bless ye," said Edith, Alice, and Roger together.

"You're welcome," said Hawk.

Edith grabbed his hand. "If ye find a girl with pale skin, raven-black hair, and eyes green as springtime grass, let her know her mum is here for her. And let her know she isn't angry with her." For the first time since they'd met her, tears glossed the older woman's eyes. She wiped them away, for they caused immense pain as they turned to crystals beneath her eyelids.

"I will," said Hawk. He turned to Gilbert. "Won't we?"

"Yes," said Gilbert. "We will."

Hawk stopped Gilbert before they exited through the door. He lifted a bundle of fabric. Bemused, Gilbert watched his best friend. He'd never seen Hawk wear such an uncoordinated outfit before, and it seemed they were about to add one additional layer.

"For extra warmth . . . and extra luck."

He handed Gilbert the white Carmelite habits they stole from the monastery. Gilbert threw it on top of everything else, just as Hawk did with his own stolen habit. With much strength and vigor, they forced open the door. The blizzard punched him in the face, flakes of snow catching in his patchy beard. Gilbert staggered back. The thunderous wind combated them for every inch. The cold was all-consuming. His teeth chattered within his head, shaking his entire skull. He lost his breath and had to brace against Hawk.

But then he thought of William. He thought of his brother braving this tempest out in the open. How long could he be out there in this storm and survive? An hour? Less?

The red moon shone brightly in the darkness around his soul. The Devil searched for him.

Those dangerous thoughts disappeared when Hawk grabbed his arm. Gilbert glanced at his best friend. "We'll save him," Hawk said. "You are brave."

"Thank ye, Hawk."

The two friends picked up the axe and hammer they had stolen from a nearby blacksmith and pushed out into the dark storm.

"I think we're here!" screamed Gilbert, shielding his face with his right arm while he kept his left firmly against the Oxford city walls. His toes and fingers were numb. It frightened him that he hardly felt any pain from his extremities—only unceasing nothingness.

"I'm behind you!" Hawk shouted.

The Lord had graced them with luck thus far, as they'd yet to run into any patrols. That didn't lessen the ominous foreboding that lingered in the pit of Gilbert's stomach like a nauseating sickness. They knew it was unlikely that they'd run into anyone around the city walls, especially given the limited visibility; however, to reach William they would have to navigate directly through King Stephen's encampment. Gilbert had gotten lost in the maze of tents even in the clearness of day. Finding where the prisoners were kept before they froze to death would be the greatest challenge they'd face.

"Jesus Christ," muttered Gilbert through his chattering teeth. It hurt to speak. Each inhale felt like he was sucking in burning spikes.

"Which way?" asked Hawk.

Gilbert simply pointed, unwilling to feel the pain that speaking brought. If he was right, they were near the Oxford eastern gate. Sometime between leaving the mill and navigating around the outer walls of Oxford, the sun rose beyond the endless tempest. The blizzard began assaulting not only their ears and skin but also their eyes. It was blindingly white in all directions, piercing his irises in such a way that made him believe he'd never see darkness again. Any time he closed his eyes, all he saw was white. If they were even a step too far away from the wall, they'd lose sight of it entirely.

Taking a deep breath, and swallowing his fear, Gilbert let go of the wall. It felt like untethering himself into a bleached void. As he stepped away from the security of the battlements, he was loosed from the world of man and became enshrouded in the elemental providence of God. And Hawk, loyal as ever, followed him.

Snow piled on the ground, sinking their feet into icy water. Each step exhausted Gilbert. He'd stop every few paces and wait for Hawk to catch up. His friend, much like Gilbert, would wrap his arms tighter around his body, his breath pluming out often and heavy, and nod that he was still alive.

They reached the first tent in the war camp. It bulged outward from the center on all sides; the soldiers from the king's army had packed themselves into their tents until they were close to bursting. Gilbert glanced back at Hawk. He was only a meter behind him, but he would periodically disappear behind a thick sleet of snow, hail, and other blown debris. He nodded beneath his cowl. This was a good sign. Perhaps the entire army was hunkered down, and no one would be out in the storm to catch them. They pushed on, passing many more stuffed tents.

Time unknown passed, and the blizzard refused to abate. Slowly, Gilbert and Hawk froze to death. The pain would cycle. At first it was a freezing agony, then it would transmute to a burning affliction. Eventually, Gilbert couldn't feel his nose, fingers, toes, or ears. Outside the occasional tent or half-buried firepit, Gilbert saw no signs of life.

Everything was white. Everything was loud. Everything was cold.

"We need to scream for him!" Hawk said from somewhere nearby. "We'll die if we take much longer!"

Gilbert gathered all the power he could muster. His knees wobbled. His stomach contorted in his gut. It would hurt to speak almost as much as it pained him to walk.

"William!" he yelled.

"Will!" Hawk followed.

They shouted and lost more feeling and yelled and searched and fell even closer to a frosty death. "WILLIAM! Will! Where are ye?! WILL!"

Gilbert felt himself failing when an echo in the wind finally responded, "... Gilbert? ..."

"WILLIAM?!"

"... Gilbert! ..."

He could barely keep his eyes open as the unrelenting tempest threw hail the size of fists at them. His whole body had frozen over. Only the tired, pulsing rhythm of his heart gave him any sense that he was still alive, that blood still flowed through him. But his heart was struggling, each beat taking a physical toll. He could feel it in his chest, thumping against his rib cage. Desperate. Terrified.

"WILLIAM!"

"... GILBERT! ..."

Finally, when he was only a few feet away, Gilbert saw the caged prisoners. There was a sorry-looking man in the wagon cell with his brother. The man was bloodied and straining just to stand upright next to William.

"Stand back!" yelled Gilbert. He brought out the hammer he carried under his habit. With a few mighty swings, he cleaved the frozen lock in two.

His brother was free.

Like a sack of vegetables leaned precariously against a closed door and, once opened, came stumbling out onto the opener, so too did William stumble out of the cell onto Gilbert. It was the first time he'd hugged his brother since that dreadful morning along the Côte d'Opale;

and even though his skin was stiff and miserably cold, Gilbert held him dearly. William, overcome with fatigue and suppressed dread, cried into the nape of his older brother's neck. Gilbert held him until the frigid skin between them warmed like hard soil turning into clay. He held him until their combined heat overcame the deadliest of the blizzard's wrath. He held him.

The other prisoner stepped out of the cell gingerly. When he came closer to the two of them, Gilbert saw that the man was deformed. He had a broken nose. Blood trickled slowly from his nose, mouth, and ears. His right hand dangled from his wrist. Many of his fingers were misshapen, broken and twisted against the knuckle. He didn't have any fingernails; the skin there appeared slimy-red. His left eye was half swollen, and his skin was bruised from the top of his head down to the tops of his feet. Gilbert felt nauseous simply looking at him.

"Thank you, Will," said the abused man hoarsely. "I must be off."

William separated from his hug with Gilbert and held out his arm to the older man. "Good luck."

The tortured man took a long look at William's arm. He slowly raised his own and gripped William's. They held there for a few seconds, each grabbing the other's forearm.

"I pray ye find her," William said.

The man's voice cracked. "I'll honor my oath," he said, before turning away and disappearing into the storm forever.

"Who was that?" asked Gilbert.

His brother ticked. Without answering, he asked, "Where's Hawk?"

Gilbert glanced around him stupidly. Caught up in the moment of finding William, he hadn't realized that he'd lost his friend. Panic rose in his chest. Gilbert stuffed it down as best he could. He had to be the older brother. He had to be brave. "I don't know, but we can't do much about it. He knows to head back to the mill."

"Don't let go of me."

"Never," Gilbert promised.

Will was doomed the moment you loved him...

Gilbert closed his ears to his mother's terrible voice. The wind picked up and carried with it were the cruel voices of his past.

No, Gilbert thought, *I am over this. I am better than this.*

He heard his sister crying. He heard his mother wailing.

William's hand tightened around his. "What's wrong?"

"Nothin'," said Gilbert, pulling his brother along, ignoring how the snow became a faint crimson color. They navigated back the way he had come. It was pure drudgery. They trudged through the rapidly stacking snow, now reaching halfway up their calves. Gilbert had never been so cold, not even back on that terrible night many, many winters ago. He focused on the only point of warmth he had left: William's hand held in his.

"What's that?!" asked William over the roar of wind.

"The fuck..."

It was one of the stuffed tents, and it was *shredded* open.

Ten soldiers lay slain. Like a perverted, blossoming rose, their bodies bloomed out from the center of the tent, the snow beneath them a bright-red color. They were mangled. Throats slit. Hearts punctured. Heads caved. Arteries spouting. Intestines steaming.

"What could have done this?!" His brother's voice was hardly a whisper.

Gilbert remembered the stories of his childhood, of the devilish fiends living in the forest that took their sister. Had they come back for him after all these years?

Gilbert saw a red moon in the expanding blood.

Hawk screamed. The two brothers spun, facing the gale that carried the wails of their friend. William's hand tightened on Gilbert's.

"He's this way!" yelled William, pulling Gilbert toward the noise.

Fear latched onto him so profusely, so tightly, that Gilbert dug his heels into the snow, fighting back against his brother's pull. William's hand slipped from his.

"William!"

But it was too late; his brother had already sprinted into the thickness of the storm. Gilbert was alone.

The world crushed in on him. The terrible storm swirled around him. He was at the epicenter of endless disasters, endless disease, endless pain. And Gilbert, he was the cause of it all. Gilbert the Craven. Gilbert the Devil. Gilbert, the spawn of a crimson moon.

"You're a coward," he admitted into the blizzard. He was about to fall onto his knees and give in when—above the storm and above the wind and above the pain—Gilbert heard Hawk's voice:

You're not for him.

Forcing himself to move one step after another, one brave act begetting the next, he followed his brother's footsteps before the falling snow could sweep them away. He went toward the sound of screams, passing the voices of his past, stepping over dead soldiers that bled half-buried in the snow, killed by whatever beasts butchered the men in those tents.

He followed until he found them.

Hawk and William stood next to each other. They weren't alone.

A circle of destroyed tents surrounded them. Some tents were on fire, their flames desperately fighting against the oppression of the storm. Others were tattered, and they made a horrendous noise as they flapped wildly in the wind. Amongst all these destroyed tents, and amongst the multitude of slain men, towered three rugged and intimidating men-at-arms.

Bandits.

Gilbert had forgotten about them over the course of the last few cold weeks. The ruffians had stuffed sacks next to them carrying their spoils from raiding the king's camp. It was an audacious and downright temerarious attack, but under the protection of a storm, when all the king's men hid inside thin linen tents, or stashed themselves away inside the city walls—when even the king himself would be safely sequestered inside Beaumont Palace—they saw an opportunity to gain immense wealth and stave off starvation for the winter.

But now they had three young witnesses in their way.

The bandits charged. Two of them held swords, which glinted silver under the tumultuous weather, while the other held an axe of considerable heft. All three were armored with quilted gambesons and *maille* coifs; the one with an axe had a steel helm protecting his head. These were fighters, army deserters like Gilbert and William—only not the cowardly type.

Hawk pushed William to the side as the axe thudded into the spot where Will had just stood. Snow exploded into the air. The other bandits shouted, swinging their swords at them. Hawk sidestepped one attack, but the other brigand clipped him with a pierce, slicing through the top of his right shoulder. He grimaced, leaped to the side, and took out his hand axe. Gilbert did the same with his hammer.

William, who remained weaponless, circled around the exterior of the battle. This drew the attention of the axe-wielder, who wanted an easy way to favorably hew their numbers. Gilbert's heart launched into his throat when the brigand moved toward his little brother. All at once, the battle became two separate frays: Hawk against the two swordsmen, and William against the axe bandit. Glancing with concern at Hawk, who was trying to distance himself from the swordsmen, Gilbert moved to save William first. He had to trust his friend to fend for himself. Hawk had been in many fights in the past, and he was a much better fighter than Gilbert.

The axe bandit didn't seem to notice that Gilbert had joined the fight, so he used that to his advantage. His muscles ached. His fingers were stiff. His mouth was dry. But Gilbert, despite it all, crying out to protect his brother, lifted his hammer and swung it down on the ruffian with every bit of strength and vigor he had left.

He missed.

Aiming for the throat, the head of the hammer slammed into the brigand's iron helm instead. The metal indented. The bandit stumbled from the blow, blood pouring from under his *maille* coif; the bright red covered his ear, covered his shoulder, covered his leg. William didn't hesitate. While the man tried to keep himself from collapsing to one knee, his brother ran forward and grabbed at the arm that held the axe. The bandit screamed, drawing the attention of a swordsman.

Gilbert ran up to the axe bandit while he was prying William off his arm. The ruffian upturned his face, staring up at Gilbert as he pulled back the hammer. Through the gale of snow, Gilbert saw him clearly: hazel eyes, scruffy beard, pale skin, dark freckles.

Fuckin' die! Gilbert swung the tool with such force that the hammer buried itself into those hazel eyes up to the handle. His pale skin and dark freckles vanished behind splintered bone and splattered blood.

"Gilbert!" shouted Hawk.

He and William turned just in time to see the swordsman charging at them. Gilbert tried to pry out the hammer, but it was stuck in the axe bandit's brain. Gilbert dropped the handle. William yelled something. He couldn't hear it over the wind in his ears. The swordsman raised his weapon. Gilbert roared.

And he charged at him.

The ruffian, surprised by the sudden attack, missed his deadly strike. The blade cut the edge of Gilbert's arm, slicing it down to the elbow. Gilbert was amazed to find that he didn't feel the pain, but his body still reacted accordingly. They collided with one another, both losing their footing on the slick surface and collapsing in different directions. Gilbert's world disappeared into complete whiteness as his body burrowed itself into a mound of snow.

He pushed himself up to his knees, wheezing, snow piling onto his back and onto the embankment around him. Wind and piercing hail slammed into his face. He cried out—reached forward—shoved off snow, shoved off despair. He saw them in bursts through the blaring tempest.

William. Hawk. Fighting and screaming against the two remaining brigands.

Gilbert's tears froze over his eyes. One ruffian swung his sword. William fell to the ground. Hawk tried to jump in front of him, but the other bandit tackled him, pinning him down, the snow exploding around them and adding to the storm.

Gilbert tried to stand. But his legs buckled, and he collapsed back into the snow. All his strength and vigor were depleted. The storm, the cold, the panic, the past that clung to him . . . it all took from him. He touched his gash that ran warm and wet with the heat of blood.

"I can't do it," Gilbert cried under his breath. "I can't . . ."

"GILBERT!" His brother's plea carried over the storm.

"William . . . I can't . . ."

His bones ached. The snow built around his legs, up to his mid-thigh. It weighed him down from above. Soon enough, he'll be buried under the burden of a million snowflakes, a million independent calamities formed from extreme pressure.

The swordsman stepped closer to his brother. Hawk fought back against the weight of the brigand on top of him; he lifted his head up from the snow. His eyes pierced through the sleet and sought Gilbert out. His best friend reached for him.

"Gilbert!" he screamed, his face a bloody mess, his eyes a haunting desperation. "Gilbert, you are not a coward! Hark my words! You are not cursed!"

Shoving his hands into the snow, compressing it to ice beneath his fingers, Gilbert pushed up. He pushed—pushed—and collapsed. He yelped, but his voice vanished in the tumult. He had nothing left to give.

It piled and piled and piled on top of him, the weight of it all. A million snowflakes, a million particles catching alight in the storm; a million judgements, a million eyes chastising him since birth. The roar of the wind blew out his ears, and all he heard was the sound of a thousand voices taunting him, berating him—pushing him into nothingness, into villainy, into devilry.

"YOU CAN SAVE HIM!"

"GILBERT!"

The snow buried him up to his waist. Gilbert's arms disappeared beneath the stacking white, submerged beneath a million ice crystals—a million truths.

He was worthless. He was evil. He was craven.

He was why they'll die.

His body ached. The truth built around him and weighed him down from all directions. He'll be enshrouded beneath the burden of a million lies, a million independent remarks formed under extreme oppression.

The bandit who pinned Hawk to the ground pulled out a dagger.

The swordsman reached William and lifted his weapon.

"No!" Gilbert forced himself onto one knee. The snow toppled off his back and shoulders like an avalanche of shedding misery. "NO!" he screamed again.

Gilbert braced his face against the sleet, against the storm, against the lies that became truths and the truths that became lies; he braced against the life that was given to him and the one that was stolen from him.

Ye took two babes from me in life, devil! And two more yet in the womb!

All your life you've used your birth as an excuse for your own cravenness.

The bandit put the blade against the back of Hawk's neck.

You're a coward, Gilbert. Look at what you've done to them. Watch them. Behold! O, how they die!!! O, how you've killed them!!!

The swordsman stood over his brother.

I will venture with him into the abyss, for that is what family does.

Gilbert hesitated.

Run, you coward! Flee into the storm! They are doomed; you are not. Flee! Run! Live!

"For what?" Gilbert asked himself. "I would live for what?"

And at the utterance of that question, the blizzard quieted around him. The suffering became trivial. The weight, tranquil.

All the million blinking eyes of his life stared at him, and Gilbert stared back.

"You're not a curse!" Hawk yelled from beneath the bandit. Gilbert met the gaze of his childhood friend. Tears formed in Hawk's eyes. "You are loved!"

Gilbert braced himself on one knee. The snow showered down on him. It wanted him to give up. It wanted him to topple over. It wanted him to die.

"You are wanted!" cried Hawk. "You are needed!"

His love is a poison that'll bury ye into the deepest pits of oblivion.

"Believe, Gilbert!"

"I believe," Gilbert whispered back.

I know your type. The moment they have you, you'll betray me and your brother and every other sin you've committed.

A million snowflakes. A million rebukes. A million regrets.

All the woes we've carried all these years come from you.

"Believe it!" Hawk shouted again. "You are *not* a curse!"

"I am not a curse..."

"You are *not* a scourge!"

"I am not a scourge..."

Gilbert stood despite the weight, despite the stares, despite the hate.

Will was doomed the moment you loved him.

The swordsman stabbed down. William rolled to the side—nearly missed being impaled.

"Be brave! Be the man I know you are!" Hawk laughed as he saw him standing against the false truths. And in the quietness that he had created in the chaos, Gilbert heard his friend's beautiful, unique cackle.

"I am *not* cursed," said Gilbert.

He saw his mother's face. He saw the emptiness of his sister's cradle. He saw the crimson moon reflecting off the snowfield around them.

"Be strong!"

"I am *not* hated."

Seek forgiveness for your transgressions, son; seek absolution in the Lord.

Hawk and Gilbert met each other's eyes one last time.

Take your soul and purify it.

"SAVE YOURSELF . . ."

"I AM *NOT* A COWARD . . ."

Purify it in the pits of Hell.

". . . BY SAVING US!"

". . . BECAUSE I AM LOVED!"

Gilbert saved them.

He ran, legs churning powdered snow, arms powering fathomless bravery. The swordsman turned too late. Gilbert tackled him over his kid brother. The two rolled, toppling over each other once—twice—slamming to a sudden halt against a boulder hidden under the surface. The brigand's neck snapped as his head careened into the rock.

The last remaining bandit screamed at the sight of his two dead comrades. His eyes burned with fury. He stabbed his knife into Hawk's back, serrating his spinal cord.

Gilbert roared. He took up the fallen sword and cleaved through the bandit's face, gushing his blood over the rich, powdery snow. Gilbert pushed him off his best friend and upturned Hawk so they could look upon his face. William kneeled next to Gilbert. He cupped Hawk's head in his hands. Hawk glared at Gilbert in horror.

"This is not your fault," Hawk said adamantly through his gurgling blood. He looked into Gilbert's eyes, pleading. "This is not your fault."

"I know," he said. And for the first time in his life, Gilbert believed that.

"Please . . . please . . ."

"Shh, Hawk, be well. 'Tis not my fault. I'm not cursed. I know that."
"You're *not* cursed."
"I know, be still. I know."

The horror left Hawk's face when he realized what Gilbert said was true. Emotion welled up in his throat. Hawk smiled. His beautiful laugh bestowed bittersweet joy to their ears. Gilbert steadied his friend's shaking hands.

"We saved him," said Hawk ecstatically.

"We did, Hawk. We did." Gilbert glanced at his brother lovingly.

"No . . ." It was now Hawk's touch that steadied Gilbert's hand. "No, my friend. We saved *you*."

Now the tears fell. Now his laugh became ingrained in Gilbert's memory. His brother wept, and the three of them held each other more strongly, more warmly, than ever before.

Gilbert understood. It was gut-wrenching.

It wasn't the fear of death that horrified his friend during his last moments, but the fear that his death would cause Gilbert to slip back into what he always believed: that he was cursed, that he was the spawn of all suffering. But upon hearing his words and seeing the truth in his eyes, Hawk could be comforted in knowing that Gilbert, at long last, was free of that delusion.

"I love you," said Hawk.

"I love you too," Gilbert said back.

In the corner of his eye, Gilbert saw the bright-red cap that his friend loved so dearly. He picked it up, flung off the snow, and placed it atop Hawk's head. All was right with the world. Hawk's eyes glimmered; salvation had re-entered their lives.

"I feel so warm," he said. "Don't you?"

The two brothers held Hawk until he died in their arms.

CHAPTER XLVII
EADRIC

Eadric felt worse than he looked, and he looked conjured from a frozen death. The blizzard hurt his eyes. Twigs and pebbles pelted his body, both unseen and unavoidable in the storm. He couldn't hear or taste or smell anything. The only blessing was that he couldn't feel his multiple wounds. He knew his ribs were still broken, that a few of his fingers were snapped, and that there must be some deep muscle bruising based on how stiff he was. But all of that was minimal at the moment; the blessed cold made all sense of self-preservation vanish. That was Eadric's biggest weapon. If he were to stop Sir Álvaro and save his daughter, he needed to fight like never before. He couldn't do that while half dead.

A flickering torch appeared ahead of him. He crouched low. The snow stacked around his feet as he waited. The light passed him by. Eadric took a deep breath. They must have been within ten feet of him, for the torchlight would've been near invisible any farther than that.

Stumbling toward what he hoped were the city walls, he wondered how Empress Maud planned to escape during this blizzard. She must be mad to attempt such a thing. Then he thought about Lucia, and he was angered that *she* would try such a thing.

Don't get yourself killed again before I reach you, thought Eadric.

He pushed on, urging his legs to step through the dense snow. A blob formed ahead. The suddenness of this immense dark shape coming out of the blinding whiteness startled him. It was like a monster of towering height had opened its jaws to reveal a black throat, awaiting its prey to enter. And Eadric, always the fool, always the one to act before he thought, was willing to do it if it meant saving Lucia.

He kept moving toward the blob until it finally formed a shape. It became less monstrous, less unknown. The Oxford northern gate. He made it.

"Halt! Who ventures forth?!"

"What the fuck are ye doin' out here?!"

Two watchmen approached from the gate. One of them held a torch with a dim flame that fought against the assaulting tempest. Eadric focused on the jittering light. It reminded him of how his heart felt. Pulsing, flailing desperately to stay alive until he held his daughter again.

"Me said, what the fuck are ye doin out here?!" The guard's voice trembled. Eadric wasn't sure if it was because of the cold, or because Eadric looked like a living corpse. When he didn't respond, the two guards glanced at one another hesitantly.

That was when he pounced.

He was slow; the guards were faster. Eadric underestimated how much stagnation had deteriorated his joints, how the months of cold and lack of food had made his muscles dull. The watchmen dodged him. Eadric pivoted on his foot, aimed a jab at one of their throats. They sidestepped and punched Eadric in the oblique. His insides mushed together; he held back from vomiting.

The blizzard surged. The torch fell out of the guard's hands, extinguishing before it even hit the snowy tundra. They launched at him. Eadric blocked one punch, but not the second nor third. They were too quick. His body shuddered with each blow.

He twisted himself and grappled at one of their arms. He bent it, the guard's bone snapping at the elbow. The watchman opened his mouth in an inaudible scream; the tempest overpowered all sounds of their struggle. It was like spectating a fight underwater, slow and agonizing and without the normal rhythm of battle.

No screams. No grunts. Just the unrelenting roar of wind.

One watchman suddenly crumbled to the ground. Eadric didn't bother to investigate why. The other guard stabbed at him; something hot pierced Eadric's leg. He ignored the sudden warmth and wrapped his arms around his victim's neck. They fell to the ground with a hard *thump*. The snow exploded around their bodies, covering them with it. Eadric constricted tighter and tighter until the guard went limp.

Once he was sure the guard was unconscious, he used the last of his strength to push him off. He glared up at the flurry of snow and debris blowing past him, feeling the hardness of the ground below him—the wonderful heat of the earth.

Eleanor appeared above him. She held an iron ladle in her hand.

"What's that for?!" Eadric asked with a frown.

"Looked like you needed help." She nodded to the other unconscious guard. His helm was dented inward at the crown. Eadric glanced at the iron ladle again and found it to be dented as well.

"You're incredible," he said.

"And you're not thinking straight. Come. We need to get to the western gate. I have everything you need."

The little barn they hid in was right outside Oxford's western gatehouse, which overlooked the frozen River Mill Stream. The discarded pewter dish that held their cold soup lay in a pile with Eadric's prisoner garb. Eleanor handed her husband a short sword and dagger. He slipped them into their scabbards.

"So, this is it then?" she asked after dressing him in his armor. "All our pain and suffering led us to this?"

"What do you want me to say?" He felt over-encumbered and dumb before his wife. He used to be fierce, used to be frightening, but now he was only a scared father. It wasn't dissimilar to the day Lucia had been born.

Eleanor shook her head. Her hair peeked out from behind her wimple. The strands looked soft and gray and so human. Eadric brushed it back into place. "I suppose I want you to say that you'll be back," she said. "That you'll survive."

"Now we're both doing this wrong. You're supposed to want me dead."

"And you're supposed to say you hate me . . . but I don't believe you feel that way anymore."

"No," admitted Eadric, "I don't."

It was easy to say. So easy. Why was he always so afraid to say that when he had the chance? He put his hand on Eleanor's cheek. She caressed his arm, pressing hard on the *maille* as if she could pass her hand through the layers and feel his warm skin.

"I want you to try," she said. "After you save your daughter, try to make it back to me. We can escape back to my kingdom, disappear for the rest of the war. If the empress wins, we can even keep Rockingham. You, me, your daughter. We can have a family."

"I'll try."

"Do you think she'd like me?"

Eadric smiled. "I think she'd love you more than I."

Eleanor laughed, and Eadric kissed away a tear that drifted down her cheek. It tasted salty and soft, and it made him feel overwhelmingly sad. They embraced.

"Can you say it now?" she asked softly. "Can you say you love me? Because . . . I'm loathed to admit it, but I find myself loving you."

Gently, tenderly, he said, "I made a promise. A promise to a little girl that she'd be the last woman I ever loved. My heart has no room left. But . . . you're as close as anyone could ever get. Eleanor, you're the best thing to have happened to me over these past ten years. You've been my everything. You're the reason I can save her, and the reason I haven't died yet."

The storm rattled the walls of the barn. Soon the empress would make her escape, and he would have to go back out into that terrible weather. But right now, he held his wife in his arms; he wanted the moment to last.

"I'm leaving everything to you. The estate. My wealth. All of it. All I ask is that if Lucia ever needs a home to fall back on, you hold the door open for her."

"Of course I will." She kissed his neck, and his heart sang in his chest. They finally pushed away from each other. She looked him up and down. "I wish this could've ended differently."

"I see them, Eleanor, all the dead I've killed. All those souls I've taken only to find out she may still be alive. I can't atone to those I've killed. There's no redeeming what's lost. All I'm left with now is a life of scars.

No words can explain sins like mine. But my daughter, she's out there, living. My daughter is here, and alive, so what else can be said?"

The morning bells tolled. It was time to leave.

Eleanor sighed. In both of their souls, they knew this was the only way this could've ended. She pulled her husband into one last hug and said the only thing left to be said:

"Go save her."

Two groups exited the hidden postern from Oxford Castle. They all wore the same white cloaks to conceal themselves in the blizzard, and they both had the same number of men—or women, Eadric supposed. They split up and raced away from the entrance. It was a dangerous passage. The river ice would be thin, and any unfortunate plunge would be deadly.

Eadric chose the group heading farther south—or at least, south by his vague reckoning—for no reason other than they were closer to him. He ran as fast as he could, trying to keep them in view. There were six of them in the group. Their white cloaks flapped wildly around them while they battled through the elements.

Eadric's eyes stung. His armor weighed heavy, and his breath caught in his throat. It was as if the cold air was suppressing his hot breath from leaving his lungs, burning him from the inside out. His feet slipped, but he caught himself at the last second before he fell face-first into the river. He could feel the water streaming beneath the ice. This was no time for caution. If the good Lord kept him alive all these years, through all the terrible things he'd done, just to have him die by falling through the ice only feet away from his daughter . . .

Well, then Eadric could relate to the Lord's vindictive humor.

The group of white cloaks slowed, and Eadric saw his chance. He sprinted and intercepted their path. Unsheathing his short sword with his nondominant hand, he stood firm in the frightening gale. They froze as they espied him.

Eadric and the group were only a mere seven-to-eight feet apart, but the intensity of the chaotic sleet made them seem separated by miles.

Their faces remained obscured under their cowls. Each of them had a scarf wrapped around everything but their eyes.

"Who goes there?!"

Two of the figures stepped forward, pushed back their cloaks, and revealed iron weapons underneath.

Eadric willed his voice to carry over the short distance. "Lucia?! Lady Lucia of Rockingham?!"

The two figures glanced back at another cloaked person—one shorter than the rest. This person stepped between the two guards and said, "Move from our path or it'll be your death!"

"Is Lady Lucia of Rockingham with you?!" Eadric saw that two additional cloaked figures also had weapons at the ready.

Four guards at minimum then, thought Eadric.

"My Lady, we must go," said one guard.

"Move or be killed!" demanded the cloaked leader. She had a feminine voice. Eadric could tell she was older and of a noble background. Her voice carried weight and power.

"I am her father, Baron Eadric of Rockingham. I will not ask again! Is she with you?!"

This caused some heads to turn. The guards glared at the woman bundled in white for guidance. She lifted her head, and Eadric sensed her penetrating gaze within the shadow of her face.

"Kill this man."

Eadric tensed. The guards advanced—

"Wait!"

One of the white phantoms stepped around the woman and kneeled beside her. He took out a short sword, which appeared more ceremonial than practical, and held it up to her.

"I know this man, my empress. He speaks true. Let you not waste men on this scoundrel that could better serve you alive during your daring escape. Allow me to escort the baron to his daughter, so that your time may not be wasted any longer. Each moment squandered is another Stephen could trounce upon you."

Eadric waited for Empress Maud's decision. The guards were tense; they kept their eyes locked on him. The moment seemed to stretch endlessly, with all the cold of the world centered on them. Finally, Empress

Maud placed her hand on the kneeling man's head. "I will remember this," she said. "Let's be off, lest this blizzard kill us all!"

And as quickly as that, the woman King Stephen and William of Ypres had spent years and countless lives scorching the realm for, passed within a few feet of the hellhound and disappeared into the storm. Only the solitary man kneeling in the blinding snow remained. Eadric was relieved not to have to fight. His muscles weren't ready, and his breathing was ragged.

"You know where Lucia is?" he asked the cloaked man as he stood.

"Yes. And if you come with me quickly, we can reach them before they cross the mill."

Eadric's heart pounded. He widened his stance so he wouldn't faint. *Yes . . .* the word echoed in his vacant soul.

Another person had now claimed her to be alive. Could it be true? He was almost too scared to believe it. What if all of this was one last cruel way for Sir Álvaro to torture him? Eadric didn't think he could handle such a revelation.

"Who are you?" Eadric asked him.

"A friend of your daughter's."

Eadric distrusted him immediately, but he was out of options. If she were truly out here, he needed to catch up quickly. And now that he had chosen the wrong group, he would be lost without a guide.

"Very well," said Eadric. "Lead the way."

"My lord." The cloaked man bowed to him.

The white figure with the ostentatious sword fought through the blistering wind. Eadric stayed close behind, careful never to remove his hand too far from the hilt of his own weapon. His body tensed. His hauberk felt like it was freezing through his undertunic and burning small rings into his skin. Eadric kept his mind focused.

He knew Álvaro was well fed. He knew Álvaro was stronger than he was. And he knew Álvaro had learned all of his combat tendencies over the years they fought together.

But the one thing he couldn't possibly know was the love of fatherhood. He didn't know the inhuman power that gave a man. Álvaro would never know that such power was a divine gift from God, and Eadric was ready to unleash it one last time.

"Which way?!" asked Eadric when they reached the Oxford woods.

The cloaked man glanced around. Snow filtered through the groaning boughs above them. The hard ground was a mix of frozen mud and fallen twigs, branches, and animal carcasses. He pointed and said, "This direction!"

They sprinted as quickly as they could, unable to keep themselves from slipping and sliding on rogue patches of muddy snow. Eadric watched the cloaked man carefully. He slid and stumbled as often as Eadric did, and Eadric's body was already pushed past its breaking point.

An older man then? Suspicion stirred in his mind.

Eadric hurdled some shrubs and nearly collided with his guide. Four white-cloaked bodies lay on the ground, freshly slain, their cadavers steaming from their open wounds and disemboweled organs. Blood pooled around them, melting the patches of snow and ice. Eadric breathed a sigh of relief as he realized these were all men—guardsmen by the look of them. The cloaked guide pulled out his short sword.

A woman screamed. Eadric didn't wait for his companion.

Tree trunks blurred past him. The snowstorm buzzed chaotically above the barren canopy, making the relative calmness of the forest floor seem serene. It reminded Eadric of the giant domed cathedrals he saw in Rome during his youth; it was as if the whole of the Oxford woods was covered by an invisible barrier, allowing them to gaze up at the magnificent white fury of God without being assaulted by it themselves.

Eadric rounded a batch of closely grouped birch trees and found Sir Álvaro. He wielded a knife and was wearing his black armor. He stood next to a slender figure on the ground, who wore the same all-white cloak that Empress Maud's group donned.

All Eadric could think, or feel, when he saw the black knight was one thing...

Ferocity.

Eadric had known hatred. He thought the moment he finally laid eyes on Duke Richard again would be the pinnacle of all his hate. But it was Sir Álvaro who truly taught Eadric the full extent to which a human could loathe another.

His bones no longer ached; the cold no longer constrained his stamina. He felt only complete and utter hostility.

He allowed his eyes to drift, for the slightest of moments, to the figure in white. The scarf around their face had fallen, and he could just perceive their features. They looked soft and delicate under the gray, even light of the forest. He sensed the figure appraising him in that instant, deciding whether he was friend or foe. Eadric wanted to rush over, throw that damnable hood off their head, and see once and for all if it was her.

Sir Álvaro laughed. His cackle was as sunken and sharp as the air around them. Eadric growled and pulled out his sword. He tried to bend into a balanced stance, but his knees buckled under his weight. His body was rapidly failing him.

"You are incredible," said Sir Álvaro in disbelief. "Why God gifted you with such resilience is beyond my comprehension. You, Eadric, are the greatest proof He doesn't exist. For if He did, He would have rid the world of you long before."

"Silence!" yelled Eadric. "Drop the knife, León!"

The knight's eyes drifted to something behind Eadric. "T'was you who helped him?"

Eadric spun around to find the cloaked man behind him. The man glanced between Eadric and the black knight. "He found me, Álvaro," he said. "It was the only way to save myself."

"Fuck yourself," said Sir Álvaro. "I'll slay you both and throw her body on top of your cleaved corpses."

Throw her *body* . . .

The woman in white tried to slip away, but Sir Álvaro swung his weapon and blocked her off. "No, no. You're not leaving. You're going to watch. Do you understand yet what is happening, or was your enslaved mind incapable of recalling distant faces?"

The woman looked among all the men in confusion. Her eyes held a darkness hidden within them, and it pulled at Eadric's heart. He breathed in the frigid air. His fingers tingled as his blood gushed through his veins in uncontrollable ecstasy. It must be true. She must be . . .

"I'd like you to meet your father, Lucia," said Sir Álvaro. "You may say hello."

Eadric waited with bated breath.

The world went still.

Was it really—?

"Daddy?" asked Lucia.

Never in his life had Eadric received a jolt like he did at that moment; he heard his daughter's voice again. It was hers. He knew it down to the marrow of his bones. It invigorated him. All their memories, the breadth of his eternal love, swarmed over him like an ocean wave, both overwhelming and powerful beyond belief. It was the cure for the deepest ailment of his soul.

He would not fail her again.

Eadric charged and swung his sword, as Sir Álvaro knew he would. The black knight parried the attack, deflecting Eadric's pierce. The knight danced around him faster than he could keep up. Sir Álvaro's blade bit into his skin somewhere. Eadric jumped away before the black knight could pierce again.

"You're getting slow, Eadric."

The blood ran hot on the left side of his back. Sir Álvaro had slashed above his hauberk and cut him on his exposed neck; luckily, the opening was only a few inches wide. It was an expertly placed cut, but mostly superficial. The fatal blow hadn't been struck.

"Come on, you Spanish bastard!" yelled Eadric, swinging his arms to taunt Sir Álvaro away from his daughter. If he were going to win this battle, he'd have to acknowledge that his body wasn't what it used to be. He was slower, weaker, and older than the knight. But Sir Álvaro had a wildness about him, one he never learned to tame. That made him vulnerable.

Eadric needed to find a way to make him wild.

And he had a plan; unfortunately, that plan burned to ashes when Sir Álvaro *and* the cloaked man attacked him together.

CHAPTER XLVIII
EMMA & LUCIA

Emma sprinted with Crispin, Mildritha, and the other workers across the snow-packed inner bailey. She couldn't see anything. The only way they could tell they moved in the right direction was by the ever-increasing slope at their feet. *Upwards*, she told herself, *forever upwards*. Eventually they reached the keep and entered within.

The main hall was packed with every man, woman, and child that still lived within the castle. Even the soldiers who'd spent the last few months defending the ramparts were inside with them. They were weaponless, and *that* made Emma very nervous. The hearth at the end of the hall had a mighty blaze, sending smoke halfway up the chimney until the tempestuous winds smothered it.

"What's goin' on?" Crispin asked his mother.

"Empress Maud has fled," she answered. She placed her hands on Crispin and Emma, rubbing their backs. "She abandoned Oxford. They're surrendering at the gates."

Emma gasped.

"Are we goin' to die?" asked Crispin.

Mildritha shushed him. That was the only answer he needed. He peeked at Emma with unadulterated concern in his eyes. She reached out her hands, and Crispin grabbed them. His palms dripped with sweat.

"Don't worry," said Emma. "We'll survive."

The multitude of servants, guardsmen, and soldiers found open spots on the ground to settle at. The keep waited for Stephen's army to arrive. They've all heard, of course, of the awful things his army had done as they swarmed the countryside around Oxfordshire. Emma prepared herself for the worst. Would they take and rape her too? Would the king, blinded by wrath for his failure in capturing Maud, slaughter them all?

A fever of murmurs infected the crowd while rumor of the empress's desertion and their inevitable capture spread. Children cried. Women wept. Men slumped over in defeat. Just as they'd all known when the Holy Roman Empress and her retinue first arrived all those months back: their destinies, wanted or not, were tied to her. Empress Maud lost; and thus, they lost.

Now all they could do was wait and see if the fiery temperament of King Stephen of Blois would rid them of their lives.

They reached the edge of the forest. Appearing suddenly from the ceaseless white around them, the towering, monstrous trees seemed like godly sentries that stood watch over the wretched weather of the mortal world. A sense of awe washed over Lucia; it was as if she'd reached the outer rim of their realm, at the precipice of the untamed afterlife.

Only, there was a demon who blocked their entrance.

Her group stopped before the figure clad in black armor. He was tall and muscular, and Lucia could tell by his stance that he was a well-trained knight. Indeed, now that the storm let up for a fraction of a second, she saw the longsword attached to his hip. His armor, mostly *maille* with some plated metal at vital points, reflected the falling snow like white stars shining against the black backdrop of space. She could not see his face under the helm. Immediately the four guards around her stepped up, unsheathing their weapons and putting themselves between her and this rogue ruffian. Doing her best to stand tall and regal, to make him believe she was the empress, she lifted her head high and said, "Begone! Remove yourself from my sight, lest you be slain where you stand."

"I will not." The black knight's voice sounded tinny and hollow under his helm. "It is you I am after."

One guard took a step closer, raising his sword at the knight. "You will respect the wishes of your empress!"

"I am not interested in that insufferable bitch. I want *her*." The black knight unsheathed his longsword and pointed it straight at Lucia.

What the Hell is happening?

"This is your last warning," said Lucia. "Remove yourself or—"

"Belt it, wench! You want to bargain? Give yourself up to me, and I will let your pitiful retinue live."

"How dare you!" Lucia put all the aggression, all the masculine power she could muster, into her voice. Sometimes that was the only way to get a man to succumb to the folly of his pride. "I am the empress—!"

"Enough! I am here for you, Lucia. And I *will* have you."

Lucia found it hard to swallow. Her hand sprang to the knife hidden in her cloak. The other guards tensed. They glanced at her for permission to attack.

"Who are you?" she asked.

The black knight lifted the helm off his head. A sudden surge of wind separated them with a curtain of snow, making their cloaks flutter, making their eyes water. When the wind subsided enough to allow them to see one another, her body went into shock.

"It's one of God's manifested miracles. He kept you alive just for me," said Sir Álvaro.

A tempest of awful memories suffocated her; all the terrible attempts at courtship, the insufferable comments. He was a detestable, rotten person back then, and she could only imagine the monster he had turned into since. Worst of all, he reminded her of the master and his sons—scheming and heinous men that spread wanton hate. He, and men like him, made her love Maud. Men like him showed her that true gallantry can be found beyond knights and decorated soldiers. It was men like him who had taught her contempt.

"Kill him!" she said. "We must reach the empress."

The guards rushed at him. Sir Álvaro blocked multiple attacks, stepping into one strike and using his momentum to guard off another. Their grunts and yells seemed distant and thin as the storm picked up.

The whole fight was a blur of upturned snow, with occasional sparks from colliding blades.

Lucia didn't wait to see who won. She turned to John FitzGilbert Marshal, an older nobleman whom Empress Maud was considering to elevate to an earl, and motioned for him to follow her. Ignoring the shouts and cries of the men protecting her, Lucia and John Marshal flew through the sharp, leafless boughs and bushes. The Oxford woods was like stepping into another realm. The sentinel trees muffled the deafening yell of the blizzard into a muted, constant drone, while the blinding whiteness of the storm vanished into a thin coat of snow and ice on the forest floor. Flurries of snowflakes danced around them in the frigid wind, but it was minimal compared to what they had just gone through crossing River Mill Stream.

"Where from here, my lady?" asked John Marshal.

She glanced around, trying to make out which way was north. The forest looked identical in all directions—falling snow and nude trees. Everything was dark and still.

"This way," she said. She was unsure if it was actually north, but she wanted to get as far away as quickly as possible. John Marshal didn't argue.

Lucia jumped from one spot of clear ground to the next, trying to avoid any snow or ice she could slip on. She hadn't moved more than forty paces before she heard John Marshal yell. She spun around. Sir Álvaro shredded his sword across the nobleman's back. The old man fell into the snow. Lucia screamed.

Sir Álvaro was a devil. Rivulets of blood carried snowflakes between his plated harness; his black armor appeared to be voids of abyssal nothingness. His harsh, visible breath blew out around the nasal protection on his helm. Lucia could not see his eyes nor his face. She took out her dagger and felt its weight in her hand. She thought back to her father's lessons.

It's an extension of your body. Let it aid your reach. It should float through the air as you swing it. Pierce fast and pierce often. Overwhelm them with steel.

Sir Álvaro tilted his head, cracking the aches in his neck. Lucia could tell he was trying to make it appear his recent carnage did not exert him, but the raggedness of his breath betrayed him. His longsword had a blood groove down the center, and it drained its namesake to the ground beneath him where it melted through the softly piling snow.

"So those men were the best fighters your empress could spare?" he asked.

"Fuck you!" She spat back. Lucia ripped off her white mask, as it was getting hard to breathe with the damn thing on. If she was going to die, she was going to do so with unimpeded airflow.

Sir Álvaro stepped toward her. She could sense the profound *want* in his eyes. The deep, passionate desire. He wished to have it all from her.

Fuck this, she thought. *Not again. I won't let it happen again.*

"I have come to rescue you," said Sir Álvaro. "At long last, my dear, you can feel warm again."

"There are a thousand colds I would endure before I succumb to the warmth of your arms," she said. It tasted raw out of her mouth, stupid and blatant. She was tired, so Goddamn tired. Why now? Why did this whoreson want her *now*?

"Let's make this quick," said the black knight.

"Yes. Let's."

Sir Álvaro lunged. Lucia dodged around a tree trunk. Distance was both her ally and her foe. If she could maintain a reach advantage, she could avoid the lustful lunacy of this degenerate. But by the same token, she'd never be able to cut him if she didn't get close. Sir Álvaro pounced around the trunk like a ferocious, feral animal. Terror burrowed into her heart at the sight of a man devoured by such carnality. He swung his sword. She ducked. The blade axed into the tree, felling bark onto the tundra below.

He had a gleam in his eye; one she had seen before. It sent shivers unimaginable down her spine, a feeling she thought she'd quartered off into an abandoned part of her soul. He pried the blade out, grunting in exasperation. Lucia caught her balance as a giant root snagged the back of her foot. The knight took advantage almost before she realized she'd tripped. She sliced her blade. It glinted in the pale light. Blood flew. Her aim was true. Sir Álvaro grimaced in pain. She hit somewhere; although nowhere near important enough, for the man was on top of her in an instant. All she could do was yelp.

Sir Álvaro punched her with a backhanded pommel strike. Lucia's hair flung across her face. She bit down on her tongue and spat out a chipped tooth. Everything went dizzy. She slammed her fists upward, trying to avoid the inevitability of unrestrained manhood. Sir Álvaro refused her dissuasion. He pounced on top of her, already shedding his belt.

"I've waited so long."

"Too long," she said.

It happened in an instant; Lucia took her blade and stabbed it at her throat...

She'd told herself a long time ago that she would never let it happen again. This was her promise fulfilled. It felt natural, *right* almost: the blade puncturing into her neck, the artery which gave life from her heart to her brain severed at its most vulnerable spot, and her life ending as it should have a decade past. Immediate and purposeful, Lucia stabbed hard...

But Sir Álvaro reacted faster.

His hand whipped to the side and deflected the dagger away from her neck. His strength was much greater than hers, and the knife flew from her hand, bouncing into the fallen leaves to their side.

"You dumb cunt," he said. "I plan on making this last."

Lucia's eyes went wide. Now she was terrified. She screamed at him. It was a clear and loud shriek. As he mounted her, she punched and roared and squirmed under the black knight. It was to no avail.

"Stop your fuckin' wailing or else I'll cut out your tongue too."

"Then you better fucking do it!" Lucia snapped back. The rage and frustration at her helplessness made her crazed with insanity.

Maybe if I make him angry enough, he'll kill me, she thought. If she fought hard enough and screamed loud enough, maybe there would still be a way out.

Sir Álvaro reached for his belt and removed a dagger. She was certain he was going to follow through with his threat of severing her tongue until two men stumbled through the frosted underbrush next to them. One of them was in the ghostly white cloak of their escape party, but the other was an older man who wore armor and carried a short sword. The other man wore his pain clearly, with a limp and an arm that he favored. His face was scarred, bruised, and battered, with wrinkles upon wrinkles that made him look much older than he probably was.

Sir Álvaro seemed to recognize this man, as he laughed and said, "You are incredible. Why God gifted you with such resilience is beyond my comprehension. You, Eadric, are the greatest proof He doesn't exist. For if He did, He would have rid the world of you long before."

"Silence! Drop the knife, León!"

"T'was you who helped him?"

"He found me, Álvaro," said the cloaked man. "It was the only way to save myself."

"Fuck yourself. I'll slay you both and throw her body on top of your cleaved corpses."

Seeing her chance to escape, Lucia crawled away while he was distracted. But Sir Álvaro twisted around and stuck his blade in front of her face. Lucia growled. She glanced between them all, thinking, *Lord Christ, I fucking* hate *men*.

"No, no," he said. "You're not leaving. You're going to watch. Do you understand yet what is happening, or was your enslaved mind incapable of recalling distant faces?"

She waited impatiently for Sir Álvaro to come to his damn point. He had a maniacal gleam in his smirk, a powerful glee in knowing the unknown. He pointed his sword at the older man in armor and said, "I'd like you to meet your father, Lucia. You may say hello."

At first, she had no reaction. There comes a point when all sensibility becomes muted. What was one more emotion stacked upon a thousand previous ones? What was another wound on a soul that had already been lacerated a thousand times? What was one last surprise in a world of unceasing astonishments? There was only one reasonable reaction to a world of endless emotion, endless pain, endless shock: numbness. The pure bliss of dissociation.

Lucia had been there before. She'd lost herself in the beautiful relief of despondency for what seemed like an eternity. It would be so easy to fall into it again. She could cease to be Lucia or Madame Beatrice. She could become a phantom again, a spectre who went through life as transparently as the fleeting seasons. In her experience, that was how most people lived. Briefly, painfully, and unremarkably.

Thus, all that being true, did it really matter if that *was* her father? Did it matter if she had loved him deeply once? Did any of this matter if life always ended with death, suffering, and perversion?

Yes, she discovered, *it* does *matter. My father was the man who made life seem possible, who made me feel safe. That was my father.*

Tears fell down her cheek; she felt the presence of her younger self, that scared girl who kneeled in the middle of Uncle Rowan's bailey with a blade pressed against her throat. She let herself experience all those affections, and re-experience that beautiful, last fleeting hope she had—that her father would single-handedly fight through the gatehouse to rescue her. She saw her father's face as it was on that night, the fear and horror of his reaction when steel bit into her neck and peeled open the skin until it ran dark with the ichor of her throat.

She thought like most girls did; she believed, wholeheartedly, until the exact moment it never transpired, that her daddy would save her. There was never any doubt in her mind. Perhaps that was the catalyst that made her mind snap—the reality that her father, the strong, powerful, and jolly Baron Eadric of Rockingham, couldn't rescue her.

But now that he was here, her fragmented memories finally fell into place. She felt whole for the first time in forever. He *did* come to save her.

Only now, in this modern day and age, she was equally capable of rescuing him, now that she was the woman she was always meant to become.

At long last, Lucia accepted who stood before her.

"Daddy?"

Her father charged at Sir Álvaro. Their attacks were quick, violent, and forceful. Sparks of fire lit the darkening forest as their blades chipped into each other. Eadric cried out; the powdered snow splattered with blood.

"You're getting slow, Eadric."

"Come on, you Spanish bastard!"

But it wasn't only Sir Álvaro who came after her father now; the cloaked figure from Maud's retinue attacked too. Lucia screamed to warn him. Within an instant, all she heard was clashing steel; all she saw were blades slicing through visible breath. The men hollered. Blood flew, but she couldn't tell from whom. They moved too fast for her untrained eye. The little girl she used to be crawled back up from the grave Lucia had buried her in. She felt the same fear of the world, and with it, the same overwhelming urge to hide and let her father take care of it. It was that old familiar feeling—to trust her father to do what he must, for her.

But she now knew that was a fool's errand. Every man and woman had a limit. Lucia stuffed her inner child back into the grave. As much as the sight of her father had compelled her to become that little girl again, to feel the awe and wonder at God's creation around her, that wasn't who she was now.

Lucia was the handmaiden of an empress, capable and willing to act against the evil that pressed back against her. It wasn't her that needed saving; it was her father.

Taking up her dagger again, she jumped into the fight... and was almost immediately decapitated. The swirl of a blade missed her by inches. Her father tried to yell something at her, but Lucia's blood rushed too loudly in her ears. Eadric deflected a blade and shoved himself into Sir Álvaro. The knight stumbled back. His *maille* coif caught beneath his helm, and Lucia saw the flesh of his neck. She stabbed at the opening, striking true. Sir Álvaro yelled as his black armor leaked red.

The knight swung his fist; it collided with the side of Lucia's head. Her jaw snapped, and her half-chipped tooth dislodged completely. The trees spun around her. She stepped out to brace herself, but her foot hit ice. She slipped. Her head slammed into the hard dirt. The next thing Lucia knew, she was on the ground with a glob of blood forming in her mouth.

She glanced up. Her father stood over her, deflecting two blows and releasing an angry roar. The cloaked man and Sir Álvaro hesitated. The knight tossed his helm and the cloaked man threw off his white mask, both of them desperately trying to breathe easier. Lucia recognized the man in white. It was exactly who she expected it to be.

"Richard," said Eadric, his eyes burning red. "You really do have a death wish."

"You would never stop coming after me," said the duke. He reached at his right leg; it was nearly cleaved in half. "If I were to fight you out in the storm, the empress would've abandoned me. This was my only option."

"You are a fool."

"Eadric, you can't win this," said Sir Álvaro.

"I know. But I'll make damn sure you can't either."

Her father swung at him. The black knight guarded against it, but Eadric had planned for that. He feinted, violently twisting his hips to switch his attack to a thrust.

But not against Sir Álvaro.

Duke Richard never saw it coming. Eadric buried his blade up to the hilt in the duke's chest. The *maille* beneath his white cloak exploded outwards, springing and clattering around Lucia like crumbling debris. It was an expert maneuver by her father, but it had left an opening.

Sir Álvaro thrust with an attack of his own, and it bit into the previous wound in Eadric's back. Her father spasmed. His useless right hand clutched at nothing. He whipped his head back in an uncontrolled twitch.

Lucia reached out and pulled on Sir Álvaro's leg, trying to trip him. It almost worked. The knight, however, caught himself at the last moment. He pulled back his foot, and the next thing Lucia saw were stars as he kicked her in the upper chest and clipped her chin. Eadric jumped at him. Sir Álvaro lowered his sword and stepped into her father's lunge. He managed to get underneath her father's attack. He flung Eadric over the top of him. Slamming into the ground a few feet away, her father groaned while blood pooled around him. Sir Álvaro, with a maniacal glee spreading across his face, lifted his sword and pierced down. Eadric held up his hands and deflected the blade away from his sternum. The weapon, instead, stabbed through his right wrist and through the palm of his left hand, pinning his arms to the earth. More blood splattered up onto the black knight. Eadric screamed.

"It's over, Eadric. Learn when to fucking quit." Sir Álvaro tore the blade through Eadric's hands. He pointed the bloodied weapon at Lucia. "Now lay there like a good bitch and watch."

Lucia tried to catch her breath. Her eyes drifted up to the bare branches way above her. The turbulent blizzard rumbled through the canopy so ferociously that it snapped whole boughs off. She glanced about her, searching despondently with her hand. She found a thick branch with a sharp, broken edge next to her. The silhouetted figure of Álvaro straddled her body.

Get up, she told herself. *You're strong. This is your body. This is your life.*

The little girl inside her curled up inside the grave. She was crying, her tears so hot that they evaporated in the blistering cold. Lucia wanted to cradle her.

Don't watch, she pleaded with the traumatized girl. *Just know we'll survive this. We're women. It's our burden to survive what men cannot. 'Tis our curse to push onwards in a world that men fight to stop. But please don't watch. You've seen too much already.*

Close your eyes, Lucia. Close your eyes.

Sir Álvaro placed his sword down and stroked her cheek. He wiped away the tears that bled from the corners of her eyes. Her father groaned at the edge of her vision. He reached his hand forward, but his strength failed him at long last.

"Álvaro, please," begged Eadric. "Please don't. I'm sorry."

"Don't cry, Lucia," said Sir Álvaro, ignoring her father. "Hark the words of your poor daddy. Don't make him feel worse. Show him how beautiful love can be . . . before he dies."

Sir Álvaro unfastened his belt and threw it to the side. She watched him lower his chausses and lift his hauberk.

Lucia smiled. What was the one useful thing about sinful men? They never change. Sooner or later, they would always let the devil out. Sir Álvaro stripped back his gambeson, revealing the skin of his lower belly.

Men are creatures of flesh.

Lucia gripped the broken tree branch and stabbed.

The jagged edge gored into Sir Álvaro's intestines. It broke off inside his stomach. Lucia, glowering at her old suitor, speared the branch deeper and deeper into his belly until her knuckles disappeared inside the gooey flesh of his mangled skin. Sir Álvaro blanched. The rush of black blood drenched her as his heart spat more and more of it out. His life ichor ran sticky and warm, and it felt perversely good compared to the frigidness of the world.

Eadric tackled Álvaro off of her. They both bounced off the ground. Lucia pushed herself up just in time to see her father land on top of him.

"I wonder," said Sir Álvaro, "will you despise me in Hell?"

"We'll find out," said Eadric.

He reached into Sir Álvaro's mutilated gut and ripped out as many organs as he could. Álvaro's eyes widened while unimaginable pain spiked through his body one last time. Maybe it was the shock that finally killed him. Maybe it was the loss of blood. It was impossible to say for sure.

But what was certain was this: in his last moments, much to Sir Álvaro's chagrin and everlasting despair, his final thought must have been, *the lady and baron of Rockingham have bested me once again.*

He died in that hellish forest as a frozen corpse, so dreadfully far from his brilliant Spanish sun.

Eadric collapsed next to Sir Álvaro. Lucia scrambled after him. She pushed the cadaver away and rolled her father over so that he could look upon her. His blood seeped out from multiple wounds, streaming between her fingers. She cradled him in her arms. He looked so much older than the last time she had seen him.

"Daddy, it's me," she said.

"Certainly death comes for me, for 'tis a ghost I see."

"Not a ghost. Feel my warmth." Lucia grabbed his hand and placed it on her cheek. Eadric smiled. And suddenly, with that stupid, silly smile known only to him, Lucia no longer saw the beaten and broken man, but saw the father of her childhood—the man who believed he had everything in the world simply because he had her.

"Could it be?" Eadric's voice choked. He was crying, and so was she. "A father's prayer answered?"

"God is cruel if this is how He answers."

"No . . . no, honey. He is not cruel. I thought Christ and His angels were asleep, but now I see they were busy protecting you."

Eadric, cautiously at first, as if he might injure her or make her vanish if he pressed too hard, traced the wrinkles that had formed on her face. He touched them with such gentle care that her heart broke even more. She realized, with a sense of overwhelming dread and anxiety, that this would be the final time she'd ever feel him or hear him speak.

Remember his voice, his touch. Remember this feeling.

"What are these lines on your face?" he asked.

"I've grown, Daddy."

"You've grown beautifully."

"'Tis well, Daddy. You can tell me the truth." She forced a laugh. Eadric gave a real one in response. His tears froze as they streamed down his cheek, leaving a trail of sparkling frost which led to his eyes.

"Do you remember, Lucia? I promised you. I promised that even as a toad, I'd still love you. And you've become so much more beautiful than I could ever imagine." She saw him grow serious. He pressed his hand firmly against her cheek. "Do not become as I have. Let your pain thaw with the winter snow. My life ended when I lost you. Swear to me you won't do the same. Let life breathe anew this coming spring."

"Yes, Daddy."

"Promise me, honey. Find purpose. Find love."

"I promise."

As the storm lessened above them, showering snowflakes to the earth in a serene dirge, she came to the realization all at once. She *had* found purpose; she *had* found love. Foolishly, Lucia had believed herself to be abandoned since her uncle's castle was sacked. But she wasn't. Empress Maud blessed her with love and purpose; meanwhile Emma, the spy with the gift of life, helped her regain her womanhood; and her father, when he finally came back for her, gave salvation to the little girl she had buried inside. Lucia was not alone. She never was. She wiped her tears away before they fell on his face.

"I promise, Daddy," she said, meaning it this time.

Eadric's eyes sparkled for the first time in a decade—the unrelenting joy of a father. In this world, he was always Lucia's beacon of light and laughter. She hadn't realized how much that meant to her, how much he made the world brighter.

And now she would have to accept a world without him.

And now he would have to accept an afterlife without her.

"You were why I lived," said Eadric, uncaring of his future, uncaring of his Hell; none of that mattered, for he had, at long last, told his daughter what she meant to him. "I love you. Forever."

"I love you too, Daddy."

Eadric died a few moments later. Lucia closed his eyes and, like a silent saint, knelt over his body until the blizzard siphoned away the last of his warmth.

Hours after bundling into the great hall, the barricaded door thundered aloud. Crispin pulled Emma close to him, and Mildritha wrapped her heavy-set arms around the both of them. The fire at the hearth wasn't much more than embers now, and the unyielding cold saturated everything. The breathing of a hundred-plus people shot visibly into the air.

The barricaded door shuddered again. Someone shouted a command.

At the front of the sea of fear, Aubrey de Vere stood up, glanced upon the multitude of families and soldiers that he was sworn to protect, and removed the barricade himself. The door swung open. A bellowing, brutal gust came with it, piercing the faces of those inside. Emma's face turned bright red. De Vere stepped back, giving room for a tall man in an ornate purple cloak that shimmering white from a thousand snowflakes. Soldiers and knights and more swarmed in around him. They held polearms, swords, maces, shields, and even bows. They pointed these weapons at the women, at the children, at the men and priests and forfeited soldiers. They were ready to kill all of them.

Emma held her breath. Crispin squeezed her hand. The last glowing embers in the hearth turned ashen white.

"Welcome, Stephen of Blois, King of England," heralded the steward. "The seat of Oxford sits vacant. It shall be bestowed upon you, if you so desire, my king."

King Stephen terrified Emma. His eyes were sullen, dark, and keen. His lips were pulled tight against his face. His hand hovered at a sword on his hip.

"Are you Aubrey de Vere?" asked the king.

"Yes, my liege. As steward of this keep, 'tis my honor to declare fealty to you. Oxford Castle surrenders to your magnificent might. I am yours to be commanded."

The hall went deadly silent. Stephen's soldiers awaited orders. The king gazed over them, his face a mixture of a few dozen emotions. He rested his hand on the hilt of his sword. Emma braced for the slaughtering, the raping, the burning. She braced herself to experience Marlborough anew.

"Tell your people," King Stephen began dramatically, "that Oxford is mine. As of now, those who wish to remain in the city, and swear fealty to me as king, may prosper. Oxford will be rebuilt! Under my kingship, this city shall become the second throne of my kingdom, only behind the powerful towers of London. Those who wish to leave may do so. I do not blame anyone here for the treachery of Maud. She made you suffer. She made you starve! Then she abandoned you and left you for the wolves. I am *not* as vindictive as my cousin! I will *not* betray you as she did! She used a woman's trick to flee early in the morn, long before the saints and angels of Christendom were awake. She will be caught. She will be brought to justice. But you have my oath: my men will not harm or touch you. All I ask of you, in honor of this benevolence, is to remember it was Stephen, King of England, who saved you from utter damnation."

Emma, Crispin, and Mildritha crossed the bridge from the inner gatehouse to the city proper. Oxford was a husk of the glory that Emma remembered. The streets were bereft of tradesmen and artisans and clergymen and maidens and all the wondrous like; instead, stationed everywhere were soldiers and knights and mean-looking vagabonds. They exited the city of burned homes with a large group of others who abandoned the castle. Emma rubbed her tender arm in its sling. She tried to move her fingers, but they wouldn't budge.

Emma sighed. She wished so badly that she could go back to that girl in the Reading bathhouse and shake her, slap her, or do whatever else it took to make her return home and never think of Tom again. She wished she could regain all the time she'd lost with her mother. She wished she would've gone to the tavern alone with Alice and Roger and enjoyed their company more thoroughly. Most of all, she wished she would've told herself that being a princess was an extremely, *extremely* stupid thing to want. Princesses lose eyes; they get traded, bartered, and sold off for political gain; they endure schisms within the family. Princesses were the most used and disused items in the world.

All she wanted, more than anything else in the world, was to once again be that happy peasant girl from a small, unimportant village. But just as she could never go back and tell her past self what she learned, she could never undo what that time had changed within her.

Scars are carried forever, and some wounds are even taken into the afterlife, for the lacerations of the soul reverberate unto eternity.

Some people, however, make those burdens easier. There are some who have the miraculous ability to ease the pain of those eternal lesions. Emma had learned to hold on to those people and never let them escape. Those rare souls, once found, are worth a lifetime of sorrow; God's greatest miracle was blessing you to exist at the same exact time as those special people. People—Emma smiled—like Crispin and Mildritha, like Madame B and Ansfride, like Alice and Roger, like her mother and Lief and Verona, like so many more souls she was still to meet.

Emma, for the first time that year, felt grateful.

"What now?" she asked, glancing back at Mildritha and Crispin. The mother and son shrugged. They looked about the barren wasteland surrounding Oxford. Where once there stood a hundred houses, barns, sheds, and workshops, remained now only charred wood and rubble—a city outside a city, destroyed by refugees, an invading army, and a snowy tempest. Where once there grew vegetables and grains in such copious amounts that their seeds littered the air, there now only remained a white blanket of impenetrable lifelessness. Snow fell softly around them. It was all so beautiful yet so haunting.

"Emma?!"

She started.

"... Emma ... Emma?!"

There were two different voices—no, three. Three voices called her name through the snowfall. *What in the—*

"Emma!"

She recognized the voice. *It can't be ...*

"Mama?" Her voice trembled.

She spun around, her feet slipping on ice, and there, about a hundred feet away, limping through the snow with such speed that it'd put young men to shame, was her mother. Behind her, another fifty paces back, stood Alice and Roger. Emma's world stopped. It was as if the Lord picked her up and placed her in Heaven, the miles of snow not more than the top of a puffy cloud. She rushed to her, feet churning through white powder. The snow and ice tried to make her slip; they tried to keep her from feeling the outstretched arms of her mother. Emma shook off the tears. Her mother's smile could brighten the darkest nights.

Edith screamed her name again. Alice and Roger trudged their way to her. Emma widened her arms, now only feet away.

"Mama!"

Mother and daughter both jumped into each other's arms and fell to their knees atop the fresh snow. Emma ignored the pain roaring through her shoulder. Her mother pushed aside Emma's wimple and sobbed into her hair, while Emma buried her face in her mother's chest. They cried together as shimmering snowflakes fluttered down from Heaven above.

"I'm sorry," Emma cried. "I'm so sorry."

"Don't be, my love," said Edith. "God, I've missed ye so."

"I love you."

"I love you too."

Alice and Roger reached them, and the embrace of two became four. They remained there hugging and crying until the snow went damp from the heat of their love and the tears of their joy.

"How?" Emma eventually asked. "How did ye find me?"

"Your mum refused to abandon ye," said Alice. "After Roger made his way back to us, we helped her cross from Sutton Courtenay to Abingdon and then to Oxford."

"But your leg—"

"This leg can't keep me from you," said Edith. "What happened to your arm?"

"'Tis a long story. How did you survive the winter? And how did . . . I mean—" Emma's words stuttered. She was astounded by all of this.

"We had some help during the worst of winter." Edith put her hand gently on Emma's shoulder and pointed her to two men who stood awkwardly a few dozen feet away. "They helped us. I'd like ye to meet them."

CHAPTER XLIX
GILBERT

G ILBERT AND WILLIAM TRIED to stand straighter, while Edith introduced them to her daughter. Gilbert flexed his fingers and toes, desperately wanting to regain warmth in them. William hung onto him shakily, for he was in worse shape after a year of captivity.

The dense cloud coverage parted in the west, but the lingering sun brought small comfort to the grieving brothers. There was no going back for Hawk now that the storm had passed. Everyone in the camp may be too distracted at the moment due to Stephen's successful seizure of Oxford and Maud's spectacular escape, but soon enough the army would turn into a furious uproar as they hunted down who slaughtered their fellow countrymen during the blizzard, stealing their food and wealth. The two brothers were staying a safe distance away from the camp, just in case. Thus, tragically, their childhood friend would remain out there in the king's camp, forgotten until the snowmelt revealed his corpse to whoever was unlucky enough to stumble upon him first.

"This here is Gilbert," said Edith. "And I presume that this is your brother?"

"It is," said Gilbert, forcing a smile as best he could.

"God bless ye," said William.

"This is my daughter, Emma." She rubbed her daughter's back, beaming with the glory only a mother could hold.

"May God bless ye," Emma said. "Thank you both for helpin' my mum during the last few weeks. I'll remain forever grateful."

Gilbert nodded awkwardly; admittedly, he didn't feel like he did too much outside brooding, stoking the fire, and catching some food.

"What happened to Hawk?" asked Roger behind Edith and Emma.

They must have noticed how broken Gilbert and William were inside, for they softened their expressions and gazed at them sheepishly. "I'm sorry," he said.

"He's with God now," said William.

Wanting to move past the embarrassment of bereavement, Gilbert changed topics and asked, "Where ye off to now?"

"I'm not sure," said Edith. "I suppose we'll take it one day at a time. Wherever life takes us."

"Oh!" Emma screamed excitedly. "Mama, look!" Emma pointed to two people who approached from the city gates—an older woman and a younger boy about Will's age. "I'd like you to meet them."

Edith tried to grab her daughter, but Emma had already run off while dragging Alice and Roger with her.

"I apologize," Edith said to the brothers. "My darling Emma has always struggled to stay still. It was a pleasure to meet ye, William. Your brother cares very deeply about you."

"Me knows it," he said.

She then gave Gilbert the coin she had promised him back in Abingdon-on-Thames and hobbled off after her daughter. Gilbert and William watched Emma introduce them to the older woman and younger boy. William smiled watching the interaction, and Gilbert smiled watching his brother smile. He grabbed William's arm.

"Come on," he said. "Let's not interrupt their moment. I'm awfully hungry. What say we find some food and water? Then we can patch up our wounds. We have much to talk about."

"Yes," said William. "Let's."

The two brothers snuck off down the southern road, leaving behind them a trail that led to the last resting place of Hawk, the greatest friend they'd ever known.

On the fifth of January, in the eleven-hundred and forty-third year of our Lord, Jesus Christ, Gilbert and William reached Wareham—exactly seven months after Gilbert first arrived at the port city. This time, however, there was much less violent fanfare, as the city was in a busy effort to repair itself after a year of hardship.

Unlike most of the countryside, due to its proximity to the coast, snow did not blanket the city; however, much like most of the kingdom, it was covered by ashes of war as well. Word of King Stephen's exploits, as well as the miraculous escape of Empress Maud, had spread to the far corners of the kingdom. It was rumored that the empress had fled west, potentially reuniting with her brother, who was said to have snuck into England sometime around the king's sacking of Oxford. Whatever the case may be, they seemed to be in a lull in the war. Having captured one of the largest castles in the center of the southern shires, Stephen appeared content to hold his position and reprieve his army until winter passed. That meant that those poor sailors and fishermen, who'd seen their livelihoods and homes destroyed by the strong wartime currents, were given a chance to steady their flooded lives. The undertow of political and religious strife would, of course, continue to reverberate as it always did, sending occasional waves to disrupt the lives of the peasantry, but this was nothing new to the poor fishermen, sailors, farmers, and laborers. And thus they lived on, watching the sea with constant speculation; for they knew, like all those who lived by the precarious grace and sorrow of the ocean, that the storm would come for them again. The clouds of war always lingered on the horizon.

It took some work to track them down, but Gilbert and William eventually heard word of two foreigners from Normandy who awaited passage back to France. They were staying at an inn located by the harbor near the River Frome. Only a few buildings still stood in that district, which reeked of mildew and rotten things. The inn, colloquially called Fromeside Inn, was a small building on the corner of two cross streets. Across the southern street from the inn, the water caps of the River Frome shimmered gently under the pale sunlight, the surface disturbed here and there by the fluttering of ducks and geese. Standing atop the quay, Gilbert wondered at the sight of such fowl during this time of year. Were they stuck on this island kingdom like himself? Were they taking a break before continuing their trek southward?

A kind breeze drifted in from the north, bringing with it a few odd snowflakes, which evaporated before they touched the ground. It was in this tranquil, quiet, and serene state that the two brothers entered Fromeside Inn.

The inner chamber was warm and comely. A well-kept hearth popped invitingly against the far wall, while a couple of well-placed chairs sat alluring in front of the heat; they were already occupied by multiple peasant men and fishwives, many of whom smoked a tingly, acidic-smelling substance from short pipes. Six bedchamber doors surrounded the main room and were guarded by an elderly innkeeper sitting atop a rickety chair. The elderly man had a mangled mess of a thin white beard, and a large bald spot atop his head. He looked scrawny, like most people during winter, and he seemed comedically small in the ancient chair he sat in. He waved them over.

"Are ye in need of a bed?" asked the innkeep.

"No—"

"Then get the fuck out! No stay, no solace."

William and Gilbert hesitated. They weren't prepared for such a rude introduction. For someone to disturb the decency of hospitality, especially during winter, was a crime in all ways but by law. It could cause an establishment to be torched.

"I don't mean to be rude," said Gilbert, "but we're lookin' for—"

"No stay, no solace!"

"Hark, we just—"

"No stay—"

"No solace," William cut in. "How much for a room then?"

"Three pence for the night."

"Three pence?!" asked Gilbert incredulously. "Who pays three pennies for a single night?"

"Ye do if ye want solace, dirty foreigners." He spat on the ground. "Dirty fuckin' foreigners pay dirty fuckin' foreigner prices. Three pence."

"One pence."

"Scrub me ass for one pence, and I may shit out a shilling."

"To Hell with ye," said Gilbert irritably. "Come, Will. We'll wait outside for them."

The elderly man grabbed them before they could turn. "Aye! Damn ye dirty fuckin' foreigners and ye'r scummy fuckin' ways. Two pence and a halfpenny then."

"Two pence and a farthing."

"Do ye see any other inn in Wareham?! Do ye see any other bedchamber not burnt to a crisp? Do ye see any other hearth staving off the frost death? Do ye?!"

Gilbert grabs William to turn away—

"Fine! Fine. Two pence and a farthing." The elderly man yanked the coins from Gilbert's hand. "Now what did ye want?"

"We're looking for two other foreigners, a couple. They go by Beatriz and Bartholomew."

"Aye, they be rentin' chamber four over yonder."

"Thank ye," said William, turning toward the room.

"Halt! They ain't well there now, ye dolt. They left this morn."

"When will they be back?"

"Why the fuck would I know? Do I look like the keeper of dirty fuckin' foreigners?"

Gilbert sighed. He glanced over at the hearth and asked, "Can we at least stay inside by the fire until they arrive?"

"I'm confused. Did I not say, *no stay, no solace*? Did ye not fuckin' hear me when I said *no fuckin' stay, no fuckin' solace*? Well, are ye fuckin' stayin'?!"

"Yes."

"Then ye have solace, ye stupid, dirty, foreign-fuckin' bugger." Gilbert grabbed William and wandered to the small group of peasants huddled around the hearth. They mostly ignored them, except for a woman with gentle brown eyes and jet-black hair that peeped out beneath her stained wimple. The orange firelight glowed reverently on her skin. She glanced up at them as they approached and smiled.

"Don't worry about Ol' Euan over there," she said in her tender voice. "He was a nice man up until recently."

"What happened to him?" asked William.

"He saw war. Not battle, mind ye, but war . . . I recognize you."

"Me?" asked Gilbert.

"You were with Father Tobias, weren't ye? During the sacking?"

Gilbert nodded. That seemed to loosen the woman up some.

"Euan's son was killed durin' the attack," she explained. "As was his granddaughter."

"By which side?"

"Both. Maud's army killed his son. Stephen's army killed his granddaughter." The woman gazed over at the innkeeper with an enigmatic look on her face. "The fire destroyed everythin' on the port but his inn. I don't know who he blames more: the king, the empress, or the Lord."

"Apparently it's foreigners," said Gilbert.

"He blames everyone. Maybe himself most of all."

Gilbert went silent. He listened to the soothing sounds of the hearth fire and let himself become distracted with the quietude of existence. William glanced back at the elderly man.

"It's not his fault that happened to him," said his brother.

"It's never anyone's fault," she said. "That's what makes all this so difficult to understand."

"All this?"

"Life." She had a blank stare that slowly consumed her. "I had a husband. I lost him to war and violence. According to him, that was never his fault either. He was right, but also wrong. Either way, it hurts."

"I'm sorry," said William. "How did he die?"

"He didn't. I lost him in another fashion. There's more than one way to lose a life."

Gilbert studied this woman with the brown eyes and the jet-black hair that sat before them. Just as he opened his mouth to ask her who she was, the main door of Fromeside Inn opened up. Cold air rushed in, and with it, came a familiar face.

But only one.

Along the marshy lowlands off the coast of Dorset, the weather-drenched brambles vibrated gently from the passing breeze. Under the softness of the winter air, the River Frome settled into its deep cobalt color, and the setting sun punctured through dense gray clouds, emitting brilliant red-orange rays which shimmered through the spectacular purples and blues that dominated the world at eventide. A double-masted ship with furled sails dropped anchor in the center of the river, and the sailors aboard chatted excitedly while they lowered the dinghies; they were the first crew to sail ashore since the king closed off England's borders.

Comforted by the gentleness of the setting sun, Gilbert, William, and Beatriz could lament the death of their friends, and lovers, in peace.

Beatriz clutched her rosary close to her chest, willing the pious beads to seep into her heart. She gazed out over the darkening waters, over the ship, over the clouds and past the sun, into that vast eternity which stretched forever and ever beyond the glistening stars that gave Christ and His angels succor within the radiant ramparts of Paradise; the three of them gazed over even those to see their friends again.

Maybe in the next life.

Eventually, Beatriz turned back to the brothers, and they stood in congenial silence as the breeze danced between the reeds and cattails that dominated the riverbank. Gilbert and William were a day late to say goodbye to Bartholomew. He had died earlier that morning. He had fought throughout the fall and winter to survive the wounds he sustained at Bampton Priory, but the rot had infected him too deeply. Beatriz had taken her husband to the Church of St. Martin's, and Father Tobias had sanctified his passage to the Lord above. A gravedigger had taken pity upon the poor widow and buried him within consecrated ground an hour after passing.

While they mourned on the riverbank, Gilbert was left waiting. He waited for the endless guilt and endless self-loathing to enrapture him with their hollow passion. But it didn't. He was angry at himself for being too cowardly to defend his friend as he should have, but he *knew* it was his fault. He knew it in his bones. And that meant he could find forgiveness in himself too. There was now a way forward to endure life, a lesson which Hawk and Beatriz had taught him.

The three of them embraced. Gilbert had never hugged Beatriz so warmly or so tightly before. In the arms of his heartbroken friend and his rescued brother, he broke down. They wept until their eyes ran dry, and Gilbert's throat went hoarse. Beatriz held him, and he held her; William comforted him, and he consoled William back. Their hug lasted as long as any of them could handle it. It was beautiful and healing and reaffirmed what Hawk had helped Gilbert learn:

I am not a coward because I'm loved; I am not cursed because I'm loved.
I am only brave because I love.

"I'm sorry," Beatriz said.

"Don't be," said Gilbert. "'Tis what I needed to hear. You were right to think so and right to say so."

"Hawk wouldn't have been so mean."

"He was when I needed it most."

The sun set below the western sky, and the moon rose low from the northeast. There was to be a full moon tonight, the first of the year.

"What now?" asked William.

"I'm getting far away from this accursed land," said Beatriz.

"Back to Caen?"

"No. I don't know. Wherever God takes me. Maybe I will become a nun after all." Beatriz scoffed to herself in a manner that suggested she was still in disbelief that this was her life now.

"I'm sorry, Beatriz," said Gilbert. "It's my fault Bartholomew died. I should've helped him, but I didn't. I'm so sorry."

Beatriz nodded her head, but she seemed to be half listening. "There are worse things to give a life for. What about you two?"

"I made a promise to Robin that I'd return with William and save him too. I think I'm finally brave enough to do that."

"And after that?"

"After that? We start living."

Beatriz smiled at him. It was brief and sad, but it showed Gilbert that she would forgive him too. One day.

She moved toward the sailors rowing ashore, planning to ask them if they had space for three extra passengers on their return voyage. William glanced at Gilbert. He ticked. Gilbert rubbed his back. The two brothers follow Beatriz down to the shoreline.

Far to the east behind them, the moon continued to climb higher and higher into oblivion, casting its full heavenly glow onto the kingdom of *middangeard*, the domain of man, littered with the filth of war and the grace of love; the moon shined off the backs of Gilbert, William, and Beatriz, and onto the consecrated snowfield that held Hawk and

Bartholomew; the moon shined off the dreamers, the avengers, and the blasphemers equally; the moon shined unabashedly.

And not once during that star-spangled night did Gilbert ever notice that the moon shone red, for he was too busy finally embracing the love graced to him.

EPILOGUE
THE SANCTITY OF SACRIFICE

1142 A.D.-1143 A.D.

CHAPTER L
LUCIA/EMMA/WILLIAM

Lucia was nearly a glacial carcass by the time she reached Wallingford, on the border of Oxfordshire and Berkshire. She couldn't bury her father; the ground was too hard and her fingers too frozen. Exhausted, grief-stricken, and completely vacant of thought, she crested the final hill and spotted the castle. She knew only what she felt, and in this particular instance, all she wanted was to see her empress.

In her previous life, her father had taught her that Wallingford Castle was one of the most impressive and impregnable castles in all of England, if not all the world. Even with that in mind, she was not prepared for the beautiful and awe-inspiring sight before her. It stood alone in a field of white; the keep, towering with clever stonemasonry upon its bleached hill, shone like an erected silver beacon amongst the hoarfrost. The moat surrounding the curtain wall was frozen over with rime and as still as the world around it. There were no birds chirping; no voices sounded from the surrounding village; there was not an ounce of noise except for the gentle breathing of Lucia, her mouth expelling white exhaust. She watched the snow fall silently onto this tranquil world she found herself in. The castle burned up wisps of smoke through its chimneys, as if its hidden hearths were tiny hearts which kindled life into lifeless stone. Lucia felt at her own breast, wondering if her pluming breath was only the heat of her heart, which kindled lifeless limbs, lifeless muscles, lifeless bones. She watched this frozen world and shivered beneath it.

A solitary figure ran from the castle's gatehouse. Empress Maud, having spotted Lucia's approach from a mile off, sprinted down the steps within the warm keep and threw herself past the housecarls and Sheriff d'Oilli and the multitude of guards keeping unwatchful watch atop the frosted-over battlements, until she was plowing a trail through the packed snow. Lucia forced herself forward, plowing a trail of her own, and slammed into an embrace with Maud. The two women held each other, their breaths commingling in the suspended air. A faint breeze whipped at them, fluttering their hair around their necks and swirling up a cyclone of snowflakes behind them.

"I found him, Maud."

"Found who?"

"My father. I haven't been truthful with you. I had forgotten myself. I'm not who I claimed to be."

"What say you, Beatrice? If that is the case, who are you?"

Who are you?

The words stopped Lucia cold. She separated from her embrace, and Empress Maud held her handmaiden's face between her firm hands. The only sounds in the world came from them. The only movement in the world came from their shivering bodies.

"I am Lady Lucia of Rockingham. My father was Baron Eadric of Rockingham."

"Baron Eadric?" The empress's expression went neutral. "Your father was Stephen's war constable?"

"Yes, my lady. I didn't know. I swear it."

"What happened to him?"

Lucia paused. Her eyes lingered on the empress. "He's dead. He saved me from a terrible man from my past. We killed him . . . and we killed Duke Richard. I'm so sorry."

Empress Maud pulled her back into a hug. "I'm sorry, *Lucia*. I know the pain of losing a father. It can be a hard loss for a daughter."

"That's not what upsets me."

"What is it then?"

"It's that I hate him," said Lucia, her tears burning her eyes. "I hate all the people he killed because of me. I despise the man he became for me . . . but I love him. I loved him so dearly that my heart breaks again."

"Ah." Empress Maud smiled wistfully. She placed her fingers underneath Lucia's chin and tilted up her face. "And that, my love, is the power of men. How they manage to make you love and despise them so thoroughly is a mystery to all but God. That is why they are so dangerous."

"And now I have to forgive him, even though he'll never live to see it."

"You'll see him, Lucia. In the life hereafter, you will." Empress Maud held Lucia in her arms until the cold became near unbearable. "You have an estate now, you realize? A home that is rightfully yours. If you wish it, I will relieve you of my service. You've not only been one of my closest advisers and one of my best handmaidens, but you've also been my friend. You may claim your home."

"No. No, my lady. That life is no longer mine. When I was a girl, that was all I dreamt of. But now I have us, this purpose of ours. I do not wish to give it up for anything. My father saved my life, and I choose to live that life for the world you'll create."

Empress Maud smiled. She pulled Lucia in closer to her and led her back toward Wallingford Castle. Empress Maud rubbed her back.

"I thank God every day for women like you," said the Holy Roman Empress. "Women like myself, like Matilda of Boulogne, like Lady Ansfride, or my young handmaidens like Theresa and Emma; I thank the good Lord for women who choose to live for themselves in a world not given to them."

Time moved infinitely slower during a war, but people changed infinitely quicker. Emma bent down and plucked a glovewort—or what some might call a Lily-of-the-valley. The one stem had multiple delicate, bell-shaped white flowers hanging from it. Emma wondered at the glovewort. How could something so pretty be so deadly? If ground up and ingested, the Lily-of-the-valley could poison a grown man.

Emma loved it though. It reminded her of herself and the other women she'd come to know over the past year. A dark black caterpillar with two whip-shaped tails crawled up the base of the plant until it reached the stem Emma had just plucked apart.

"Sorry," she said. "I didn't mean to take your lunch."

She placed the glovewort on the ground and the caterpillar next to it. The insect chewed hungrily at the plant. Wasn't it funny how something that could kill a man wouldn't harm a simple creature like this?

"There ye are!" Crispin said from behind her.

Dusting the soil off her brown dress, Emma stood on the outer edge of a disarrayed flower garden. Spring was quickly coming to a climax. The sun shone alluringly at their zenith, and the vale they were in was alive with every flower, insect, and bird that can be found in their kingdom. Next to them, behind the garden, a simple hut was being constructed. Edith and Mildritha had pooled their resources and paid a desperate carpenter and his son to help construct it for them—a home that would soon be transformed into an inn.

Emma smiled. Over the course of the winter, her mother and Mildritha had drawn close. They decided that they should combine their skills—Edith as a bartender, Mildritha as a cook—and create their very own place. Of course, they would need a man eventually to take care of their taxes; women couldn't be expected to own their own tavern. That would be crazy. But they *could* easily find a nobleman who wouldn't mind earning some extra revenue regularly. It was simply another tax for being a woman. What else was new?

"The carpenters said the inn should be finished this time next week," Crispin said.

"Lovely! Did our mums decide on a name yet?"

"Methinks they were still partial to Crippling Respite."

"I like that one." Emma rubbed her right shoulder. Her right hand hung uselessly at her side. She was like her mother now, a right and true cripple. It made her love Edith even more.

"Is Alice and Roger visiting today?" asked Crispin.

"Yes. They should be bringing bread and fresh water."

Emma spotted their mothers heading up the road. Next to them, a donkey dragged a wagon carrying hay and empty barrels to be placed into their inn-house. Emma smiled as she watched her mother work. She wore a simple green dress with a white apron over it, tied together with a cowhide belt. It was elegant and egalitarian and bespoke her beauty and passion.

"That dress makes your eyes look really pretty," said Crispin.

Emma peeked over at the boy, and when she realized he was staring at her, she blushed. She gazed at him. Crispin wasn't a boy in her eyes, not any longer. He was taller than he had been when she met him a year ago; his Adam's apple was more pronounced, and a few thin hairs had sprouted along his chin and above his lips. She didn't care that he had a larger belly either; in fact, she found it quite homely and charming now.

"Thank ye," she said stupidly.

Now it was Crispin's turn to blush.

"C'mon, let's go help them."

Emma took Crispin's hand and walked with him through the flowering garden to Crippling Respite, their little inn at the edge of the dirt road to nowhere—the kingdom of Emma.

William's nerves still got the best of him more often than not. And even a year removed from his captivity at the hands of the Hellhound of Rutland, he still found himself longing for the perverse tranquility of being chained. He didn't have to make choices. He didn't have to let anyone down. He didn't have to fail his brother.

The ocean waves thrusted themselves upon the docile shore of Normandy, dousing the duchy—and the Kingdom of France at large—with its white foam. After rescuing his half-brother, he, Gilbert, and Robin fled as far north as they could when the Angevin army invaded farther into the duchy. They left Caen in the early months of spring and hoped war wouldn't find them again. Their efforts were in vain.

Geoffrey of Anjou conquered one city after the next, from Pontorson to Saint-Lô and now, at last, to Cherbourg. Everyone wondered how long the city could hold out.

It only lasted two days. The city had been under occupation ever since. William, Gilbert, and their younger brother waited nervously.

William discovered he found comfort in watching the ocean churn endlessly, especially during dusk. He ticked. William groaned and rubbed his neck. The tics were happening less often than they used to, but whenever they occurred, they would cause an uncomfortable amount of pain. William rubbed his eyes. He needed to get home soon or Gilbert would start to worry.

"Mind if I join you?"

William jumped at the sound of the voice. He twisted around; the waves crashed onto the earth behind him. A young boy stood before him. Still donning the odd, asymmetrical body of adolescence, he couldn't be older than twelve or thirteen. His hair was bright red and curled so tightly that it bounced on his head when he moved. His skin was tanner than most redheaded boys, and he had chubby features that made William think of a squirrel. The boy was an aristocrat, though, for he wore flamboyant, ornately detailed clothes. Standing a few meters behind him were eight housecarls, each holding pikes nearly three meters tall.

"You're the one they call William?"

William ticked. He tapped his thigh nervously. "Yes . . ."

"I'm Henry. Care if I join?"

"No, my lord."

Henry strolled up next to him and glanced over the sea. It was getting extremely dark, even for the hours of dusk, and the approaching storm clouds would envelop the duchy in a matter of hours. Henry breathed in the crisp ocean air.

"Do you know who I am?" he asked.

"The Lord of Anjou. You're Count Geoffrey's son."

"*And* the empress's." He pointed across the channel, and when he did so, a flash of lightning scorched the horizon. The lord's eyes sparkled with an animalistic glee. His cape flapped behind him. "She's reclaiming my grandfather's kingdom for *me*."

"That's very kind of her, my lord."

"My father calls her names. He says she's a weak bitch. Did you know she nearly died when I was born? Only a weak woman bleeds to death during childbirth. Don't you think so?"

He waited for an answer. William, hesitant to say the wrong thing, simply replied, "Yes, my lord."

"So, you believe my mother to be a weak bitch?"

"... No, my lord. I mean..."

Henry glared into William's worrisome gaze. Then, the boy laughed. It was a maniacal, high-pitched screech that only a child before puberty could boast.

"She has mighty dreams like a true queen should," said the boy, "but she has an infirm, womanly mind. She doesn't know war like my father. Did you know my father now controls as much land as King Louis?"

William was deeply disturbed by this turn of events. Henry's flippant mockery of propriety and his unseemly acuity thoroughly unnerved Will. The way he spoke alone was something far beyond his years. William ticked again. The boy laughed.

"What was that?" he asked.

"I'm sorry, my lord."

"That was funny! Do it again."

William froze. His eyes danced to the lord's housecarls. He decided, then and there, that he was done with the games. If he was going to die tonight, or be imprisoned, he'd rather have it done now than dragged out.

"How do you know me? Why did you come for me, my lord?"

Henry frowned when he realized William wasn't going to be his personal jester for the night. The boy sighed in annoyance and glanced back out at the sea.

"A fortnight past, my father's army stopped a vessel from England that carried a chest of substantial wealth. My family's wealth. Coins. Jewels. *Titles*. A courier aboard claimed it to be of another's fortune. Your fortune. They said it was a gift given by the widow of Rockingham on behalf of her late husband. Did you know this man?"

William nodded.

"Of course you did. You were held captive by him, were you not? Father and his men wanted to know, of course, why a war hostage would be gifted such immense wealth. Eventually we came to learn that you are a bastard of Richard. That makes us cousins, you realize? Richard was my mother's second cousin, which makes you my cousin, and which makes Richard's remaining coin and lands, *our* coin and lands. Do you understand?"

William remained silent. Henry smiled.

"I heard you trained under Uncle Robert for a time. You know what Father says? He says, one day the whole of France and England will be *mine*. But Father also says that there'll be those who try to tear me down, like those in Anjou who rebel against us. Father says it is nearing time for me to start leading, and that means finding people who can help me fight.

"I want you to join my retinue. Uncle Richard says good things. Said you were gifted in battle planning. When he has finally won England for me, he'll come here and help Father and me take all of this kingdom. There's still much to do. Father wants to take over Brittany next, and we need to quell the rebels in Anjou. King Louis will fight back, so we need to be ready."

One of the housecarls near the back stepped forward with a trunk. He placed it at William's feet.

"A token of my good word," said Lord Henry. "It was your father's. And although it belongs to our family rightfully, I'll bless you and your half-brothers with it."

"I don't know what to say—"

"Say, 'yes, my lord.'"

The thought of it made William's blood burn hot. He didn't want to hurt anyone. He didn't want to make any decisions. What would Gilbert think? What would they do with baby Robin?

"I'm sorry, my lord, but . . . I don't think—"

"We know you deserted."

William's heart nearly stopped.

"I can have you arrested. Hung. Torn apart. It's quite fun, actually. I can do it to your brother first, so you can see. Do you know who my other grandfather was? He was King of Jerusalem. Did you know that? He died a few weeks ago."

"I didn't know, my lord."

"In five days, my father marches to Rouen. Once we capture it, the whole duchy will be ours. This is the only offer you'll get."

Henry kicked the chest on the beach. William was overcome with a thousand different emotions, a thousand different thoughts. The storm picked up across the ocean. Lightning struck. Thunder rumbled. The sharp, cool wind blasted into them.

"What will it be?" asked Henry, Lord of Anjou, son of Count Geoffrey and Empress Maud, grandson of the late King Henry of England and King Fulk of Jerusalem.

William glanced between the lord, the chest of coins, and the slumbering coastal city of Cherbourg, where his brothers would be anxiously awaiting his return. He took a deep breath, glared at the boy lord, and made his decision.

THE END

The Anarchy Saga will continue in Part 3

THE ANARCHY SAGA

WHAT IS *THE ANARCHY SAGA*?

The Anarchy Saga will be a five-part story that follows the plight of numerous eclectic individuals (and their ancestors) throughout the 12th century—specifically through the turmoil of the Anarchy. Each novel will work as its own standalone story; however, the collective whole will deliver a complete narrative that gives a fully realized depiction of life during the High Middle Ages (in western Europe, at least!). You can expect the same level of horror, violence, religious and political intrigue, twists, and betrayals to be present throughout the subsequent novels.

While Part 2 of *The Anarchy Saga* was focused around southern England and northern France, expect future installments to be set in other kingdoms around the world as well. But, of course, you can expect your favorite characters from the first two parts (and even their ancestors) to make appearances throughout the saga.

WHAT'S NEXT IN *THE ANARCHY SAGA*?

Part 3, the follow up novel to *Virtuous Sins* and *A Battlefield of Scarlet Snow*, will be a contained political thriller set in the historic city of London. It'll span over two decades of the succession war, exploring how King Stephen and Empress Maud must convince the warring factions of nobility and peasantry to their side if they're to be crowned as king or queen.

Part 3 will combine an intense love story with complex political intrigue. The streets of London are bloody with the filthy scorn of oppression, and it is here that the heart of England must be won. Uprisings, backstabbing, and passion abound in the next chapter of The Anarchy Saga...

WANT TO STAY UPDATED ON *THE ANARCHY SAGA*?

If you enjoyed *A Battlefield of Scarlet Snow: a 12th Century Revenge Odyssey* and want to stay up to date for the next installment of *The Anarchy Saga*, then consider joining Derek Roy's mailing list (including exclusive access to sneak-peak chapters of future novels):

https://www.derekroystories.com/anarchy-mailing-list

APPENDIX I

GLOSSARY — 12TH CENTURY TERMINOLOGY

Armor:

Chausses: protective leg coverings, either quilted or made of *maille*

Coif: padded protection around the head that goes under the helm, sometimes made of *maille*

Gambeson: a padded tunic quilted of linen, worn under the hauberk

Harness: a protective set of armor comprising coif, helm, mittens, splinted armguards, gambeson, hauberk, and chausses

Hauberk: full coat of *maille*

Helm: a helmet made of thin sheets of steel, often with a nose guard to protect the bridge of the nose and upper cheekbones

Maille: metal rings chained together to form protection

Plated Armor: small metal plates strapped around the *maille* (back/chest/thighs) for additional protection

Plated Harness: full harness set with addition metal plates for the chest and back

Splinted Armguard: sheets of thin metal on a linen backing used to protect the forearms

Surcoat: worn above the hauberk to show insignia or allegiance

Fortifications:

Crenellations: a wall around the top of a castle, with regular spaces in it through which the people inside the castle can shoot

Garderobes: a toilet that hangs off the side of a castle and dumps into a pit or moat (sometimes used as a closet to kill mites on clothing)

Hoard/Hoarding: a temporary wooden gallery projected out from castle walls during sieges

Parapet: a low wall along the edge of the battlements

Portcullis: a strong gate made of bars with points at the bottom that hangs above the entrance to a castle

Postern: a back or side entrance to a castle, usually hidden to make for an easier escape

General:

Cog: a single-mast ship of Viking heritage, often used to transport goods and people rather than naval use

Mendicant Orders: a religious group who survives by begging for alms

Priory: a building where monks or nuns live, work, and pray

Sea-coal: mineral coal collected from the sea, as opposed to mined

Tithe: a tenth part of someone's produce or income that they pay as a tax to the Church

Military:

Fyrd: an Anglo-Saxon militia

Housecarl: a household bodyguard

Miscellaneous:

Middanearde: Anglo-Saxon word meaning "middle dwelling", used to describe the earth/world as the middle ground between Heaven and Hell

Titles, Trades, Offices & Positions:

Circator: an obedientiary monk who punishes those who go against/act against Church doctrine

Prior: a man who is in charge of a priory/monastery or who is second in charge of an abbey

War Constable: a high-ranking military official, granted only to a privileged few

APPENDIX II

GLASTONBURY PRIORY MATINS CHANT, LATIN-ENGLISH TRANSLATION

Kyrie eleison, **Christe** eleison. **Kyrie** Eleison.

(**Lord** have mercy on us, **Christ** have mercy on us. **Lord** have mercy on us.)

Domine Jesu Christe, **Rex** gloriae!

(**O Lord Jesus Christ**, **King** of Glory!)

Defunctorum de poenis inferni et de profundo lacu.

(Deliver the souls of all the faithful departed from the pains of hell and from the deep pit.)

Requiem aeternam dona eis, **Domine**,

(Eternal rest give to them, **O Lord**,)

Et lux perpetua luceat eis.

(and let perpetual light shine upon them.)

Qui audis orationem,

(You who hears our prayers,)

Ad te omnis caro veniet propter iniquitatem.

(To you all flesh must come with its burden of wicked deeds.)

Requiem aeternam dona eis, **Domine**,

(Eternal rest give to them, **O Lord**,)

Et lux perpetua luceat eis.

> (and let perpetual light shine upon them.)

Etsi prævaluerunt super nos
impietates nostræ,

> (We are overcome by our sins;)

Tu propitiaberis eis.

> (Only you can pardon them.).

Requiem aeternam dona eis, **Domine**,

> (Eternal rest give to them, **O Lord**,)

Et lux perpetua luceat eis.

> (and let perpetual light shine upon them.)

Kyrie eleison.

> (**Lord** have mercy on us.)

Christe eleison.

> (**Christ** have mercy on us.)

Kyrie Eleison.

> (**Lord** have mercy on us.)

Domine Jesu Christe, Rex gloriae!

> (**O Lord Jesus Christ, King** of Glory!)

AFTERWORD

H ERE, HERE!

I hope you enjoyed your journey through one of the most infamous civil wars in European history. This afterword is for my historians, especially those who've done extensive research on this turbulent time period. You'll no doubt catch some liberties I took.

Starting off, I would like to touch on my portrayal of linguistics. After the Norman conquest of 1066, Europe underwent a significant and prolonged transformation of the English language. There was a clash between a mixture of five languages: Old English, Old Saxon/Old Norse, the assimilation of Old French, the nascent formation of "middle English" (as well as the very beginning of the Great Vowel Shift), and, of course, the lingering remnants of Latin. It was important to me that the peasantry spoke differently from the educated highborn; however, it was equally vital that I didn't succumb to common "Hollywood" tropes of peasantry—often depicted as filthy beggars without any intellectual thoughts. For this novel, I chose a stylish version of classic "Shakespearean" language, one that (mostly) nullifies the "thee's" and "thou's" for "ye's" and other simplified, streamlined words. I wanted the semantics to be absorbing and modern while still giving the impression that you are hearing archaic syntax.

Now, a quick note on names and language barriers. I've decided to use the modern-English names for all characters (when applicable), regardless of where they were born. A prime example: instead of using the French version of the name "Guillaume," I use the English version, "William." This change was done to make the novel easier and quicker to read; in the same regard, unless it was dreadfully obvious and egregious not to do so, every character in this novel can understand the speech of others. Since the many languages of medieval western Europe were so muddied and routinely intermixed, I took the liberty of allowing those in the region to, at minimum, vaguely understand all three of Old French, Old English, and Old Saxon/Old Norse. They were probably similar enough during the twelfth century that aristocrats and commoners knew many words from all three.

Next, I'd like to touch upon religion. Spirituality and the Church played major roles in the lives of everyone during this period, and I wanted to emphasize that without diving too deeply into the structure of the clergy (that'll be done in a later book!). Consequently, my focus is on the impact the divine had on the individual rather than the Church's effects as a whole. It's important to acknowledge that religion was paramount to everyone and everything, while also acknowledging the complex hypocrisies that individuals felt due to this fact.

Lastly, this novel holds a significant amount of dialogue and characterization of real historical figures. I believe it to be the responsibility of storytellers to handle the depictions of real people with tact and some semblance of empathy. Obviously the social and political norms of the twelfth century differ radically from today. I don't think it does audiences any justice to try to modernize historical figures to match current social standards. Thus, I tried my best to characterize these historical kings, queens, dukes, earls and archbishops as authentically and impartially as possible.

I hope with the aforesaid you can understand why I wrote the story I did, with the characters I did, and with the emphasis I did. My hopes are that the historical setting helps people realize that, while foreign, the lives and dilemmas of humans almost a millennium ago weren't that different from ours today.

ACKNOWLEDGMENTS

No novel is easy to complete. I think any writer will attest to this. A historical fiction novel set in a time period notorious for its lack of first- or second-hand accounts is especially difficult. Hence why it took twice as long as I would have liked to complete this book, and a degree of (multiple!) magnitudes more thought power than any one person would like to commit to any single project.

Thus, I would like to express my sincere gratitude to the following individuals for dealing with me as I stumbled through life while wrangling this behemoth.

To my family: I love you. Thank you for listening to my rambles. Thank you for believing in me through the ups and downs, even if you never read my work. Thank you for never giving up on me.

To my friends: you guys are my rock (and I love you too). Without each one of you distracting me daily and giving me a reason to escape my own imagined worlds, I would truly become a phantom in real life. You're all the reasons I'm not insane.

To my supporters: you give me hope. Every time I sit down at the keyboard, I think of you. Your words, your encouragements . . . it's all a storyteller can ask for.

To authors Alison Weir, Paul B. Newman, and the fathomless unsung historians who update historical articles online: I adore your effort and hard work. How you manage to shine a light on such a dim, distant time period—in such glorious detail—is beyond my comprehension. Your research effort doesn't go unappreciated nor unnoticed. This novel wouldn't be possible without you.

ABOUT THE AUTHOR

 Derek Roy is an international award-winning filmmaker, screenwriter, and author. He's written three feature film spec scripts, as well as multiple short film screenplays, and is hoping to find representation for his writing/directing in the film, television, video game, and streaming industries.

Derek Roy loves to tell stories in any medium he can. Along with writing *Virtuous Sins* and *A Battlefield of Scarlet Snow*, he plans on writing a whole saga of five standalone novels depicting a complete picture of life in 12th century western Europe.

He dreams of one day becoming a showrunner, while maintaining the luxury to pursue any medium that one of his stories might fancy.

You can find a link to his other writings and directorial work at: https://www.derekroystories.com/

www.ingramcontent.com/pod-product-compliance
Lightning Source LLC
LaVergne TN
LVHW031220080526
838199LV00092B/6453